RUTHLESS KING

KINGS OF TEMPTATION

SIENNA CROSS

Copyright © 2023 by Sienna Cross

All rights reserved.

No part of this book may be reproduced in any form or by any electronic or mechanical means, including information storage and retrieval systems, without written permission from the author, except for the use of brief quotations in a book review.

ISBN: 9798854235990

Created with Vellum

To all the women who find it perfectly acceptable to be kidnapped by a gorgeous Italian mobster…
~ Sienna Cross

CONTENTS

1. Sold to the Mob — 1
2. Cazzo, We're Screwed — 7
3. A Surprise and a Twist — 14
4. On My Knees — 20
5. What's the Worse They Could Do? — 25
6. The Boss Is Coming to Get You — 31
7. Taking Out the Trash — 37
8. C.E.O and King — 43
9. An Unexpected Encounter — 52
10. She's Mine — 60
11. A Gun Is Much Better than Pepper Spray — 66
12. This Complicates Things — 73
13. An Offer I Can't Refuse — 81
14. Best Punishment Ever — 88
15. She Has Me by the Balls — 96
16. Pretty Woman Gone Wrong — 102
17. I Stop Breathing — 108
18. The Devil in My Bed — 114
19. One Night — 120
20. The Heart Ball — 127
21. Dirty Dancing — 135
22. A Lion in the Ladies Room — 143
23. Ruined — 149
24. Breakfast in Bed — 155
25. Groveling 101 — 161
26. The Ride of My Life — 167
27. A Grand Gesture — 173
28. A Sucker for Punishment — 181
29. Painting the Streets Red — 190
30. The Worst Day — 196
31. Retribution — 203
32. Only Once — 209
33. Tell Me You're Mine — 215
34. Love? — 222
35. Coming Home — 229

36. Official Relationship Status	237
37. My Coglione Brother	243
38. Hope Is Dangerous	250
39. A Ticking Timebomb	256
40. Time's Up	263
41. Torture	271
42. Because of Me	278
43. Pain Is Better Than Fear	284
44. Payback	290
45. Love Kills	297
46. Amore Mio	303
Epilogue	308
47. Sneak Peek of Savage King	314
Also by Sienna Cross	319
Acknowledgments	321
About the Author	323

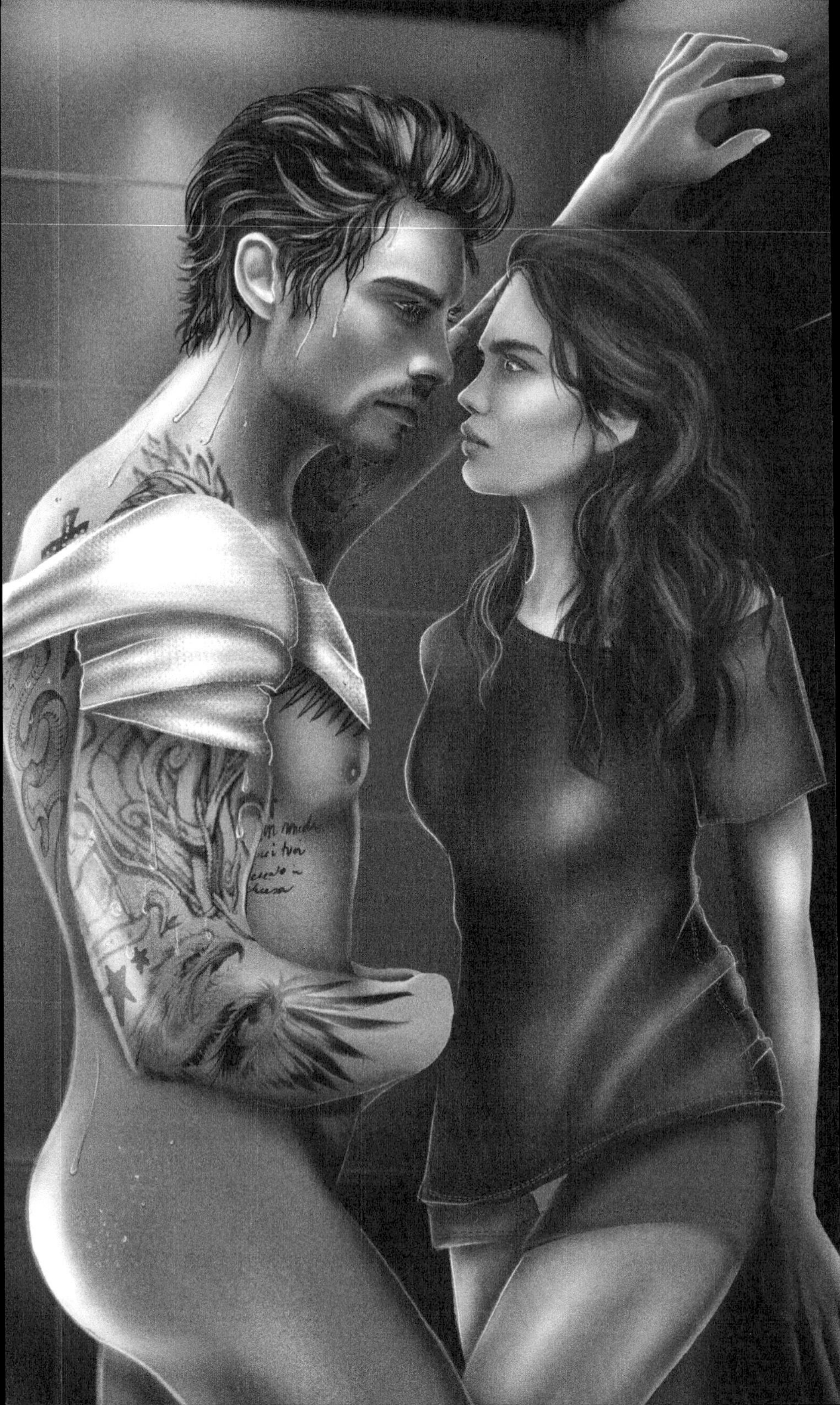

RUTHLESS KING

CHAPTER 1
SOLD TO THE MOB

S*tella*

Sold to the mob.

Sold to the mob.

Sold to the mob.

Cazzo. Fuck my life. How did this happen? I glare at my father, tears welling in my eyes. Three guys in black suits with matching red pocket squares stand across the table from us. The taller one in the middle, Tony, hands my father a stack of papers.

Another man stands behind us. He's the one with the keys to the handcuffs digging into my wrists. The keys jingle in his slacks' pocket, a sickening taunt. He takes the keyring out, the clanging of metal cutting through the tense air, and unlocks Dad's cuffs.

"Sign on the dotted line," says Tony, as Dad winces at the angry red marks on his wrists. "All your outstanding debts to the Kings will be forgiven in exchange for your daughter, Stella McKenzie, within the time period previously discussed."

What the hell does that even mean? I'm not property. I am a damned person. I couldn't be sold, could I? I struggle against the cuffs, the chair legs squealing against the cement floor.

My father's eyes dart to mine, and for an instant, he actually looks ashamed. For that one crappy moment in my life, he seems sorry for all the shit he put me through. I almost feel bad for him. Almost. That's how stupid I am.

Dad reaches for the packet, flips to the last page, and scrawls his initials along the line. He doesn't ask any questions, doesn't inquire what the hell will become of his only daughter. Then he leaps up from his chair, tosses the papers at Tony and darts out of the room. He doesn't even spare me a passing glance as he jets out of there with his tail between his legs.

Liam McKenzie is a piece of shit.

I struggle again, but two firm hands press on my shoulders, shoving me down on the chair. "You're not going anywhere, sweetheart. You're now official property of the Kings."

Seconds pass, hell, it could have been hours. Everything is a blur, muddled by the roar of my pounding heart.

The door swings open, and a dark shadow looms in the threshold. An electric presence fills the small, murky space, and I'm suddenly acutely aware of every single heartbeat. Piercing midnight irises rake over me, and goosebumps spill across my arms.

One Week Ago

"*Buongiorno*, Stella bella!" Mrs. DeVito's warm smile greets me as I stumble down the stairs of our fourth-floor walkup.

"Morning, Mrs. D." I haul my backpack strap over my other shoulder.

The cute little old lady is our long-time neighbor and like the grandma I never had. My own passed away before I was old enough to remember much about her. Technically, Mrs. D is also my boss at *Nonna Maria's Pasticceria*. She barely works at the Italian bakery anymore, but her name is still above the red and white awning which she reminds her son, Giuseppe, of when she stops by daily. She reaches for my cheek and gives it a pinch before I can scramble away. I used to hate it when I was little, but now, it reminds me of a happier time. Before Mom and Vinny... I press my hand to my chest and picture the two small hearts tattooed just over my real heart. I bury the thoughts before they threaten to pull me under.

"You getting so big, *bella*. You got a fancy job lined up after you graduate?"

"It's just an associate degree in business, Mrs. D. Once I get that, I'm out of here. I've already applied to the University of Florida, and I'm just waiting to hear if I get in." At twenty-one, it was about damn time to live on my own.

"Oh, Florida? What are you gonna do so far away without my cannoli?"

I laugh. "Probably die of starvation."

She pats my cheek with a warm smile. "No worry, bella, I send you some in the mail." Her pale gray eyes turn wistful as she regards me. "You know, you look more and more like your mamma every day."

"Thanks. That's what I hear." My throat tightens, the pang of loss still acute despite all the time that's passed. I glance up at my reflection in the cracked mirror over the mailboxes in the rundown foyer. It hangs askew, the frame chipped but still, if I close my eyes just right, I can see her in me. The long, dark brown hair and bright blue eyes. Some of the light has dimmed in the past few years, but I held on as best I could. For her memory. "I gotta run," I rasp out. "Don't want to be late for my last month of class."

"Of course, bella. Go, go." She pats my cheek again, a little rougher than necessary. "I make spaghetti and meatballs tonight. I make extra for you."

"*Grazie*, Mrs. D.," I call out over my shoulder as I barrel through the door. The rusty hinges whine in protest. I can still hear them squealing as I dart down Mulberry Street, weaving between the tourists.

Little Italy is nothing like it once was. Most of it has been overrun by China Town, but still a few treasured blocks remain. We are one of the few Italian families that still reside in this neighborhood. Most had moved on, moved up in the world. Not us. Dad was never the same after Mom, and then after Vinny … well, things went straight to hell.

I turn onto Canal Street and keep my head down as I pass the Red Dragon. *Please don't let him be in there.* I send the prayer up to a God I'm not sure exists, but I hope nonetheless.

"Where you going in such a hurry, Stella?" Feng emerges from the entrance of the Chinese restaurant and leans against the crimson dragon statue. The red paper lanterns sway in the warm breeze, reminding me summer is nearly here.

"Class," I shout without stopping.

"Bo's been looking for you."

I quicken my pace, my chest tight from the effort. I reach for my inhaler, but I don't want to stop and give my ex's cousin a chance to catch up. I draw in a deep breath instead, willing the tension away. It's taken me months to shake Bo Zhang, and avoidance is the best option.

Why I ever screwed around with that *stronzo* is beyond me. It was a new low.

The Canal Street subway sign is like a shining beacon in the darkness. Just a few more steps, and I'm home free. Tightening my hold on my backpack strap because petty theft has been through the roof around here lately, I descend onto the subway platform. Between the Red Dragons, the Kings, and the countless other gangs littering the streets of downtown Manhattan, it's become a battle zone.

Swiping my pass through the turnstile, I reach the A train platform and release a breath. The overhead blinking display catches my eye, mocking me. Nine minutes. A groan slides through my clenched teeth. With a huff, I plop down on the graffiti-covered bench, pop in my earbuds and rifle through my backpack for my Econ textbook. At least I can get some studying done.

I flip to the last chapter, my nose buried in the massive textbook, and a hand slaps down on the page. My heart stills. I don't dare look up. Not when I know exactly who that gaudy silver dragon ring blotting out the paragraph on supply and demand belongs to.

"Why have you been avoiding me, Stel?" Bo's words are muffled by the lyrics of Taylor Swift's latest and greatest.

I remain perfectly still, pretending I can't hear a damned thing over my cheap earbud knockoffs. Bo's hands close around my textbook, and the massive weight disappears from my lap. I stare in shock as my book goes flying onto the subway tracks.

"Hey!" I cry. Tearing the earbuds out, I glare up at my asshole ex. "What the hell, Bo?"

"You can't just ignore me like that."

"Yes, I can. We broke up, remember?" I dart to the edge of the platform and cringe at the rat racing over my two-hundred-dollar textbook. I whirl at him, jabbing my finger into his obnoxiously hard chest. "Go get it."

He lets out a dark laugh, the corners of his eyes crinkling. I used to love the way his eyes thinned when he laughed. It made him look sweet, adorable even. But this laugh wasn't a genuine one, not like when we first met, and things were full of hope and promise. And I was full of naïve bullshit.

"Bo!" I snarl. "I need that book."

"You should've thought of that before you ignored me." Venom laces his words, his eyes narrowed to angry gashes.

"I never thought you'd be psychotic enough to toss it onto

the tracks." Okay, so I should have known that. He didn't rise to his position in the Red Dragons for being a freakin' saint. I glance up at the display—three more minutes—then back to my book.

"If you want me to get it for you, give me another chance." He reaches for my hand, but I snatch it away. "Don't you remember how good it was?"

"Fuck, no."

Darkness rages across his pitch irises, his thin lips curling into a sneer. His hand shoots out, long fingers closing around my hair. He jerks my head back, and a cry tears from my lips.

An old Chinese man leaning on a cane stands at the end of the subway platform, but he doesn't make a move to help me. I don't blame him really. The Red Dragons terrorize everyone down here, and they don't discriminate based on age or health.

"Let go of me," I snarl.

"Not until I teach you some respect, you little bitch." He drags me off the bench and forces me to my knees. The jolt of hitting the cement floor races up my legs, and I bite back another curse. "Beg *me* to take you back."

His junk is at my eyelevel, and I can already see the shape of his tiny cock pressing against the zipper. *Ugh.* He's actually getting off on this. I steel my nerves, shoving the trickle of fear back, and will myself not to crumble.

"Never," I grit out.

"I'm going to have you one way or another, Stella. Your choice."

That looming fear races across my body at the malice in his voice. Bo had always been a possessive and verbally abusive asshole, but he'd never forced himself on me.

The ding of a subway pass barely registers across the roar of my thundering pulse as I struggle against him.

"Let go of her." A lethal voice cuts through the panic, and the calm, icy tenor sends a chill up my spine.

CHAPTER 2
CAZZO, WE'RE SCREWED

*S**tella*

Bo spins at the stranger, fury roiling off his slender, muscled form. "Mind your own fucking business," he spits.

I try to catch a glimpse of the man, but Bo's long legs block my view. The only thing I can make out are a pair of expensive looking loafers. The flickering fluorescent light catches on the hardware atop the soft leather and the interlocking G's. Growing up a block away from China Town and the myriad of knock-off purses lining the streets, I'd recognize that Gucci logo anywhere. And this one looks legit.

"You are my business. Anyone who treats a woman like that deserves my full attention," the stranger says, his tone chilling a few more notches around a distinctive Italian accent.

Bo turns to him and finally releases the iron grip on my hair. Rubbing my scalp, I crawl toward my backpack.

"Who the hell are you to tell me what to do?" Bo growls as he stalks toward the man.

I hazard another peek, but the guy's wearing a black baseball cap and a dark trench coat, obscuring his features. He's built like a freakin' Greek god with broad shoulders and a barrel chest. Even the oversized coat can't hide that.

The ground begins to rumble, and the familiar sound of the approaching subway sends my heart leaping up my throat. I eye my textbook one more time before resigning myself to the loss. I'll figure something out.

The subway races into the station, and I hazard another peek at Bo and Gucci guy. My ex still blocks him, but the man is tall, towering over him by a few inches. The sudden crunch of bone against bone freezes the blood in my veins. Bo's head snaps back, and a curse rings out over the rumbling subway. *Holy cannoli.* I'm torn between the fight and my getaway, my eyes bouncing back and forth between the men and the subway car. The doors glide open, and I only dawdle for an instant. Bo's going to be pissed. And I can't count on my Italian knight in shining armor to rescue me again. I dart inside, lingering by the doors as they slide closed.

The subway surges to life as my gaze remains fixed on my subway savior. He's nothing but a blur as we speed away.

Once we've passed the station, I collapse into a seat and reach for my inhaler. Taking a quick puff, I lean my head back and close my eyes. Just a few more weeks, and all of this will be nothing more than a bad dream.

Jiggling the old knob on our apartment door, I mutter a curse when the overhead deadbolt blocks my entrance. "Dad!" I knock once, then twice, taking out my frustrations on the old timber. My professor called me out when I told him I'd accidentally dropped my textbook on the tracks. He was a total douche. Like it would've killed him to let me photocopy a few pages from his. I'd already studied for most of the Econ final. I only needed a few more chapters.

Deal with it, he'd said.

"Open the door, Dad!" I shout.

"Stop yelling, I'm coming." My father's voice seeps through the cracks, and I wrap my arms across my chest, still stewing. Somehow, I'd managed to avoid Bo on my way home. He was probably nursing a shiner. That guy had gotten him good. Wish I would've had a front row view of the smackdown. I couldn't help a smile from curling my lips as I picture it.

The door finally whips open and Liam McKenzie stares down at me, eyes bloodshot and wisps of graying hair darting in all directions. "Good, you're home. I'm hungry." A wave of whiskey breath crashes over me as each word flees his lips.

"*Cazzo*, Dad, it's only one o'clock. How much did you drink already?"

He glares at me, the haze of alcohol lifting. "Don't use that foul language with me."

"Italian?" I smirk.

A sharp sting sears my cheek, and my neck snaps back. I mutter another curse, this one in English so I'm sure he understands it. Hot tears burn my eyes, but I refuse to let them fall, to give him the satisfaction. He's been trying to break me for years. My best friend, Rose, the aspiring therapist says it's because he wants me to be as miserable as him. No, I'll never let it happen. I'll cry in the quiet of my room later, over a pint of ice cream like a respectable girl.

"Sorry," he grumbles and folds his hands behind his back. He's not always a total asshole. He just gets worse with the booze. And he just lost his job at the bowling alley so that's been shit. "I'm just on edge ...."

"I know, Dad." I cup my bruised cheek and attempt a cheerful smile. "I'm sure you'll find another job soon." I cross my fingers and pray to St. Anthony. He's the saint of finding all things so how hard could it be to find my dad a semi-decent job? Mom was a hardcore believer in good old St. Anthony, one of the few remnants of her deeply Catholic upbringing. I wish I had her faith, but after all the loss, believing in some benevolent higher power seems like a joke.

I march into our crappy living room and toss my backpack on the plastic-covered couch. Which is ridiculous. There is nothing worthwhile under that plastic left to protect.

"You think you can run down to the corner store to grab some cold cuts and bread? It'll help with the um…."

Hangover. He's probably been drinking since he woke up. I turn on the sink and fill a chipped glass with cool water. "Here, take this."

"I'd go out myself but—" He drags his knotted fingers through his thinning hair.

"But what?"

My dad's expression sends irrational fear crawling up my spine.

"But what?" I repeat.

"I didn't want to worry you, but I called Jimmy the other night after I got canned—"

"No, Dad, you didn't!"

"It was a sure thing. He swore there was no way I'd lose."

"And let me guess, you lost?"

He nods, heaving out a frustrated breath, and the stench of stale alcohol fills my nostrils.

"You didn't even have any money to bet." The total sum in our bank account was a paltry four dollars and twenty-six cents. I knew this because I tried to buy a venti coffee yesterday morning, and my debit card was declined. It was a damned good thing I was getting paid tomorrow. "Where did you get the money from?"

He runs his palm down the back of his neck, his fair skin turning rosy and accentuating the smattering of freckles he'd inherited from his Irish blood. "I told you, Jimmy said it was a sure thing, so I took out a small loan."

"What?" I shriek. "Not only are you gambling again, but you're using borrowed money?" *F.M.L.*

He grabs my hands, his eyes desperate. "The situation is bad, honey. I didn't want to worry you, but I owe more …."

"How much exactly?"

"Twenty k."

All the air punches out of my lungs, and my mouth gapes. I try to suck in a breath, but my lungs have stopped functioning. "Are you shitting me, Dad? How the hell are we supposed to pay that?" Twenty thousand dollars is more than I make in a year at the bakery.

He drags his hands over his face and huffs out a breath. "That's why I did it, honey. Don't you see? It was our only way out."

"But you lost, didn't you? Now, how much more do we owe?"

"Five more."

"Hundred or thousand?" I squeal.

"Thousand."

"Damn it, Dad." Tears sting my eyes, but again, I will them back. How am I ever going to get out of here? Even with scholarships, it suddenly seems impossible. A horrifying thought wriggles its way into my mind. "Who did you borrow it from?"

"I'm not sure exactly. Jimmy brokered the deal."

"And how much time do you have to pay it back?" That niggling fear intensifies. The Red Dragons were into all kinds of shit. What if he owed them? Everyone knew they were brutal enforcers. That would explain the deadbolt and Dad's reluctance to make a run to the freakin' corner store.

"End of the week."

Cazzo. Shit. Fuck.

I pace a quick circle around our kitchenette, cursing with

each turn. "You have to find out who you owe. If it is the Red Dragons, maybe there's something I can do. I can talk to Bo and—" Oh, *merda*. He's going to want me back for this. Would I be willing to tie myself to a man I hate to save my dad's ass?

I shake my head out, burying the dismal thoughts. There are plenty of loan sharks in Manhattan. What are the chances it's his gang, right?

"I'll talk to Jimmy. I was supposed to send him the money directly, but I'll tell him I'm in a bind." He reaches for my hand and gives it a squeeze. "We'll figure this out somehow."

A deep rumble shakes his belly, drawing my attention to his stained t-shirt. I have to get some food into this man. I search the pantry and come up empty. Not even pasta—a staple when Mom was around. *Shit*. I really don't want to risk another encounter with Bo, not until I know for sure about the loan.

Pasta! *Grazie a Dio*. "Oh, Mrs. DeVito made spaghetti and meatballs. I'll just run over and grab it."

"Thanks, honey." He gives me a smile, a hint of some unguarded emotion seeping through the boozy haze. "I'm so sorry, Stella. I swear I only did it for us. I hate that we live this way. Your mom would've been so disappointed in me." His voice is thick with emotion, and he lowers his gaze to the floor.

Sometimes, I barely remember the old version of my dad, but every once in a while I get tiny glimpses. It only makes it worse.

"Be right back."

"Hmm," he mumbles without looking up.

I trudge to the door, doing my best to keep my feet from dragging. No matter how hard I try, sometimes I'm sure we're cursed. Just when I start to see a light at the end of the tunnel, someone slams the door shut in my face.

Once I'm out in the hallway, I stop and lean against the peeling wallpaper and exhale a slow breath. A tear trickles out despite my best efforts. I blink quickly to force the deluge back. After I get Dad fed, I can disappear into my room and let it all out.

The click of the deadbolt behind me sends my heart jolting up my throat. *Geez, chill, Stella.*

Cazzo, we are so screwed.

CHAPTER 3
A SURPRISE AND A TWIST

S*tella*

I'm still trying to convince myself some knee-busting loan shark isn't coming after us as I walk up the steps with the heaping tray of spaghetti and meatballs. *Grazie a Dio* for Mrs. D. She is not a big fan of my dad, so I had to lie and promise the delicious meal was for my mouth only.

I pause on the last step and peer around the corner. All clear. I release a breath, chastising myself for being so paranoid. So Dad owed twenty-five k to some unnamed organization? It didn't mean we were going to get killed for it, right?

As I creep down the hallway, something catches my eye in front of our door. I narrow my gaze and inch closer. A book? I hurry the last few steps as my pulse accelerates. My eyes finally settle on the massive text and the post-it note taped to the cover.

How did Bo rescue it from the subway? I should've been thankful, but it would've never ended up on the tracks if the dickhead hadn't chucked it on there in a jealous fit.

Gently lowering the heaping container of pasta to the floor, I nearly crumple up the note until I focus on the smooth penmanship. It's not from Bo. I'd recognize his choppy writing anywhere. Bending closer, I scan the neatly penned words.

You forgot something when you ran off without thanking me.

An unexpected chuckle bursts from my lips. I turn the note around to search for a signature but only find a crude design—of a crown, maybe? For someone with such neat writing, my subway savior couldn't draw for shit.

I pick up the book and the attached post-it and press it against my chest. That new book smell wafts up my nostrils. My rescuer hadn't just recovered it before it got smashed to smithereens by the subway; he'd bought me an entirely new one. That was pretty decent of the guy. These textbooks are expensive as hell.

"If you wanted me to thank you, you should've at least left me your name," I mumble out loud. Great, now I was talking to myself. Dad's gambling problems were already getting to me.

Between the book and the platter, I don't have enough hands to open the door, so I give the worn wood a little kick.

I hear the squeak of the peephole opening a second before the front door whips open, and Dad's wide eyes bore into me. He scans the empty corridor, then releases a breath. Damn, how bad of a situation had he gotten us into? Did he really think his booky would be coming for us already?

Before I can ask, Dad grabs the platter from my hands and dips back inside. He either doesn't notice the huge book or doesn't care enough to ask. Probably the latter. "Save me some!" I call out as he disappears into the kitchenette.

Mrs. DeVito's spaghetti and meatballs are almost as good as Mom's. Or at least that's how I remember it. I trudge into my bedroom which is actually the living room with a makeshift wall to give the pretense of privacy. Not that I'd ever bring a guy home with me anyway. After Bo, I'd sworn off all men. They just weren't worth the hassle.

Maybe the sun-kissed surfers in Florida would be different. I could hope, anyway.

Dropping the brand-new textbook on my desk in the corner, I heave out a breath. Just a little over a month and school would be over. I'll finish out the summer working at Mrs. D's and hopefully I'll have enough money saved for my grand escape. I sure as hell wasn't giving a penny of my savings to Dad for that gambling debt. After my run-in with Bo today, I'd decided that even if I didn't make it into any of the universities in Florida, I was out of here one way or another.

"Shit." Dad's muttered curse tears my thoughts from sunny beaches to my dismal reality.

I hurry out of my room and catch him with a mouthful of spaghetti glaring at the screen on his old flip phone. "What's wrong?"

"We're fucked that's what."

My head snaps back at the bitter edge to his tone. He curses like a sailor when he's drunk, but his gaze is clear now.

He swallows down the big bite and drags his hand over his balding head, pacing the small length of our apartment. "That Jimmy screwed me over big time."

"What does that mean?" The guy was a booky; he made money on screwing people over. What the hell did he expect?

His eyes meet mine for only a second before they drop to the floor. "That 'free' money and 'sure thing' came from the Red Dragons."

No ... my stomach takes a nosedive, nausea clawing its way up my throat. *No. No. No.* Of all the scumbags in

Manhattan why did my dad owe twenty-five grand to my ex and the Chinese Triad? A horrifying thought races to the forefront of my mind. Had Bo planned this whole thing? Was this all some twisted attempt to get me back?

I grab my dad's phone and throw it at him. "Ask Jimmy if Bo Zhang had anything to do with this *sure thing*."

He eyes the cell I just tossed him like it's a live grenade. "What are you talking about, Stella?"

I keep most of my life hidden from my father. He's too wasted to remember what I tell him anyway. He kind of knew I was dating the asshole and that we broke up but that was the extent of it. He had no idea I was seconds away from filing a restraining order against the guy. After weeks of harassment, today was the last straw. I didn't care if I got shit from the Red Dragons, but now … now that Dad owed them money, we were royally screwed.

"Remember Bo? The guy I was dating? He's been trying to get back together with me since we broke up. I wouldn't be surprised if he planned the whole thing." The guy is a devious little *stronzo*.

A flash of hope sifts through the gray haze. "This is it, then, our chance. He's one of their leaders, isn't he? You can talk to him and work out a deal or something."

"No way," I snarl. It took me almost a year to get out of that train wreck of a relationship. Bo was crazy jealous and possessive. He abused me in every way possible. It had taken me hours of online therapy to realize what we had wasn't healthy. That's how badly my dad had effed me up. I thought abuse was normal in a relationship.

Dad drops to his knees, the old floorboards creaking under the sudden weight. "Please, Stella, please." He reaches for my hands, squishing my fingers between his. "You don't know what those guys could do to me …. We've already lost your mom and Vinny." He chokes up, and hot tears well in my eyes.

Cazzo, this man knows how to get to me. "Do you really want to lose me too?"

I huff out a breath and wriggle free of his hold. His hands are moist and clammy, and pity surges to the surface. I should let him pay for his mistakes, but he's right, I can't risk losing him. He's all I have left. "Fine, I'll go talk to Bo." I pause and inhale a steadying breath. Just the idea of seeing him again has me wanting to reach for my inhaler. "Under one condition."

"Thank you, Stella, thank you. I'll do anything."

I sear my father with my steeliest glare. "No more gambling. For real this time. Delete Jimmy's number, cancel your subscription service for weekly tips, all of it."

His watery eyes latch onto mine, and that damned pity rears its head again. "I swear, Stel. It's done. I'll never waste a single penny again. I only did it for you, you know. After all you've suffered, I just want a better life for you."

My heart clenches at his words despite knowing better. He's an alcoholic, addicted to gambling, and a liar. I've heard this story countless times before, but still, I want to believe him. "If you want a better life for me, then let me go."

He nods slowly. "Once this is over, I'll do anything you want. You want to go to Florida? I'll help you get out of here; I swear."

"Good," I grumble. "Now go take a shower, Dad. You stink."

The hint of a smile curls his lips, and for an instant, the ghost of my dad reappears. The sober one, the one that was happily married with *two* kids. As much as I hate him sometimes, I can't help but think back on that version. Mom's death knocked him down, and Vinny's was the final knockout punch.

He slowly rises, shoulders rounded as he attempts to straighten. "You deserve so much better, Stel."

"Yeah, I know, which is why I'm trying so damned hard to get the hell out of here."

Dad cups my cheek, his rough palm so different than the soft touch I remembered as a child. "You will. You always accomplish whatever you set your mind to." With one final lingering glance, he turns away and shuffles toward the bathroom.

The minute the door slams closed I slump down on the couch. Angry butterflies batter my insides at the thought of groveling to my ex. Bo is a manipulative bastard, and somehow, I just know he planned this. It's his way of ensuring I'll be bound to him forever.

Little does he know I'll be out of here in a few short weeks anyway. Forcing myself off the couch, I trudge to my half of the living room. If this is going to work, I'll have to make it believable. Rifling through my closet, I pick out my sexiest dress. It's the one I wore on our first date. With a plunging neckline and soft, slinky material, it hugs all my Italian curves. It's Bo's favorite. He always said Asian women were too skinny, and he liked a little meat on his girl. All that stupid shit I bought into.

My stomach churns at the thought of his hands on me. Shaking my head, I force the nauseating images away. It won't come to that. I'll make empty promises, anything to erase my father's debts. With any luck, I'll be long gone before I have to pay up.

CHAPTER 4
ON MY KNEES

*S*tella

I hurry past Mrs. DeVito's door, praying to God she doesn't see me in this outfit. Poor woman would have a heart attack at the plunging neckline and indecent hem. Not to mention the fiery red stilettos.

I can practically hear her in my mind, her thick accent coming through in stereo. *"You crazy, Stella? You want some man to think you a puttana?"* She wouldn't be wrong either in these hooker heels. I'm only wearing them because Bo bought them for me, and I'm ready to pull out all the stops to buy my father's freedom.

Once I pass the bakery, I slow my pace. At least now I won't run into Mrs. D. or her son, Giuseppe. I turn the corner onto Canal Street, and further down the block, a man in a black suit is climbing into a dark town car. His gaze flickers in my direction, and our eyes meet for an instant. There's something familiar about the intensity in his dark gaze, the hard set of his jaw. The glint atop his fancy leather shoes.

I squint to make out more details, but he's too far. His brows furrow as we stand there locked in an epic staring contest, neither moving. I finally blink, and he darts into the car.

"Hey!" I call out, unbidden, but the car takes off, tires screeching. I watch it race down the street and disappear around the corner. I'm filled with the strangest and most overwhelming need to follow it.

What the hell's going on with you, Stella?

Shaking my head, I continue down the street until the savory scent of fried dumplings and sweet and sour sauce invade my nostrils. The mouthwatering Chinese food is the only thing I miss from the year spent shackled to Bo. The pair of gaudy red dragons eye me as I grow closer to his family's restaurant. Drawing in a steadying breath, I attempt to tame the monster-sized butterflies whipping around my belly. The idea of begging Bo for mercy makes me want to vomit.

But I suck it up and force my feet up the steps of the Red Dragon.

The bright scarlet door swings open, the jingle-jangle of the overhead bell like a death knell. Feng leers down at me, dark bangs plastered across his forehead. "What are you doing here, Stel—"

His words are cut off as my ex marches in, a satisfied grin on his lips as his eyes rake over my scandalous dress. If it weren't for the purple shiner darkening his cheek and the split lip bringing a smile to my face, I would've turned tail and run. No, I tell myself to enjoy the moment of triumph. Short-lived, but still.

"You got a little shmutz under your eye." The words pop out before I can stop them. *Merda.* Dammit, Stella. You're supposed to be winning the ass over, not pissing him off.

His expression sours, the satisfaction on his lips melting into a scowl. "It was worth it just to see your face when that book hit the tracks, and the fear in your eye when I had you on your knees."

I contemplate a witty comeback, namely, mentioning I

already got a brand new book from my mysterious savior so he can suck it, before I remind myself I'm here to play nice. Inhaling a calming breath, I bat my lashes and don my sweetest smile. "I didn't come to fight, Bo. I came for a favor."

He snorts on a laugh, dark eyes gleaming. "Miss my cock that much, huh?"

I bite back the slew of curses poised on my tongue. The *bastardo* knows exactly why I'm here. "It turns out my dad owes the Red Dragons some money."

Bo leans back against the counter and crosses his arms over his wiry, muscled chest. "Is that so?"

"Yeah. You wouldn't happen to know anything about that, would you?"

His lips slant into a thin line. "Not a thing, Stel." He moves closer, a wicked grin taking shape. "It's a nasty business gambling." He pauses, letting the embarrassment sink in. "How much are we talking?"

"Twenty-five g's," I grit out.

A sharp whistle echoes across the quiet restaurant. "That's more than *some* money, babe."

I cringe at the old pet name. How the hell did I ever find that cute? Slapping my hands on my hips, I swagger closer despite every nerve in my body recoiling at his proximity. "So can you help me out?"

"What exactly are you asking?"

"Can you make the debt go away?"

A throaty laugh bursts through his thinned lips, and a second, higher pitched one detonates from his cousin's mouth. Feng had been so silent I'd forgotten he was here. The pair of idiots laugh at me, and anger burns my cheeks. This is so humiliating.

No, what comes next is going to be much, much worse. "I'll do whatever you want," I grit out.

Bo's eyes light up, and he hisses at Feng, "Leave us."

His cousin's thin brows shoot up, and my ex barks at him

in Mandarin. Feng turns heel like a beaten dog with his tail between his legs and slinks through the metal doors to the kitchen.

Bo stalks closer, and bile rises further up my throat with each step. *You can do this, Stella.* I clench my fingers into tight fists and force my body to still. My fight or flight reflexes are kicking in, and all I want to do is get the fuck out of here.

"Anything?" The corner of his split lip tips up. "Will you be a good little whore and suck my cock?"

His hands close around my shoulders, and he forces me to the ground. My knees hit the cold tile, and pain streaks up my legs. I grit through the ache and plaster a smile on my face. "I will if you erase my father's debt."

Bo barks out another harsh laugh as he unlatches his belt buckle and sneers down at me. "Twenty-five thousand for one blow job? How good do you think you are, babe?"

A swirl of anger and embarrassment heats my cheeks, and I'm a second away from punching the *stronzo* in the throat. There must be another way out of this. I close my eyes and Dad's miserable face darts across my mind. I have to do it for him. Steeling my resolve, I smile wider, flashing my teeth. "Then what would it take to expunge the entire debt, Bo?"

He snatches my chin with his thumb and forefinger and jerks my head up, forcing my eyes to his. "You're mine till the end of the summer. To do with as I please."

The hiss of metal grinding across the teeth of his zipper sends goosebumps racing down my back. I shake my head, black encroaching into my vision. I'd never survive. "A week," I counter.

"Your tight little pussy isn't worth twenty-five k, Stel. The whole summer." He tugs his cock from his pants, and nausea claws up my throat at the pale, veiny thing. "Today will be day one."

Oh, God, I can't do this. I swallow hard, the idea of sucking him off sending tremors up my spine. If I did this, I'd be no better than the Canal Street *puttana* that Mrs. D. is always warning me of.

The front door whips open, the sharp jingle sending my heart catapulting up my throat, and three large males fill the red-rimmed doorway. A sea of black suits and matching crimson pocket squares. I leap to my feet barely able to get my stilettos out from under me as the three dark-haired males eye me.

Bo slips his dick back into his pants, and I exhale a sigh of relief. Saved by the freakin' bell.

"Leave, pretty girl," says the taller one whose chest reminds me of a wine barrel. "We've got business to discuss."

"No problem," I mumble as I race to the door.

"Stella, wait," Bo barks.

With one hand on the doorknob, I cant my head over my shoulder and school my lips into something resembling a smile.

"If you still want to take me up on the deal," he calls out, "come back tonight."

I force my head to bob up and down despite every bone in my body wanting to spit in his face. Then I race out the door whispering a dozen Hail Mary's and thanking all the saints that those thugs had shown up.

CHAPTER 5
WHAT'S THE WORSE THEY COULD DO?

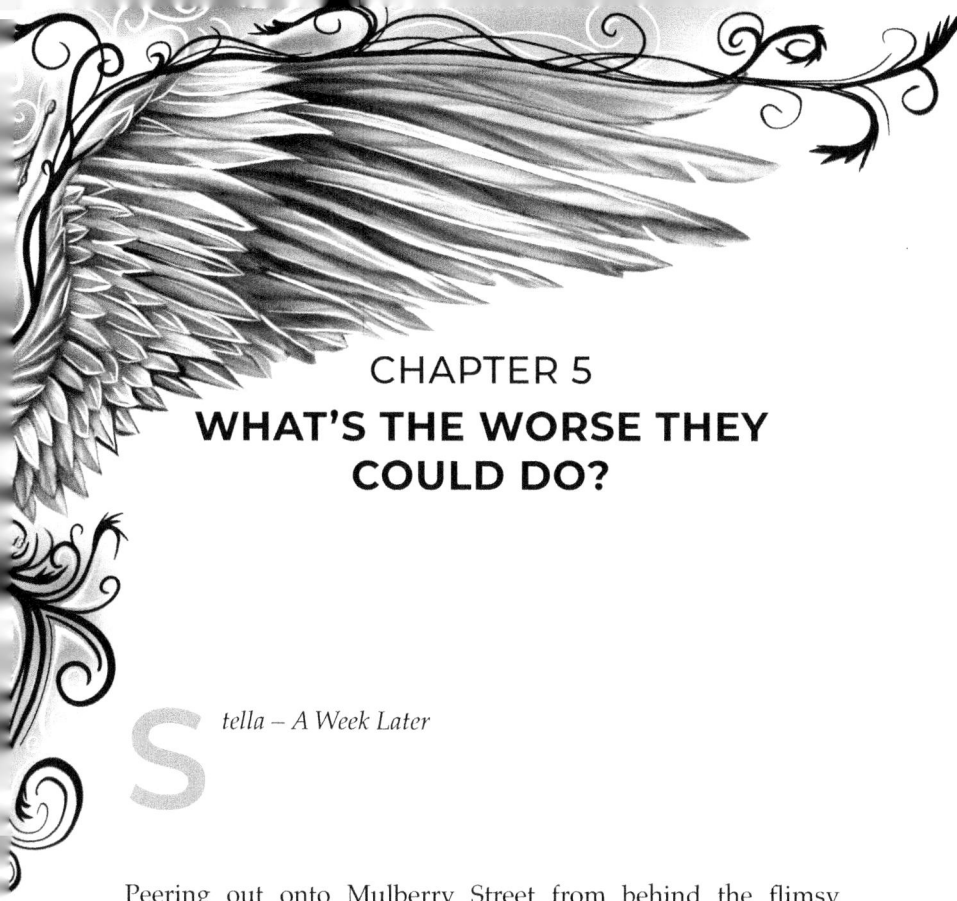

Stella – *A Week Later*

Peering out onto Mulberry Street from behind the flimsy curtain, I huff out a breath. I'm not going to be able to hide from Bo forever. Plus, the *pezzo di merda* only extended my service of indenture when I told him I was deathly ill. It wasn't entirely a lie. The idea of physically being with him did make me want to vomit.

But a week off work is more than we can afford, especially right now. Which means, I'm going to have to come out of hiding. With any luck, I'll be able to avoid Bo today between classes and my shift at *Nonna Maria's*.

My mind flickers back to a man I met at the café nearly a week ago. He'd left me a fifty-dollar tip which had bought us groceries for the week. It was the only reason I'd been able to take the time off. A pair of dark eyes flash across my vision, and my stomach lurches. For a second, I could've sworn I'd met him before. There was something so familiar about his touch, those eyes, that penetrating gaze that seared right through the ridiculous oversized hat and sunglasses I'd worn to hide from Bo.

Pazza. That's what Mrs. D would say. I'm going crazy.

Pulling the curtain across the window, I eye my phone on the bed. A string of unanswered text messages awaits. Who am I kidding? There's no way I'm getting out of this thing with Bo. Is my virtue worth twenty-five thousand dollars? I'm starting to think no.

There's only one text message I do answer. The one from my best friend, Rose. She's been in Long Island for the week visiting her mom. A part of me is happy she's missing out on all the drama with Bo. She'd kill me if she knew what I was considering after all I went through to escape him.

"Hey, Stella, are you feeling better yet?" Dad's voice seeps through the makeshift wall separating my bedroom from the tiny living room.

Instead of telling my father the truth, I'd resorted to lying to him too. My father wasn't a great man, but I didn't think he'd approve of me selling my body to pay off his debt. "Yeah, Dad. I'm going back to work today."

He pokes his head around the plaster barrier, eyes bloodshot. Dragging his hand over the back of his neck, he smiles sheepishly. "Oh good. Because I've got to start paying back that loan—" He smothers the rest of his words, burying his face in his hands.

Cazzo. Bo probably has his goons harassing Dad because I haven't upheld my end of the bargain. "What's the new payment schedule you worked out?"

His eyes dart down to the floor. "Two grand a month."

"Two grand?" I shriek.

And still, it would take over a year to pay it off. Not to mention the interest. Dammit, I'm really going to have to do this. I'd have to submit to Bo's depraved fantasies to get us out of this debt. Worse, I'd have to delay my move to Florida until the end of the summer.

"Get out … please," I add after a beat. "I need to get dressed."

"Sure, honey, I'll get out of your hair." Only he doesn't move.

"What?"

"I know you've been sick and all, but did you ever get a chance to talk to that Red Dragon guy about giving us a break?"

"Yes," I grit out. "I'm handling it, okay?"

"Sure, thing. Thanks, Stella." He backs up a few steps, then finally turns heel and disappears into the kitchenette.

If he asks me what's for breakfast, I'll lose my mind. *Grazie a Dio* he remains silent as he shuffles through the empty cabinets. I throw on a shirt and a pair of jeans, tie my hair back into a high ponytail out of my face like Mrs. D. likes it and head out.

Hours later, I huff out a breath of relief when I make it back inside my building. Spinning around to make sure the front door locks, I lean against the worn timber with my bagful of Italian pastries. Somehow, I'd survived a full day of work, but just barely. Bo's cousin, Feng, spotted me when I went outside to deliver a plate of cannoli to a customer despite my clever hat-and-sunglasses disguise.

I'd quickly scooted back inside *Nonna Maria's* and never came out again. I must have looked terrified because Giuseppe, Mrs. D's son and my boss, asked if I was okay. I told him Bo and Feng were giving me trouble, and he stood guard at the door for my entire shift.

The man was a godsend.

As are these cannoli. I'm starving. My stomach grumbles

on cue, but I force myself up the steps before giving in to the tasty treats. Dad must be hungry since I doubt he's left home all day, and our cupboards are bare.

I reach the top step, and my eyes land on our battered door halfway down the hall. *Cazzo*. I sprint the rest of the way, dropping the warm bag of pastries. With my heart jackhammering against my ribcage, my hand closes around the doorknob which hangs on by only one rusty hinge.

"Dad!" I call into the quiet apartment.

No answer.

My mind flashes back to a similar scene from the past. A dark room. Blood splattered across the floor. Tears sting at the corners of my eyes, but I will them back. I'm not a little girl anymore. And *Nonno* was gone. He couldn't be responsible for this.

Silently, pushing the door open, I tiptoe inside. I'm half-certain I'll meet the barrel of a gun the moment I cross the threshold. But I'm greeted only by silence.

And a ravaged apartment.

Couch cushions are tossed to the floor, every single drawer and cabinet is open, a broken lamp lies on its side, the glass from the bulb scattered across the linoleum. *Merda*. I can barely keep the tears back now. "Dad?" It comes out as more of a whimper.

As shitty as my father can be, he's still my only living relative left.

Terror seizes my lungs and I drop to my knees, scanning the floor for blood. My heart begins to function again when I find none. Breathe, Stella. Inhale, exhale. I reach for my inhaler in my pocket and take a long pull.

You can do this, Stella. It has to be Bo. He's trying to make a statement because I've been hiding out. Well, fuck that. I'm done hiding. I'm also done pretending I could ever do any of the vile things he'd expect from my summer of servitude.

I'd find another way to pay off this damned debt if it killed me.

Pushing myself off the ground, I draw in another breath and march to my bedroom. Like the rest of the apartment, it's in shambles. From across the room, a yellow post-it note clinging to my desk catches my eye.

I immediately recognize the dark scrawling. Mom always used to say Dad should've been a doctor with his chicken scratch. An insane bubble of laughter tumbles out at the idea of my father responsible for someone's life. I scan the note, my chest tightening with each word.

Stella,

They found me. You gotta help. Ask Mrs. D. for a loan if you have to. If you bring two thousand dollars, they said they'll release me. This is the address:

103 Canal St.

I'm sorry.

I love you, Dad

I drag my hand through my hair, hot tears pricking at my eyes again. What the hell am I supposed to do now?

I know Mrs. D. will give me the money if I ask, but it's just not fair. *Nonna Maria's* hasn't been doing great with the sudden increase in crime. It's been scaring all the tourists away. How can I put her in that position?

I pace the length of my shitty bedroom, mind whirling. "What do I do, Mom?" I stare up at the ceiling and pray to a God I've long given up on. "What do I do?" I cry.

Mom loved Mrs. DeVito as much as I do. She loved Dad too, but the man that she knew was gone. I wouldn't take advantage of our friendship. I'd just have to go down to Canal Street and reason with them. There had to be another way to get my dad out of this mess without selling my body or risking *Nonna Maria's* business.

What's the worst they could do to me, right?

CHAPTER 6
THE BOSS IS COMING TO GET YOU

*S*tella

I stare up at the address stamped across the aluminum grate covering the entrance of 103 Canal Street. With a deep breath to steady my nerves, I lift my knuckles to the metal. The harsh clanging sends my heart shooting up my throat.

A faint buzz catches my attention, and I glance up at the security camera over my head. A red light blinks, and the lens clicks and spins. A moment later, a middle-aged man in a black suit appears behind the barred door.

He opens it a crack, and dark beady eyes meet mine. Wiry gray hair creeps up his temples, mixing with the black. "You Stella?"

I nod.

He takes a step back and ushers me inside. From the first look at the interior, it's an old pawn shop. The dusty glass cases hold a treasure of gold and silver jewelry and watches.

"Give me your phone." He extends a meaty palm as I fumble for my cell.

"When will I get it back?"

"Don't worry about that right now." He snatches it from my hand and slides it into his jacket pocket. "Now come with me." He hitches his thumb over his shoulder and leads me toward the back. The hair on the back of my neck rises, and I dip my hand into my pocket, fingers closing around the pepper spray. I'd swapped it out for my inhaler in a last-minute attempt at self-preservation.

As I follow the big man down the dark corridor, my thoughts reel. First off, I've never seen this guy at the Red Dragon, and after a year of dating Bo, the asshole, I was pretty familiar with the major players. I was certain I'd find Bo here himself. So who was this guy?

He holds the door open and ticks his head into the dim room. From the crack, I can just make out a hunched figure on a chair. "Dad!" I cry out and race for him, but a firm hand closes around my upper arm.

Another dark-haired male glares down at me, this one a few years younger than the first and with arms so thick his suit clings on like spandex.

My dad lifts his head, both eyes bruised and puffy. "Don't hurt her, Tony."

"I'm not a monster, you prick. I wouldn't hurt a lady." He releases his hold and motions toward the chair beside my father. Two other males in black suits and matching ruby pocket squares stand in the shadows. Were these the same thugs I'd seen at the Red Dragon? Or did they all just wear the same uniform?

I shoot the first guy a narrowed glare before marching over to check on my dad. His lip is split, and dried blood splotches line his collar. I spin around and glare at this Tony guy. "So you wouldn't hurt a lady but a middle-aged man is okay, *bastardo*?"

A flicker of a smile curls the man's lip. "I didn't know you were Italian. Not with a father like that."

"Well, I am. My mother was an Esposito."

The entire room is blanketed in silence. *Yeah, that's right fuckers. Nonno*, my grandfather was kind of a big deal. Way before the Kings and the Red Dragons, and the Chinese Triad ruled these streets.

The man dips his head. "I'm sorry for your loss. I didn't know Isabella was your mother."

An odd, strangled sound erupts from my father's lips, and a knot of emotion thickens my throat. I shove it down. Hard. Now is not the time for sentimental bullshit. I need my wits about me if we're going to survive this.

Tony reaches into his jacket pocket and pulls out his phone. After shooting off a quick text, he pockets it again and rounds the table we're seated in front of. "Do you have the money?"

I shake my head. "If we had the money, we would've given it to you a week ago. Didn't Bo tell you we were trying to work out a deal?"

"Bo?" The big guy's thick brows slam together.

"Yeah, Bo Zhang. Aren't you all Red Dragons?" The moment the words are out I feel like a total *stronza*. With dark wavy hair, prominent noses, and thick New York accents, there's nothing Asian about any of these men.

A deep chuckle erupts from Tony's thinned lips. "No, sweetheart, we ain't Red Dragons. We bought out some of their old debts. So now, you owe the Kings."

Well, shit. On one hand I'm beyond relieved I wouldn't have to beg Bo for a break, but on the other, the Italian mafia is just as ruthless as the Chinese Triad.

"Stella, damn it," Dad snarls, "you should've gone to Mrs. D. like I told you."

"I couldn't," I whisper-hiss. "She doesn't deserve to be dragged into this mess."

Tony cracks his knuckles, the sound sending ripples of

goosebumps up and down my arms. "Well, Mr. Liam McKenzie, you owe my boss money, and my job is to collect."

"Please ...." I chomp down on my lower lip to keep it from trembling. I'd rather beg to this guy than Bo any day. "There has to be some other payment schedule we can work out. I've been sick and out of work and Dad lost his job. Can you give us another month?" I grab my purse and pull out my checkbook. Not even Dad knows about my secret savings account. I've been squirreling away every penny for my grand escape. I still had just shy of a grand. "I can give you five hundred now and the rest at the end of the month."

Dad's eyes light up as they scan the crisp checks.

Tony's phone dings again, a sharp cry in the thickening silence, and he scans the screen before turning his gaze back to me. "My boss has a better idea."

"What's that?" Dad leans forward but the cuffs pinning his hands behind his back restrict the movement.

"You give me the five hundred today, and you, Liam, get to walk out of here with all your limbs intact, and we keep your daughter as collateral until the debt is paid."

A sharp gasp escapes through my clenched teeth. "What?" I finally blurt once my brain is able to process the words.

"Done." My father's voice sends ice surging through my veins. I barely recognize the frosty tenor through the roar of my heartbeats.

"What?" I squeal again. Before I can get another word out, a dark shadow appears over me and big hands clamp down on my shoulders. I try to wriggle free, to reach for the pepper spray, but the man is like a freakin' ox. Another guy grabs my wrists and forces them behind my back. Metal bites into my skin, and I let out another screech followed by a string of colorful Italian curses.

Tony smirks again, and the urge to punch the *figlio di puttana* in the throat is overwhelming.

"*Vaffanculo!*" I scream at the top of my lungs. "You can't do this!"

He rounds the desk and pulls a stack of paper from the drawer, then places it in front of my father. I can't even look at him. The sight of the man who raised me, who is supposed to protect me, sends my stomach roiling and nausea clawing up my throat.

The meathead that led me into this godforsaken place unlocks Dad's handcuffs and remains at his side, looming dangerously.

"Just sign here." Tony points at the dotted line. His lips twist, in what I could swear is disgust, as my father signs my life away without a second thought.

The *pezzo di merda* doesn't even look at me as he slides the papers back to Tony and leaps up.

"Dad?"

Nothing.

"Make the payment as required, and you'll see your daughter at the end of the month."

Liam McKenzie nods and races out of the room so fast he's nothing more than a cowardly blur.

I lean back against the chair, numb. He left me. My father, my last living relative just sold me off to the Kings.

Tony sinks into the chair across the desk and runs his large hands over his face. With a grunt, he watches me as a thick silence pervades the small space. "Piece of shit," he mutters.

My eyes dart up to meet his. Was he talking about my dad? I almost open my mouth to ask, but I'm too fucking spent. All the anger seeps out of me like a leaky tire. How could he do this to me?

I was ready to sell my body for him. I would have done anything to save his sorry ass despite the shitty way he's treated me for the past ten years.

Tony's phone pings again, but I'm too numb to care. My

heart is broken, a bottomless chasm opening up in my chest, and I have nothing left.

"... coming to get you, sweetheart." The man's words blur in the distance. It sounds like he's underwater or maybe I am. I'm drowning.

I stare at him blankly.

"I said, the boss is coming to get you."

CHAPTER 7
TAKING OUT THE TRASH

Luca – *A Week Earlier*

Pezzo di merda. I glare at the piece of shit bleeding on the subway platform whose family has ruined everything good about lower Manhattan. The Red Dragons have no finesse, no style, no purpose in their business dealings. Rape, burglary, assault. It makes no difference to them if it's a woman or an eighty-year-old grandpa. It's just wrong.

"Get out of here," I hiss and throw in another kick for good measure.

Bo Zhang lets out a grunt, his body curling in on itself. "Fuck you, guido. I should've known it was you." My blood boils as a snide grin tilts the corners of his lips. "The Kings are old news. You've gone soft, everyone knows it. It's only a matter of time until the Dragons rule everything south of Harlem."

I snort on a laugh. "You're delusional, Bo. That last punch must've hit something important." I button up my trench coat, about done with this *bastardo* and this conversation. The roar of the approaching subway spins my attention to the tracks. That woman's book.

My feet compel me forward to the edge of the platform. It's already destroyed from the last train that passed but the cover is still legible. Taking my phone out, I snap a quick pic and send it to Tony. That guy can track down anything.

Hmm … Economics.

From the corner of my eye, I catch Bo pushing himself off the ground. I cock my head over my shoulder and glare at the shithead. I try to be civil with these goons to keep the peace with the Chinese Triad but today, I can't. "Who was that woman? It sounded personal."

He staggers closer, wiping blood from his lip. "Just some whore I used to fuck."

Dio, the man has no respect for anything. "She have a name?"

Bo shakes his head. "Can't remember it." His eyes narrow as he regards me. "What are you going to do Robin Hood, save her book?" He ticks his head at the ravaged remains below. "If you jumped on the tracks you'd sure as fuck be doing me a huge favor."

The rushing winds of the approaching train jostle the torn spine and ripped pages. Dark black letters catch my eye on the inside of the front page. A name. I snap another quick picture and send it to Tony a second before the train rolls in. If anyone can figure it out, it's my righthand man and one of my oldest friends.

The subway charges into the station, and I inch closer to the yellow line. The doors glide open, and I slip through. Bo makes a move toward me, but I hold my hand out. "Take the next one," I snarl.

"Are you fucking kidding me, Luca?"

"Does it look like I'm kidding? And that's *Signor* Valentino to you, shithead." I shove him back, and the sleek doors slam closed. A satisfied smile curls my lips as the train car lurches forward. Bo's furious expression blurs, his irate curses falling away as we speed out of the station.

Once my temper simmers, I fold into the empty seat beside the door. It isn't often I make use of the city's underground transportation system anymore. It must have been fate that brought me here today. There was something about that girl … I close my eyes and her face, pressed to the glass doors of the subway car, whizzes by.

Opening my eyes, I shake my head out and dismiss the images. I've got enough to worry about without adding some girl Bo's screwing to the list.

As soon as I'm back on the streets of the Upper East Side, the tense set of my shoulder blades eases. Up here I'm Luca Valentino, respected businessman. Down there, in my old hood, I'm something else.

My cell phone pings, and I glance at the string of messages from Tony. In my rush, I hadn't actually explained what any of the pictures I'd sent him meant. Filling him in on my encounter with Bo, I ask him to track down the woman and find her a new textbook.

Economics had always been a favorite of mine.

Yes, that had to be it. It has nothing to do with the gorgeous brunette kneeling on the ground or the look on her face that had roused an indescribable emotion in my hollow chest. Another wave of anger pummels into me, and I lengthen my stride and turn down the next street toward The Plaza. I need a release.

A hidden gem, the famous Plaza Hotel houses the super exclusive gym I belong to, *La Palestra*. With my Italian roots, when I'd heard the name, it was a no-brainer. I spent most mornings there working out my explosive temper, but I'd missed my session today.

After that run-in with Bo, I need to hit something. Again.

Taking the steps two at a time, I nod at the bellmen

stationed in front of the classic hotel. "Morning, Mr. Valentino." One of them rushes to open the door.

"Morning … Vic." I glance at his nametag, and he rewards me with a smile. I slip him a twenty and the grin only grows wider. "Put it towards your college fund, kid. I used to save up every penny I earned." And I'd done just about everything when I was a teenager: from waiting tables, to valet parking, to petty theft.

"Thanks, Mr. Valentino."

I dip my head, cross the glittering foyer of the bustling hotel and head toward the stairs. As I descend the private stairwell, the scent of disinfectant muddled with lavender assaults my nostrils.

"Good morning, Mr. Valentino." The cute blonde behind the counter flashes me a brilliant smile.

"Morning, Grace." She opens her mouth to continue the conversation, but I zip past her. The girl is sweet, but it's obvious she likes me. And I have rather particular tastes and rules regarding my sex life. It was just sex. And that was it.

Plus, I love this gym, and I don't want to have to stop coming here if I fuck around with this girl. I dip into the locker room and strip out of my suit and tie. That is the one thing I hate about being Luca Valentino, C.E.O. of King Industries. I much prefer jeans and a t-shirt. Sure, Armani jeans are my favorite, but I have to support the motherland, right?

Once I've changed out of my restrictive clothing, I head out of the quiet locker room and straight into a familiar face in the hallway.

Merda.

The blonde lights up as her eyes raze over me. "Luca Valentino, I did not know you were a member here."

Neither did I. Or I never would've fucked you. "*Ciao*, Caroline. I had no idea."

She creeps closer, and her hand finds her way to my stomach. I take a step back, and she traps me against the wall, her big fake boobs pressing against my chest.

"Caroline," I whisper, "you do remember what we talked about before we …."

Her grin widens. "Before you fucked me senseless?"

"Hmm." I nod.

"Yes, yes, I know, no strings." Her hand creeps lower, until it brushes my cock.

I squirm but her hold only tightens, fingers wrapping around my now hardening dick. We're in the middle of the hallway and anyone can walk by at any moment. Public displays are *not* my thing. Besides that, I am a man of my word, and I stick to my rules. For reasons.

My fingers latch around her wrist, and I tear her hand away from my cock. "I said no, Caroline."

"But why?" she whines. "I thought we had so much fun the other night."

"We did, but that's all it was. One night. Like I warned you."

She pouts, sticking her full lower lip out. My mind whirrs to the other night when that pouty mouth was wrapped around my dick. Great, now I'm impossibly hard, and all I wanted was a fucking workout.

"Just one more time?" She bats her long, sooty lashes and ticks her head at the locker room door. "Please, Luca, I'm already so wet just thinking about you. I'll let you fuck me wherever you want." She presses her body flush against mine, and hell, yes, I'm tempted. But there are reasons I stick to my rules. I don't need to get emotionally involved with women. And if you screw around more than once, things start to get complicated.

I close my hands around her shoulders and gently push her back, until she peels her body off mine. "I'm sorry, Caroline. The other evening was great, but it's over. And if you'll excuse me, I'm late for my workout session."

"You're an asshole, Luca," she hisses as I hurry down the hall.

I release a frustrated sigh and dart around the corner to find that punching bag. I'm in desperate need of it now.

After an hour of relentless punching and kicking, I feel remotely better. A twinge of guilt still eats at my core about Caroline, but I shove it down. I was very clear with her as I am with all women before I take them to my penthouse. Most accept my rules, but there are always the exceptions.

I'm about to jump into the shower when my cell phone vibrates, echoing across the locker.

Tony: *I found the girl and her address. You want me to drop off the new book now?*

Me: *No, wait. I'll see you at the office in fifteen.*

Tony: *Will do, capo.*

That odd sensation fills my chest as I shove my phone into my pocket and decide to forego the shower for now. I need to find out who that woman is. If only to fuck with Bo.

CHAPTER 8
C.E.O AND KING

L*uca*

A new wave of anger rushes my veins as I stare at my reflection in the fogged-up bathroom mirror. A scratch bisects my dark brow from my encounter with that piece of shit, Bo, and a faint bruise is beginning to form in the middle of my tattooed torso. I run my finger across my brow and scowl. It better not scar. The last thing I need is a permanent reminder of that asshole. I already have more than enough across my body.

The Red Dragons have gone unpunished for long enough. First, they invade Little Italy, then they spread their venom across the Lower East Side. It's not even safe for a woman in the subways anymore.

My mind flickers back to the brunette at the station, and that unfamiliar sensation tugs at my chest. There was something so familiar about her, but I just can't place the girl. She definitely wasn't any of the women I associated with. None of the models or socialites I casually dated would ever be caught in a shitty subway station in Little Italy. So who was she? The feeling was so insistent I'd had Tony call in more than a few favors until he tracked her down from the name I'd gotten out of the destroyed textbook. Then, I had him follow her to find out where she lived.

I stare at the post-it note on the vanity. Stella M. 356 Mulberry St. The heart of Little Italy. I knew a Stella once, but it had been nearly a decade since I'd seen her. Bands tighten around my chest, and I draw in a haggard breath. *It couldn't be her.*

Mulberry Street wasn't far from where I'd grown up actually. And a far cry from my new penthouse in the Upper East Side. Old memories invade my mind, and I'm tossed back in time.

"*Come on kick the ball, Luca!*"

"*I'm planning my shot,* bastardo, *give me a second.*" I dribble the soccer ball between my feet, eyeing my friend as he blocks the goal.

"*Hurry up, those prep school kids could come out any minute.*" He glances over his shoulder at Cambridge Prep.

We'd ditched school and taken the subway to the Upper East Side for a little fun. "*What's the matter, Vinny, you scared of a little tussle?*"

"*Course not. I'd just rather not piss off Dad. Sometimes he takes it out on me or Stella. He hasn't been in the best mood since—*"

His words cut off, and I wished I'd kept my big mouth shut. It had only been a couple months since my best friend lost his mom. Idiot. *Papà's right, I am a* cretino.

I curl my knee back, and my foot explodes forward. The ball sails toward the net. Vinny leaps to the right, but it flies right between his hands.

"Gol! Gol!" *I shout.* "Forza, Italia!"

Vinny pushes himself off the ground, a scowl on his pretty boy face. "Lucky shot."

I jump at him, throwing my arm around his shoulders. It's rare I get one past him. The kid is a soccer superstar. I'd never admit it, but he was even better than me. "Luck had nothing to do with it, my friend. Now, come on, I'll buy you a beer at O'Shea's."

He eyes me incredulously, those pale blue eyes shimmering in excitement. "How?"

I reach into my back pocket and pull out my newest prized possession. One of Papà's new hires is a counterfeiting genius. Money, IDs, checks, you name it, and he can forge it.

Vinny's eyes are so wide they're a second from popping out of his head. "I want one too."

"Stick with me, kid, and maybe one day you'll have one." I toss him a smirk and lead the way off the field. He races behind me like an overeager puppy.

My heart clenches as the memories fade away. *Dio*, I hadn't allowed myself to think about my childhood friend in ages. My gaze refocuses on the familiar address, and I force the old, painful images to the back of my mind. Who still lived in Little Italy anyway? I'd moved *Mamma* out of there when I made my first hundred grand. Then after my first million, I bought her a house in the suburbs, away from the hustle of the city and a safe distance from my life.

"You ready, *capo*?" Tony's voice seeps through the door.

"No," I grit out. "If I was ready, would I still be in here?" It's my own damned fault for having a bathroom built into my office, but in my line of work, sometimes a shower in the middle of the day is necessary. And today, after the gym, I definitely needed it.

"Sorry, Luca," he mutters. Tony's a good guy, just not the most perceptive at times. He'll stand beside me until the very end, do anything to protect me. He's an old family friend and as loyal as they come.

I reach for the shirt and clean suit hanging from the back of the door and spear my hand through the sleeve. The five numbers scrawled within the crowned skull tattoo across my chest draw my eye. After the unexpected rise of old memories this morning, I can't tear my gaze away from it. Shaking my head, I button up my shirt and bury my past.

To distract myself, I focus on the yellow note taped to the vanity. Maybe I'll drop off the new textbook myself. It's been so long since I've visited my old neighborhood, it could be nice. At the very least, I could grab some cannoli from *Nonna Maria's* and remind those bastard Red Dragons who controls Little Italy.

Yes, that's what I'll do.

I slip on my favorite cufflinks, the gilded crowns bringing a smile to my face. Mamma always used to call me her *piccolo principe*, her little prince. Now I was all grown up, and I was the king, or rather the C.E.O. of King Industries.

With one last glance in the mirror, I adjust my black tie and slip the note into my pocket. I whip the door open and the frosty air from my office mingles with the fog from the hot shower. Tony eyes me, quirking a brow. "You know, boss, they say cold showers are best for the circulation."

"My circulation is just fine, thanks." I spend enough hours at the gym to ensure that. It's the only way to relieve the stress. Well, there are other ways of course, but that involves dating and with my schedule, it's difficult. Case and point: Caroline. I'd rather keep my interaction with women casual, sex without strings.

Marching to my desk, I glance over the leather chair to Park Avenue and the sprawling city below. Once I'd constructed my empire, only the best office space would do. I'd crawled my way up from the bottom and built everything from scratch.

Papà, God rest his soul, had been in the canned tomato business back in Italy. He had a decent brand, but when he died, the company crumbled. I did my best to keep us afloat, but I was only a kid back then. I quickly learned that money wasn't in the tomatoes, but rather the machinery. Before long, I'd developed the most high-tech equipment out there and sold it to every cannery in the U.S. Now King Industries had their hand in just about every production plant out there.

Sure, I'd made some enemies along the way, but that was the nature of the business. And that's what I had Tony for. He runs my *other* enterprises.

I settle into my chair and glance up at my friend. "So, what's the status on the new project?"

"Not good, I'm afraid." He scrapes at the thick, dark scruff on his chin. "The commissioner is blocking our petition for the gambling cruise."

"Didn't you speak to him?"

He nods. "He's not interested in the money."

I scoff. Everyone is interested in money. He must be getting greased by another player. "Show him the pictures of him and his mistress. I'm sure that'll interest him."

"Will do, boss." He glances at his phone, scanning the notifications and scowls. "What about that asshole from Meatpacking that owes you for last month's shipment?"

"Take him to the pawn shop. If he won't pay with money, he'll pay with his damned blood."

"Right-o, I'll get Eddie on it." He scrolls across the screen and glances up again. "And that debt Jianjun offered you to acquire?"

"Yeah, let's go ahead and take him up on that."

"Good, that's it for me then." Tony ticks his head at the textbook at the end of my desk. "I'll drop the book off after I visit the old man?"

I reach for the Economics book and shake my head. "Nah,

I'll take care of this. I've been meaning to take a walk in the old hood."

His dark eyes chase up to my brow, and his lips twist. "You sure you want to risk a run-in with the Red Dragons again?"

"I'm itching for it, Tony." My fingers clench into tight fists. A light purple hue darkens my knuckles. It's been a while since I've handled my own dirty work, but damn, did it feel good today.

"Behave yourself, *Signor* Valentino." Clara pokes her head in without knocking.

If I didn't love my assistant like a second mother, I would've chewed her head off. No one comes into my office without warning. It is essential to my business.

She saunters in, swinging her hips like she's some diva. In an office full of males, she knows she runs the place. "Don't you think one fight is enough for a day?" Her warm brown eyes lock on the cut across my brow.

I shoot Tony a narrowed gaze. "Is nothing private around here?"

He shrugs, a sheepish smile crossing his lips. He's about a decade over my twenty-seven years, but we all know who's the boss around here. Clara.

"Luca, you know very well if I don't keep your mother apprised of the situation, she'll come down here herself."

"*Oofa*, that's the last thing I need, especially with this shit with the Red Dragons going down." My mamma is the love of my life, but for her safety, I keep her out of my business. She has little knowledge of my back-alley enterprises.

"Damned Dragons are trying to take over the docks again. Phil just called, and they've offered him twice what we're paying."

"*Merda*," I mutter. "Are the Red Dragons still operating out of that shitty restaurant in Chinatown?"

Tony nods. "Jianjun will be there, likely with the other members of the Chinese Triad. I wouldn't just swing by alone, *capo*. Especially if you want to keep things on the up and up with the new debt acquisition."

I crack my knuckles, the slight bruises sending a twinge up my hands. "I can handle myself, old friend."

"I know you can, but we wouldn't want to mess up that pretty little face of yours."

I can't help but grin. Tony's like the big brother I never had. My biological older brother is an ass so we're not exactly close.

"All those hot models will stop coming by if you ugly up that mug."

"And you won't get any of my sloppy seconds." I shoot him a wicked grin.

"Hey, I'm not complaining, Luca. No way any of those gorgeous models would look at me otherwise." He laughs, his broad shoulders bouncing.

"Oh, you two, *smettila*! Stop it. The way you treat those women, really, Luca, your mamma would just die if she knew."

I cock my head at my executive assistant. "I'm perfectly honest with every woman I meet, Clara. When *they* approach me, as is most often the case, I am very direct with what to expect. I'm not tricking these women into my bed. They know very well I'm not interested in dating or relationships."

She claps her hand over her chest and sighs dramatically. "What a waste of perfect genes. Who will continue the Valentino bloodline?"

"There's still Dante, don't forget."

Clara rolls her eyes. "*Che peccato*, the Valentinos are doomed." I'm not the only one who thinks my brother is an idiot. It's the reason why I sit atop the throne of the Kings empire instead of him. When *Papà* died, everyone assumed Dante would take the role, but he never stepped up. So, I did what I had to.

"Don't be so dramatic." The woman is a total drama queen but she's smart as a fox. "With all the shit going on in this world today, bringing another life into it would only be selfish."

"Maybe, you're right, Luca. But it wouldn't hurt to have an intelligent, attractive woman at your side when you attend all these important galas."

"And it would keep all the other hungry ladies off you," Tony adds.

Hmm. They're not wrong. Perhaps I'll look into a high-end escort service, just for the company, not the sex. If it's all business, it would keep things simple.

"Speaking of hungry …." Clara hands me the manila folder tucked to her chest. "Sister Margarita just called from the orphanage. They're in desperate need of a new roof. It would be a good tax write off for the company."

"How much is that going to be?" Tony blurts.

My assistant's brows knit as she stares at the figures from over my shoulder. "About eighteen grand."

Tony lets out a low whistle.

"Take some of the money from the gambling boat project and siphon it over," I reply as I hand her the folder.

"You're kidding me, Luca," my friend barks. "We need that money to pay off the state's gaming commission."

"Get it from somewhere else."

"But—"

I throw my hand up cutting him off. "Get. It. Somewhere. Else." I punctuate each word with ice. "Those kids deserve a decent place to live. End of story."

Clara throws me a beaming smile, and my frosty heart thaws. There's so much bad in this world, hell, I've done so many bad things, when I get the chance to do some good, I've got to take it. I have to tip the balance on the scales in my direction at least a little, right?

I reach for the textbook on the corner of my desk and rise. "I'm going to Little Italy. I'll be back later."

Tony rushes behind me. "You sure you don't want me to come?"

"No. I need that cruise project back on schedule. Go take care of the commissioner first, and we'll meet up later."

"Got it, *capo*."

I'm going to do my own digging about the first woman that has truly intrigued me in years, and I need to go alone.

CHAPTER 9
AN UNEXPECTED ENCOUNTER

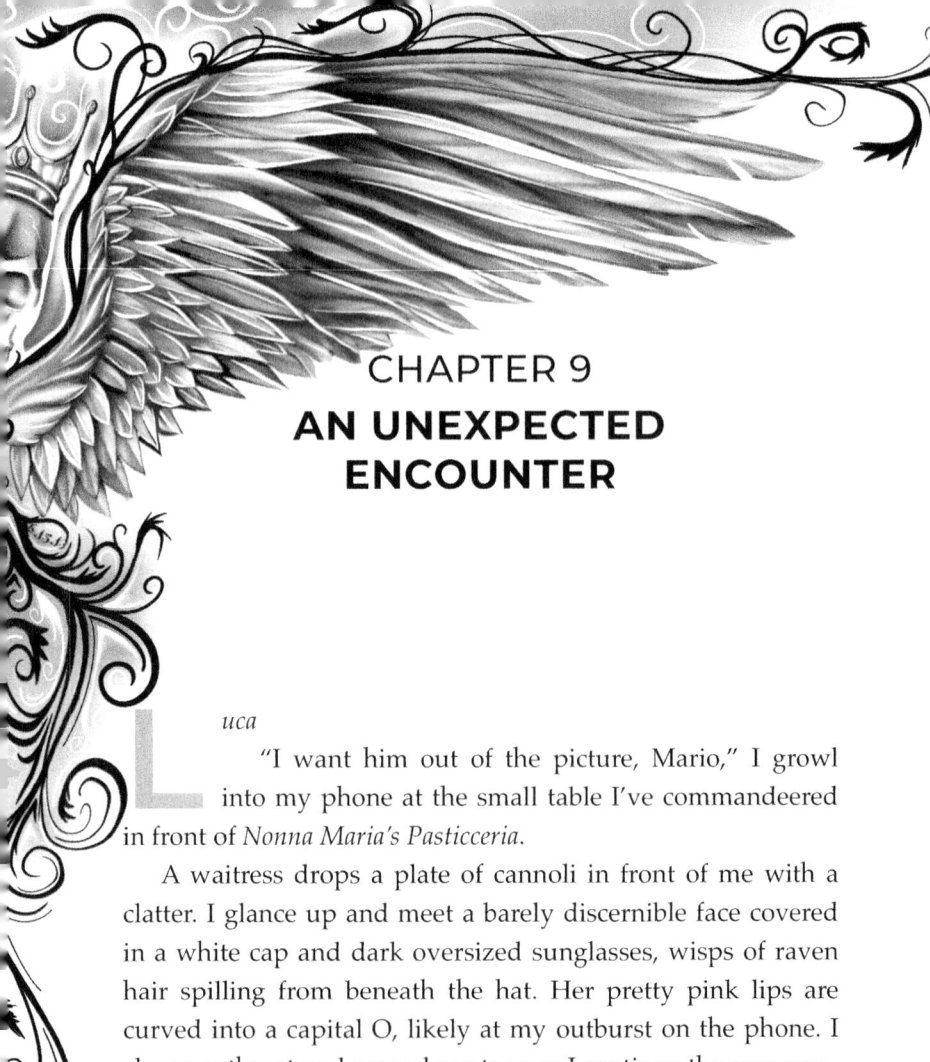

Luca

"I want him out of the picture, Mario," I growl into my phone at the small table I've commandeered in front of *Nonna Maria's Pasticceria*.

A waitress drops a plate of cannoli in front of me with a clatter. I glance up and meet a barely discernible face covered in a white cap and dark oversized sunglasses, wisps of raven hair spilling from beneath the hat. Her pretty pink lips are curved into a capital O, likely at my outburst on the phone. I clear my throat and amend my tone as I continue the conversation, and she sets the small cup of espresso beside the plate.

"Sorry," I mouth.

She nods, keeping her head down. My eyes lift to the bright red nametag. *Stella*. A whisper of a childhood memory flickers to the surface. That name seems to be following me everywhere lately.

Mario continues to squeal like a pig on the slaughtering line, but my attention is fixed on the curvy brunette who refuses to meet my eye. I certainly don't consider myself conceited, but the ladies tend to react a certain way around me, but this one, *niente*. Nothing.

I reach for the espresso, and my hand grazes hers as she drops a heap of napkins. A faint gasp parts her lips, and my dick twitches at the sexy sound. Images of those lips wrapped around my hard cock flash across my mind. What the hell? I blink quickly as heat streaks low beneath my belt.

I open my mouth to say something as she regards me with what I can only assume is a matching expression of surprise. I've never had such a primal reaction to a woman. She spins away, but my hand captures her wrist, fingers closing around her soft skin before she can get away. "Wait," I mumble.

Her gaze darts over my shoulder, and her hand trembles beneath my touch. I follow her line of sight to a pair of shadows creeping in the adjacent alley. Damned Red Dragons, like rats infiltrating every corner of my city.

"Let go," she hisses and wriggles free of my hold. There's something so familiar about her voice.

I want to stop her, find out who she is, but she darts back into the *pasticceria* before I can get another word out.

Tony strolls up, and I force the odd encounter with the waitress to the back of my mind and swallow another bite of the *cannolo* before whatever my enforcer has to say ruins my appetite. "It's done, *capo*."

Clearing my head, I focus on the matter at hand. "How did Jianjun take it?"

My old friend grabs a chair from a nearby table, the sharp squeal of wrought iron against asphalt making my teeth itch, and he sinks into the tiny thing. The man's a beast, dwarfing the small chair. "Not great, but not bad." He eyes the empty plate between us and sticks his finger in his mouth then swipes it clean of the remaining powdered sugar.

I shake my head, barely suppressing a smile.

"It was a fair deal. And to be honest, we're better equipped for dealing with repayment of small debts. Honestly, I don't know why they assumed it in the first place."

"It was probably his idiot son, Bo," I snarl. My fingers jump up to the scratch across my brow then flashes of our altercation on the subway platform race across my mind. And that girl….

I almost knocked on her door when I went to drop off the book. To what end, I had no idea. Somehow, I just wanted to make sure she was okay. I'd stopped myself before doing something rash and left the textbook on the welcome mat, but I couldn't help myself from leaving that stupid note. A hint of a smile curls the corners of my lips.

And then I could've sworn I saw her again when I was leaving the Red Dragon. And now the waitress? Why did she seem familiar? Was I losing my mind?

"Why are you smiling, boss?"

I bring the espresso to my lips, smothering the grin. "Was I? I'll have to stop that. We wouldn't want any members of the Triad thinking I've gone soft."

He follows my gaze over his shoulder and catches the two figures in the shadows of the alleyway up the street. Squinting, he turns back and mutters a curse. "Who is it now?"

"Pretty sure it's Bo and his cousin. They're probably waiting for an opportune moment to get their revenge."

"Clara was right, Luca. You gotta be careful."

"I don't give two shits about those *bastardi*. Let them try to come for me in public. I'll have Jones on their ass for assaulting the C.E.O. of King Industries."

Tony chuckles. "That lawyer of yours sure is a shark."

"He's worth every penny, *amico*." I tip back the cup and finish off the espresso. Mmm, just like Mamma makes it. This alone made my trip to Little Italy worth it. "Speaking of pennies, Tony, make sure you and the guys get all these new loans squared away. You know the drill."

"Will do, Luca."

I stand and throw a fifty on the table. Tony eyes the bill, his dark irises widening. "It's for the waitress, not you, *stronzo*."

He chuckles and licks the remaining powdered sugar off the plate. "I would never."

I toss him a twenty, shaking my head. "Do yourself a favor and go buy a dozen cannoli for you and the guys so you can stop lapping up my leftovers like a mongrel. It'll make your job a little sweeter."

"Thanks, boss, you're the best." He shoots me a smirk, and I drop my sunglasses from my head down to settle atop my nose.

I consider going into the café to search for the waitress but pitch the crazy thought out before I do something stupid. There's a reason I don't date. Sticking to my rules is critical to my life and my line of work.

As I march down Mulberry, burning glares sear into the side of my face. *Make your move, figlio di putana. I dare you.* Neither Bo nor his chicken-shit cousin take a step from out of the shadows. Hiding like cowardly rats.

The train doors slide open, and I draw in a breath of fresh air, the tension immediately seeping from my taut shoulder blades. This is exactly why I moved Ma out of the city. A quick thirty-minute ride on the Metro North and the chaos of the surging metropolis is nothing but a distant memory.

Shrugging off my jacket, I bypass the line of taxis and opt to walk the fifteen-minute stroll today. I skipped the gym to deal with Bo myself today and without it, I have extra energy to burn. My visit to Mamma's this afternoon is two-fold: it's the anniversary of King Industries so I've come to surprise her with a gift, and I'm checking out an investment property for myself. There's too much money coming into my *other* businesses, and I need a way to divest.

Plus, Ma will be ecstatic when I tell her we'll be neighbors again.

The stroll goes by quickly with my fevered pace. The tickets are burning a hole in my jacket pocket. I owe everything I've become to my mother, but she's so proud and stubborn, she never lets me spoil her. There's no way she'll pass this up though.

I practically sprint up the stone walkway once I reach the quaint two-story home. With roughhewn gray stone walls, pristine white siding and a small porch, it's a modest house, but it was the most Mamma would allow me to spend on her.

Before I reach the last step, the aroma of roasted garlic and tomatoes wafts over me. My stomach rumbles despite the cannoli from only an hour ago. Nothing beats Mamma's cooking.

"*Ciao, Mamma!*" I shout as I walk in. She always leaves the door unlocked, something that we fight over constantly.

"*Luca, sei tu? Ma cosa fai qui?*" A huge smile lights up her face as she races from the kitchen. "What are you doing here?" Flour powders her cheek and dark hair, the pungent scent emanating off her housedress in thick waves. "*Che bella sorpresa.*"

"Yeah, great surprise." A familiar voice echoes from beyond the narrow hallway.

My gaze lifts to my brother's, and my pleasant mood sours instantly. "What are you doing here, Dante?"

"Just came to see Ma. And you?"

"Same."

"*Che piacere* to have both of my sons home." She moves between us, lacing an arm through each of ours and tugs us to the kitchen. *La cucina* was always the heart of our home; it didn't matter the size. Even when we lived in that tiny walk-up off Mott Street, we'd all crowd around the crappy table and eat, drink, and laugh.

Dante used to be semi-decent back then. I eye my brother as we sit around the table, and Ma goes back to making her homemade fettucine. An old Frank Sinatra number plays in the background, and my mother begins to hum as she works.

"Why'd you really come?" I whisper to my brother. "Out of money again?"

"Fuck you, Luca. It's not like that. I just came to see her like I said. It's a special day." He jabs his fingers through his wild hair, eyes narrowing. Though we share the dark brown coloring of our mother's hair, Dante's is a touch curlier than mine which has a soft natural wave. My brother always hated those tight curls, typically choosing to buzz them off. Right now, they're longer than I've seen them in a while. Which leads me to believe there's something going on.

Dark circles line his eyes, the whites bloodshot. A twinge of pity rattles my insides. After Papà died, Dante took to drinking and dabbled in some hardcore drugs. I thought it was all in the past.

"If you need something I can help you," I offer on a frustrated exhale.

"Nah, I don't need nothing from you, Luca."

Clearing my throat, I sit up and reach for the jacket slung over my chair. "Ma, I've got a surprise for you."

She puts down the pasta dough, wipes her hands and saunters closer, swaying her hips to the Frankie classic. "What surprise, *figlio mio*?"

"I don't know if you remember, but today is the anniversary of *Re* Industries. Papà started the business fifty years ago."

"Don't you mean *King* Industries?" Dante hisses.

I renamed the business when I took over, translating from the original Italian. "It's still Papà's company."

"Right."

"Anyway," I pull the tickets from my jacket pocket and hand them to her. "I'm taking you to Italy in the summer. We'll stay in Naples for a few days then go to Capri and Ischia. Just like old times."

Dante snorts on a laugh. "Yeah, like old times? When could we have ever afforded a villa in Capri?"

"Dante, *basta*," Ma snaps. "Your father gave us everything he could. It's because of him that we are living in this country today. He risked everything to bring us here, and your brother has worked hard to continue that legacy."

He scoffs again, and my fingers curl into my palm, fingernails digging into the skin. "I'm the eldest, I should have assumed that role."

"So why didn't you?" I bark and shoot up looming over my brother. "I didn't ask to take over the family business. No one else stepped up."

"You're deluded, Luca."

"*Vaffanculo*, Dante."

He leaps up and the chair flies out from under him, skidding across the kitchen.

"*Basta*! Enough!" Mamma cries. "We will not fight today. It is a day of celebration, of good memories. Papà loved you both very much, and I know how proud he was of his two boys. So please, no more." She takes the tickets from my hand, and a rueful smile curls her lips. "This is too generous, Luca. I cannot accept it."

"Mamma!" I press them back into her chest. "This is a gift, and it's non-refundable. I already bought the two tickets, booked the villas, rented the car, and I have no one else to take."

"How about Concetta's daughter, Gianna? Weren't you dating for a while?"

I barely suppress a grunt. Ma set me up with her neighbor's daughter a few months ago, and I took her out one night in the city out of obligation. I'd wanted to end it at dinner, but she insisted on going back to her place. She practically threw herself at me. Like always, I'd been very clear on my rather specific sexual preferences. She'd been more than happy to oblige after hearing my rules.

I was shocked honestly.

But then she failed to obey rule number one. One night only.

She'd become that desperate, needy, clingy girl. She texted, called, even showed up at my penthouse one night. Since she was a friend of Mamma's I didn't want to be rude, but *merda* she was persistent.

"We never really dated, Ma," I finally grumble. "It was *one* date."

"There has to be someone, *figlio mio*. I don't want to die without the joy of ever hearing my grandchildren's laughter."

Dio, Mamma knew how to lay it on thick. Unbidden, my thoughts flicker to the waitress at *Nonna Maria's* again. Those pink pouty lips, the shot of electricity that went right to my dick when her hand grazed mine … *Shit, where did that come from*?

"Yeah, right, Ma." Dante chuckles. "Who'd put up with all of Luca's rules?"

I shoot my brother a glare. The last thing I need is my mother getting into my sex life. No, keeping it casual with women was the safest bet for all involved.

CHAPTER 10
SHE'S MINE

Luca – Present Day

I barrel into the old pawn shop, my heart pounding out a manic rhythm. When Tony texted me a few minutes ago, I'd had my driver cut across three lanes of traffic to race back down here. Isabella Esposito's daughter is here? I couldn't fucking believe it.

I hadn't heard that name in nearly a decade, and just like that the past surged to the surface. I eat up the small space between the front door and the back room where Tony handles business and nearly tear the door off its hinges. I force myself to stop, to inhale a deep breath. I'm not little Lúca Valentino anymore. I'm the fucking C.E.O. of King Industries. Pausing at the metal door, I draw in a deep breath and force the frenzied beats of my heart to subside.

I slip on a cool mask and wrap my fingers around the handle. I count to ten before jerking it open. The handle nearly comes off, despite my best efforts. Fury rages through my veins as my gaze lands on the brunette cuffed to a chair in front of Tony's desk.

The girl at the subway.

The waitress at *Nonna Maria's*.

"Uncuff her now, Mario. *Sei un vero stronzo*." Fucking idiot. "From now on, I'm the only one who touches her." My tone is lethal, barely constrained fury flooding my system. My boys know better than to question me ever, but this time, Mario's so fast he's nothing but a blur. The handcuffs clatter to the floor, and the young woman hisses out a curse between clenched teeth.

From the shadowed entry, my gaze locks on the heart-shaped face, the full pink lips, those piercing blue eyes. Which look like they're about to murder me. Can it really be her? *Dio*, last time I saw her we were only kids. Well, hell, I thought I was a big deal, but I wasn't shit back then. She was the whore Bo had been fucking around with? It couldn't be.

Stella M. was Stella McKenzie *and* Stella Esposito. How could I have missed it? She must have gone by both names at school.

"He signed the contract, *capo*." Tony holds out a thick stack of pages. I immediately recognize my lawyer's signature. That *pezzo di merda* sold his own daughter to be free of twenty-five thousand dollars in debt? I couldn't wrap my head around it. This was exactly why I never wanted to have children. People were too fucking selfish.

My fingers close around the contract, but my gaze remains glued to hers. *Stella*. If I'd known it was her in the subway, I would've ripped Bo's head off with my bare hands. That darkness bubbles up, and my fingers clench into tight fists. She continues to glare at me, not a hint of recognition flaring within those bottomless blue orbs.

Had I changed that much in ten years?

Or maybe she'd erased everything from that terrible day at the cemetery up until the bloodied chaos of the dark alley. My hand moves to my chest, unbidden, my palm pressing against those numbers inked across my heart. The day I'd lost my best friend.

"I'm not some piece of meat you can ogle, *bastardo*," she spits, jerking me from my dark musings. "A person can't be bought or sold, so whatever the fuck my asshole dad just signed can't be legal."

A tiny smirk pulls at my lips. She was always feisty.

My lawyer is the devil in a Prada suit. If he'd laid out the contract, it was legit and airtight. "Let's call it an arrangement then." I step out of the shadows, and her mouth curves into a perfect O. Again, my cock throbs at the sight. Only this time, I want to fucking slap myself because this is Stella. This is my dead best friend's kid sister. And for the next thirty days she belongs to me.

"You?" she squeals.

For a second, I'm relieved she's finally recognized me. It'll be easier this way. Maybe she'll be more amenable to the idea—

"The guy that left me a fifty-dollar tip at *Nonna Maria's*?"

A scowl flips the corners of my lips.

"And the guy who sav—"

I cut Tony off with a sharp wave. "Yes," I answer. "I must say I'm surprised to see you here too."

"Are you the guy in charge?" She puts on a smile and bats her dark lashes. "I know my dad owes the Kings money, but I swear I'll pay it. I just need a little time, that's all."

"Do you have any idea who you're talking to?" Mario cuts in.

"*Zitto!*" I hiss at the idiot. I need a second to process this. A minute ago, she was just a mystery girl I could use to get revenge on that idiot Bo, but now … Now, she is Stella, and she is so much more. An image from the past floats to the forefront of my mind. A ten-year-old girl broken, sobbing, on her brother's shoulder with a wooden casket looming behind her petite form.

Now she's a full-grown woman, a gorgeous one. I focus on those blazing irises, and my cock throbs with need. *Madonna mia*, what is it about this girl that has me as horny as a teenager back when we first met? "I'm sorry," I force out. "A deal's been made, and if anything, I'm a man of my word. You'll remain as my guest for a month and if the money is paid as promised, you'll be free to go."

Those luscious lips curl into a snarl as a slew of curses erupt from that pretty little mouth. "So I'm your prisoner, basically?" she growls.

"My penthouse has been called many things but never a prison."

Tony's jaw drops. I catch the overly dramatic gesture from the corner of my eye.

"I'm going to be staying with *you*?" she screeches.

"Mmm, yes. For the next month, you're mine, princess." This little unfortunate predicament could be the answer to my dating dilemma. If Stella decides to cooperate. "Come with me."

Defiant, brilliant blue irises glare up at me. "*Vaffanculo.*"

"Please," I amend.

Mario pales, a fine sheen of sweat coating his upper lip.

"I'm not going anywhere with you." She plants her ass in the chair and crosses her arms over her chest.

"Stella…," I growl.

Her dark brows lift, and for a second, a hint of recognition streaks across her pinched expression. And then it's gone. "You think you scare me, *capo*? You think a little growl is going to make me come running? I've dealt with assholes like you my whole life. If you want me to come like a good little hostage, you took the wrong girl."

"Fine," I grit out.

"I got this, *capo*." Tony steps toward her, but I slap my arm across his chest before he moves an inch.

"I said no one touches her. She's mine to deal with, *only mine*."

"I'm not fucking yours, you male chauvinistic pig," she spits. "I'm a person, and I don't belong to anyone, least of all you."

This woman will be the death of me.

I march over to the chair and glare down at her. It's a terrifying look I've mastered over the years. One that would have even Tony pissing his pants. Stella doesn't even flinch.

Loosing a frustrated breath, I wrap my arms around her middle and toss her over my shoulder. An explosion of Italian curses bursts from her lips as her surprisingly strong fists pummel my back. She kicks and squirms, and damn, she's a feisty little thing. Again, my damned cock twitches as visions of handcuffs and silk sheets flood my mind.

I carry her out the back with Mario and Tony trailing behind me. Neither says a word, but I know what they're thinking. I've fucking lost my mind taking this wildcat home with me. But they have no idea….

Mickey's waiting in the black town car in the back alley. He peers over his sunglasses as I approach, and the hint of a smile tugs at the corner of his lip.

"Don't," I snarl.

"I didn't say nothing, *capo*."

I crouch down to get into the car, but Stella's arms are flailing, derailing my efforts. I don't want to break her arms, but I'm about a second from losing my shit.

"You need help?" Tony pops his head up beside me.

"No," I grit out. "I'll see you back at the office tomorrow."

"Let go of me, you *coglione*! *Figlio di puttana*!" Stella screams. She kicks and lands a booted foot in my crotch.

"*Porca miseria*!" I roar and cup my balls with one hand

while clenching my arm around the devil woman. "Get in now, Stella, or I swear to God…."

She punches my back with both fists and continues wailing. Releasing my wounded family jewels, instinct takes over. I slap her on the ass. Hard.

The crack reverberates across the suddenly silent air, and Stella immediately goes still. I'm not sure who's more surprised: her or me. But I only stop to dwell on it for a second, before shoving her into the car.

She lands on all fours on the soft leather, then whips her head back and glares up at me. "Never touch me again."

And damn, if it isn't the hottest thing I've ever seen.

"Sorry," I mumble. "I swear the next time I spank you it'll be because you begged for it." I press my lips into a tight line the moment the words are out. Fuck, this is Vinny's little sister. What the hell's wrong with me?

Not to mention, I am not the type of man who touches women without their permission. I don't apologize either. I've done my fair share of spanking but only with full consent. Hell, full enjoyment. I crawl onto the bench across from her and reach for my briefcase. I have two meetings this evening that I'll have to cancel. It's clear my new houseguest will require my full attention tonight.

Merda, what did I get myself into?

CHAPTER 11
A GUN IS MUCH BETTER THAN PEPPER SPRAY

S*tella*

A tremor races down my spine as we zip up the FDR to the Upper East Side. I clench my jaw to keep it from shaking. There's no way in hell I'll look weak in front of this *minchione*. My thoughts begin to spiral with each passing moment of silence.

What is he going to do to me?

The other two idiots keep calling him *capo*, which means boss in Italian. Could this guy really be the head of the notorious Kings? Why the hell would he want me? And for what?

Another shiver surges down my back, and a wave of goosebumps puckers my flesh. I eye the man from across the roomy back seat. He's jabbing at his laptop, eyes fixed on the luminescent screen. Dark, wild hair tumbles over his forehead, obscuring those midnight irises hidden beneath long, sooty lashes. His strong, stubbled jaw flexes and strains, a tendon twitching with each inhale. If the *figlio di puttana* hadn't kidnapped me, he would've totally been my type. Asshole and all.

In any case, he doesn't seem like the type of man who'd need to force himself on a woman. But who the hell knows what this guy is into? If he gets me to his penthouse, I am screwed.

The pepper spray. In all the commotion, I'd nearly forgotten about it.

Before digging my fingers into my pocket, I glance across the back seat, and my captor's dark eyes meet mine from over his laptop. *Dammit, stop looking at me.* Diverting my gaze, I skim the sleek leather upholstery and the gleaming wood accents of the fancy town car. Crystal bottles full of liquor and polished tumblers line the left side of the backseat. It's practically a full bar back here. On the opposite side, bottles of water and soda jut out of a cooler filled with ice. And just beyond that, a hidden compartment catches my eye. Something silver and shiny glistens beneath the dim lighting.

A gun? So much better than the pepper spray.

Dad used to keep a Glock hidden underneath the mattress. He'd even taught me how to use it once the old neighborhood started getting rough. I inch closer, and the mob boss's eyes lift to mine again.

Shit.

I point at the bottles lamely. "Can I get a water or are prisoners not allowed?"

The ghost of a smile curls his lips, and fuck me, if it doesn't make him ten times hotter. A devil with the face of an angel. "Help yourself." And that accent….

I reach for the farthest bottle, the one closest to the hidden compartment. With my knee, I nudge the cover open and a shiny, silver handgun stares up at me. My heart catapults against my ribcage, and time slows. *You can do this, Stel.* Grab the gun, point it at the *bastardo,* and force him to let you out of the car. Easy.

With one hand, I reach for the water, so my arm blocks the other one inching toward the gun. My fingers close around the cold metal, and I jerk it free.

Capo spins at me, eyes wide as I point the barrel at his face. "*Che cazzo fai?*"

"What the fuck am I doing? I'm getting the hell out of here." I inject steel into my tone, but it does nothing to mask the trembling of my hands. Both are wrapped around the weapon, strangling the handle.

The computer slides off his lap, and he holds his hands up, the hard set of his jaw softening. "Stella, you don't want to do something you'll regret. Put the gun down."

I hate the sound of my name on his lips. It triggers something deep inside, something long buried. I inhale a deep breath and shove the impractical thoughts away. "Tell your driver to pull over and let me out."

The divider is up between the backseat and the front, and for a second I wonder if the guy has any idea what's going on back here.

"I can't. We're on the middle of the highway."

"Then tell him to get off!" I shout, shaking the gun.

"Stella, easy!" He swallows hard, his Adam's apple jogging down the long column of his throat. He pushes his laptop further away and slides to the edge of the seat. "Give me the gun, and I promise I'll make Mickey stop as soon as it's safe."

"I don't believe you." My throat tightens, and hot tears prick at my eyes. Dammit. *Do not cry. Do not cry.* My finger wraps around the trigger.

"*Lo giuro*, Stellina."

My throat closes up at my old nickname, my chest so tight my lungs cease to function. My brother Vinny used to call me Stellina when I was a kid. *My little star.* No one has uttered the name since. My hand instinctively clamps across the tattoos over my heart.

"I swear," he repeats, his voice so soft I'm certain it doesn't belong to the same man who's kidnapped me.

A sharp horn blares, and the car jerks to the right. I stumble, my arms shooting out to steady me. The loud bang rings out across the small space before I know what's happening. I fall back on my ass from the kickback of the gun.

My captor winces and clutches at his shoulder as the car careens off the road. "*Cazzo*, Stella, you shot me!"

Merda! My fingers are still clenched around the handle, my knuckles white from the strain. Blood gushes down his fine suit, so much blood. I squeeze my eyes closed as long-buried memories rush to the surface.

I suck in a sharp breath, and darkness edges into the corners. My fingers itch to dig out my inhaler from my pocket, but I swapped it out for the damned pepper spray. No matter, I shouldn't let this guy see any hint of weakness anyway. If that's one thing I learned growing up, it was to never show fear.

The car slams to a halt, and I keel forward and the gun slides through my fingertips. The back door opens a second later, and the driver pokes his head in.

"Fuck, *Signor* Valentino, are you okay?"

Valentino? The name strikes a faint memory, but it's too fleeting to grasp.

"No, I've been shot, you asshole. Of course I'm not okay." He grits his teeth, hand still firmly clenched around his shoulder. Blood seeps between his fingers.

My stomach roils, and a bout of nausea crawls up my throat. *Oh, please don't puke. Please, don't puke.*

"Call Dr. Filippo and tell her to meet us at the penthouse immediately." *Capo* shrugs out of the jacket, wincing as it passes over his wounded shoulder. His white shirt is painted in blood, and my stomach flip-flops again.

"Yeah, boss, of course." Mickey tugs his cell phone from his black jacket and jabs thick fingers along the keypad.

"I can't believe you shot me," he mutters as he starts to unbutton his shirt with his good arm. A thick, braided gold chain and a cross appear nestled in a smattering of dark curls.

"You kidnapped me!"

"It was a deal, a binding contract."

"One I had no say in," I snap. Is this guy delusional? In what world is selling a person normal? Crossing my arms, I stare at my boots. Deep crimson splotches the black pleather. *Oh, no*. Blood on my shoes… I squeeze my eyes closed again.

By the time I glance back up at *Signor* Valentino, he's shirtless. And a freakin' ripped god. Abs ripple beneath perfectly tanned skin, and even the old scars and bloody mess across his right pec don't detract from his flawless form. Black ink tattoos his flesh, a myriad of spirals and symbols surrounding a skull with a tilted crown in the center. More ink traces his upper arms, completing the entrancing design. Tiny numbers embedded within the ink over his heart catch my attention, but they're bathed in blood and I'm too far away to make them out. Plus, I'm fucking staring at his bare torso. Shit, stop that.

He lifts his gaze, expression turning feral. "See something you like, princess?" he rasps.

"Never," I hiss.

I force my eyes to the door opposite where the big thug stands on the phone. This is it. My chance to escape. Sure, the door would open to the FDR, and I might get hit by oncoming traffic, but I'd just have to risk it. I'm on all fours again, and I start to crawl backwards. One knee slides back, then the other. I hazard a quick glance at my kidnapper.

He flashes me brilliant white teeth clenched so tight the tendon in his jaw pulses. "Hand me some ice."

"What?"

He ticks his head at the bar just a few inches away from my hand. "Ice, now. It'll numb the pain. From the bullet that you just fucking shot me with."

"How am I the bad guy here?"

"*Please*, Stella, the ice," he grits out. A tiny prickle of guilt stabs at my stupid heart. What the hell is wrong with me? He's the one who kidnapped me!

My gaze darts between the car door and the anguish on his face. I could still make it. He'd never catch me, not with that wounded shoulder.

"Don't even think about it. You open that door, and the first car that zips by will take you with it."

Dammit. "Sounds like personal experience. Is that how you take out the competition?"

His eyes narrow, and his mouth twists into a sneer. "You know nothing about me or my life, Stella."

Mickey's head pops in again, meaty hands stuffed in his pockets. "The doc said she'll be at your place in twenty minutes tops."

"Good, let's get the hell out of here."

The goon eyes his boss, big lips screwed into a full pucker. "Do you think I should leave you back here with *her*?"

"*Mannagia alla miseria*, she's only a girl, Mickey. I'll be fine, just drive."

I can't help the tiny smile from parting my lips. That's right, he should be scared. He's got another thing coming if he thinks I'm just going to roll over for him because he's some badass mafia king. I have no idea where this newfound bravery is coming from, but I'm rolling with it.

I'm tired of being treated like shit. Dad selling me out to the Kings was the final straw. It broke me, but in a way that needed to happen. It's time to rise from the rubble.

"Mickey," he barks before the driver closes the door.

"Yeah, *capo*?"

"Some ice?" *Signor* Valentino ticks his head at the bucket.

"Yeah, sure thing." He dips his big hand in and scoops out a few handfuls, filling a glass tumbler. After he gives it to his boss, his dark eyes skim over me. "I've got my eye on you, girl."

"Leave her alone, Mickey," *Signor* Valentino barks.

My brows leap up, nearly reaching my hairline. For a kidnapping asshole, he was being oddly gracious considering I'd just shot him.

The door slams shut behind our friendly driver, and I'm left alone with a bleeding mob boss.

CHAPTER 12
THIS COMPLICATES THINGS

L*uca*

I still can't believe that wild little thing shot me. *Dio*, I am off my game. I never would've let anyone get the drop on me like that. She had all the blood rushing to the wrong head. I underestimated her, not something I'd ever do again. Especially now that she will be living under my roof.

Stella sits on the couch, every muscle tense as Dr. Filippo finishes stitching me up. Normally, I would've had her fix me up in private, but I couldn't risk letting Stella out of my sight. Mickey has a few jobs to finish up, and my housekeeper, Magda, is out running errands.

I watch her from across the room as she curls a dark lock of hair around her finger. She's nothing like the sweet, innocent, freckle-faced little girl I remembered. Then again, I'm not the same person either. She still hadn't even recognized me, her own brother's best friend. We'd been inseparable for nearly two years when I'd landed fresh off the boat in Little Italy.

"All set, Luca." Dr. Filippo's appreciative gaze lingers over my bare chest for a few seconds longer than appropriate. She's a beautiful woman, but I have strict rules about mixing business and pleasure. Having a doc on call is critical in my line of work, and I'd never risk that for a fun fuck.

Stella's eyes flicker to mine. It's just occurred to me it's the first time she's heard my first name aloud. Maybe now she'll remember.

As I button up my shirt, I walk the doctor to the elevator that opens up into my foyer, intensely aware of Stella's trailing gaze. Would she try to make a run for it again? If she did, maybe I should tell Alberto, the guard stationed in the lobby, to let her go this time. Already, this arrangement is shaping out to be more trouble than it's worth.

Dr. Filippo presses a kiss to each of my cheeks, and I hand her the envelope of cash. The woman is well-paid for her off-the-books work. I'm fairly certain the monthly fee is more than what she makes a year at the hospital.

"Thanks again."

"Any time, *bello*."

I force a smile and press the elevator button. Luckily, it quickly glides shut behind her, blocking the main escape route. Only a select few know about the secondary elevator tucked away in my bedroom for emergencies. I spin around to meet those scrutinizing blue eyes. Earlier, I could've sworn I caught her checking me out, but maybe the blood loss was affecting my mind.

Right now, she keeps her narrowed eyes pinned to mine.

The silence lengthens, and I march to the kitchen to make myself a stiff drink. My shoulder aches, and I could really fucking use one after the day I've had. I hate disorder; my life is all about control. It's necessary in all aspects of my business and personal life. Less than a day, and Stella's reduced it to chaos.

As I pour, I lift my gaze to my new houseguest. "You want a drink?"

She scoffs.

"What?"

"Are you trying to get me drunk so I'll be a more pliable prisoner?"

"*Che palle*, Stella. I'm simply offering you a drink to take the edge off. I know I need one."

"To stave off the guilt?"

A dark chuckle escapes through my thinned lips. "It's cute that you think *this* would cause me even the tiniest amount of guilt. Do you have any idea the things I've done?" I snap my jaw shut, cursing my loose lips. What the hell is wrong with me? A beautiful face from the past has me spilling all my sins?

"So I should be thanking you for keeping me prisoner?"

"The way I see it, I saved your *cullo* from Bo and the Red Dragons. From what my men saw at the restaurant, you were destined for a much bleaker fate."

Her dark brows furrow. "Those were your guys at the Red Dragon last week …." A deep pink hue blossoms across her cheeks, matching the warm color of her lips.

I nod and take a long pull of the perfectly aged scotch. Yes, Tony told me exactly what that *pezzo di merda* was forcing her to do. The thought of Stella on her knees and that dickhead's hands on her makes my blood boil. She is mine now. Official property of the Kings. No one would ever touch her again. *No one but me.* A dark voice echoes across my mind. The things I want to do to her.

No. No. No. I would wreck her, destroy her innocence. She did not deserve that.

"Well, don't expect a thank you any time soon." Her soft voice distracts me from the onslaught of dark thoughts. She settles onto the couch, the tight set of her shoulders relaxing a smidge. Her gaze lands on the bouquet of calla lilies on the glass table, and her lips pucker.

"You disapprove of my floral arrangement too?" I snap.

"No." Her voice is quieter than I've heard yet. Her mouth thins out into a harsh line, and I opt for a change of subject. "If you were so concerned about your safety here, why didn't you tell the doc I was keeping you prisoner?"

"I figured she was on your payroll. Any respectable doctor would have to report an incident like a gunshot wound."

"That's what you wanted? For me to report you? You'd rather spend years in jail than a month with me?"

Her lips screw into a damned irresistible pout. *Gotcha.*

"You're blackmailing now? A bullshit contract isn't enough so you're going to force me to stay by lording a shooting in self-defense over me?"

"Self-defense?" I bark. "That's laughable."

"You *kidnapped* me!"

I raise my hands and a twinge races across my shoulder. Gritting my teeth, I motion around the sprawling penthouse with views across Central Park. "I'm sorry, you're right, Stella. I am a fucking monster. Forcing you to spend an entire month here with me instead of at the mercy of Bo and your alcoholic father at that shithole on Mulberry Street."

She leaps to her feet and lunges. "*Vaffanculo!*"

I catch her wrist with my good hand before she swings at me. "Don't," I snarl.

"Or what?" Her hand is an inch from my face, her body pressed against me. "You'll rough me up like your goons did to my dad?"

"I don't hit women."

"No?" She splays out her fingers and runs her nails across my cheek. Hard. I can feel the blood oozing to the surface.

"Damn it, Stella." I jerk her hand behind her back, pinning her body to mine. She wriggles against me, those penetrating eyes throwing daggers. "Stop it." Her breasts are pressed against my chest, spilling over her tank top. I can't help my gaze from dropping to her tempting cleavage. A hint of a tattoo peeks out from beneath her top, and a lethal mix of rage and excitement streaks through my veins.

Every wiggle has me growing harder.

She lifts her knee and aims for my crotch again, but this time I see it coming. With one hand holding her and the other still nursing my cocktail, I kick my leg out to dodge the blow. Our legs get tangled, and with her incessant squirming and my bad shoulder, I'm knocked off balance.

And we're falling.

The tumbler crashes to the ground, scotch, ice and glass spraying all over us and across the marble floor. I'm about to land on top of her, but I throw my hand out at the last minute so I don't crush her. Instead, fiery pain races up my shoulder and blossoms across my wound. *Merda.*

I hover over her, all my weight on my forearms. I'm sticky and wet, and pissed. I shift to my good arm, and my cock brushes against her panties. I glance between us, and her skirt is up to her waist, exposing a lacy pink thong.

Shit.

I can feel myself hardening against her. Every wiggle, every squirm sends heat racing down to my stupid dick. Her narrowed gaze widens, two pools of endless blue fix to mine and horror streaks through.

"Let go of me!"

She tries to roll out from under me, but I bend my forearms, pinning her down to the floor. A wicked grin slashes across my face. She reaches for something in her pocket, but I catch her wrist before her fingers disappear into the denim. I palm the top of her skirt, just above her hip and meet something hard.

"Stop!" she shrieks.

"What is that?" I dig my fingers into her pocket, and she hisses out another curse. Jerking the little cannister out, I stare in awe at the pepper spray. "Were you really going to use this on me?"

"Maybe," she spits.

Dio, what have I gotten myself into? I force myself off the ground and jerk her up with me. "What else are you hiding in there?" I eye her tight tank top and frayed jean skirt.

"Nothing."

"I don't believe you."

She pulls her pockets inside out and glares up at me. "See? *Niente*."

My eyes lock on her full breasts, then trail down her slim waist and curvy hips. She could definitely be hiding a knife in there, and after earlier, I wouldn't put anything past her.

I back her against the wall and run my hands down her sides.

"*Che cazzo fai?*" she screeches.

"What the hell am I doing? I want to make sure you don't try to knife me in the middle of the night, princess."

"Well, you're not the damned police, and I don't consent to you frisking me."

With one last slow scan over every inch of her, I lean in close, my body flush against hers, trapping her against the wall. I speak slowly, deliberately. "If you ever try to shoot me again or spray me with that shit, hell, if you look at me the wrong way, I *will* punish you."

She glares up at me, and her palm lifts. I see it coming, but I do nothing this time. She's earned it for the fight she's put up. I never expected her to be so wild. The crack sears across my cheek, and a smile parts my lips.

"So you like it rough?" she hisses with the slap still echoing between us.

"I'm pretty sure I'd like it any way with you, princess." A wicked grin curls the corners of my mouth. She's hot as fuck, especially like this, and she's not wrong, I do like it rough. And in this moment, there's nothing I'd like more than to tear her wet clothes off, bend her over the couch and fuck her until she screams my name.

"Dream on, *bastardo*. Never happening." Her mouth is a heartbeat from my own, her hot breath ghosting over my lips. She struggles against me, palms pressed to my chest. Heat races from her fingerprints, branding me with each touch.

Her mouth says one thing, but her body betrays her. Her dark pupils are blown out, nipples peaked against my chest. Hell, she's breathing heavier than I am. Here I thought she'd be a safe bet. An answer to my dating dilemma. I never thought sweet, innocent Stella would have a dark side.

This certainly complicates things.

Energy crackles between us, but I finally peel my body from hers. My cock curses me out as I slowly back away. Stella still watches me, eyes wide, as she adjusts her skirt to cover those irresistible pink panties. I swear I see a twinge of disappointment. I should've expected it. If she dated Bo, she had to have a thing for morally gray, fucked up men.

Leaning against the wall, she crosses her arms over her chest and inhales a deep breath. "Now what?"

I eye the mess on the floor. "Now we clean that up."

She scoffs. "So I'm supposed to be your maid too?"

"No. I have a housekeeper, thank you very much. Magda is a lovely young woman who I'm sure you'll meet shortly. She's just stepped out to run some errands."

"Figures."

I glance down at my white shirt and scowl at the tan splotches from the scotch incident. My hand is sticky from the liquor, and to be honest, I could use a nice, cold shower. "I'm taking a shower. Clean it up or don't. Magda will take care of it when she returns." I spin toward the hallway that leads to the bedrooms.

"Wait." Her footsteps echo behind me. "I'm drenched in alcohol in case you didn't notice, and I don't have any other clothes. You didn't really give me time to pack before you kidnapped me." She fishes into her top and pulls out an ice cube. Her white shirt is soaked through, revealing tight peaked nipples.

Squeezing my eyes shut, I force in a deep inhale. "Come with me."

She follows me down the hallway, eyeing the array of paintings lining the white walls. They're all landscapes of Italy: Naples, my hometown, the islands of Ischia and Capri, the Amalfi Coast, the most beautiful places on earth, in my opinion.

"Beautiful," she murmurs, her voice so soft I'm not certain I hear the word.

From what I remembered, Stella and her brother were born in New York. Her mom had met her bastard father in the U.S., and Stella had never been to Italy. "Have you ever been?" I ask without turning.

"No."

It's the fucking stupidest idea ever, but for a second, I imagine the two of us there. Strolling down the *lungomare*, eating *gelato* at the *piazza*. I'm definitely losing my shit.

I finally stop at the end of the hallway in front of the double doors that lead to my bedroom. I pause, my hand curled around the handle. I've never brought a woman inside. If they even make it into my penthouse, I usually fuck them in one of the guest bedrooms. It's clean, sterile, and outfitted with an array of toys. It's silly really, but it's one of my rules. Letting someone in feels too intimate.

"Are we going in or what?" Stella's breath ghosts over the shell of my ear.

I cant my head back, and my nose nearly brushes hers. She's on her tiptoes, peering over my shoulder. "Yeah," I mutter and turn the handle.

CHAPTER 13
AN OFFER I CAN'T REFUSE

S*tella*

I walk into the uber-modern bedroom, a spicy, musky scent thick in the air. I've only spent a few hours with Luca and already I recognize it as his. It was all I could smell when the *bastardo* had me pinned to the ground.

He treads behind me, so close his warm breath brushes the shell of my ear. I wait for the fear, the icy fingers crawling up my back at his proximity, but I feel nothing but excitement. I should be terrified. I'm alone in an empty penthouse with a stranger who's been dubbed the most ruthless man in New York City. Only, I feel none of those things.

I must have suffered a psychotic break when Dad abandoned me.

I scan the floor-to-ceiling windows with sweeping views of Central Park, and the twinkle of city lights in the distance. Sure, it wasn't a traditional prison, but I was still his prisoner. The bedroom is immaculate with more paintings of Italian cities, but not a single personal touch. Except for a framed photograph on the nightstand. I move toward it, but he jumps in front of it, cutting me off.

"The closet is that way." He points to another set of double doors across from the massive bed. Of course, he has black silk sheets. He opens the door and lets me peruse the wide selection of sleek black suits and classic button-down shirts. It's like *Saks Fifth Avenue* exploded in this man's closet. I've never seen so many designer names in one place. Does this guy not own any t-shirts? "I can have Magda buy you some clothes tomorrow."

"Or I can just get mine from home."

He raises a dark brow.

"What?"

"I may need you to accompany me to certain events in which you'd require a specific type of attire."

"What type of events and what type of attire?" I hiss.

He leans against the doorjamb, looking unfairly hot with his partially unbuttoned shirt and the myriad of tattoos curling around his tanned flesh. He lifts his eyes to mine, and dark hair tumbles over his brow. "I'd hoped to discuss this tomorrow once you were more settled."

"I don't think I'll ever get used to being your prisoner. So you might as well just tell me now."

He huffs out a breath and palms the back of his neck. "Given my position, there are numerous social commitments I must attend. Having a beautiful woman on my arm would make things easier."

Beautiful. My traitorous cheeks blush at the compliment. "Easier how?"

"I don't date, Stella. When I go to these events, the women tend to get … aggressive."

I snort on a laugh, unable to contain myself. "The big bad mafia boss is scared of *aggressive women*?"

"No," he growls. "I'd just prefer to spend the evening

focused on business instead of shooing off women I have no interest in pursuing."

"So you're into men?"

He blanches, his mouth curving into a satisfying scowl. "*Cazzo*, no!" he snaps. "I simply don't have time for that sort of relationship right now. Nor do I desire one."

"That's really all you want from me? Arm candy for a few parties?" With all the rumors I've heard about the ruthless Kings, I find this hard to believe. This man could have any woman, why me?

His lips press into a hard line, and he watches me for a long moment, those bottomless midnight irises piercing. "Yes." The answer is loaded and tension fraught as if there was so much more behind that one word.

"And you don't expect anything … sexually?" I swallow thickly once I get the word out.

"No." His mouth twists. "I don't need to force women to sleep with me."

A rush of air expels through my thinned lips, and I nod slowly, discreetly eyeing the gorgeous man. I wouldn't think so. "And in exchange for that, and payment from my father, I'll be free to go at the end of the month?" It seems too good to be true.

"Yes, that's the deal."

I swallow hard again and take a good look at the man in front of me. I'd just called him a mob boss, and he hadn't flinched. Is this guy really the infamous head of the Kings? He seems awfully young to lead such a powerful organization.

Luca stands beside me, oddly silent. *Luca. Luca.* Something about that name sends a chill tattooing up my spine. Fuzzy images whirl through my mind, and I blink quickly to chase the unnerving feeling away. He still watches me, the fine lines around his eyes crinkling.

What choice do I have other than to agree in this moment? The next chance I get, I'll escape.

"Fine," I finally murmur. "But let's talk some ground rules."

A chuckle escapes through his pressed lips, the warm, rich sound like melted mozzarella on Mrs. D's lasagna. I lick my lips as heat fills my belly. "You are in no position to make any demands, princess." He ticks his head at the far corner of the gigantic closet. "You'll find some t-shirts in those drawers. And boxers in those." His gaze rakes over me, and another explosion of goosebumps puckers my skin. "They might be a little big, but they should be okay for tonight."

Judging by the width of his shoulders, they'd be gigantic on me. "I still have to go back to my house for something."

"Whatever you need, I can buy for you. I don't want you going back there right now."

"I need my inhaler," I grit out. If today was any indication of how things would play out for the next month, I'd need it to survive.

"Oh." His tongue inches out and glides across his lower lip. And fuck me, it's so damned sexy. "I'll send one of the guys for it tonight."

I nod, the image of one of Luca's goons showing up at my place and scaring the shit out of my dad ridiculously satisfying. With a half-smile, I scamper to the back of the closet, passing an array of Gucci loafers. An image flickers across my mind. The subway. The glint of the silver hardware on my savior's shoes. Glancing across the space, I meet dark eyes tracing my every move. Was he the man who'd saved me from Bo? And bought me a new textbook?

I shake my head, dispelling the errant thoughts. Tons of men in Manhattan wore Gucci loafers. It just couldn't be …. Mafia bosses don't go around saving shredded Economics books and dropping cute notes at your doorstep.

My gaze travels to the discarded, bloodied shirt on the floor beside the hamper and to a flicker of gold. Cufflinks in the shape of crowns. My thoughts fly back to the note and the crude drawing in the place of a signature. *No… it couldn't be.*

Forcing my attention away from the shirt, I refocus on finding some clothes. As soon as I open the drawer, a musky scent fills my nostrils. I worked at the Macy's at Herald Square one summer when I was a stupid kid thinking I could make it in the fashion industry. I'd ended up in the fragrance department. Luca's scent is a heady mix of bergamot and hot pepper.

Grabbing a shirt at random, my fingers close around the softest material I've ever touched. I have to restrain myself from moaning as I finger the silky cotton. Hugging it against my chest, I move onto the dreaded underwear drawer.

Heat seeps up my neck as I fiddle with the array of boxers, boxer briefs and dare I say, a few bikini briefs. Typical Italian male.

"Are you doing inventory or are you going to pick something?" Luca's breath trails across the shell of my ear, and my heart leaps up my throat. When had he gotten so close?

Without looking, I grab the first pair of boxers my fingers find and slam the drawer shut.

He eyes the underwear pinched between my thumb and index finger and smirks. My stupid heart staggers at the sight. When had the kidnapping mafia asshole gotten so hot?

"Those are my lucky boxers, princess, so you better not lose them."

I glance down at the flashy green, white and red underwear, horrified. Great, I was going to sleep with the Italian flag on my ass. "How would I lose them? It's not like you're going to let me out of this penthouse, are you?"

He cocks a dark brow. "We'll see how you behave."

A streak of heat races down my core at that wicked grin. Suddenly, all I can think about is his thick erection pressed against me when he pinned me to the floor. *Dio*, I was fucked up. I should be terrified. This man has imprisoned me in his home, and I'm getting wet just thinking about his impossibly hard length between my legs.

Between my dad and Bo, I'd gotten so messed up in the head. I couldn't wait for Rose to get her psychology degree and fix me. *Rose*! My best friend would freak out once she returned from Long Island and found out what happened.

Would Dad tell her the truth?

"What about my phone?" I ask. The idea of being isolated from the outside world is more frightening than the smirking mobster looming over me.

"What about it?"

"One of your goons took it. Can I have it back?"

"His name is Mario, and he's not a goon. He's worked for my family for over thirty years."

"Fine," I grit out. "So?"

"Same answer as before. We'll see how you behave."

This asshole is enjoying this.

He stalks across the closet and rifles through the drawer, picking out some clothing. "Now, I'm going to shower. Can I trust you to behave?"

I nod and give him a sweet smile. "I need a shower too." I pinch the wet material against my bra. It clings to my hard nipples, and a wave of embarrassment sends heat spilling across my cheeks.

He swallows hard, his Adam's apple bobbing along the long column of his throat. *Dio*, even his neck is sexy. Who's ever heard of such a thing?

"Follow me, I'll take you to the guest bath."

This is the perfect opportunity to make my move. I trail along behind him like a good little captive. If he thinks he's won, maybe he'll let his guard down. As soon as he gets in the shower, I'll make my escape. My heart raps out a thundering rhythm as my mind spins with ideas.

If he wanted to kill me, he would've done it already. I shot him for god's sake, and I'm still standing. I've already been alone with him in his bedroom, and he hasn't forced himself on me either. *Grazie a Dio.* The mob boss may not want to hurt me, but I certainly don't want to be his prisoner for the next month either. I have to at least try to get away. Steeling my resolve, I scan the quiet hallways and the foyer that opens up to the elevator.

With my thoughts whirling, he leads me to a bedroom right beside his, but unlike his, splotches of pink and another bouquet of fresh calla lilies brighten up the stark space. My heart pinches as memories of Mom's funeral bubble to the surface. The mahogany casket. Covered in calla lilies. They're a symbol of rebirth, a new chapter in one's life. Or death. I shake the dark thoughts out and focus on the handful of photographs that line the washed oak dresser.

My eyes flicker to the gilded frames. They look like old family photos. I'm drawn to them, so curious to take a closer look, but Luca ushers me straight to the bathroom. He points at the shower and deep soaking tub. "Take your pick. There's a ton of toiletries so help yourself."

"Thanks," I mumble.

He nods and spins toward the door.

"You don't have hidden cameras around this place, do you?"

He grins before he stalks out. "Not in the bathroom."

As soon as the door slams closed, I lock it. Leaning against the timber, I draw in a breath to slow my racing heart. This has been the most insane day of my life, and it's not even over yet. I march to the tub and turn on the faucet. Then I wait.

Five minutes and I'm out of here.

CHAPTER 14
BEST PUNISHMENT EVER

Stella

With the water still running, I tiptoe out of the bathroom and streak across the bedroom. I reach the door, my heart hammering against my ribs. I can just make out the rush of water from the neighboring door. Good. Luca's still in the shower. Peering through the doorway, I scan the hall one more time. Empty. My eyes lift to the ceiling, searching for the eyes of a roving camera, but there's nothing. Probably hidden, duh.

Praying to all the saints my mom so fervently believed in, I creep out into the corridor and sprint toward the elevator. I jab my finger at the button, and it lights up, sending my hopes soaring.

Come on, come on.

My foot taps out a manic beat as the floors tick by at a snails' pace. Of course, he has to live in the penthouse. How high are we for fuck's sake? Ninety-one. Ninety-two. Ninety-three. I glance over my shoulder at the master suite. Doors still closed. Ninety-six. Ninety-seven. Ninety-eight. I didn't even know a building could be this high. The elevator doors finally glide open, and I dart inside.

The slap of footsteps across marble sends my heart catapulting up my throat. *Cazzo*. I stab the L button, and the doors glide closed, the echo of heavy footfalls inching closer. The elevator descends at an alarming rate, and I brace my hands against the gilded walls. My stomach leaps up, and I'm totally regretting that last cannolo from Mrs. D.

Get a grip, Stella. You're almost home free.

I haven't quite had time to form a plan, but the gist is easy enough. Disappear. Dad screwed me over big time so I shouldn't feel guilty about abandoning him to deal with the Kings, right? No. I should not. My stupid heart pinches all the same. Ignoring it, I continue to formulate my plan. I'll just take my measly savings account and hop on the first bus to Florida. Done. Plan made.

The elevator dings, and the doors glide open. I choke on a gasp as my gaze lands on a wet, completely naked Luca barring the doorway to the empty lobby. I gasp and stumble back, my heart hammering.

So much skin. So much perfectly toned, muscled, scarred and tattooed with a smattering of dark hair leading down—I force my eyes up.

Luca glares down at me, fury raging through those bottomless pits of darkness. "Oh, princess. I'm going to have to punish you now…."

I'm speechless. My brain can't seem to form a single word with all that fine nakedness sprawled before me.

A big guy in a suit appears behind Luca, jerking my attention from the miles of carved perfection. Even the white bandages across Luca's shoulder don't detract from his flawless form. "You want me to take care of this, boss?"

"No, Albie," he grits out. "She's mine."

A chill cascades down my spine at his tone. I should've been scared, hell terrified, but all that godly nakedness has my brain muddled and my hormones raging.

He steps into the elevator, and I stagger back until I hit the wall. My heart kicks at my ribs, desperate for an escape. *He hasn't killed you yet.* There's no reason he'd do it now, right?

The mob boss glares down at me, rage pulsing across those midnight irises. "I told you to behave." His tone is lethal, barely restrained fury ticking the tendon across his scruffy jaw. I try to pull myself together.

"And I told you I never agreed to be your good little captive," I rasp out. *Cazzo*, why do I sound so out of breath? I lie to myself and blame it on the spiking adrenaline and my missing inhaler. But that doesn't explain the heat pooling between my legs.

My gaze drops to the minute space between us and rakes down his muscled chest, the whirling tattoos, then I get distracted by those rippling abs, and that deep V….

"Eyes up, princess." Luca's fingers close around my chin, and he tips my head back, capturing me in his piercing gaze. "If you fight me on this, I'm going to have to treat you like my prisoner. Is that what you want?"

I release a shuddering breath.

"Don't make me a monster. I don't want to be that man with you, but I *will* be if you push me. Your absolute obedience is not only expected, it's necessary. For the safety of us all." He drags a hand through his wet hair, and tiny droplets cascade down his broad shoulders and across the white bandage. "This deal could be beneficial for both of us, trust me." His warm breath ghosts over my lips.

He inches closer and something smooth and hard nudges my belly. The desire to look down is overwhelming, but Luca keeps my eyes pinned to his, fingers locked on my chin. My heart pounds out a ragged beat. "Now, answer me, Stella. Do you want me to punish you?"

My thoughts flicker back to the town car and that spank. To the feel of his palm on my ass, and the heat that had raged as a result of it. I'd never been spanked … not in the sexy way anyway. Now it's all I can think about.

"No," I finally grit out. "I'm not some disobedient child. I don't need to be disciplined."

He grunts. "You're certainly acting like one."

The elevator doors glide open, and he takes a step back, freeing me from his intoxicating presence. I draw in a breath untainted by his musky scent, and my heart stops thundering. He spins around, giving me a close-up view of his magnificent ass, and my traitorous eyes trail his perfect form. More scars riddle his back, but somehow they only enhance his raw, untamed beauty.

I swallow hard and force my feet to move. Where exactly? I'm not sure. Maybe he's right, and I should just suck it up for the next month. If I behave, I'll be free. How bad could it be to live in this penthouse and go to a couple of fancy parties? It certainly beats Bo's proposal.

"Come with me." Luca's command echoes across the quiet hallway.

As I cross the living room, a thought niggles to the forefront of my mind. "How did you get downstairs so fast?"

Luca stops in front of the guest room door and swings it open. "I have my own private elevator in my bedroom. Having only one exit would be risky in my line of work."

"Which is what exactly?" I cross my arms over my chest and meet his hard gaze.

"C.E.O. of King Industries."

Holy cannoli. How did I not make the connection before? Probably because my life was enough to handle without understanding the inner workings of the mob. I may not know much about big business in Manhattan, but even I'd heard of

King Industries. That name was stamped all across New York City, including that brand new towering skyscraper on Park Avenue.

And Luca was the C.E.O.? He must've been a freaking millionaire, and from the look of him, he probably only had about five years on me.

I must have been staring like a gaping idiot because his finger ends up under my chin again, tipping it up this time. My jaw snaps shut. His hand slides from my face down to my upper arm before he finally releases me.

He watches me for an endless moment. "Any more questions, princess?"

I inhale a steadying breath and force out the words I've been too nervous to voice. "If I *behave*, you promise not to hurt me?"

"I don't hurt women," he barks, his tone so sharp my head snaps back. As if he senses my discomfort, he clears his throat, and the tense set of his jaw softens. "You still want that shower?"

I nod quickly and he tows me into the bathroom once again, the scent of stale scotch swimming beneath my nostrils.

He reaches for a towel and wraps it around his narrow hips, and a deep, dark part of me is disappointed. I tell that lusty little vixen to shut up. Then he jumps up on the countertop, and with a wicked grin, ticks his head at the glass stall. "Go ahead."

"Excuse me?"

"You lost your privilege of showering alone."

"*Sei un pezzo di merda*, Signor Valentino," I growl.

"I'm a piece of shit?" His grin only grows wider. "Trust me, with that stunt you pulled, this is the gentlest punishment anyone's ever endured. If one of my guys had disobeyed me like you did…." He shakes his head, an evil glimmer in his eyes.

"So now I'm an employee?"

His head dips slowly. "Mmm, yes. I like the sound of that, princess."

"You just promised not to hurt me," I snap.

"Have I touched you? Laid a hand on that beautiful face or perfect body?" He grins. "Some would enjoy a steamy hot shower."

I cross my arms over my chest and scowl at the smirking *bastardo*. "I'm not stripping in front of you. That was not part of the deal."

"Why not? You've seen mine; I think it's only fair."

"I did *not*—" Heat surges up my neck and blossoms across my face.

"Please, you couldn't get enough of it."

I whirl around, teeth clamping over my lower lip before I say something stupid. I eye the shower and the massive rainfall showerhead. *Dio*, after the day I had it would be like heaven.

"Or you could try the bath. The bubbles would probably cover more…." Without turning around, I can hear the smile in the *idiota*'s voice.

He's not wrong either. I can't remember the last time I took a bubble bath. Our shitty apartment had no such luxuries.

I spin at him and stalk toward the tub. "Will you at least be a gentleman and close your eyes until I'm in?"

"Then I'd only be punishing myself, princess, and this is supposed to be *your* punishment." He smirks wider, and irritation gathers along my brow.

"Seriously, Luca?"

A dark chuckle splits his full, pouty lips. "Fine. But you've got ten seconds before I open my eyes."

I spin both faucets until steamy heat pours out and dump a capful of scented bodywash into the tub.

"I'm starting now," he calls out. "Ten, nine…."

I cant my head over my shoulder to make sure his eyes are closed before peeling off my sticky tank top and tossing it onto the marble floor. Then I shimmy out of my jean skirt and hazard another peek. Even with his eyes shut, every nerve ending prickles at his scrutiny. Unclasping my bra, the weight of his unseeing stare bores into me.

"Five, four, three…."

I slip out of my panties and tuck it under my skirt.

"Two, one…."

Dipping my toes into the warm water, a faint groan escapes my lips. *Dio*, this is heaven. I sink into the bubbles, and the sweet scent of lavender fills the room. My eyes slowly close, and I lean my head against the edge of the tub. For an instant, I forget all about the broody mob boss perched by the sink.

A piercing gaze rakes over me, the intensity so powerful it forces my lids to open. I meet a pair of dark, bottomless orbs, pupils so blown out they completely eclipse his irises. My center begins to throb at that unrelenting stare, and I'm filled with the most overwhelming desire to touch myself to relieve that aching pulse.

Dio, I've never had such a primal reaction to a man. My own father abandoning me to the mob must have broken something. I'm completely *pazza*.

Luca's tongue glides over his bottom lip, and I imagine that tongue licking up my center. *Cazzo*, what is wrong with me? This man is keeping me here against my will. Sure, he says he won't hurt me, but how can I believe this criminal? And still some stupid gut feeling trusts this man that I've only known for a few hours. This must be some sick Stockholm's Syndrome or something.

"Do you mind?" I hiss as I strategically move some bubbles around to make sure all my important parts are covered.

"No, not at all, princess."

"It's kind of hard for me to wash myself with you staring."

"Why's that?" A devilish grin curls the corners of his lips. "You prefer to touch yourself in private?"

"Yes … I mean, no!" Ugh. I sink beneath the bubbles to

escape his piercing stare. When I finally emerge, it's only because my lungs are about to explode. Those eyes latch onto me again, and the sparks only grow hotter. "Stop staring," I hiss.

"I can't help it. You're all beautiful and wet…. Why shouldn't I enjoy it, and why shouldn't you?"

"Oh, I don't know, a perfect stranger, the head of a freaking criminal organization, nonetheless, watching you bathe shouldn't be uncomfortable at all, right?"

"I'm not a—I can't believe you don't remember…." His jaw snaps shut a second later, and I'm not certain I heard him correctly.

"Remember what?" I blurt.

He shakes his head, the mischief lighting his eyes only a second ago vanishing, and his expression shutters. Then he slides off the counter and stalks toward the door. "Punishment over. Finish up and get ready for bed." Without another word, he slams the door behind him.

What the hell was that?

CHAPTER 15
SHE HAS ME BY THE BALLS

L*uca*

I stare at the clock on the nightstand and hiss out a breath. I'd barely slept all night. Every creak had my heart jolting up my throat. Despite the security system and Alberto being stationed on the ground floor, I was terrified Stella would escape somehow.

The idea of losing her sends a stab of pain through my chest. Which is insane. I'd only just moved her in yesterday. How could her potential absence send me into such a panic? I don't get attached; I'm never encumbered by bothersome feelings. After ten long years, this girl shows back up in my life, and I'm already breaking my rules for her.

I wasn't lying yesterday, if one of my guys had disobeyed me the way she did, they would've lost a finger. Or a toe at the very least.

My mind flickers back to the tub, to her naked, wet body covered in those indecent bubbles. God, it had taken every ounce of restraint not to jump in there with her. Every so often, her pretty pink nipples peeked through the foam, and I imagined dragging my tongue over them, tasting, nibbling, until I teased them to tight peaks.

My cock hardens at the vivid images.

I groan and bury the thoughts to the furthest corners of my mind. This is Stella, *cazzo*. Vinny would fucking kill you if he were alive. Only he's not ….

I reach for my phone on the bedside table and open the home security app. Flipping through the cameras, I stop at the one in Stella's room. She's splayed across the bed wearing my shirt and boxers. Damn, she looks good in them. My tee rides up just under her breasts giving me a perfect view of her fine torso, that slim waist and those curvy hips. My boxers have slid down low, giving me a sneak peek of her lacey panties.

Shit. I'm hopelessly hard now.

What is it about her that drives me so wild?

I slide my hand beneath the sheets and throttle my dick. Beads of moisture already cover the head, and I glide my palm up and down, imagining my cock buried deep inside her. I haven't even touched her yet, and I already know she'll feel like heaven and taste like sunshine and rainbows. My sweet, innocent Stella.

I'd ruin her.

A hint of movement draws my eye to the video as I continue to stroke my dick. Her eyes open, and she stretches leisurely. Then her hand skates down her stomach, and her fingers sneak beneath *my* boxers.

Oh, *merda*.

Heat rushes down my cock as she wriggles on top of the sheets. Her hips begin to move and mine pick up a matching rhythm as I fuck my palm. I turn up the volume on the camera, and her faint moans fill the air. Her free hand closes around her breast over *my* t-shirt, and she pinches her nipples to tight peaks. Fiery heat blazes through my veins.

Is she thinking about me?

I close my eyes and picture her pretty little mouth on my cock, licking and sucking, lapping me up.

Shit, I'm going to come.

My head tips back, and I let out a grunt as an orgasm rips through me. It's so violent and powerful, my free hand clenches the sheets, nails digging into the mattress. *Cavolo*, I can't remember the last time I came so quickly.

I draw in ragged breaths as I watch her pleasure unfold. She wiggles and grinds her hips against her palm, and I imagine my fingers inside her, coated in her fragrant juices. A few minutes later, she cries out as she orgasms, riding the waves of pleasure, and I picture my name on those lips.

A deep, dark part of me wants to be the one coaxing those sounds out of her. My cock buried balls deep in her slick heat.

Porca miseria. What have I gotten myself into?

She'd never agree to my rules, never be okay with my darkest desires … would she?

I shake my head, tossing out the impossible thoughts. *No.* This is a business transaction and nothing more. I need a woman on my arm, and she's the perfect fit. She doesn't belong in my fucked-up world, and I won't give into temptation because I already know one taste of Stella would never be enough.

I wouldn't just ruin her, she'd devastate me.

When I finally abandon the safety of my bedroom, I find Stella propped on a barstool at the oversized marble island. She's still wearing my shirt and boxers, and I'm instantly hard again as images of her wiggling on the bed when she touched herself fill my mind.

Magda shuffles around the kitchen, banging plates and cupboards, dragging my thoughts to the present. The savory scent of bacon and eggs fills the penthouse, and my stomach growls. I usually only have coffee for breakfast, so she must have prepared all of this for my new roommate. Magda drops a brimming plate of food in front of our new houseguest, and Stella rewards her with a warm smile.

Come to think of it, she's likely only a few years older than Stella. "I take it you've met Magda?" My gaze darts between the two women.

"Yes, she's been quite lovely. She even gave me a tour of the penthouse this morning, something you conveniently forgot to do last night."

"Perhaps I wouldn't have forgotten if you hadn't shot me and then attempted an impossible escape." The corner of my lip twitches, unbidden.

Magda's eyes widen for only a fraction of a second before she schools her face to neutrality. The young woman has been under my employ for nearly five years now. Her mother worked for my father, and when she turned eighteen, she inherited the role. There isn't much that surprises her. I'd sent her a message last night and warned her of our surprise guest.

Stella's appreciative gaze rakes over my suit until she catches me staring. Her lips pull into a frown, and she returns her focus to her eggs. "So where are you going?" she asks without looking up.

"It's seven-thirty in the morning on a Wednesday. I'm going to work, princess, where do you think?"

"What am I supposed to do?"

My lips purse as she eyes me. I hadn't actually considered the day-to-day logistics of her stay. "Whatever you want, I suppose."

"Can I go home?"

"No," I growl.

Magda reaches for a yellow envelope on the counter. "Mr. Tony dropped this off last night with Mr. Alberto, Signor Valentino."

I rip it open and a small white and orange cannister rolls out. I'm tempted to test it out to ensure it's not pepper spray in the guise of a harmless inhaler. Instead, I hold it out to Stella who snatches it from my fingers. "You're welcome."

"Thank you," she hisses.

Grabbing my phone from my jacket pocket, I scroll through the notifications then scan my calendar. The Heart Ball is right around the corner. At least an outing would give Stella something to do.

"Magda, would you like to accompany Clara and Stella today to pick out a couple gowns for the next few events?" Along with my security team. The more eyes on her the better if she's leaving the safety of the penthouse. Maybe if she's busy, she'll stay out of trouble.

The woman's pale gray eyes sparkle. "It would be my pleasure, signore."

"That won't be necessary," Stella responds around a mouthful of bacon. "Since Tony is so familiar with my apartment, he can just go pick up my clothes."

"I already told you—"

"How do you know I don't have any fancy gowns?" she snaps before I can finish.

I roll my eyes and heave out a breath. "I don't, but I'm giving you the opportunity to pick out new ones. Anything you'd like."

Her brows slam together, and unexpected irritation darkens her expression. "I don't want anything from you. We already owe you enough, I don't need to add to the debt."

"This is a gift."

"Why?" she shouts.

The elevator dings, drawing my attention away from this ridiculous argument. My executive assistant, Clara, looking flawless as always in a perfectly tailored Chanel skirt suit, saunters into the foyer and makes a beeline straight for Stella.

"*Grazie a Dio*, Tony wasn't exaggerating, *é bellissima*, just gorgeous." My overly eager assistant squeezes Stella's hands and spins her on the barstool.

Stella's eyes grow wide as she swallows down a big bite. "Who are you?"

"*Scusi, bella.*" She swats at my shoulder and tosses me a glare. "I thought Luca would have told you about me. Where are my manners?" She extends a hand and a beaming smile. "I'm Clara, Luca's executive assistant."

"She'll be taking you shopping today," I add.

Both women stare at me like I've grown a second head.

"It's been decided. No arguments."

"But Luca, I came to discuss the matter Tony has been working on…."

"I'll handle that, Clara, you handle this." I jerk my thumb at my scowling princess. "And keep a firm grip on her while you're at Bergdorf. She has a tendency to run." I pin Stella in my dark gaze, clenching my jaw. "Mario will escort you, and if I hear you gave him a hard time, I will punish you for real this time, princess."

She snorts on a laugh, staring up at me defiantly. And damn, if that look doesn't make my dick twitch.

"Clara, you have the social calendar, please make sure the gowns are appropriate."

"Of course, signore."

My gaze lingers on Stella for a long moment before I reach for my briefcase on the table and force my feet toward the elevator. "I'll see you tonight," I murmur over my shoulder.

She doesn't respond, or perhaps I don't hear it with the elevator doors gliding closed. Either way, the moment I'm alone an unfamiliar emptiness invades my chest.

Cazzo, one night alone with this woman, and she already has me by the balls.

CHAPTER 16
PRETTY WOMAN GONE WRONG

S*tella*

I feel like I'm a freaking curvy, Italian Julia Roberts in *Pretty Woman* with the three salesladies hovering around me like flies on shit. Only they're offering me champagne and chocolate-covered strawberries, and I haven't even had to screw Luca.

Which I thoroughly have no intention of ever doing.

Despite the face that kept popping into my head all night and again this morning. It was only because of his damned shirt. It was seeped in his spicy, musky scent and I'd woken up horny as hell, my clit throbbing with images of his perfect naked body seared into my mind.

I've been in kind of a dry spell in that department. After Bo, I'd sworn off men for a while, and after the tension of being kidnapped, I'd desperately needed some sort of release. It had to be that lethal combination. There is no other sane reason.

"Stella?" Clara's voice tears me away from my insane musings.

"Hmm?"

"Is there anything else you'd like to try on?"

I stare at the mountain of designer gowns on the chair, the tower of shoeboxes and the dozens of shopping bags and shake my head. "No, I think I'm good." For the rest of my life. There's no way I'll use all these designer clothes in one month even if I changed outfits three times a day.

Clara hands the saleslady the black AMEX, and again I'm floored as she signs multiple thousands away. I've never seen so many zeros on a receipt.

"God, Luca really is a millionaire, huh?" I mutter to Magda.

"Billionaire actually."

Holy cannoli.

"The youngest billionaire in all of Manhattan." Clara beams, pride flashing across her expressive irises. "When he took over King Industries, he tripled its market share and quadrupled earnings. His papà would be so proud."

My chest tightens at the word. My own father was trash. What kind of piece of shit sells off his only daughter? I couldn't even start to unpack that baggage. If I let myself think, really think about this situation, I'd curl into the fetal position and just bawl.

Instead, I'll tuck away all the pain, fear and uncertainty to deal with later. Right now, survival is key.

"You really look beautiful in all these gowns, Stella." Magda's pale eyes sparkle.

"Thanks," I mutter.

I wanted to hate both of these women, but after spending the entire day with them, I couldn't. Magda is sweet and shy, and never says a harsh word, and Clara with her overprotective, mother-hen routine reminds me of my mom.

I had to keep telling myself these two ladies worked for

Luca, and they too had a hand in keeping me hostage. Not as much as Mario, who lingered just outside the private fitting room with a gun in the holster beneath his black jacket, but still.

After the accidental shooting the other day, he never took his eyes off me.

Once we load up all the shopping bags, each of us carrying three apiece and Mario toting the rest, we descend onto the busy streets of Fifth Avenue. The traffic is so bad from rush hour we have to walk up the block to meet Mickey in the town car by Central Park or we'd be stuck for hours in gridlock.

"I can't wait to see you in that blue gown," says Clara as we weave through the mob of men and women in sleek business suits. "Luca's going to have a heart attack."

I choke on my spit as I try not to laugh. "I didn't think he had a heart."

Clara's warm gaze turns icy as she regards me. "Luca has a heart of gold, *ragazzina*. He might be a ruthless businessman on the outside, but inside, there is no one better. He doesn't let many people in, but when he does, you could never find a more generous man."

An unexpected wave of guilt rushes over me. The man had just spent close to ten thousand dollars on me, nearly half of what my father owed him. Why would he do such a thing? It makes no sense.

My footsteps slow as I attempt to process the insanity that has become my life in the last forty-eight hours and fall behind the others.

A thick shoulder slams into me, and I'm knocked off-balance. As I try to right myself a hand weaves between my fingers and wrenches one of the shopping bags free. "Hey!" I shout as the man reaches for another.

Mario spins around but two men with briefcases dart between us, rushing to catch a cab. I clench my fingers around the shopping bag handle and curse at the robber. But damn the asshole is strong. He pulls a gun out and shoves the barrel into my belly.

"Give me the damned bags," he hisses.

I freeze, fear paralyzing the blood rushing through my veins.

Pocketing the gun, he yanks me forward, and the paper bag breaks. I lunge to reach for it, but my legs tangle and I go flying across the cement.

I hit the ground with a smack, my forehead bouncing off the concrete and all the air squeezes from my lungs. The rough cement bites into my cheek, and I let out a little squeal. My beautiful clothes scatter across the sidewalk as the thief grabs what he can before darting into the thick mob.

Mario drops the remaining shopping bags and races after the *ladrone*, but the guy already has a block on him. Clara and Magda rush to my side, clearing a space around me. My head is already starting to pound.

"Are you okay?" Magda kneels on the ground and offers me a hand.

"Oh *Madonna*, your face." Clara's pinched expression says it all.

I sit up and gently raise my hand to my cheek, then the knot on my forehead, and I wince. My fingers come back sticky with blood and dirt.

Some random guy in a navy suit bends down with his cell in hand. "I saw the whole thing, are you okay? I called 911, they should be here any minute now."

I nod numbly. A prickle of heat burns the corners of my eyes. Which makes no sense. I was sold to a mobster, and I didn't cry, and now *this* would break me?

I bring my knees to my chest and curl into a ball. I'm vaguely aware of Magda gathering the remaining sparkling gowns from the sidewalk.

"Here, *bella*." Clara bends down beside me, clutching a Duane Reade bag. She presses ice to my forehead then opens a bottle of peroxide and cotton balls. "This will sting a little, but it will disinfect the cut." How she'd bought all the necessary first aid supplies so quickly was beyond me. Did I black out? How long had I been sitting on the ground?

The thunder of approaching footfalls jerks me from the haze. Strong hands cradle my face, and penetrating eyes meet mine. "Stellina, *stai bene*? Are you okay?"

Stellina. That voice reaches deep inside me, and that nickname pierces through to my very soul. It's the second time Luca has called me that.

He snatches the cotton ball from Clara's fingers and gently dabs it across the scrape. I hiss as the peroxide burns my skin. His lips pucker, and he blows a cool breath over the wound. Goosebumps ripple across my arms, and a tremor races up my spine. The depth of emotion surging beneath the dark surface steals the remaining air from my lungs. I'm trapped in his piercing gaze, and I just want to lose myself in the endless abyss.

"Where did you come from?" I mumble.

"My office is nearby. I was grabbing a coffee …."

Nearby? Park Avenue is two long streets away. Even if he'd sprinted it should've taken him longer to get here.

Mario appears over Luca's shoulder, drawing my eyes away from those mesmerizing midnight globes. "Sorry, *capo*, I lost him."

Luca hisses out a curse and spears the man with a withering glare. "Get with Tony and find out who that lowlife scum was immediately. No one touches what's mine and lives." His eyes meet mine for an impossibly long moment before jerking back to Mario. "And I'll deal with you later."

Another tremor surges across my body at the violence in his tone. I'm tempted to remind him that I don't actually belong to him, but the scolding dies on my tongue.

Luca's arm snakes around my shoulders, the other beneath my thighs. I gasp as he lifts me off the ground and cradles me against his chest. His warmth seeps into me, immediately stilling the ragged thrumming of my heart. He winces slightly and shifts to carry the bulk of my weight on his uninjured side, making it seem effortless.

"I can walk, you know," I mutter half-heartedly.

"I know. That doesn't mean you should."

That spicy pepper, musky scent envelops me, and an odd sense of home warms my insides. I haven't felt anything like it in years, not since Mom and Vinny …. The hint of a memory stirs, but the images are too fleeting to grasp. I blindly clutch at my chest, fingers drawing a circle over the inked hearts. June fifteenth. Two years apart, but I lost them both on the same damned day.

"Relax, I've got you, princess."

"What about the police?" I mumble.

"No police. I'll take care of this myself."

Luca's long strides lull me with their steady rhythm. I'm suddenly so tired, my eyelids so heavy, they begin to droop. A scruffy chin tickles my cheek, then soft lips press against my forehead, or at least I think they do. But I must have imagined it, because why would the infamous Luca Valentino kiss me?

CHAPTER 17
I STOP BREATHING

Luca

Blinding fury races through my veins as my eyes lock on the asshole cuffed to the chair. The man who dared touch what is mine. My entire body trembles with rage, the feeling so intense, so out of control, I force a drag of air into my lungs before I proceed. Control. My life, both business and personal, is all about control. A few days with Stella and I'm spiraling.

When Mario texted me about the robber, I'd raced right out of my meeting with the city commissioner. The meeting I'd been waiting for all month. Getting in his good graces was integral to my shipping operations, both legitimate and not.

Tony and Mickey loom in the shadows, guns cocked and ready. It's been years since I've involved myself in this aspect of the business. But today, this is personal. I would make this motherfucker pay for pointing a gun at Stella, the knot on her head, for that bruise on her cheek. He'd drawn blood and broken skin, and now I'd break him.

I shrug out of my jacket, slowly, purposefully and toss it on a chair. I stalk across the room, dark gaze fixed on the trembling idiot. He's gagged but not blindfolded. I want him to see exactly what's coming. To know the fear intimately, until it strangles, suffocating.

I stop right in front of him, my legs nearly hitting his knees, and roll up my sleeves. Deliberately. Methodically. His eyes bulge and sweat beads off his brow. He mumbles something, but I ignore him, carefully folding my sleeves and tucking in my favorite cufflinks with the gilded crowns.

Then I pull my arm back and release. My fist smashes into his cheek, the crack of bone against bone reverberating across the silent space. *Dio*, that felt good, and I am just getting started. "That was for her cheek."

Reaching into my pocket, I pull out the gold-plated brass knuckles. They were custom-made in the shape of a crown, each circle adorned with a pointy tip. The man's trembling becomes more violent as I slip it over my fingers.

I hit him again. Anger pours out of me, much like the blood from his mouth. "That was for the bump on her head."

He wiggles and squirms, blood dribbling from his chin and perspiration pouring down his forehead, into his eyes. He mumbles again, and a wicked grin slants my lips. "I'm sorry I'm having a hard time understanding you." I pivot to Tony. "Knife, please."

The *bastardo*'s eyes widen to the size of saucers. "No, no!" he mutters.

Tony tosses me the blade which I catch by the hilt with the honed precision of a ninja. I spin it around in my hand, reveling in the familiarity of the worn wood. When I was a young, little thug, I used to carry this thing with me everywhere. I thought I was tough shit. Me and Vinny ....

The dark thoughts threaten to pull me under, but I focus my rage on the man before me. The *stronzo* who hurt her. I inch closer, glimmering blade pointed at the guy's face. He tilts his head back, but he's got nowhere to go. He's trapped.

I slice the blade across the gag, and his scream echoes through the dim chamber. I barely nicked him. Coward. Most men who attack women are. They're the scum of the earth in my book.

"What's your name, piece of shit?" I snarl.

Tony opens his mouth, but I wave him off. I want this man to talk to me and only me.

"Sean," he chokes out.

"You got a last name, Sean?"

"O'Malley."

Ugh, fucking Irish. As if the Chinese Triad wasn't enough to deal with, I had to worry about the rising Irish mob. "Do you know why you're here?"

He ticks his head at Tony and Mickey. "They said I stole from you, but I didn't know. I swear to God, I didn't fucking know."

"Are you new in town?"

His head whips back and forth.

"Then how the fuck did you not recognize my guy with *my girl*?"

"I—I didn't know ... I'm sorry...."

I jerk my arm back and release again, the satisfying crunch of bones breaking satiating the rage. "I'm going to do you a favor Sean O'Malley. I'm going to let you live, but you're going to do one for me in return, got it?"

His head dips, one eye nearly swollen shut already. "Anything you want."

"You're going to spread the word that Stella Esposito McKenzie is mine. Anyone talks to her, comes near her, anyone fucking lays a finger on her, and I'll gut them from spine to sternum. You got it?"

"Yeah, yeah, I got it."

"*Signor Valentino*," I hiss.

"I got it, Signor Valentino."

I tug a handkerchief from my jacket pocket and wipe my hands, then remove the brass knuckles and tuck them into my pocket. My fingers curl around the knife. I spin around and strike, dragging the blade across his forehead until I hit bone.

He lets out a wail, muttering curses.

"And that's for pulling a gun and scaring her. A permanent reminder for all those to see what happens to anyone who fucks with what's mine." I spit on the scum's shoes and march out.

I should be at the office tonight. I'd spent all day tracking down that asshole with Tony and now I should be working with Clara to move things around my calendar to reschedule the meeting with the city commissioner. If we don't get the rights to the docks' redevelopment project, we're going to lose out big. Instead, I'm lingering outside Stella's room like a *minchione*. Peering through the crack in the door, my eyes settle on her figure splayed out on the bed. She's still in my shirt, despite the fact that Mickey had dropped off a suitcase of her old clothing.

My ribcage tightens, the space suddenly too small for my constricting lungs. I'd watched her all last night on the monitor. Her sleep had been plagued by nightmares brought on by that asshole. And I'd let it happen under my watch.

A wave of guilt pummels through me. Stella had already suffered so much; she didn't deserve any of this. Bringing her into my life was only making things worse. Fuck. I should just let her go.

My heart riots at the idea.

What is it about this woman that has me so fucking rattled? My eyes close, and my mind drifts to the past. A smiling little girl with freckles and a contagious laugh fills my vision.

. . .

"You again, Luca?" A fiery, tiny thing glares up at me. She's in a My Little Pony bathing suit, splashing around the busted fire hydrant.

"Yes, me again. You think you're going to get rid of me that easily? I'm your brother's new best friend." I hitch a thumb at Vinny. He's sitting on the front steps of the barber shop, a black and white ball between his feet.

"Just ignore her, or she'll follow us everywhere for the rest of the day." He stands and kicks the ball around.

"I will not," she hisses. "I don't care what you guys are doing anyway."

"Good." Vinny pats her on the head, and she shoots him a scowl. "Stay here where Mrs. D. can see you, piccola. We don't need you getting into any trouble, Stellina."

"Don't call me that. I'm not a baby anymore."

"You'll always be my little Stellina."

She plants her hands on her hips and mutters what I swear is a curse in Italian. "Where are you guys going anyway?"

Vinny doesn't answer, just keeps walking down Mulberry Street. So I turn back and shout over my shoulder, "We're just going to play some football, kid. We'll be back soon."

"Football? I thought it was soccer."

"Ah, vero. That's right, I always forget it's called soccer here in America." I quicken to a jog to catch up to Vinny, and his sister trails behind. I stop abruptly and spin around. "Hey, kid, your brother said to stay put."

"He's not the boss of me."

A laugh tumbles out despite my best efforts. "Fine but stick close. I don't want to lose you." Vinny puts on a good façade pretending not to care about his little sister, but I know she means the world to him.

. . .

The vivid memories fade, and I draw in a breath to ease the tension in my chest.

"Luca …." A quiet murmur in that sweet voice brings it all flooding back. I slip my head through the opening. "Luca," she cries out, "where are you?"

My feet propel me forward before I can stop myself. The room is dim, blackout curtains drenching the room in darkness. I can just make out her form as my pupils adjust to the obscurity. Her eyes are still closed, but my name is on her lips.

"No, please, don't!"

As my eyes grow accustomed to the lack of light, they focus on the welt on her head and the scrape across her cheek. Another round of anger floods in as tears roll down her cheeks. My fingers clench into tight fists. She's having another nightmare. Is it from the past or that *bastardo* yesterday? She whimpers, and it doesn't matter which; I ease myself onto the bed beside her.

A part of me knows this is about more than just the mugging the other day. She probably went through hell the past ten years. While I did nothing. "Shh, it's okay, you're safe," I whisper. "No one will ever hurt you again."

She rolls toward me, lids still sealed. My arms ache to wrap around her, to take away the pain I caused. I should've sent more guys with her. I know what the streets are like these days, even in broad daylight. More than that, I should have been there for her all these years.

"Luca, help…."

My heart staggers on a beat, and my body moves without my permission. My arms lace around her soft form and tug her into my chest. She curls into me, her soft curves fitting perfectly against my hard planes. She exhales softly and weaves her arm around my waist. I freeze.

Then, I stop breathing.

CHAPTER 18
THE DEVIL IN MY BED

Stella

I turn my face, and my cheek presses against something hard. The bruise pulses, and my eyes snap open. A golden cross nestled in a tangle of dark hair and tanned skin fills my vision. And that familiar white bandage. What the …? Steel bands are wrapped around my torso, a muscled leg entwined between my own.

My heart springs up my throat, and I barely suppress a squeal as my hazy thoughts come to focus. Luca. In my bed. Worse, my arm is wrapped around his bare waist. I'm torn by the urge to scream or cuddle closer into his warm, spicy scent.

After a nightmare riddled first night after the mugging, this was the best sleep I'd gotten in years. But why? Why is the devilish mob boss in bed with me? Again, indecision wars with my sanity. I should shove him off and get the hell out of here. My body betrays me, curling into the oddly familiar touch.

I try to stretch out my leg, and my knee accidentally rubs up against a particularly hard part of his lower anatomy. Panic freezes my movements.

A dark chuckle rips through the thick silence. "Good morning, princess."

I gasp and peel my body from his, shooting straight up. "What are you doing in my bed?"

"Well, technically, it's my bed, as is all the furniture in this penthouse."

Shooting him a narrowed glare, I reach for the comforter and pull it up to my chin. He lays across the mattress in only boxer briefs. I send up a quick thank you to the Virgin Mary he's not in those skin-tight bikini bottoms. As it is, I can already see the perfect shape of his dick. *Oh, Dio.* I drag my eyes away from his thickening erection.

"Why are you here?" I blurt again.

A look I've never seen on the smug C.E.O. splashes across his handsome face. Fear? Regret? I can't quite tell. "You were crying last night, and you called my name." He shrugs nonchalantly, and the raw moment of insecurity vanishes. "I thought something was wrong, so I came."

"And crawled into bed with me?"

"You pulled me onto the bed!"

"Liar," I hiss.

"I'm not lying, you can check the footage—" His mouth snaps shut, and unease prickles across my spine.

"There's a camera in my bedroom?"

"I told you there was … just not in the bathroom." A smirk crawls across his lips as embarrassment steamrolls over me.

Oh God, please don't tell me he saw when I …. The thought is too horrifying to complete even in my mind.

"Don't worry, princess, this was the first time you've cried out my name in bed. But hopefully not the last."

I reach for a pillow and chuck it at the smirking *bastardo*. He ducks, and the fluffy projectile sinks to the floor.

"We'll have to work on your aim so you can defend yourself better next time."

"Next time?" My tone hitches up a notch.

"I meant because of the mugger, not that you'll find me in your bed again. Unless you ask that is."

"I will *never* ask that of you." *Liar.* A dark voice in my mind calls me out on the bullshit.

"Never say never, princess." He rises, revealing that ripped torso and the swirl of mesmerizing tattoos. My eyes instinctively drop to take in every inch of his caramel-skinned perfection. *Dammit.* He saunters toward the door but spins back at the last second. His easy expression hardens, jaw clenching. "About that thief… you'll never have to worry about him or anyone else hurting you again." A lethal ferocity skates through his tone, thickening his accent, and the hair on the back of my neck prickles. Not just at the sound but the familiarity.

My eyes close, and I'm back on the subway platform, the cement digging into my knees and Bo's fingers twisted in my hair. That voice.

"It *was* you," I whisper.

His eyes widen, a hint of surprise flashing before his demeanor returns to neutral. "I'm afraid I don't know what you're talking about."

"In the subway, with that asshole Bo Zhang about two weeks ago."

The corners of his eyes crinkle, lending a hint of humor to his dark gaze. "I'm not in the habit of taking the subway, princess. Too many scumbags."

My chest tightens with an unfamiliar emotion. It's been years since I've felt cared for, no, taken care of. After the cancer ripped through Mom and then Vinny's attack, I was the one who held us together, who stepped in when Dad was too drunk to see straight. And in only a few days with this man, he's managed to fill a void I hadn't even realized was there. A man who's holding me captive against my will.

Dio, I am *pazza*.

Luca watches me from across the room for a long moment, midnight irises smoldering. The air crackles between us, an electric charge filling the space. It was him, I'm certain. Heat zips over every inch of my body as that scrutinizing gaze rakes over me. That look is like a lethal caress, the intensity enough to send warmth pooling between my legs.

Madonna, it should be illegal.

"What?" I finally blurt because in a second I'll melt into a puddle from that piercing stare.

"I like my shirt on you." His jaw clamps shut the moment the words are out, as if they'd escaped without his approval. He drags his hand through his hair and mutters something I can't quite make out. "You did get the suitcase of clothes Mickey dropped off?"

I nod. "Yeah, I think Magda put it in the closet." I chew on my lower lip for another second before muttering, "Thanks for that."

"So why are you still wearing my shirt?" His dark brow lifts, and amusement brings a twinkle to his eyes.

I shrug. "I didn't even notice I had it on." *Lie.* "I must have grabbed it off the floor last night in the dark without thinking. I was exhausted …." I stop talking because the twist at the corners of his mouth tells me he's not buying it. Hell, I know I don't. I'd never admit it to the arrogant mob boss, but his scent calms the raging storm of nerves. It must have been because he was the one that picked me up off the streets after that robber assaulted me. It's misplaced hero-syndrome or something. That's a thing, right?

He steps closer, and my spine snaps to attention. *Cazzo*, my whole body does, forcing me to stand. "I meant what I said before, I took care of that *pezzo di merda*. No one touches what's mine."

My core clenches, and I release a shuddering breath. I should be insulted by the way he talks about me, like I'm nothing more than a toy, one of his shiny possessions. But the dark glimmer in his eye, the curve of his lips, the hard clench of his jaw has heat racing below.

To distract myself from the ache, I blurt the first thing that comes to mind. "Did you kill him?" I was too young to remember much about my *nonno*, Michele Esposito, but his reputation preceded him. Even though Mom had never been in the business, I'd grown up hearing countless stories. I knew what happened when you crossed the big boss.

He stalks closer still, and my body thrums with anticipation. He towers over me, the sinister curl of his lips doing unspeakable things to my insides. His warm breath ghosts over my mouth. "Did you want me to?" he whispers, the question much more seductive than it has any right to be.

My pulse accelerates, vision blurring as I'm back on that crowded street. The man barrels into me, holds a gun on me and then I'm falling. I hit the floor and my mind swims, the edges of my vision darkening. I'm catapulted back in time to a similar smack, to all the times my father took out his drunken rage on me. For a second, I thought I was going to pass out. Did the guy deserve to die for that? Probably not, but a deep, dark part of me wants to say yes. I finally shake my head.

He cracks his knuckles and fury surges across that handsome face, sharpening his features. "I wanted to." He drags his thumb across my bottom lip, and a tremor roars through me at his touch.

That air thickens again as our gazes remain entangled for an endless moment. If he only tipped his head forward another inch his lips would capture mine. I hold my breath in anticipation, battling with the knowledge that I want this. I want his mouth on me. Everywhere.

There's something in that dark gaze, something hidden deep beneath those pools of onyx. I try to grasp onto the feeling, but it withers away until there's nothing left but that look, those eyes boring into me.

"Instead of killing the lowlife," he finally says, releasing my lip, "I decided to make an example of him. Now, everyone will know that you are under my protection. If anyone so much as looks at you the wrong way, I'll kill them with my bare hands."

I swallow hard. Without truly knowing this man, I understand he's not trying to impress me with his threats. I feel the certainty down to my core. He would really do that and more because he believes I do belong to him.

And as fucked up as it is, a swell of exhilaration blooms at his words. At the idea of not being alone anymore.

He hitches his thumb over his shoulder, taking a step back and signals toward the hallway. The overwhelming tension dissipates, and I finally release the breath I've been holding and sag back down on the bed. "I'm going to get dressed. I have a conference call in half an hour."

"You're not going into the office today?"

He shakes his head. "Nah, I thought I'd work from home. Someone has to make sure you stay out of trouble. I can't have you all scratched up for the big Heart Ball next week. What's the point of arm candy if it's all banged up?"

I shoot him the middle finger, and the tense set of his jaw softens until it melts into a smile. Luca smirks a lot, but a smile, a true genuine smile on the man is devastating. I dart into the bathroom to keep myself from staring like a silly fool.

Dio, one night in this man's arms, and I'm starting to forget that I'm actually a prisoner here. A prisoner in a gilded cage, captured by a man who makes my body thrum and my heart sing.

CHAPTER 19
ONE NIGHT

Luca

Stella sits by the window, her dark hair aglow beneath streaks of mid-day sunshine. The scent of calla lilies strewn across the stark penthouse mixes with her intoxicating natural fragrance. She's got her luscious lower lip snagged between her teeth as she flips through the pages of her Economics textbook, and I'm jealous, fucking jealous of those pages because I want her fingers on me, envious of those teeth because I want *my* mouth on that full, pouty lip.

Fuck. It hasn't even been a week since Stella blew back into my life, and already I can feel the shift. Like the ground beneath me isn't quite as steady, the black not so black and the white ten times brighter.

Tomorrow is the big Heart Ball, and the true test to determine if this arrangement will actually work. So far, it's been nothing but headaches and blue balls. The hint of a smile creeps across my mouth as her image on the monitor consumes my vision. I spend every night watching her like a *pazzo*. She hasn't touched herself again, not since that night. I keep waiting, waiting for her to sink her fingers inside her sweet pussy and moan *my* name.

My cock instantly hardens. I shift uneasily and reposition the laptop across my legs.

Instead, every night she just crawls into bed wearing my t-shirt and sleeps like a fucking angel. Like she doesn't have a care in the world. How is it possible? As much as she complains about being a prisoner, she's adjusted quite well to her new life. She doesn't even seem scared of me anymore.

I'll have to do something about that soon. I can't have her getting all comfortable here. Despite how good she looks in my home. This is strictly business and only temporary. Maybe if I repeat it enough, it'll get through my thick skull.

My phone vibrates on the side table, and I shake my head out to dislodge the all-consuming thoughts of Stella which have taken permanent residence in my mind. "Hello?" I growl.

Stella's head spins toward me, likely unnerved by my tone. *Good.*

I mutter a curse at Albie before gritting out, "Fine, let him up."

When I slam my phone down, Stella's gaze is still intent on mine. She scoots to the edge of the chaise lounge, still nibbling on that lip. "Who's coming up?" she finally asks.

"Dante."

Her dark brows knit together, a flash of recognition brightening her irises before it dissipates completely. "Who's that?"

"My brother."

Her pretty pink lips screw into a pout, and even though I'm no mind reader, I know exactly where her thoughts go. To the brother she lost. Too bad my brother is nowhere near the man that Vinny was or could have been.

Her mouth opens again, and I know she's going to delve

into the past, something I cannot deal with right now. The shadows are too dark, the memories still too raw.

"Keep your mouth shut when he gets here." I immediately regret the sharpness in my tone, but it's too late to say anything else.

The elevator doors glide open, and Magda appears, racing across the penthouse to the entrance foyer. She dips her head. "Hello, Signor Dante."

He drops his coat in her arms without so much as a greeting and marches toward me.

"Hey *bastardo*, I know Mamma taught you better manners than that." I tick my head at Magda who lingers by the entrance, cheeks rosy.

With an eyeroll, Dante whirls around and gives my housekeeper a tight smile. "Morning, Magda." His gaze pivots to meet mine for an instant before landing on Stella on the chaise. Her textbook is splayed out beside her, and her curious eyes are fixed to my brother. "I couldn't believe it when Clara said you were working from home today, but I guess now I understand why." He smirks and takes a step toward Stella. I move in front of him. "How very unlike you, Luca. A quickie in the middle of the workday? Or did you break one of your precious rules and allow the pretty girl to spend the night?"

"I'm not some *puttana*—" Stella shouts, but I shoot her a narrowed glare. Shockingly, she obeys my unspoken command. Good, she's learning.

Undiluted fury pounds through my veins. I can feel Stella's questioning stare boring through the back of my head, but I don't take the bait. My brother is simply trying to rile me up, and I refuse to let him win. "*She* is none of your business," I grit out. Inhaling a deep breath, I don the cool mask, the one of the C.E.O., the enforcer. "What's so important that you came all this way?"

"I need to talk to you about the Red Dragons."

"So talk."

He motions to Stella. From the corner of my eye, I catch the tense set of her shoulders, the faint quiver of her lip. Dante's right of course, I shouldn't be discussing my business in front of her, but a tiny fucked-up part of me wants her to know what sort of monster she's dealing with so she'll stay away when our arrangement is over.

"I said talk," I rasp out.

His eyes flicker back and forth between us before he discharges a frustrated grunt. "Jianjun Zhang is getting too ballsy. His kid took out half a dozen of our guys in the Meatpacking District last night."

I hiss out a string of curses. Fucking Bo. I'm going to end that *rompicoglione*. I should have that day in the subway. Hell, I would have if I'd known that was Stella on her knees. "Did he get into our warehouses?"

He shakes his head. "No, the guys were able to take the fuckers down before they found the merch. The cops showed up and Tony handled it, but it was close."

"Why is this the first I'm hearing of this?"

"I don't know." He shrugs, his eyes lifting over my shoulder to Stella once again. I puff out my chest, broadening my shoulders to block her from his view. "Guess Tony thought you were otherwise occupied." A smirk pulls at his lips.

I ignore the jab and begin to formulate my plan for retaliation. Those damned Red Dragons need to be put back in their place. I try to play nice, negotiate, make deals, but they don't know how to act like gentlemen. "Tell Tony to ransack their warehouses on the Lower East Side. I want all of their shit burned down."

Dante blanches, jaw nearly unhinging. "All of it?"

"Did I stutter?"

"Luca, that's easily half-a-mil in blow."

"I'm well aware of that, brother. And I don't want that shit on my streets." I might be a man of questionable morals, but I do not peddle drugs. Never have, never will. There are plenty of other ways to make money without destroying the brains and rotting the bodies of this city's future.

"You do this, and you'll have the entire Chinese Triad on your ass."

"Don't worry about my ass. Just do it."

He shakes his head, hissing out a breath. "Will do, *capo.*" He just stands there staring at me. His dark gaze flashes to Stella again, and the desire to gouge his eyes out for even looking at her rushes through me like a runaway train.

"Anything else?" I grind out.

"Nah, nothing else, bro. I'll see you at the Heart Ball tomorrow?"

I nod. "See you there."

"Hope to see you again, gorgeous," he calls out over my shoulder, and a wild tremor races up my spine. I grit my molars to keep from biting his head off.

Dante smirks again as if he can feel my rage before he whirls on his heel and saunters toward the elevator, grabbing his jacket from Magda. Again, he completely ignores her when she offers a murmured goodbye. *Idiot.* Just because he hates me for stealing his birthright by assuming the role of C.E.O. in Papà's business doesn't excuse his behavior toward my employees.

The moment the elevator doors slide closed, Stella appears in front of me, jabbing a finger at my chest. Luckily, she's just shy of hitting the nearly mended bullet wound. "What the hell was that? I'm not some piece of furniture you can just talk around."

"You're pissed because I didn't introduce you to my piece of shit brother?"

"Yes," she hisses. "He thought I was some *puttana* you picked up off the streets."

"And you'd rather him know you're my hostage?"

Her lips press into a thin line.

"Dante and I aren't exactly close. I don't keep him up to

date on everything that goes on in my life, business or otherwise."

"So it wasn't true what he said about you not allowing women to spend the night?" Her cheeks burn an enticing crimson, the same shade I imagined she would turn if I was plunging deep inside her.

A dark chuckle rumbles in my chest, and her cheeks flush a deeper red. "Why do you care, princess?"

"I don't," she snaps.

"You could've fooled me." I reach for her, dragging my thumb across her lower lip to free it from her gritted teeth. "Trust me, one night is all women need." My feet propel me closer.

She swallows hard, the elegant column of her throat bobbing. Her dark eyes lance into mine, pupils so wide they nearly eclipse the blue. She draws in a sharp breath and actually leans into me. *Dio*, she wants this. Despite the fucked-up things I've done to her, her body craves mine as much as I desire hers.

What happened to the sweet, innocent Stella I'd known all those years ago? What did Liam McKenzie do to make her want a monster like me?

We remain perfectly still for an endless moment, locked in a battle of wills. Electricity thickens the air between us until it's so heavy my breaths come out in ragged spurts. Stella's chest is heaving too, her nipples erect beneath her new silk blouse. It would be so easy to take her right now. I'm fairly certain she'd let me toss her over the back of the couch and fuck her until nightfall.

I'd steal her innocence, and she'd capture my cold heart.

But in the end, we would both lose because villains don't get happy endings. And as fucked up as I was, I wouldn't rob her of that.

So I pry my fingers from her soft flesh and take a big step back, creating some much needed space between our heated bodies. "Tomorrow at the ball, I'll introduce you as my girlfriend. Happy?"

The sound of air catching in her throat fills me with an immeasurable amount of pleasure.

"As per our arrangement," I add before she starts imagining this concession is something more.

She licks her lips before clamping them shut.

"And if you're a good girl, you may get a reward."

Her eyes sparkle, the brilliant blue deepening a few shades. "I'm not your fucking Golden Retriever," she bites back.

I can't help the chuckle that erupts from deep inside. "No, you're not," I finally answer. "But damn, would I love it if you rolled over for me."

Her eyes narrow, fury zipping through those expressive orbs. "*Vaffanculo*, Luca!" she hisses before storming toward her bedroom.

Go fuck yourself. I'd probably have to now that I was harder than hell. Luckily, I'd saved the video footage from the other night so I could get off while watching her touch herself as many times as I wanted.

Mmm. One day, princess. One day, it'll be my *cock coated in your juices instead of those fingers….*

CHAPTER 20
THE HEART BALL

Stella

A maddening bout of butterflies lash their wings across my insides as I stare at my reflection in the mirror. Magda zips up the deep emerald gown with the plunging neckline, and I barely recognize the woman in front of me. Soft, dark curls cascade down my shoulders resting along the silky fabric of the gown. Dramatic eyeliner and smoky shadows make my blue eyes pop against light caramel skin. Not only is Luca's housekeeper a whiz in the kitchen, but she is also an absolute miracle worker with hair and makeup. Though the bruises from my run-in with the robber have begun to fade, her expert strokes made them completely disappear.

I feel like I just stepped out of the cover of W Magazine.

Her pale gray eyes catch mine through the mirror. "You look beautiful."

"Thanks to you," I offer. The girl has been a godsend over the past week. Though she claims Luca has spent much more time at the penthouse since my arrival, business meetings keep him away most of the day. Despite studying for final exams, which Luca somehow convinced my professors to allow me to take virtually at the end of the semester, most days I was pretty damned lonely. If it wasn't for Magda, I would've gone insane. I begged Luca for my phone back, but every day I got the same answer. *Not yet.*

I missed my best friend, Rose, and wanted more than anything to talk to her.

I'd been here for over a week now, and I hadn't tried to escape again. Honestly, I didn't have anywhere to go. Not until I graduated with my crappy associate degree. With any luck, I'd survive the month with Luca, and then I'd get the hell out of here. I could finally put all of this behind me. A pang of something I refuse to accept niggles at my chest.

"Can I help you with anything else?" Magda's question derails my spiraling thoughts, and I take one last quick look in the mirror.

"Nope. This is as good as I get."

She smiles. "Signor Valentino will be very happy when he sees you."

I snort on a laugh. "Like I care what he thinks."

A hint of amusement curls the corners of her lips, but I don't dare ask what's so funny. I'm too scared of the answer. I march into the bedroom and slip on the uber-expensive designer stilettos. The rhinestone-encrusted, gold Jimmy Choos cost more than my first car. I teeter on the high heels before I get my balance and send a quick prayer to the Virgin Mary to keep me from busting my ass tonight. Not only could I break an ankle, but I'd also likely rip the slit up the back of the tight dress and give everyone a front row view of my lacey thong and bare cheeks. These designer gowns are not made for curvy Italian women with an irrational penchant for cannoli.

A quick knock at the door has my heart launching itself at my ribs. "The limo will be here in five minutes, Stella." Luca's voice sends another wave of mad flutters through my gut. He's been giving me the countdown every five minutes for the past half hour.

"Be right out," I shout. Grabbing my new gold Gucci clutch, I throw my lip gloss and inhaler in and wrap my fingers around the soft leather. *You can do this, Stella.* One night out on the town with the mob boss. What could go wrong?

Magda stands by the door, holding it open. I'm paralyzed by the bed, unable to force my feet to move. "Go, Stella. Signor Luca is waiting."

Right. Just walk, *cazzo.* You've been doing it for nearly twenty-one years. Inhaling a lungful of air, I steady my nerves and place one stiletto in front of the other. Magda offers a nod of encouragement as I cross the threshold into the hallway.

A sharp hiss lifts my gaze to a pair of piercing, bottomless irises. Our eyes lock, and my heart trips on a beat. That one look is more invasive, more lethal than any man's touch. It should be illegal. I force my spine to straighten to keep from trembling. Luca in normal clothes is gorgeous, but in a tux, he's devastating. The fine fabric molds to his broad shoulders, tapering down to narrow hips and powerful thighs. I already know what lies beneath the expensive threads, the body of a god. My heart races, heat pooling below my bellybutton, and he's all the way down the hall. If he simply touches me, I'll explode.

"*Sei bellissima,*" he finally murmurs, and his legs propel him closer.

I move too, my feet thrusting me forward of their own accord. Like the earth and moon, we're helplessly drawn to each other. On a deadly collision course. I'm not sure how I know he feels the same compulsion, but I do. It's written across his face, in the tense set of his coiled muscles.

I stop mere inches from him, his warm breath ghosting over my lips. His typically scruffy jaw is shaved clean, and I stare at his smooth skin to focus on something, anything, instead of the riot of emotions pummeling my insides. His chest rises and falls quickly, the emerald pocket square that matches my dress bouncing up and down in an erratic rhythm.

"I—" His eyes bore into me, devouring me whole. And for an instant, that's all I want, to drown in Luca Valentino.

"The limo is here, signore." Magda's voice breaks the spell, and he releases me from that unrelenting gaze.

The look of wonder, of awe, disappears replaced by the cool mask of the C.E.O. and mob boss. He clears his throat and offers me his arm. "Come, we don't want to keep Mickey waiting. We already know he doesn't like you."

His quip dispels the thickness in the air, and I release the breath immobilizing my lungs. "I'm not overly fond of him either."

He smirks and leads me toward the elevator. As we enter, it dawns on me that this is the first time I've left the penthouse since my disastrous shopping trip right after my arrival. Luca must realize it too because he corners me against the cold metal wall and levels me with a narrowed glare. "My men will be crawling around the event tonight, so don't even think about making a run for it. If you try anything tonight, I will punish you. Do you understand, princess?"

An involuntary shudder races up my spine. My stupid body now equates punishment with a very naked Luca and a warm bubble bath. Somehow, I'm fairly certain he wouldn't allow me to get away a second time quite as unscathed.

I run my tongue across my lower lip and his eyes trace the movement, heat flashing across the darkness. "I understand."

"Good. And if anyone asks how we know each other, let me do the talking."

"Fine," I grit out. "Any more rules? Or was Dante making that up too?"

He pauses, eyes pinned to mine. "Oh, princess, there are many more rules, so many they'd make your head spin." A wicked grin spreads his lips, revealing a hidden dimple. And

Dio, that panty-dropping smile should be illegal. The elevator doors glide open, and he leads me to the limo.

Mickey shoots me side-eye as he holds the door open, and I slide into the backseat. Luca glides in beside me, his muscled thigh pressing against the silky satin of my gown. Heat radiates from his leg and sears into mine. I scoot over and squeeze my eyes shut to steady my breathing. I'm tempted to reach for my inhaler, but instead focus on deep breaths. Inhale. Exhale. Images of the first time we rode in his town car fill my mind. Surely, his driver has cleared all guns from the vehicle tonight.

Luca sits quietly beside me, the silence oddly comfortable. After a week of living together, I've learned to sense shifts in his mood. The man is mercurial at best, manic at worst. Perhaps, his mind is also on the last time we rode together.

"Why are you going to this Heart Ball anyway?" I finally ask, curiosity getting the best of me.

"It's a charity I support."

"How noble of you."

He cocks a dark brow. "One of many."

"How extra noble then." I slant him a cheeky smile. I can't believe how much our relationship has changed in the short span of a week. "Do these lovely, charitable men and women know you keep hostages in your penthouse?"

"Of course not," he grits out.

"I didn't think so."

"Stella…," he growls.

"I know, I know. It's an agreement, a business deal and that's it. I promise to be your gracious arm candy all night."

"Thank you."

Before long, the limo slows and spotlights dance across the tinted windows. Despite my bravado, my pulse skyrockets at the sight. The New York Public Library is aglow with lights, spotlights, flashlights, and camera lights flickering through the darkness. Mickey opens the car door and I freeze, a deer trapped in headlights. The click-click of cameras and bulbs flashing has me on the verge of a panic attack. I reach for my purse but find warm fingers instead. Luca's hand wraps around mine, and he guides me out of the backseat, grabbing my clutch with his free hand. He leads me between the iconic stone lions and up the red-carpeted marble steps, effortlessly weaving me through the mob of guests and paparazzi.

Holy cannoli.

So, this is how the other half lives?

I stare up at the imposing marble columns and ornate details of the national landmark. As a born and bred New Yorker, I hate to admit it, but I've never actually been inside. A travesty really.

"Mr. Valentino!"

"Over here, Luca!"

"A quick picture, please."

The paparazzi call out his name, but the C.E.O. of King Industries doesn't bat an eye. His hold on my hand only tightens as he steers me through the real-life pages of Society Magazine.

"Luca, come on, remember you owe me one. For *The New Yorker*?" A female voice cuts through the onslaught, and my escort pauses. From the corner of his eye, he scans the woman in a fitted red pantsuit.

"Just one picture, Kerry."

"One good picture," she counters, "and the name of your date."

With a frustrated sigh, he wraps his arm around my waist and turns us toward the camera. "Stella Esposito," he grits out.

The sound of my full name on his lips makes my stomach somersault. And the fact that he used my mother's maiden name instead of my asshole father's loosens the tightness in my chest. I take in a lungful of air and plaster a smile on my face.

"That's my good girl," Luca whispers, his warm breath skating over the shell of my ear. A delicious tingle races up my spine, and a genuine smile parts my lips. His grin reflects my own, and an inexplicable giddiness fills my chest.

"Got it!" The reporter gives us an enthusiastic thumbs up as she glances down at the camera. "It's a *really* good one. The smile even looks genuine, Mr. Valentino."

With a grunt, Luca rushes us away from the crowd. He leads me up the final steps through the archway, my head tilted back, completely absorbed by the endless beauty. We stop at the foot of the ballroom, and I barely suppress a gasp. Every corner is exquisitely decorated from the finest linens to sparkling chandeliers and gilded centerpieces twinkling with candlelight.

"It's something, isn't it?"

"Yeah," I murmur, unable to take it all in fast enough. "Do you attend a lot of these events?"

He nods. "I've got three more this month."

For an instant, I'm sad there aren't more. Clara bought me dozens of beautiful gowns. What would become of them all? A devastating thought spears me in the heart. What if he's done this before? What if there are other women with whom he's made arrangements like these? Maybe the next one would inherit my dresses.

Logically, I shouldn't care. I should be happy when this twisted bargain is over.

Luca hands a cream envelope to a smiling female standing behind a podium. The blonde doesn't even open it, batting long fake lashes at my escort. "Of course, Mr. Valentino and guest, please come this way," she croons.

And guest? Seriously?

The woman leads us to a table in the center of the room, right in front of the dancefloor and mere inches away from the stage. "I hope this table suits you, Mr. Valentino. It's reserved for our most honored guests."

"It's fine, thank you." He offers her a cold smile.

"If there's *anything* else I can do for you, my name is

Mitsy." The emphasis on the word anything has my hackles rising.

"Noted. However, I'm certain my date will be more than capable of tending to *all* my needs." She blanches and skitters away as a smile tugs at the corner of my lip. He turns his back to a quickly retreating Mitsy and pulls out my chair. I have to clench my jaw to keep it from dropping. When did the mob boss become a chivalrous gentleman?

I'm about to call him out on it when a muttered curse tumbles from his gentlemanly lips. I look up, following his line of sight. A murderous expression hardens the sharp lines of his jaw as they raze over Dante and a leggy blonde.

Luca whirls at me and jerks me out of the chair. "Let's dance."

CHAPTER 21
DIRTY DANCING

Stella

Luca's fingers latch onto mine, his hold nearly punishing, as he drags me to the dancefloor. For a second, I forget I'm supposed to play the role of doting girlfriend, but a sharp tug quickly reminds me as he jerks me against his chest. I crash into him, my hand escaping his, and both palms press against the fine silk of his suit.

His breaths are uneven, ragged spurts vibrating his ribcage.

"What the hell is wrong?" I hiss.

"Nothing."

"You just had an overwhelming desire to dance with me?" I tease, trying to lighten the mood.

"Yes," he growls. "You're mine, remember? To do with as I please until the end of the month." *Dio*, this man's mood swings are giving me whiplash. He peels my hand from his chest and spears his fingers through my own, then his arm tightens around my waist, bringing me flush against him.

I clench my teeth to keep the faint gasp from escaping. He's all over me. His scent tickles my nostrils, his chest presses against mine, his arms caging me in. My body's reaction to his is unfair. Perhaps, he's not the only one with an erratic mood.

He's all I see, all I sense, all-consuming. I can barely focus on keeping time with the music, not when each point of contact violently thrums between us. Luckily, he's a masterful dancer, another completely unexpected quality of the mob boss, and he guides me across the gleaming parquet like a puppet on a string.

Luca's eyes are locked on mine, every twirl, every dip, they never deviate. Heat consumes the minute space between our bodies. The anger flashing across those bottomless irises slowly wanes, replaced by something raw and far more dangerous. Something shifts between us, something I'm too terrified to name. Because what I feel for this man is not normal. No one should feel this way about someone who's keeping them prisoner.

The melody continues in a blur, one song merging into another and another. I'm held captive in that dark gaze, that firm hold that makes my blood sing. Minutes or maybe hours pass. I have no concept of time beyond this intense moment between us.

He leans his forehead to mine, our lips only a heartbeat away. "Oh, princess...," he murmurs, the rough edge to his tone accelerating my pulse. *Dio*, I want to capture those lips, to taste him just one time. It's fucked up, and I'm well aware what that means for my own sanity, but I can't seem to bring myself to care.

With the shitshow my life has been over the past few months, I need this. A little release. Who cares if I'm being reckless? I've been responsible my whole life, and tonight, I want to lose myself in this man.

I press my body closer and grind my lower half against him. His arm tightens like a vice around my waist, hand skating toward the curve of my ass. I can feel him hardening against me, and fiery heat rages between my legs.

"You're playing a dangerous game, princess," he whisper-hisses in my ear.

I rock my hips against his erection, too far gone to heed his advice, and another sharp hiss seeps through his lips. Everything else around us disappears, muddled in the background and drowned out by the mad roar of my thundering heart.

Dio, I've never wanted anything more.

The tune morphs into a slow, sultry one, and he leads us into a smooth transition. We sway to the sweltering rhythm, his cock rubbing dangerously close to my center with the additional height the stilettos afford. He licks his lips, our heated breaths mingling.

Luca's hand digs into the hair at my nape and tugs, exposing my throat. The scrape of his teeth across the sensitive flesh sends goosebumps cascading down my arms. A faint moan escapes, and a wicked grin flashes across that clean-shaven jaw.

"If you keep making sounds like that I'm going to lose it." He runs his hands down my ass and cups my soft curves.

It's hard to remember we're in public as I shamelessly grind against him, but with his strong arms around me, I feel like no one can touch us, like we're in our own private bubble. Luca has that quality about him, that all-powerful aura that no one can match. He oozes authority and dominance, and *Dio*, it's so damned sexy.

I lift my chin and meet that devastating gaze. "What if I want you to?" I breathe out.

He slowly shakes his head, hard lines carving into his jaw. "Me losing control wouldn't be good for anyone."

I press my chest against his, my breasts spilling over the top of the gown. His eyes drop, and he lets out a groan. "Oh, Stella, what are you doing to me?"

"Just playing the part of doting arm candy."

"You're going above and beyond."

I smile. Seeing the calm, collected Luca lose his cool because of me is doing things to my insides that should be criminal. I grind my hips against his cock to ease the fiery ache. Only it has the opposite effect, and I rub harder. His fingers tighten around my ass and guide my hips over him. There are layers of clothes between us and still, I'm fairly certain if we keep this up, I'll come right here on the dancefloor.

The smoldering fire in Luca's eyes reveals the same.

"We should stop," I pant out.

"Yes, we should." But he doesn't. Instead, he drops his head and flutters kisses across the swell of my breast. He pauses, and I barely restrain myself from shoving his mouth back to my burning flesh. He runs his finger over the top of the heart tattoo peaking from beneath my gown.

"What's this?" he murmurs.

"A tattoo," I snap. My dead mother and brother are the last topics I want to be discussing right now.

Pressing his lips together, his finger dips beneath the indecent neckline and traces the outline of the interlocking hearts. His eyes meet mine, and something unreadable flashes across the dark abyss. I'm certain he's about to spill something earth-shattering, but instead, his lips find their way to my chest again.

He resumes his exploration and the heat building below rises, rushing across my cheeks. All thoughts vanish, and all I can do is feel. We're in the middle of a crowded dancefloor, in perfect view for all to see. I should be much more embarrassed than I am. But it's hard to form cohesive thoughts with Luca's warm tongue lavishing me.

I want that tongue everywhere.

"Ah, there's the happy couple." The voice splashes ice across the fiery embers raging in my core.

Luca glances up from his spot nestled between my breasts,

dark eyes murderous as they lance over his brother. "Dante," he grits out. "And Caroline, what a surprise." The cool mask slips into place, and he releases me. A frosty chill rakes over my body at the sudden absence of his.

The blonde squirms beside Dante, hand resting on his shoulder, but her gaze is pinned to my escort.

"I didn't realize you knew each other," Luca says smoothly.

Dante wraps an arm around the woman and draws her into his side. "We just met a few weeks ago at *La Palestra*."

"Oh, imagine that." Luca's glare razes over his brother, and I know I'm missing something. Which I hate. It's bad enough he refused to introduce me the other day at the penthouse.

I throw my hand out at the blonde who eyes it like it's covered in dog shit. "I'm Stella, Luca's girlfriend."

Her eyes nearly pop out of her head, and I'm incredibly satisfied by her reaction. Dante looks like he's about a second away from a heart attack. I'm confused because wasn't that the whole point of this arrangement, to be the good little girlfriend?

"Girlfriend?" Caroline ignores my offered hand and glares at Luca. Her cheeks redden, and her breaths come out in haggard spurts. "You really are an asshole, Luca Valentino," she hisses before spinning away and darting off the dancefloor.

My escort doesn't even make a move to stop her, instead lets out a frustrated breath and whirls on his brother. "What the hell are you thinking bringing her here?"

"What? I had no idea you fu—knew each other intimately."

I've known Luca's brother for all of a second, and even I can smell the lie. I try to focus on that instead of the inappropriate pang of jealousy at his insinuation.

Luca shakes his head, irritation sharpening the hard lines of his jaw. He turns to me and wraps firm fingers around my arm before bringing his lips to my ear. "Meet me in the women's bathroom in five minutes. I'm not done with you."

The rough edge to his tone sends a chill up my spine. I steady my nerves and meet his hard gaze. "Why? Where are you going?"

"I need to talk to my *fratello* in private first."

Dante stiffens beside him, and for the first time I take a good look at his brother. He looks older, but not by much. They have the same dark eyes and silky hair, but Dante's expression is harder somehow. I don't know anything about him besides the obvious fact that he's not Luca's favorite person. Before he showed up at the penthouse the other day, I didn't even know he existed. When Vinny was alive, he was all I talked about. He wasn't just my brother, he was my best friend, my hero ….

I bury the thoughts, this night chaotic enough without digging up dark memories of the past.

"Go, Stella," Luca grits out.

I shoot the *bastardo* a narrowed glare before spinning on my heels. I march off the dancefloor, lifting my chin to keep my pride intact after being dismissed like a dog. *Cazzo*, I will never survive this. This man's mercurial temper is enough to send me to an early grave. As I search for the damned ladies' room, I'm cursing myself for allowing Luca to touch me the way he did when we danced. And *Dio*, I wanted it so bad. If Dante and that Caroline woman hadn't shown up, I'm fairly certain I would've had an orgasm from rubbing against his hard cock in the middle of the crowded dancefloor.

Merda, I'm a disaster.

Meet me in the women's bathroom in five minutes. I'm not done with you. Luca's words echo across my mind as I traverse the grand ballroom and finally spot the gilded restroom sign. What does that even mean? Is he pissed I introduced myself as his girlfriend or was that threat something else entirely?

A tremor rolls through my body as his hands ghost along my hips, hugging my ass, and those lips ….

Stop it! I blink quickly, but I'd have to carve those images out of my mind with a knife before they ceased to exist. Pushing through the bathroom door, I nearly barrel into a familiar blonde.

Ugh. Shit.

Caroline eyes me, her deep green irises scanning over every inch of my designer wardrobe. I pull my shoulders back, refusing to be intimidated by the woman. Sure, she probably bought her own Jimmy Choos and Dior purse, but she has no idea my new ridiculously expensive accessories were a gift from Luca.

"What?" I bark.

"Classy…," she murmurs. "I've never seen you at one of these events. What did you say your last name was?"

"I didn't."

Her lips screw into a sneer as she flashes pearly white teeth. "How do you know Luca?"

I internally curse him for not letting me create a backstory before we arrived. "Old family friends," I blurt. I have no idea where that came from, but it's probably true. My *Nonno* was the don of all of Manhattan back in the day. He must have known Luca's father. "How do you know him?" I counter.

"We fucked once. And you know Luca—one time is all you get. Right?"

My brows knit, a hint of an emotion I refuse to name settling in the pit of my stomach. She must read the confusion on my face because a wicked grin stretches across her face. "Oh, I get it. You haven't fucked him yet. Now, this makes more sense." She leans against the vanity, her smile growing. "I'm going to do you a favor and warn you to stay the hell away from Luca Valentino. He has all these rules when it comes to screwing: no kissing, no face-to-face, and most important, only once. He'll fuck you senseless, leave you craving him like a drug, but he's unbendable. And he sure as hell doesn't date. So do yourself a favor, little girl, run far away before he ruins you."

I stare at her, completely numb. All the words tangle in my throat, my brain on overdrive. I shouldn't be surprised by what she's said. It seems every bit in line with Luca's controlling character, and still, it hits me like a freight train. My heart stalls, my ribs suddenly too tight. I can't drag in a breath fast enough.

"Trust me, sweetie, you're not his girlfriend, and you never will be." With that, she twirls on her stilettos and marches out.

The moment she's gone, my knees give out and I barely make it to the upholstered bench along the wall before I crumble. Heat burns the corners of my eyes, and I hate that her words could have that effect on me. Because that only means one thing … one thing that I refuse to accept. I'm falling for my captor.

The bathroom door whips open, and Luca fills the entryway, his overwhelming presence sucking all the air from the room. He slams the door shut, and the click of the lock cuts through the thickening silence. Blazing dark irises fix to mine, and he stalks toward me.

CHAPTER 22
A LION IN THE LADIES ROOM

Stella

I shrink back on the chaise and bump the mirror behind me as Luca stalks closer, a lion focused on one thing: his prey. Piercing irises raze over me, and a shudder roars up my spine. That single, feral look leaves me completely exposed, bare before him.

He stops only inches away, his legs nearly brushing my knees. I draw in a breath to slow the thundering beats of my heart. His expression is lethal, but I can't tell if it's anger or lust burning through those midnight irises.

The same is true for me. My mouth is dry, pulse skyrocketing, but heat flares between my legs. The familiar ache from our dance returns, pulsating below.

He steps closer and forces my legs apart. The rip of expensive fabric has my heart kicking against my ribs. "My dress!" I cry. Of all the things to say at that moment, it's the only thing that comes out.

"I'll buy you a new one." A mischievous grin curls his lips as he bends down, eyes smoldering. His hands close around my thighs, and he spreads them another few inches apart. I gasp at the sound of another rip. He glances down at the indecent tear, and fire surges down my belly. If he bends any further, he'll have a front row view of my sheer, lace thong and everything hidden beneath.

He licks his lips and *Madonna mia*, it's so sinful and sexy, I chomp down on the inside of my cheek to keep myself from tangling my hand around the back of his neck and dragging that mouth to mine. His fingers sear into my flesh, and every ounce of restraint teeters on the edge. I need to focus on Caroline's warnings because I know if I let this happen, we can never go back. And I need to know if she was telling the truth, and only the smirking asshole in front of me can confirm that.

"Wait…," I murmur, my voice rough and way too needy.

He crouches down further bending his knees, hands digging into my heated flesh. He's too close now, another inch and he'll get an up close and personal of all of me. His nostrils flare, and he breathes in deeply. "Mmm, you smell delicious, princess."

Dio. All the heat flaring below races up my cheeks, burning my face. And *cazzo*, if it isn't the hottest thing anyone's ever said to me. "Caroline," I blurt. Because my brain is too overcome with lust to string together an entire sentence.

His gaze turns savage. "What about Caroline?"

I heave in a breath and focus. Which is so damned hard when his fingers are inching up my thighs. "She said you had rules—"

His lips slant into a hard line, and the tendon in his jaw flutters. His nostrils flare again, his pupils distending. "I do," he finally rasps out as if saying the words are physically painful. Endless silence pervades, our gazes locked in an epic battle I'm fairly certain no one will win.

"Like what?"

He shakes his head. "It doesn't matter right now."

"It does." Because if what she said was true, and I could only have him once I had to prepare my heart.

Another never-ending minute of silence passes with the air only thickening between us. "What do you want from me?" he murmurs, the softness in his tone so unlike the one I've come to expect from the ruthless mobster.

Everything. The errant thought frightens the *merda* out of me. How could this man I barely know stir such strong feelings? I want to let loose. I want to forget. "I want you to fuck me." The words flow from my lips beyond my control. The moment they're out, I snap my traitorous jaw shut and bite my tongue.

A dangerous glint sharpens his irises, and a hiss slides free through his pursed lips. "Oh, princess, you have no idea what you're asking for."

"Then explain them … your rules."

He shakes his head, sinking his teeth into his lower lip. Then his hands close around my waist, and he spins me around so I'm facing the mirror. I suck in a breath as he drops to his knees in front of me. "Keep your eyes on the mirror."

"Wha—?" The rest of the word dies in my throat as his head dips between my legs. He slides my damp thong to the side and runs his tongue across the inner seam of my leg. I gasp and dig my fingers into his hair.

"Mmm, that's my good girl, you're already soaked and ready for me." He slips my panties down to my ankles.

His warm tongue drags through my center, and a moan parts my lips. "Luca," I groan, my fingers tangling in his dark locks.

He dips a finger inside me, and my hips buck against his palm. "Keep your eyes on your reflection, princess," he murmurs against the bundle of nerves at my apex. Lifting his head, his blown-out pupils meet mine. "I want you to watch every tantalizing second as I fuck you with my tongue and allow you to come in my mouth. I want you to memorize your exact expression, the sparkle in your eyes, the flush of your cheeks, the curve of your lips, every moment of pleasure so that you never forget you are *mine*."

I swallow hard. No one has ever talked to me like that, and fuck, it's got me hot as hell.

His head disappears beneath my gown once again, and his tongue flicks at my clit. My hand threads through his hair, and the other grips the edge of the chaise. His tongue runs circles around the sensitive bud, driving me to the precipice of insanity. Then he dips a second finger inside me, curling it until it hits *the* spot. Between his tongue and his fingers, I'm a squirming mess. I grind my hips into his palm, into his mouth. I'm an explosive ball of lust and pleasure and another few expert flicks will have me on my knees.

"Stella, you're not looking …," he murmurs against my sensitive flesh. *How the hell does he know?* The vibrations against that taut bundle of nerves are nearly enough to throw me over the edge.

I force my eyes up away from his silky hair and meet my reflection. My lower lip is swollen from biting it, my cheeks flushed. I've never seen myself on the brink of orgasm. There's something oddly erotic about it.

Luca's free hand glides up the front of my gown, and my focus pivots to those strong fingers moving toward my breast. He jerks the fine silk down and slides his hand inside, cupping me, fingers working my nipple to a taut peak. He pinches, and I let out a squeal. The rush of desire is too much.

I gasp as raw pleasure tears through me. "Luca," I moan. "I'm going to—"

"That's right, princess, come for me." His words reverberate through me, throwing me over the threshold.

My body constricts around his tongue, his fingers, as I ride out the storm, desperately rubbing up against his palm. He doesn't let up until he's squeezed out every ounce of pleasure, and I'm nothing but a writhing puddle of vibrating desire.

I grip the chaise, a boneless mess. Luca's head pops up from between my legs, chin covered in my juices, smiling like he just discovered gold buried deep inside my pussy. He runs his tongue over his lips, and *cazzo*, I was wrong, that is the sexiest thing I've ever seen. I hate to even think about Bo in a moment like this, because his image will only ruin the high, but that *bastardo* never went down on me. He was the most selfish lover I'd ever had.

He licks the two fingers that were just inside me before running his thumb over my bottom lip. "Mmm, just like I thought, sunshine and rainbows." That rough timbre forces all thoughts of Bo to vanish.

"What?" I finally manage.

"Nothing." He shakes his head as he tugs my soaked thong back up my legs and drags down my torn dress, the ghost of a smile curling the corners of his lips. He offers me a hand and pulls me to my feet. Standing behind me, his eyes meet mine through the mirror. "My sweet princess." His heated breath skates over the shell of my ear, and my body instinctively leans back to rest on his chest. He stiffens for an instant before his hand moves to my hip and fingers dig into my side possessively. His rock-hard cock presses against my ass, kindling another rush of desire. "You're mine, do you understand that? No one else can ever touch you."

I don't want to state the obvious and ruin this—whatever this is—I'm his prisoner, who else would I have access to? Not to mention the fact that our time together has an expiration date. So I nod slowly. I desperately want to ask about his rules, but before I can gather the nerve his mouth skates down my ear and stops at the crook of my neck. He sucks hard, then nibbles at my soft flesh. I let out a squeal when his teeth sink in. "What are you doing?"

His warm tongue replaces his teeth, and he lavishes my

sensitive skin. "Marking you as mine." He smirks as my gaze lifts to the mirror to find the deep red hickey.

"What are you sixteen?"

A deep chuckle rumbles his entire chest, the sound so warm and inviting, I sink deeper into his firm hold. The hand on my hip tightens, then his free arm laces around my waist, drawing me closer so that his arousal drives into my ass. I'm so tempted to turn around, to meet that hungry gaze. But I force myself to keep still. I'm already in way over my head, and if I go any deeper, I'm terrified I'll drown.

CHAPTER 23
RUINED

L*uca*

Merda, I was right. One taste of Stella would never be enough. What the hell was I thinking? My hand tightens around hers as I lead her back to the ballroom. Dozens of curious gazes dart in our direction as we pass. She looks sexy as hell beside me, wearing my jacket to hide the rip in her gown, her cheeks still flushed, dark hair wild. I wish I could have seen her face as I drew the orgasm out of her. *Next time....*

Cazzo. There wouldn't be a next time, remember you, *scemo*? You have rules. You must stick to them.

Technically, I didn't actually fuck her though. Not with my dick anyway. So really, am I breaking the rules?

I run my hand over my face, and Stella's sweet scent lingers on my fingers, on my lips. I can't get it out of my mind. I can't get *her* out of my mind. *Porca puttana*, this is bad. Vinny would string me up if he knew what I'd just done to his sister, if he knew all the fucked up things I wanted to do to her.

But he's not here. He's dead. *Because of you.*

I swallow thickly and bury the dark thoughts before they threaten to pull me under. I'm ready to get out of here. I showed up, I donated, and now it was time to take Stella home.

And do what with her? That same dark voice asks.

Lock her up in her room and away from my throbbing cock.

"Let's get out of here," I whisper.

She nods, a shy smile only making her look more gorgeous. *Dio*, I want to kiss her. Right here, in front of everyone. And then I want to fuck her on my bed, in the tub, on every surface of my cold-ass penthouse until she fills it with her warmth.

"Well, shit, look who's slumming it with my leftovers." That irritating, nasally voice sends the hair on the back of my neck bristling. I whirl around, fury pounding through my veins as my gaze settles on Bo.

Stella's fingers tighten around mine, and she takes a step closer to me. I'm not sure if she's even noticed it, but it fills me with an absurd amount of happiness. The moment is short lived.

Dante and Tony flank me before Bo takes another step. I tick my head at Tony, and he moves beside Stella when I'm forced to release her hand. I close the distance between Bo and me and loom over the *figlio di puttana*, daring him to utter another word about her. Unbridled fury rages through my veins. If we weren't in the middle of a public event, I'd strangle the little shit with my bare hands. "Never speak about her like that again." I drop my tone to lethal levels. "She's mine, and any insult you hurl in her direction is a direct assault on *me*. Are we clear?"

From over Bo's shoulder, I catch a few of the Red Dragons skulking closer. No one's going to make a scene at a gala of this caliber, and we all know it.

My hands fist around Bo's shirt collar, knuckles pressing

into his neck. Barely restrained rage surges to the surface as he glances over my shoulder at Stella and grins. "Are. We. Clear?" I punctuate every word with an increase of pressure to his throat.

"Yeah, we're clear, *capo*."

I release him and readjust my bowtie.

He leans in, that smirk growing in confidence, and whispers, "Just remember my cock was in her mouth first. Every time you kiss her, it's like sucking my dick."

Blood red seeps into my vision, and a storm of emotions crashes over me until I'm hurtled over the edge of logic. I pull my arm back and ram my fist into Bo's face. A crack echoes over the sweet melody of the orchestra, and he screams like a pussy. Deep crimson spurts across his pristine shirt, and satisfaction fills my vacant heart.

I inch closer and he flinches, his hand covering his broken nose. "When I'm done with her, my cock will be the only one she remembers. Trust me."

Bo's cousin, Feng, grabs him by the shoulder. "Come on, man. Now is not the time or the place." Across the dancefloor, I can just make out Jianjun and his men. He dips his head, lips drawn. He must be dying to get revenge for the fire we set that took out hundreds of thousands of dollars in cocaine. Good thing Bo's father knows better than to make a public scene. Usually, I do too.

Fuck.

One little taste of Stella's sweetness, and I am ruined.

Dante steps beside me and nudges me in the ribs. "It's time to go, *fratellino*. We've got dozens of eyes on us."

I shake him off and spin to Stella, trapping her hand in mine. Her eyes are wide as she regards me. "Are you okay?" I whisper.

She nods. "Yeah, fine. You?"

It's only then I notice the tremor vibrating my entire body. I draw in a deep breath and search for the icy calm, but with

Stella at my side I can't numb my feelings. For the first time for as long as I can remember, I don't want to.

I glare at my brother from across the elevator. If the *rompicoglioni* had an ounce of sense, he would have left the ball with Caroline instead of following me home. I have enough on my mind with Stella; I don't need to add his silent disapproval to the mix. She's tense beside me, the raw, vulnerable woman from the bathroom retreating beneath the surface. She must sense the tension in the air.

I know I fucked up with Bo, but I couldn't care less. I won't let anyone insult Stella like that. My phone vibrates in my jacket pocket, but I ignore it. Dante's cell pings a second later, drawing my attention to my scowling brother.

He has a lot of nerve with that holier than thou expression. That asshole has screwed up more times than I count. "And it begins," he mutters as he scans his phone.

"What?"

Dante turns the screen to me, and a shaky video comes to focus. Me punching Bo at the Heart Ball on TMZ. *"Merda."*

"What?" Stella inches closer and tries to get a look at the screen.

Dante snatches it away, muttering curses. "I can read the headline now: C.E.O. of King Industries Assaults Known Gang Leader. Are the rumors true? Could the notorious Luca Valentino's mob connections be legit?"

"Vaffanculo," I hiss.

The elevator doors glide open, and I wrap my hand around Stella's and tow her into the foyer. Dante stalks behind, trailing us down the hall. "What are you going to do about this? We have to issue a public statement—"

I spin around and loom over my older brother, fury heating my blood. "I will handle it," I grit out.

"How?"

"*Cazzo*, Dante, give me a minute." I jerk my chin at Stella who stares wide-eyed at both of us. "Call Jones and wait for me in the study. He'll have every damned video taken down and wiped out of existence before morning."

He eyes Stella, his gaze trailing down her bare shoulder to our clasped hands. A sneer curls his lips. "You going to fuck your new toy and then tuck her in while I take care of your shit?"

Blinding rage compels my arm back, fingers curling into a fist. Fury uncoils, and my knuckles smash into my brother's cheek. Stella lets out a gasp and takes a step back trying to squirm free of my hold, but my fingers only tighten around hers.

"What the hell is wrong with you?" Dante wails.

I hadn't even hit him hard. My knuckles barely hurt.

I close the remaining distance between us, my chest bumping his. "I don't want her name sullied by your lips. Don't ever talk about her, don't look at her, and *Dio* help me if you ever lay a fucking finger on her, Dante …."

He eyes me, rubbing his jaw like I've lost my shit. Maybe he's right.

Silence looms between us, a stare down I know I'll win. It's the same reason I became C.E.O., usurping his birthright. He has no determination, no drive. He doesn't know how to play the long game.

"I'll get him some ice." Stella's voice surprises me, and I nearly blink, losing focus. Instead, I finally release her. The click-clack of her heels across the marble eases the deepening tension, and Dante steps back, exhaling a frustrated sigh.

Ha. I knew I'd win.

"What is your deal with her?" he snarls. "I've never seen you strung so tight around a woman."

"There's no deal," I snap and drag my hand through my hair.

A knowing smile parts his lips. "You haven't fucked her yet …. That's what it is, right?"

"I'm not discussing this with you."

"Why is she here? In your apartment? I've never seen a woman in this place more than once."

"It's business, Dante. Leave it alone."

"I won't leave it alone when it interferes with your head in the game. Did you forget we just burned half a million worth of Chinese Triad coke? Retribution is coming, and it's going to get ugly. I need you at your best."

"I'm always at my best," I growl.

"No, you've been different lately. I didn't know what it was until I saw you two dancing tonight. It's her, she's screwing with your head. So just fuck her and get on with it."

"She means nothing to me," I hiss. "She's business, and that's all you need to know."

A sharp intake of air spins my head around. Stella stands in the hallway with a bag of ice in her hand, and a look in her eye that'll haunt me tonight. Betrayal. Anger. Pain. It lances through me so acute I stagger back a step.

She tosses the ice at Dante and darts past us.

"Stella, wait." I reach for her, but she's too damned fast. And pissed. She's halfway down the hall by the time I realize she just disobeyed me, in front of my brother, nonetheless.

My legs compel me forward, to chase after her, but I can't. Not with Dante staring down at me with that smug smile. "Right, just business, *fratellino*."

Shooting him a glare, I tear the bag of ice from his hand. "I hope it bruises."

His laughter follows me down the corridor, echoing behind me even after I slam my door shut.

Fuck. What have I done?

CHAPTER 24
BREAKFAST IN BED

S*tella*

Ugh. I look like *merda*. Staring at my reflection in the bathroom, I run my finger over the dark, puffy skin beneath my eyes. *She means nothing to me.* Luca's words ping-pong across my mind. I swallow hard and shove back the unwanted emotions, focusing on my weary reflection. The ugly swelling is *not* a result of crying myself to sleep last night. No, I would never shed a tear for that *bastardo*. It's gotta be allergies or something respectable like that.

Hiking up my towel, my gaze catches on the patch of mottled purple skin at the base of my neck. Heat races below my navel, and I squeeze my eyes shut as memories of the Heart Ball flit to the surface. Luca's firm arms around my waist, holding me against his chest as we danced. That wicked tongue flicking over my clit until I had the best orgasm of my life. And those lips on my neck, claiming me, as we stood in front of the mirror together. For a second, for a stupid, stupid minute I was happy. I thought that we could actually have something.

Dio, I am so messed up.

How could I ever dream of wanting anything other than freedom from this man?

A soft knock at the bedroom door has my heart tripping on a beat. I skulk out of the bathroom and pad across the plush carpeting. I stop at the door, awareness prickling the hair at the back of my neck. I don't need to open it to know who's standing on the other side. Somehow, I can feel him. His spicy scent invades my nostrils, seeping through the cracks in the door, but I refuse to let it crack my defenses.

I draw in a steadying breath. "What?" I bark.

"Um, it's me. I have breakfast."

I eye the calendar on the wall, the one on which I've been marking off the days since my arrival. Today is Sunday, Magda's day off. My heart kicks at my ribs, and my hand closes around the knob.

I've never seen Luca set foot in the kitchen other than to reach for whatever Magda offered him. Did he actually make breakfast? I waffle for another minute until curiosity trumps the anger, and I twist the handle before I lose my nerve.

The door swings open, and Luca leans against the doorjamb holding a tray of assorted fruit and Italian pastries, looking unfairly sexy wearing only low-slung sweatpants. Black ink sneaks out from beneath the white bandage still criss-crossing his chest and shoulder, the intricate patterns drawing my eye down his carved abs. Then further down to the deep V that disappears into his waistband like an arrow directing my twitchy fingers. My traitorous clit begins to throb, and I squeeze my thighs together to quell the unwanted surge of heat.

"Good morning, princess."

"Morning," I mutter, injecting ice into my tone. I will not let that smoldering gaze erase the memories of his words last night. I meant nothing to him. I was just business.

I needed the reminder.

Forcing my eyes off his body and onto the tray, my gaze settles on the *cannoli*, *sfogliatelle calda*, and *cornetto* with Nutella oozing out. My stomach lets out an embarrassing growl, and warmth floods my cheeks.

"Breakfast in bed?" He jerks his chin toward the tangle of sheets.

"I'm not hungry," I grate out.

He hitches a dark brow, and the corner of his lip lifts. "Don't lie to me, princess. I can practically see you salivating."

"I don't want anything from *you*." I fold my arms across my chest and assume a fighting stance. "It's just business, remember? I'll do my part and you do yours. If I'm not needed on your arm at some event, I'd prefer if you just kept your distance."

His broad shoulders round, and that irresistible smirk melts away. "I don't know what you want from me, Stella…." His voice is soft, nothing like the typical deep tenor. It stirs something deep inside.

This entire argument is insane. A part of me knows that very well. What the hell do I want from him? Besides more of that wicked tongue, I can't even say. This situation is miles beyond fucked up and still, last night, his words cut deep. Especially after what he'd made me feel in that damned bathroom.

He steps closer, and I stagger back. "Tell me what you want." He drops the tray on the desk and closes the distance between us until he pins me against the wall. His scent floods my senses, bathing every inch of me in him.

His palms smack the wall on either side of my head as he cages me in. With his body this close to mine, a tremor races down my legs. "Don't," I murmur.

"Don't what?" His breath ghosts over my lips.

"Don't mix business with whatever this is …." My lower lip trembles.

"Pleasure?" He cocks a dark brow, and that elusive dimple appears.

The air catches in my throat, and an embarrassing whimper escapes. "Luca, please …." I'm not even sure what the hell I'm asking of him.

He drops to his knees, and those piercing irises lock on mine. The hunger in his gaze steals the remaining air from my lungs. "I—I don't know how to apologize. I'm not even quite certain what I'm apologizing for, but I'll do whatever it takes to fix what's hurting you. I'm not used to feeling powerless, and fuck, I hate it." Genuine fear darkens his eyes, carves into his strong jaw. "What do you want from me, princess?" he repeats.

I know I can't have what I want, not to mention how fucked up the idea even is. Discussing emotions with this man is forbidden territory, but there is one thing he can give me, the only way we can connect. "Your mouth on my pussy again." I'm startled when the words so easily dribble out. Until that very moment, I wasn't sure what I needed from him. Not to mention, I've never been so forward in voicing my sexual desires—except with him.

A devastating smile parts his lips, and a glint of wickedness flashes across those darting eyes. His hands slip beneath the towel and grip my bare ass, fingers digging into my flesh. His mouth covers the juncture of my thighs, and his words vibrate through the plush cloth. "It would be my pleasure."

A tremor skates up my spine, spilling goosebumps over my arms and legs. Already, they feel like jelly, and he's barely touched me.

"I dreamt about this sweet pussy all night, princess," he growls against my mound. "*Dio*, what you do to me. Your taste is … addictive." He catches my gaze and his tongue flicks out, devastatingly slowly, he drags it across those full lips.

I'm trapped, caught in that smoldering look that has my core on fire. Every part of me wants to drop down to the floor beside him and capture his lips. Not only because Caroline told me it was forbidden, but because I need to taste him.

Luca rips my towel off and tosses it onto the bed.

"*Madonna, sei bellissima,*" he whispers the words like a prayer. "More beautiful than I ever could have imagined." His heated gaze streaks up my body and pauses on the hearts inked across my left breast.

Cool air hits my heated skin and another wave of goosebumps puckers my flesh. He diverts his gaze and presses his nose to my dark curls. And inhales. Oh, *Dio*. I suck in a sharp breath along with him.

"Mmm, sunshine and rainbows," he murmurs.

My hazy thoughts flicker to last night. It's the second time he's said the exact same phrase. I make a mental note to ask him about it later because right now all I can focus on is his nose running through my damp folds.

His tongue flicks out again, short quick bursts as he tastes me.

"Mmm, you're so wet for me, princess, so ready." His hand crawls up my torso, blindly searching. It finally finds my breast and settles around the sensitive spot. His fingers tease and twist my nipple into a tight peak.

A moan tears free, and I reach for his hair, twining my fingers through the thick waves. Then he slows, licking in a sultry, leisurely pace, up and down my center as he clings to my ass and drives my hips to his face.

He *devours* me.

That tongue is pure sin. It circles my clit, faster and faster, then slows, drawing out the roaring pleasure. I can barely stand anymore.

"Luca …," I pant.

His hands move to my thighs, and he must feel the quiver because he drops to his stomach and slides between my legs then spins around. His eyes lock on mine as he wedges his head between my bare feet. "Sit, like a good girl."

"Excuse me?" I rasp out.

"I want your delicious pussy on my face. I want to see all of you. Can you do that for me?"

No ... I don't think I could. What if I smother him?

"Stella," he warns. "It wasn't a question." His hands wrap around my knees, and he gives them a gentle tug. It doesn't take much. They're already as loose as linguine. I buckle forward, but somehow, he catches me and settles my knees on either side of his head so I'm straddling his face.

The rest of his words are swallowed up inside me as his tongue resumes its devastating dance. I groan again. His tongue slides across my center before pausing at my clit and circling like a maddening shark.

My gaze drops to the giant erection tenting Luca's sweatpants. My fingers itch to touch it, to feel its hardness. I've already felt it bare against my thigh the night I'd tried to escape, but I need more.

I'm panting now, my head falling back as pleasure rips through me. He slips a finger inside me, and my hips roll, desperate for the friction. In and out, in and out. He fucks me with that long, thick finger. I'm a writhing mess, but I don't want to give in yet.

If this is his apology, I'm going to soak in every last minute of it.

He fills me with his second finger, the tips curling to find my G-spot. Oh *Dio*, I'm so close. Between his tongue and those expert digits, I'm seconds away from plunging over the cliff.

But I want more. I want his cock inside me.

CHAPTER 25
GROVELING 101

S*tella*

With Luca lapping me up like a hot fudge sundae, I force myself to focus, biting down on my lower lip until I nearly draw blood. Not yet. I can't give in yet. Glancing down, I focus on the outline of his erection. *Mannagia alla miseria,* he's huge. He's tenting his baggy sweatpants like a freaking flagpole. It seems even bigger than it was a moment ago.

My hand reaches for him, moving without my control. My fingers wrap around his hardness, and a sharp hiss skates across my pulsing center.

"Stella …" My name on his lips vibrates through my clit, and another moan breaks free.

I grind my hips against his face as I stroke his cock over his sweatpants. His hips begin to move against my palm. They rock forward meeting each fevered pump. I inch my free hand beneath his waistband to draw his pants down, but he snatches my wrist, fingers clamping tight and drags it away.

"No," he snarls.

"Why not?" Fuck me, I just *whined*.

"This is *my* apology," he murmurs against my clit.

I shudder. "So I should get what I want," I barely manage. "And what I want is you inside me. Now."

He freezes beneath me, his fingers still inside.

I wriggle against his palm, the orgasm so close …. "Don't stop," I pant.

"I won't, if you behave." His fingers tighten around my wrist. "No touching me today."

"Is this one of your stupid sex rules?" I blurt.

He stiffens beneath me, withdrawing both fingers. I nearly scream. *Son of a bitch.* After an endless moment of silence, he mutters, "Yes."

I push myself off the ground and wrap my arms across my chest. Wetness dribbles down my legs, and dammit, it's impossible to look indignant with saliva mixed with your own juices sliding down your inner thigh. "I need to hear the rules. Now."

Luca heaves out a frustrated breath and sits up. "Are you sure you want to do this right now? You were so close—"

I lift my hand, cutting him off. "The moment has passed. Now talk. Why can't I touch you? And why won't you have sex with me?" I cringe as the last part comes out. I sound like a total *puttana*. This is what one week with the mob boss has reduced me to.

He stabs his fingers through his hair, tugging at the wild ends. His jaw ticks, and an unreadable expression darkens his features. "I don't fuck women more than once." The moment the words are out, his entire body softens, the tense set of his jaw, his shoulders, even his hands. His fingers uncurl from around the thick carpeting as he searches my face for a reaction.

That's why he doesn't want me to touch him … "Technically, we didn't have sex," I finally mutter.

"Exactly."

"So everything Caroline said was true…" *No kissing, no face-to-face, and most important, only once.* My head spins, and suddenly, there's not enough air in the room. My lungs constrict, and I search non-existent pockets for my inhaler.

"Caroline?" he barks. "What exactly did she say to you?"

"I told you I saw her in the bathroom last night before you came in. She confronted me." I'm panting now, every breath labored.

Luca must notice my panic because he mutters a curse, then he's on his feet searching my drawers as I struggle to drag in a breath. "Where is your inhaler?"

I point at the nightstand, forcing my manic pulse to slow. He darts across the room and nearly knocks the little side table over when he jerks the drawer open. Leaping over the bed, he places it in my palm and steadies me, those strong hands closing around my shoulders.

"Breathe, Stellina, breathe."

I bring the inhaler to my mouth as hot tears prick my eyes. I hate looking weak, especially in front of him. Especially after what he just said. I take two quick puffs and toss the little cannister back onto the bed.

Luca stands in front of me, still holding me steady. Tiny beads of sweat line his brow, and his own chest is heaving. His mouth is still shiny from my arousal, lips swollen.

My stomach churns.

"I'm sorry," he mutters. "I never should have started this. It's my fault. Lines are getting blurred, and it's not fair to you."

"No, it's not," I spit. "Why are your fucking rules so important anyway?"

His gaze drops to the floor. "They're all I have."

"Caroline was right. *Sei un vero bastardo*, Luca Valentino." I shrug free of his hold, grab my towel and dart into the bathroom. I slam the door with such force the entire wall shakes.

Luca

Porca miseria. What the fuck is wrong with me? I've been standing here like an idiot staring at the bathroom door for an entire hour. Stella never emerged. If it wasn't for the occasional muttered curses that seep through the door, I would've been certain she'd found a way to escape somehow. Clearly impossible.

What has this woman done to me? One week in my home and I'm ready to throw out every single rule just to be with her. My lips crave hers, my dick so fucking hard it aches to burrow inside her until I can't tell where I end and she begins.

I'm obsessed.

After she overheard my conversation with Dante last night and stormed off, I thought about her all night long. I watched her on the cameras, every twitch, every sigh. I almost raced into her room and climbed into her bed again when she murmured my name in her sleep. *My* name. Was she thinking about me between her legs in the bathroom? It was *all* I could think about. Hell, I'd been up so damned early, I'd gone all the way to Little Italy to buy those *pasticcini* from *Nonna Maria*'s as penance. And she hadn't even tasted them because she was so angry at me.

For telling Dante she meant nothing to me.

A fucking big ass lie.

Dio, she means *everything*.

If I give into this, nothing will ever be the same. For either of us. She has no idea what she's getting into. I'm the reason for one of the hearts tattooed across her chest. I'm not so completely caught up in my own world to ignore her pain. Though she hasn't admitted it, I know those hearts are for Vinny and her mother. Already, I've put her in danger. Now that the Red Dragons know she's mine, they'll try to use her to get to me. Bo saw how I reacted last night. If he's too stupid to notice, his father most definitely is not.

I stomp out of Stella's room, making extra noise just so that she hears. I don't want her to spend all morning trapped in that bathroom. Besides, I need to check in with my lawyer, Jones, to ensure he's destroyed all versions of that video of me pummeling the shit out of Bo Zhang.

Bastardo deserved it and so much worse.

When I reach my study, my gaze lands on the note taped to my computer screen. *Dante*.

> *Fratellino,*
> *No worries, Jones and I took care of your little Bo problem. I hope you took care of yours and got the girl out of your system. You've worked too hard to risk what you have for a hot piece of ass. Remember that. And you're welcome.*
> *Dante*

"*Stronzo*," I mutter and crumple up the note. The last thing I need is Stella finding it. I sink into my desk chair and stare at the screen, but all the words blur together. Clara was finally able to reschedule the meeting with the commissioner for tomorrow. That would be a huge win, and a big blow to the Chinese Triad. A few more key moves and they'll be out of my territory for good.

That thought alone would've had me giddy as a fucking schoolgirl before. But now, all I can think about is Stella locked in that bathroom. I reach for my phone on the desk and open the home security app. I wasn't lying to her; there really wasn't a camera in the bathroom. But maybe she'd come out since I left ….

I toggle through the cameras until I reach her bedroom, and a stupid grin stretches across my face. She's still in that towel, and she's eating the cannoli. I zoom in, so the camera focuses on her mouth, on those luscious lips closing around the pastry. *Dio*, just watching her makes me hard again.

I can almost imagine the sounds coming out of her mouth. I'm not sure she even realizes that she moans when she eats. It's so damned sexy. Before I'm hopelessly hard again, I close out the app and shove my phone into my pocket.

Pushing back from the desk, I jump up. Screw it, it's Sunday; I can work tomorrow. Even *Dio* took a day of rest. And besides, I never finished apologizing to Stella. Now I have some major groveling to do.

CHAPTER 26
THE RIDE OF MY LIFE

S*tella*

Dio, those *pasticinni* were to die for. I'd recognize *Nonna Maria's* pastries anywhere. I couldn't believe the *coglione* had gone all the way to Little Italy to get my breakfast. A growl of frustration vibrates my throat as I fan mascara across my lashes.

I hate him.

My teeth grind together as I apply a hint of lip gloss.

I *don't* hate him.

And that is the big problem. Besides that skillful tongue and the best orgasm I've had in my life in the bathroom at the Heart Ball, I'd grown to like the broody asshole. The past ten days had started to feel normal, comfortable. We'd fallen into a routine so quickly it made my head spin. Sometimes, it felt like I'd known Luca my whole life.

I'm certifiable. It's literally the only answer.

My bedroom door whips open, and Luca darkens the entryway. My arms instinctively wrap around my middle as if

I could somehow protect myself from this powerful, relentless man.

"You don't even knock now?"

His brows furrow as if the idea is so wild. "This is my house—sorry," he mumbles around an exasperated sigh. "You're dressed." His piercing gaze rakes over me, and I couldn't feel more naked.

"I didn't realize remaining in the nude was one of your rules," I grit out. "Perhaps you should educate me."

"It's not," he hisses through clenched teeth. "*Dio*, Stella ...." Despite his unusually casual look, the soft heather gray Henley and worn whitewash jeans, tension radiates from each twitching muscle. "I'm glad you're dressed because we're going out."

"We are?" My gaze flickers to the calendar on the wall. "For what? I don't have another event on my schedule until next week."

"Last minute pop up."

I arch a skeptical brow as I regard his casual attire. I've never seen him leave the penthouse in anything but a suit. "And you're going like that?"

"Yes, princess. Now, quit it with the third degree and let's go." He wraps his hand around my forearm, and his fingers sear into my flesh. Those clever digits that had worked me close to oblivion just a few hours earlier.

"Can you at least tell me where we're going so I know if my attire is appropriate?" I'm in cutoff jeans and a tank top for fashion's sake.

Again, those eyes skim over me, that lethal caress sending a shudder up my spine. "Mmm, you're perfect."

I shake my head and toss him a good eyeroll. The man is infuriating, and yet I can't seem to stay mad at him. Mostly because this situation is so screwed up what could I possibly expect?

His gaze tracks down my legs and settles on my bare feet. "I suggest sneakers; you'll be more comfortable."

"Okay." I dart toward my closet and pass on the designer sneakers he insisted I needed and decide on the old Converse I'd worn the day Liam McKenzie sold me to the Kings. Bile oozes up my throat at the memory. Like all things I refuse to accept, I shove down the images and bury them in the dark corners of my mind. I slump down on the bed and tie the frayed laces. When I lift my head, a pair of pitch irises capture mine.

Luca's lips are only a heartbeat away, his minty breath lingering between us. The faint line between his dark brows puckers, and my finger itches to reach up and smooth it away. An epic battle is being fought in that twisted mind of his. I only wish I knew which side would win.

"You're going to ruin me, princess." His whispered confession sends goosebumps spilling down my spine. He closes the distance between us, and his lips brush mine. The chaste kiss only lasts for a second, but it feels like an eternity to my shuddering heart.

His hand clamps around mine, and he tugs me to my feet. A playful smile brightens those midnight irises as he watches me. "Are you happy?"

I screw my lips into a pout. "Why would I be happy?"

"Because I broke another rule for you."

"You call that a kiss?" I cry.

The cocky mob boss looks genuinely insulted, and I'm practically giddy. "Our lips touched, didn't they?"

"I had better kisses in middle school." I wrench my hand free from his and march out of the bedroom.

He follows behind me, the slap of his approaching footfalls speeding up my own. I'm sprinting, and a laugh bubbles up my chest by the time I reach the elevator, my breaths coming in uneven pants. I jab my finger at the button, but the damned thing crawls up the ninety-plus levels.

When Luca reaches me, he traps me against the elevator doors, pinning me against the cool metal. He runs his nose up my neck, then nips at my earlobe. "Just for that, you won't get another kiss until you beg for it."

I let out a shaky laugh, his warm breath spilling across the sensitive shell of my ear. "I'll never beg you for anything, Luca Valentino," I rasp out.

"We'll see about that, princess."

The elevator doors slide open, and I stagger back, but a firm arm snakes around my waist keeping me upright. He holds me like that until we reach the parking garage, and the doors open again, revealing the mysterious Albie.

Does the man live in the garage down here? The elevator pit bull seems to be eternally fixed to his post.

"Signor Valentino." He dips his head at the boss then offers me a tight smile.

"Is everything ready as I requested?" Luca asks.

"Yes, *signore*." Albie steps to the side, revealing a tomato red Ducati with two helmets atop the seat.

"We're going on that?" I tug on the frayed edges of my jean shorts, fully aware I'll be flashing my ass cheeks to anyone behind us.

"You're not scared, are you?" A twinkle of mischief lights up that dark gaze.

A whisper of a memory sparks to the surface. The wind in my hair, my thundering pulse as we weave across crowded city streets, a smile plastered on my face. I blink, and the images are gone, but the odd sensation tightening my chest remains.

"Stella?" Luca ducks to meet my eyes, his thumb and forefinger closing around my chin. "You used to—" His jaw clamps shut, and that cold mask I hate slips into place. "If you don't want to ride it, we can just take one of the cars."

I step closer to the sleek beast and run my hand over the glossy metal. "No, I want to."

A panty-dropping smile splits his lips, and I understand very well why women accept only one night with the C.E.O. There's just something about being in his overwhelming presence. *Dio* knows I lose all my sanity when I'm around him. I'm still supposed to be pissed about his callous remark, his stupid rules ….

Luca reaches for the smaller helmet and slips it over my head. I try not to focus on the countless other women who have likely worn it before me. I really am *pazza* so I sniff the helmet once it's on in search of female perfume. Surprisingly, it smells brand new.

He must notice because his mouth puckers as he regards me. "You don't like new helmet smell?"

A stupid laugh bursts out. "Is that like new car smell?"

"Only ten times better." He grins, and for an instant he looks younger, not the hardened mafia boss or the shrewd businessman. He's just Luca. A soft smile curves his lips, and I'm gripped with the desire to press my mouth to his. Only now I can't because he'd expect me to beg.

And I refuse. I had to keep at least an ounce of dignity intact.

After securing his own helmet, Luca elegantly drapes his long leg over the seat and grips the handles, so the motorcycle roars to life. Then he offers me his hand. I wipe my sweaty palm on my jean shorts before accepting, and he swings me onto the seat behind him.

Our bodies touch in at least a hundred places, and I can feel each and every one acutely. I inch back to place a little much-needed space between us, but his hands clamp around my thighs and a sharp hiss escapes my lips.

"Arms around my waist, princess."

"Do I have to?" I grumble.

"Do you value your life as much as I do?"

My traitorous heart trips on a beat before I smack some sense into it. "Mmhmm," I mumble.

"Then hold on like a good girl."

My arms encircle his waist, and my body instinctively leans into his. I'm not sure where exactly to put my hands so I hover them just above his navel.

He threads my fingers together, presses my palm against his rock-hard abs, then clamps his hand over mine. "Tight. Like this."

"Got it," I rasp out.

With his free hand, he pulls my thighs in tighter around his. "And I want these legs glued to mine, understand? Like I'm buried balls deep inside you, and you're clinging onto my hips like your fucking orgasm depends on it."

I gasp at his wicked tongue, and a dark chuckle vibrates Luca's whole body, reverberating across my own.

"Get ready for the ride of your life, princess."

CHAPTER 27
A GRAND GESTURE

S*tella*

The roar of the motorcycle engine cuts off, and I peel my body from Luca's. My arms are sore from holding him so tight and still, I find it hard to pull away. He's parked the bike in front of a sprawling empty lot in an upscale part of Eastchester. Only thirty minutes outside the city and already I can breathe better.

"What are we doing here?" I tug off my helmet and eye the stretch of green over his shoulder.

"Just needed a change of scenery." He hooks his helmet on the handle and jumps off before offering me his hand.

I slide off and my legs are still buzzing from the engine's vibrations, my knees shaky. I wobble a little, and Luca's arm laces around my waist as naturally as if it belonged there. He holds me for an endless moment, eyes pinned to mine. The leader of the Kings is a complete enigma, a monster one minute and a chivalrous gentleman the next. A few hours ago, he was devouring me like an animal, and now the gentleness in his touch has my heart pinching.

"Come on." He tugs on my hand and breaks the spell that dark gaze casts over me.

"Um, isn't this trespassing?" I ask as he weaves us through the towering evergreens scattered across the property.

"Trust me, princess, trespassing is the least of my sins." The corner of his lip hitches up, that mischievous smirk more tempting than one of Mrs. D's cannoli.

I can't decide what I want more: to kiss that smile off his face or just bask in its beauty. I should be satisfied with myself for forcing him to break one of his precious rules, but now that I've had a taste of those lips, I only want more. Would he let me have it? Or would he really make me beg?

As we reach the edge of the property, the woods thicken. Already, my breaths are coming hard and fast from our jog across the clearing. Luca must notice because he slows and throws a concerned gaze in my direction. "Almost there," he murmurs.

The gnarled, climbing trees part and reveal a small clearing beside a rippling pond with a rickety old dock. A red-and-white checkered blanket is spread out on the grass and a cute wicker basket sits beside a champagne bottle immersed in an ice bucket. Next to it, is a bouquet of pure white calla lilies.

My breath catches, and this time my asthma has nothing to do with it. "You did this?" I rasp out.

He shrugs, and a flash of crimson coats his cheeks. *Dio*, I didn't think it was possible. The mafia boss blushes? And *cazzo*, it only makes him more gorgeous. Waving a nonchalant hand, he mutters, "I had Tony pick up a few things."

The idea of Luca's righthand man setting up a picnic sends a fit of the giggles cramping my belly. I do my best to suppress the laughter, but I finally buckle over as a laugh escapes.

Luca's cheeks burn brighter and damn it, he's so beautiful

my heart reels. "What's so funny?" He's trying his best to hold in a smile, but the amusement sparks across his dark eyes.

"I'm sorry, but the idea of big, tough Tony setting all of this up is just hysterical."

"I'll be sure to tell him you laughed at his grand gesture."

"*His* grand gesture?"

Luca rocks back on his heels and drags his palm down the back of his neck. "Or mine, whatever."

I take a step closer. "Is this all part of our business arrangement?"

He nods. "I have to find some way to keep my arm candy happy, right?"

My lips pucker. Each day that passes, the lines between us grow blurrier. I want more from him, so much more. But I know how ridiculous that sounds. "Right," I finally mutter.

"Sit, we don't want the champagne to get warm."

I fold down on the colorful blanket and run my fingers over the delicate calla lily buds. "Why do you like these flowers so much? They're the only ones I've ever seen in the penthouse."

Luca shrugs as he strips the bottle of the gilded foil covering. "I like their simplicity."

"You know they're a symbol of resurrection and rebirth, right?"

"Um hmm." He nods, eyes avoiding mine.

Could the infamous mob boss be secretly hoping for redemption? A new life?

Luca pops open the bottle and the cork flies across the blanket. The *Dom Perignon* bubbles out, and he brings the tip to my mouth. I wrap my lips around the rim and swallow the fizzy liquid.

"Mmm, that's my good girl." His eyes lock on my lips as I swallow it down, and all thoughts of redemption vanish.

Once it stops foaming over, I run my tongue around the rim. His heated gaze bores down on me with each slow circle.

My lusty vixen has already joined his dark thoughts, imagining my mouth on his cock. Licking him, tasting him.

"Stella …," he warns, a jagged edge to his tone that wasn't there a moment ago. "Hand over the bottle before I lose what little is left of my sanity."

I release the rim and throw him an exaggerated pout. "Maybe I like you better when you lose control." The bubbles must have gone straight to my head because I had no intention of saying those words out loud.

He clucks his teeth as he reveals two crystal flutes from the basket and fills them with champagne. "You have no idea what you're asking for." He hands me the glass, and smoldering irises find mine.

I take a long pull, nearly draining the flute in one gulp.

"Easy, princess." He brings his glass to his lips and takes a small sip. I reach for the base of the stem and tip it back, forcing him to drink more.

"Now who's trying to get whom drunk?" Mischief sparkles through the dark abyss of those soul-penetrating eyes.

"I told you I like it when you let loose."

A deep chuckle vibrates the air between us. "You haven't seen me when I let loose, princess. I'm not sure you would enjoy it."

"Maybe you have no idea what I like, Signor Valentino." I drop the empty glass and crawl closer until I'm kneeling between his powerful thighs. I curl my hands around the collar of his shirt and pause, a hairsbreadth from his lips. "I like you," I whisper.

And just like that, a dam bursts.

Luca's hand wraps around the back of my neck, and he jerks my mouth to his. Our lips crash in an explosion of fury and raw desire. His mouth engulfs mine, his lips punishing, teeth gnashing against my own. He draws my lower lip between his teeth and bites down. Hard.

"Ow," I squeal.

"This is what you wanted, right, princess?" he pants against my mouth. "You wanted me out of control, now you've got me." His hands clamp around my thighs, and he winds them around his waist so I'm straddling him.

Even through our jeans, I can feel him rock hard against me. I grind my hips into him, reveling in the friction.

He captures my mouth again, hand fisting my hair to position me to his liking. His other hand travels down my back and curls around my ass. His fingers slip past the frayed edges of my shorts and dig into my bare flesh. Then his thumb finds my slick heat, and he runs it through my wet folds. I moan at the unexpected invasion.

He grinds me into his erection, and another groan fills his hungry mouth. "You want me to fuck you, princess? Is that what this is about?"

God, yes. Thank goodness I somehow manage to keep my stupid thoughts to myself this time. Mostly because I can't seem to form a single cohesive sentence with his cock between my legs.

His thumb circles harder, bordering on the precipice between pleasure and pain. "You want me to strip you bare right here and nail you to the ground?" I let out a whimper. "You want my cock pounding into your sweet pussy in the middle of fucking suburbia for any nosey housewife to see?"

"No," I finally pant out.

He freezes, eyes widening.

I lace steel into my tone despite the growing tremors. "Because that'll be it, right? Just one time and then you'll be done with me. Like Caroline said."

He withdraws his finger, and I barely resist the urge to growl in frustration. His dark brows knit as he regards me with the fire of a thousand suns. Endless seconds pass, then torturous minutes. He doesn't utter a word as a battle plays out in his mind. I don't understand why his rules are so important, why he refuses to give in. He wants this as bad as I do, somehow, I'm certain.

Unthreading his hand from my hair, he slides it down to my ass and lifts me up as he rises.

"What are you doing?"

"We need to cool off." His long strides carry us off the blanket, and before I have a chance to scream, he runs across the old dock and leaps into the pond.

Icy water envelops me, only the warmth of Luca's arms driving away the chill. I splutter as he straightens, and we're wading in the middle of the shallow pool. "*Sei pazzo*?" I shriek as I push out of his hold. This man has completely lost his mind. "Why would you jump into the lake?"

A ridiculous grins splits his lips, softening the typical tight set of his jaw. "I told you we needed to cool off."

"Maybe you did!" I shout. "I was perfectly fine."

"Please, I would've had you coming on my lap in a few more seconds."

"*Bastardo*," I snarl.

"And don't get me wrong, I'm going to make you come again, just on my terms." He shoots me a wicked grin, and it's a damned good thing I'm already soaked.

I smack the water and send a wave across that stupid smirk.

He shakes his head out like a wet dog and runs his hands down his face. "Behave or I'll dunk you again, princess."

"I'd like to see you try."

That smile morphs into something truly wicked. Those eyes flash, and he's on me before I blink. His arms wrap around my torso and pull me under. I struggle against him as the icy water tingles across my skin, but my blood still burns from his touch.

He pulls me back up to the surface, and I gulp in a breath of air. With his arms still enveloping me, all I get is a lungful of

Luca. That spicy, musky scent of bergamot and hot pepper does nothing to quell the burning in my chest.

He licks his lips as he watches me. "You know, you forgot to beg."

"What?" I squeal.

"Back there—" He jerks his chin at the blanket. "You kissed me without having to beg for it per our previous conversation."

"First of all, you kissed me. Second of all, like I said before, I'll never beg for anything from you, Luca Valentino." *Liar.* A dark voice in my mind calls me out on the complete and utter bullshit. I was already so far gone for this man I'd done a number of idiotic things, and I had a nasty feeling this was only the beginning.

"Never say never, princess." A devious smile pulls at those perfect lips. "I also said I'd follow my rules till the day I died until you blew back into my life." He wades closer, and I take a step farther. Confusion at his words freezes me to the spot.

"Back?"

His dark brows slam together. "What?"

"You said *back* into your life?"

His jaw clenches, a faint tendon pulsing beneath the five o'clock shadow. "Yeah, after the day I met you at *Nonna Maria's*." That cool mask slips back on, and I'm certain I've missed something. "Who knew my cute waitress would end up as a bargaining chip at the pawn shop?"

I regard him for a long moment, but his expression is unreadable.

"Come on, we better get you out of those wet clothes."

I eye him, my soaked t-shirt clinging to my skin. "You brought us a spare set?"

He nods. "Of course, I did. I used to be a boy scout, the Italian version anyway. Always prepared."

A laugh tumbles out because never in a million years could

I picture the mob boss as an innocent twelve-year-old boy, let alone a boy scout.

The murmur of approaching voices sends Luca's gaze darting over my shoulder. His jaw tenses, and he mumbles a curse. I whirl around to find Dante and an older woman walking toward us.

CHAPTER 28
A SUCKER FOR PUNISHMENT

L*uca*

Cazzo, what the fuck is Dante doing here with Mamma?

I glance over at Stella, her wet tank top sticking to her skin and revealing perfectly erect nipples. Dante's gaze locks on her chest, and I roll my fingers into tight fists to keep from clawing his eyes out. A growl of frustration rumbles out, and I step in front of her, blocking her translucent shirt from his roving gaze.

"I thought that was your bike parked out front." Dante's smile is predatory. Like he's caught me with my hand in the cookie jar. A few minutes earlier and he would've caught my fingers in a much more dangerous place.

Mamma on the other hand is smiling so wide I'm afraid she'll split her cheeks. "Luca, *che bella sorpresa*." Nice surprise, my ass. My conniving brother probably brought our mother here on purpose. "Who is this beautiful woman?"

Stella's cheeks flame an enticing pink, and I'm thankful for the icy water dousing my hard-ass erection.

"Mamma, this is Stella Esposito," I finally reply.

I can see Ma itching to hug her, and again, I'm grateful we're still waist-deep in water. Introducing Stella as my girlfriend at a public event is one thing, but to my mother? The last thing I want to do is get her hopes up.

"Esposito?" I can almost see her ears perk up. Stella's grandfather was a legend in our circles. Papà and I even worked for him for a time. Luckily, Ma had no idea about any of it. She also knew nothing about Vinny McKenzie, my old best friend, being an Esposito. Their mom had always wanted to keep them safe from our world. Until he wasn't … because of me.

"Yes, Michele was my *nonno*," Stella answers, interrupting my spiraling thoughts. "*Piacere di conoscerla*, Signora Valentino." She steps out of the water, and my brother's gaze immediately latches onto her see-through top.

"Dante," I growl. "*Se la guardi così un'altra volta, ti ammazzo.*" And I would. I would fucking kill him if he kept looking at her like she's a slab of meat.

"Luca!" Mamma scolds. Though her tone is reprimanding, a faint smile flashes across her face. She knows me well; well enough to notice my insane reaction over Stella. She probably hasn't seen it since I was a sappy teenager in love.

Damned Dante for bringing Mamma into this fucked-up situation.

I climb onto the dock and trail Stella toward the remains of our picnic. Digging through the basket, I pull out a towel and wrap it around her.

Mamma's curious gaze watches every move. "Why don't you come to my house to change?"

"No, *grazie*, Mamma, we'll be just fine."

"But where will Stella get dressed? She can't take off her

clothes in the middle of the woods? What kind of gentleman would allow that?"

A faint smile curls Stella's lips as she regards me from the corner of her eye. She's not the only woman in my life I can't refuse.

"Yeah, *fratellino*, why don't you bring Stella to Ma's house?" Dante sneers as I tug my wet shirt over my head. "You know how much she loves showing your baby pictures."

Stella laughs and tosses me a look over her shoulder. "Baby pictures?"

"There will be no baby pictures," I growl.

"But you were such a cute little *bambino*." Fucking Dante.

"*Vieni*, Stella." Mamma takes her hand, towing her free of my hold. "You come in the car with me. We can't let you catch a cold in those wet clothes. Besides, we have a lot to catch up on, *bella*."

I glare at my brother as Mamma ushers Stella toward the Mercedes SUV I bought for her birthday last year. As soon as they're far enough away, I wrap my hand around my brother's arm and whirl him around. "*Che cazzo fai?*"

"I'm not doing anything, Luca. I told you, Ma and I were out for a drive, and we just happened to see your motorcycle. I never thought I'd find you with her again." He jabs his thick finger into my chest. "I guess you didn't fuck her, did you?"

I shake my head, and I don't even know why I'm dignifying him with a response.

"You never listen to me. Get that girl out of your system. There's something not right …."

"I don't need advice from you, Dante," I hiss and slap his finger off. "Not in my business and certainly not in my love life."

His eyes taper at the edges. "Guess you didn't see the headline of *The New Yorker* then? Too busy with your head between your new toy's legs?"

My heart kicks at my ribcage. Did Jones not pull through after all? "What was it?"

"You and your Italian princess on the cover."

I heave out a breath of relief. At least it wasn't of me knocking the shit out of Bo. A fake girlfriend I could handle.

"I wouldn't breathe easy yet, little brother. I was scrolling through the comments online, and the Chinese Triad is calling for your blood. Hers too."

All the remaining air squeezes from my lungs.

"And one of the commenters claims he's got a video of your new girl acting like a *puttana* with Bo Zhang."

Red hot fury uncoils in my gut, and I let my fist fly. Right into my asshole brother's face. He staggers back and lets out an indignant cry. No one calls Stella a whore and gets away with it. Even my own flesh and blood. "It's a lie," I roar. "And I already told you to keep her name off your filthy lips."

"Damn it, Luca, stop fucking hitting me!" Dante rubs his jaw and wipes away the dribble of blood from his cracked lip. He spits on the ground and shakes his head. "Get your fucking head in the game. That girl should be the last thing on your mind. You turn on me, for what? Because I called it as it is. Get a handle on yourself before this all blows up in our faces."

"I'll handle my fucking business, Dante. Just like I have all my life." I spin around and stalk back to my bike, rage surging through my blood. Could Bo really have a compromising video of Stella and him? The image makes my gut roil. His dirty hands on her perfect form, defiling her, spoiling what's mine.

As soon as I reach my bike, I grab my phone and shoot a message to Jones. I need him to remove every blasphemous comment from that article. Then when I return to the city, I'm going to pay Bo Zhang a personal visit.

Once Dante leaves Mamma's, I breathe a little easier. Having one nosy relative to deal with is more than enough. And at least I like my mother. Stella sits across from Mamma at the table, sipping an espresso. The pair have gotten along like long lost sisters. I've never seen this relaxed, chatty side of Stella before. And I can't get enough.

At home, there's always tension, even when she doesn't know I'm around. I've caught her and Magda talking, but Stella never seems truly at ease, not like she is now with my mom. The realization pricks at my heart, and I have a hard time swallowing down the unwanted emotion.

A few weeks with Stella and the vision of my future is muddled, blurry like never before. Everything was so clear before she was dropped into my life. Now, I find myself wanting things I know I don't deserve.

"... *certo*, Luca?"

I glance up, Mamma's words drawing me from my thoughts. "What?"

"I said, you'll bring Stella up for a visit more often now that we've met, *certo*?"

"Mmm." I nod.

"Luca likes to keep me prisoner in his penthouse." Stella's cunning gaze meets mine over the rim of the small cup.

"It's true," I retort with a grin. "I hardly ever let her out of that gilded cage."

Again, Mamma's smiling so hard; the guilt of deceiving her is like a punch in the face. I clear my throat abruptly and push out of the chair. Wrapping my hand around Stella's forearm, I tug her to her feet.

"Luca!" Mamma scolds. "*Sei impazzito?*"

Yes, I have absolutely gone crazy. There's no denying it. But right now, I need to get Stella away from my mother before she starts planning our wedding. "I'm sorry," I say to Stella and loosen my grip. "I just want to show you something before we go."

"Go already?" Mamma rises and wrings her hands in her apron.

"*Si*, soon. But first I want to show her my old room."

She nods, that happiness sparking in her weary eyes. "I'll wait for you down here and get the leftovers ready."

"Mamma, remember we only have the motorcycle so please, don't give us too much."

"You have to feed this girl, she's wasting away." Mamma pinches Stella's cheek, and despite the faint wince, she seems happy too. Happier than I've seen her since she moved in with me.

Dio, that sounds like we're together. Since I took her hostage, I amend. *Fantastico*, I'm having internal arguments on the status of our relationship now.

My hand closes around Stella's, and I tow her down the hall and up the stairs to my old bedroom. It's not in fact my old bedroom, as this beautiful house is a far cry from the little shithole we grew up in. But when I bought Mamma this home, she recreated it to the most elaborate degree. Every single detail of my childhood bedroom came to life in this new version. She said it gave her something to do, a way to remember the past.

I pause at the door, wary to let Stella in on this intimate detail of my life. The closer we get the harder it will be for us to let go. I'm fully aware that bringing her up here was my idea because I'm not only a monster but also a masochist.

"So are we going in or what?" Stella peeks over my shoulder, her chin brushing my shirt.

I force my hand to turn the knob and reveal my childhood.

Two twin beds line the back wall, my side of the room covered in posters of Italian *calcio*—soccer legends Totti, Maldini, and Del Piero. I nearly choke as my gaze lands on the framed picture by my bed. Shit. I'd almost forgotten that was there. I'd already had to remove all traces of Vinny in the penthouse. I race to the nightstand and pretend to bump into it, knocking the frame over. Instead of picking it up, I shove it underneath the bed. "Oops, I'll pick that up later," I say lamely.

But Stella barely notices. Her eyes are fixed on the desk in the corner, the one covered in my art.

"You drew these, didn't you?" She picks up a few of the scattered pages.

"A long time ago."

"They're beautiful." She steps closer, admiring the old charcoal sketches.

It's almost painful for me to look at them. They bring back too many old memories of when we first came to New York without a dime. Of watching Ma struggle to make ends meet, of being forced to color with charcoal because it was the only thing I could get my hands on, of being the new kid who spoke broken English and the son of a man the other kids called a gangster. And the things I was forced to do as a result ….

Stella's eyes meet mine as if she senses the raging turmoil I've fought so hard to hide behind the icy mask. No one can touch Luca Valentino. Never again.

Except for this woman.

One look and those walls crumble.

"What's wrong?" Her voice is too soft. *She's* too soft, too perfect to be with me. But I'm a selfish *bastardo,* and I can't stay away from her.

"Nothing," I mutter through clenched teeth.

The worn paper she holds slips from her grasp as she closes in on me. Her hand lifts to my cheek, and her soft thumb caresses my bristly jaw. Beneath her touch, it loosens, softens until I'm seconds away from spilling words that would ruin us.

"Why did you bring me up here if it was only going to upset you?" The fine line between her brow puckers.

"Because I'm a sucker for punishment I guess."

"What did you want to show me?"

All my dark, broken pieces. I shake my head, trying to force her gentle touch free, but it only tightens. Her fingers curl under my jaw, and she frames my face with both hands now. I breathe her in. I can't get enough.

"I just had to get you away from Mamma," I finally force out, "before she falls even more in love with you."

She pauses, nibbling on her lower lip. "Right, and we can't have that since this is only a temporary arrangement."

"Precisely," I bite out.

Her hands linger on my face, eyes scrutinizing as if she could pry the truth from my dark soul. "Kiss me," she breathes against my lips.

It's so far from what I expected her to say that my mouth moves on autopilot. I claim her lips, like they're my only hope of salvation. But unlike by the pond, I take my time, tasting, exploring, nibbling. Last time was fueled by lust and a raging desire to possess her.

Now I just want to revel in her touch, in her taste. My fingers weave through the soft hair at her nape, fisting the dark locks. I deepen the kiss, tilting her head so I can take all of her. Her hands slide down my chest and settle around my waist. Her thumbs dip beneath the waistband of my jeans and remain there, perfectly tucked in.

Much too soon, she pulls away, and it takes every ounce of my willpower not to keep her locked in my arms and never let go. "Now that was a kiss," she whispers, a heart-stopping smile on those swollen lips. "And I didn't even have to beg."

A laugh spills out, shaking my shoulders. I'm certain no one has gotten so many lighthearted chuckles out of me in years. "Stop gloating."

"I can't help it." She rises to her tiptoes and brushes her lips against mine once again. "I'm staking my claim on virgin territory."

A deep roar of laughter bubbles out this time, and I nearly

buckle over. "I hate to break it to you, princess, but you're not my first kiss." My teenage years were wild ones.

Her lips pucker into an irresistible pout.

"It's just been a very long time," I finally admit.

She remains quiet for an endless moment before she summons the courage for her next words. "Who hurt you, Luca?" Her hand cradles my cheek again, and for a second, I'm that insecure thirteen-year-old boy. "Why do you feel the necessity to create these rules to protect your heart?"

I heave in a breath and lower the wall I've fought so fiercely to build. "Because I know real pain, real struggle, Stella, and once I survived it, I vowed I would never let anyone hurt me like that again. And the only way to accomplish that is to never let anyone in here." I press my hand to my chest, over my heart and the numbers tattooed to my skin.

CHAPTER 29
PAINTING THE STREETS RED

Luca

Tony eyes me as we walk up Canal Street toward the Red Dragon. "You sure about this, *capo*?"

I pat my old friend on the back and toss him a teasing grin. "What's the matter, Tony, are you going soft?"

"Of course not." He drags his palm over the back of his neck. "I just don't think you should poke the bear in his den. Especially after all the shit that's gone down in the past few weeks."

"If Jianjun has something to say to me, he can say it to my face. Right now, he's not the one I'm interested in."

"You really think Bo will just hand over this supposed sex video?"

My hands curl into fists at my side as a surge of anger floods my system. It's bad enough I even have to think about that asshole's hands on my girl, but now there's a video? Just the thought makes me want to rip Bo's spine out from his throat and paint the Red Dragon in his blood. "I have to find out if it's true," I growl. "Jones already had all the inappropriate comments deleted, and he's having the story monitored for more. But if there *is* a video …." I can't even complete the sentence. Bile creeps up my throat at the idea of his hands on her, on my princess.

The red and gold awning of the Red Dragon looms closer, those stupid Chinese lanterns swaying on a breeze, and I pick up my pace, anxious for this to be over. The pair of ruby dragons sneer down at us, and I hurry up the stairs, each step intensifying my rage.

I whip the door open, and Tony quickens his step to meet my angry strides. A hostess stands at the podium, and her crimson lips slide into a smile. The hustle and bustle of lunch hour hums along behind her. Damn it. The few times I dragged my ass over here were during non-business hours. This thing with Stella is driving me so mad I hadn't even realized what time it was. "Welcome to Red Dragon—"

I raise my hand, cutting her off. "I'm here for Bo Zhang. Tell him Signor Valentino needs to have a word with him."

Her eyes widen, that flash of fear in her gaze only stoking the burning rage in my core. *Be afraid, be very afraid.* She spins on her heel and scrambles between the tables of the packed dining room.

From across the room, my gaze lands on the far corner table. Jianjun and the two other leaders who make up the Triad. Tony nudges his elbow into my ribs. "You see that, *capo*?"

"Mmm."

"You think they're going to let us walk in here and beat the shit out of Jianjun's son?"

"I don't really give a fuck." I lick my lips and slide my hand behind my back. My fingers settle on the cool metal of my handgun. I'll put a bullet in each of those *figli di puttana* if I don't get what I want.

The hostess stops at Jianjun's table and dips her head. As she whispers something, all three pairs of dark eyes slant in our direction. I respond with a shit-eating grin. "I want Bo," I mouth across the room.

Jianjun's eyes narrow before he whispers something to the girl. She scampers down the hall into the back room, and seconds later, reappears with that *bastardo* Bo at her side.

Tony stiffens beside me, and without looking at my right-hand man, I already know he's reaching for his gun.

The old man crooks a finger at his son and mutters something in his ear. Whatever he says pisses him off. Bo glares at me from across the room, burning hatred lancing through that shifty gaze. A faint shadow still darkens the skin beneath his eye, and a scar bisects his upper lip from our run-in at the subway station. He stalks closer, and I revel in the anger twisting his features.

I school my expression to neutrality, waiting for that lethal, icy calm to wash over me. It's that control that has allowed me to get where I am today and continually climb higher.

Bo reaches us and jerks his chin at the door. "Let's take this outside."

"I was hoping you'd say that," Tony answers and unbuttons his jacket, revealing his revolver.

Bo's jaw tightens, the faint flicker his only tell. Does he have any idea what's coming for him today? He marches down the steps then turns at the corner to the alley behind the restaurant. His cousin Feng and another guy, one of the idiots from the Heart Ball, stand in the shadows.

"So what brings you here today, *capo*?" Bo's busted lip snarls around the last word.

I tilt my head to the side, the sharp crack making Feng flinch. I can't help the smile his reactions brings. I step closer to Bo, so close his loud ass cologne makes my nostrils twitch. "I've heard a disturbing rumor that a video of you and Stella may exist?"

The asshole grins so wide it takes every ounce of restraint not to knock his teeth in. "You still fucking my leftovers?"

My hand juts out, fingers wrapping around his throat before his men can move a muscle. Tony pulls out his gun and trains it at Bo's head. "I already warned you what would happen if you talked about her like that."

I apply more pressure to his Adam's apple. He still smirks, but his throat bobs like mad beneath my thumbs.

"I'll snap your windpipe right now, Bo. Tony will take out these two idiots before either of them make a move. Is that what you want?"

"You'll start a war," Feng hisses.

"Maybe it's time for the unavoidable." My voice is deceptively calm. Inside my blood boils at this asshole's disrespect. Of all the men Stella could've been with, why this *testa di cazzo*?

"What do you want?" Bo rasps out.

"I want the truth. I need to know if such a video exists."

Again, that fucking smile.

"Don't!" I snarl.

"Don't what?" The grin falters as I squeeze harder.

"Don't even think about her, about the two of you together." Crimson seeps into my vision, my chest rising and falling faster. *Dio*, I can't fucking handle the image. The two of them together coalesce in my mind, the sickest torture. "Damn it, Bo. Does it exist or not?"

Tony cocks the gun and presses the barrel to Bo's temple. "Answer the man, *coglione*."

Feng and the other guy both go rigid.

"Is there a problem here, Luca?" Jianjun's withered voice snakes through the thick silence.

"Nope, no problem," I answer without turning. "I'm just trying to get an answer from your son."

The old man hisses something in Mandarin.

Bo heaves out a breath. "No."

"No what?" I hiss.

"There's no video."

"You sure?" I press my thumbs into his throat, and he chokes on a breath.

"That prude would never let me tape her," he pants. "The few times she did let me fuck her she just laid there in the dark, under the covers."

I swallow down the fury as more images rush through my mind. This motherfucker didn't deserve her, not for a second. My fingers tighten, and Bo's face glows a satisfying crimson.

"Luca …," Tony warns.

Dio, I want to end him. But damn it, Feng is right. I'd start a war, and I'd only end up putting Stella in harm's way.

"*Lascialo*!" he grits out.

I'll let him go when I'm damned good and ready. I sear my gaze to his, eyes narrowing. "I warned you at the ball, and I'll do it one more time and that's it. Erase Stella from your mind, don't think about her, don't talk about her, and most importantly never lay a hand on her. If I find out you so much as breathed around her, I'll choke the life out of you and everyone you've ever met. *Capisci*?"

"Yeah, I got it, man."

I slowly release my hold on his throat, and Tony lowers the gun from his head.

As I turn away, he mumbles under his breath, "That pretty little thing must be putting out a lot more for you than she ever did for me."

I whirl around and slam my fist into his throat. He staggers back, choking and spluttering. Feng and the other guy move in, but Tony's gun makes a hasty reappearance and the cowards back off.

"Enough," Jianjun calls out. "Signor Valentino, you've made your point. Now leave or I will have you removed from my property."

I finally turn around to face the old man. "I appreciate your understanding, Jianjun. I believe I've already made it abundantly clear to your son, but I have a feeling he's a bit hard of hearing, so I'll repeat it to you." I stalk closer until I can make out the wiry gray hairs in the leader of the Triad's long beard. "Stella Esposito McKenzie is mine. Anyone talks about her or looks at her the wrong way, I will take it as an act of war. Are we clear?" I punctuate each of my final words with venom.

He offers me a tight smile. "Crystal."

"*Perfetto.*" I march out of the alley with Tony at my heels, my heart a little lighter.

CHAPTER 30
THE WORST DAY

Stella

I stare at the calendar on the wall, at the fourteen exes glaring back at me. I slash another line across today, the somber black ink matching my mood. How is it possible that I've changed so much in such a short period of time? Instead of counting down the days to my freedom, each X brings me closer to the expiration date of whatever this thing is between Luca and me.

The mercurial mob boss hasn't touched me since that day at the pond. Not even when he'd dragged me to yet another fancy ball. No dancing, nothing. *Dio,* I'm dying. He's like a drug, and I'm a helpless addict. The connection I feel to this man runs bone deep, and it's absolutely insane. How can I be falling for a man I barely know? A man who keeps me prisoner in his home. A place in which I feel more at home than any of the shitholes we lived in after Mom.

From the bits of information I'd gathered while eavesdropping, Luca's lawyer had managed to remove all evidence of

Bo's public beatdown. A part of me is pissed. I wanted that *bastardo*'s humiliation live for all to see. He is a coward. Any man who takes advantage of a woman is, in my opinion. What the hell had I seen in that asshole?

Oh, right, he'd given me attention and his possessiveness at the time had made me feel needed, wanted. Not to mention Dad would've hated the idea. Extra bonus. The power Bo held gave him an aura I'd found attractive, a tiny sliver of the one Luca Valentino possessed.

With Luca, I felt invincible.

Although lately, it was more like invisible. I tried to convince myself it was only his all-consuming work, but a prickle of dread told me it was something more. He'd started opening up, breaking his precious rules for me, and now he was backpedaling. Did he regret all of it?

A sigh parts my lips, and I replace the black sharpie on the nightstand and force myself out of my bedroom. I walk through the quiet corridor, admiring the beautiful art. Final exams are in three short weeks, and if I could only manage to study, I could prepare for my escape when this is over. Only now, the idea of leaving New York carves up my insides.

"Good morning, Miss Stella." Magda offers me a smile as I emerge from the hallway.

"Please don't call me *Miss*, Magda." I slump into the bar stool and lean on the marble countertop. My cappuccino awaits, the frothy milk shaped into a heart. The woman is a life saver. How she manages to time the perfect delivery of my coffee when I don't even know when I'll wake up blows my mind.

"Right, sorry, Stella." She blushes and hands me a plateful of cannoli.

Two more weeks of this and I'll be rolling out of Luca's penthouse. I stuff the delicious cream filled pastry into my mouth as I mentally curse myself. There's a home gym tucked away past Luca's bedroom, but I haven't worked up the desire to use it. Thoughts of the gym remind me of Caroline and Luca's membership at *La Palestra*. With his bullet wound nearly healed, he's slowly resumed his workout routine.

Does he see the leggy blonde when he escapes the penthouse for his pre-dawn workout? A wave of jealousy crashes over me at the thought of his hands on her. Which is insane for multiple reasons… first and foremost, we're not together. And secondly, the part I hold on to with every fiber of my being, she made it clear they'd already fucked and per Luca's rules, it was one and done.

But what if he changed his mind?

He'd kissed me… also, against the rules. What if he decided to mess around with her again?

"Are you okay, M—Stella?" I glance up to find Magda's curious gaze heavy on me. She wears a reusable grocery bag on each shoulder as she regards me. "I have to run some errands, but I can go later if you want to talk?"

I shake my head. I've already relied on the girl enough. I'm sure she's tired of hearing me pine about her boss. "No, it's fine. I'm fine. Go ahead, Magda."

"Can I get you anything from *Dean & Deluca*?"

A good slap in the face. "Nope, I'm good, thanks."

She nods and hikes the bags further up her shoulders. "I'll be back soon. Alberto is downstairs if you need anything."

I'm shocked I'll be left with only one guard. Luca must have noticed how pathetic I've become. He's got me wrapped around his little finger. I haven't even attempted an escape since my disastrous first try. Because let's be honest, where would I go?

I'm happy here with Luca. Mostly.

How screwed up am I?

I sip on my coffee and scan the front page of *The Wall Street Journal*. Luca is weirdly old-school like that. Who gets newspapers delivered anymore? The black print blurs, and my mind wanders to my father. Somewhere I've forbidden it to go for weeks. But she's a traitorous little bitch and starts unearthing dark thoughts. Is he okay? Does he feel even the slightest bit of guilt for selling me to the Kings? He has no idea I've been living it up in the lap of luxury. For all he knows, I could be imprisoned in a dank dungeon.

Will he have the two grand at the end of the month?

A sick, twisted part of me hopes he doesn't. Would that buy me more time with Luca? *Ugh.* I'm nauseated with myself.

The ding of the elevator sends my hopes soaring. Maybe I should've taken up Magda's offer to stay. Or better yet, convinced her to let me go with her. I'm in no state of mind to be alone right now. I drop my coffee and race across the sprawling space to the foyer.

The elevator doors glide open, and Dante darkens the entryway.

He shakes his head, thick brows twisting as he regards me. "You're still here," he growls.

I wrap my arms across my chest, shielding my nightie from that intrusive gaze. "What are you doing here? Luca's not home."

"Home? Is that what you think the penthouse is to you?" He sneers, and goosebumps ripple across my flesh. He steps closer, and I take one back. There's something about the dark look in his eye that has warning bells ringing. "Why are you really here, Stella? What is this deal between you and my brother?"

A trickle of fear wraps around my lungs like a noose. I steel my spine and force the words out. "You'll have to ask him."

Dante grunts and rakes his hand through his dark hair. The mannerism reminds me of Luca. They have the same wavy, midnight hair and long, thick fingers but this cold man is nothing like my captor. "I have asked him, and I get the same damned answer every time. That it's none of my business."

"So maybe you should listen to your boss." I toss him a sweet smile.

"*Puttana*," he mutters under his breath.

"Watch your mouth," I hiss as the swelling fear transforms to anger. "If you have an issue with this situation, take it up with your brother. I'm not getting in the middle of your little pissing match."

His eyes flash and he lunges, fingers curling around my throat. "You know what I think? I think you're nothing but Bo's little whore, and he sent you to fuck with my brother."

I whip my head back and forth, the panic returning in full speed. "No …."

"Everything changed since you showed up, little girl. Luca's not thinking straight. He's got his head so far up his ass, he's going to ruin everything. The Triad is coming after us, he lost the deal with the city commissioner and when I call him out on it, I get the brunt of his wrath. He's turning on me, and it's all because of you. I want to know why," he shouts, his hot breath assailing me. His hold tightens, and darkness seeps into the corners of my vision.

I gasp.

"I'm his brother, and he uses me like a damned punching bag. He dismisses me like the help. No, worse, he treats his employees ten times better. And you, you're like his fucking queen. Why?"

"I don't know," I rasp out.

"Tell me the truth! Are you working for the Triad?"

"No!" I hiss. His thumbs dig into my throat, and I can barely gulp in a breath.

"He says it's just business between you, but I know there's more. You've gotten under his skin somehow, and I need you out of his life." His free hand travels to my hip. "You can't possibly be that good of a fuck." His fingers slide beneath my nightie and dig into my skin.

"Don't touch me," I shriek. I smack my palms to his chest, but it's like hitting a wall. A lethal mix of fear and revulsion battle it out in my gut.

"Why not? Maybe if you give me a little taste, I'll understand what has Luca so *impazzito*. Maybe I won't care anymore if Jianjun puts me ten feet under after I sample that sweet little cunt."

My chest constricts, unbridled terror closing my airways. Dammit, my inhaler is in the bedroom. Too far away. "Don't you dare lay a finger on me, Dante," I snarl. "Luca will tear your heart out."

A rueful chuckle slides out as he presses his body against mine. I'm trapped against his unyielding form and the couch. "You know, I believe that. And it makes no fucking sense to me. Do you have any idea how many women throw themselves at my brother? And sure, he gives in from time to time. We all have needs, right? But he fucks them and escorts them out. He doesn't allow women to get into his head, let alone his heart. But you… *cazzo*, I just don't get it." His hand moves up my throat and squeezes my cheeks. Then his mouth descends on mine. His tongue forces its way between my gritted teeth. I squirm and push against him, but he's too damned strong.

His mouth smothers mine, teeth gnashing. I can barely breathe against the assault. I kick and punch, lashing out with everything I have, but his hold only tightens. His rigid body is like a cage around my frail one. I'm completely at his mercy. Nausea oozes up my throat. No, I won't let this *bastardo* have me.

Somehow, I manage to free my leg and jerk it up, and my knee sinks into his balls. He lets out a curse and releases my lips. I suck in a haggard breath, pulse pounding.

"You bitch," Dante roars. "Admit that you're a spy for Jianjun, or I'm going to make you pay." He spins me around and tosses me over the side of the couch. With my ass up in the air and my face pressed against the cushion, another wave of terror spikes through my veins.

No. No. No!

"Admit it!" he shouts.

"I'm not a fucking spy," I mumble, my words swallowed up by the plush cushion.

Through the panic, I barely register a familiar ding. It cuts through the maddening roar of my heartbeats and ignites a sliver of hope.

"Let go of her now." A lethal voice slices through the air.

CHAPTER 31
RETRIBUTION

L*uca*

Stella is folded over the couch, her nightie yanked up to her waist revealing bare cheeks. Panic is carved into her jaw, and tears spill down her face. Pain lances through my heart, and the stab is so acute I nearly buckle over. Instead of the stinging ache, I focus on the rage. That motherfucker. Unearthly fury surges through my veins as I lunge at my brother.

I pummel into Dante and knock him to the floor. He stares up at me, eyes wide. "I did it for you, *fratellino*. She can't be trusted."

I yank my arm back and let it fly. The smash of crunching bones only fuels my rage. I hit him again. And again. All I see is red. Then glimpses of Stella's terrified face.

"I just wanted to rough her up a little and find out the truth," he rasps out.

Dante's words are nothing more than a muffled mess in the distance. He tried to hurt her, to force himself on her in my own home. "What the hell is wrong with you?" I roar. "How dare you touch her!" I punctuate each word with another hit.

Dante's head whips back and forth, his eyes closed, face already swelling.

"I warned you never to touch her."

Blood covers my knuckles and more spills onto the marble floor, splattering the silver veining. Crimson consumes my vision. I hit him until I'm numb.

Punch. Punch. Punch.

The slap of skin and the crack of bones rings out in a steady rhythm. Again. Again.

There's nothing but darkness.

"Luca, enough." Stella's voice barely registers through the insanity. "Luca, you're going to kill him."

A soft touch on my shoulder releases some of the wrath. I heave in a breath, and it's only then I notice the tremor coursing through my body.

"Luca, please." Stella's face coalesces, and then the feel of her hands cupping my cheeks pushes through the overwhelming anger. She kneels beside me, her hair wild and tears still trailing down her beautiful face. I stop and just stare. My chest is heaving, but somehow her presence calms the raging storm.

Heavy footfalls echo across the living room, and Tony and Albie materialize.

"Oh, shit, *capo*," Tony mutters.

He yanks me up off the floor and Albie sees to Dante. Stella follows me as Tony ushers me to the couch. I slump down, the adrenaline from a second ago waning, then morphing to icy numbness. It creeps in slowly.

"You okay, *capo*?" Tony eyes me, his dark brows gnarled.

"Yeah, I'll be fine," I manage.

"What the hell happened?"

I shake my head, unable to even speak the words. My own brother had assaulted Stella… what the actual fuck?

"Can you take care of this?" Stella points at my mangled sibling.

Tony nods. "Of course."

"I've got Luca." She slides her shoulder under my arm and helps me stand. I feel like a complete *scemo*. She was the one that was attacked, and now she's taking care of me?

"I'm okay," I mutter as she leads me down the hall. Her arm is curled around my waist, supporting nearly all my weight. She's surprisingly strong for such a little thing. Now that the fury has passed, all emotion dribbles out of me, and I'm left with nothing. Barely the strength to walk.

Once we reach my bedroom, she closes the door behind us and leads me to the bed. I slump down, the last few minutes a blur I try to piece together. If Albie hadn't called me about Dante when he did, I never would've made it back in time.

Would my own brother have really raped her?

Nausea claws its way up my throat, my stomach churning.

Stella moves between my legs, and I lift my gaze to meet hers. I should be taking care of her right now. Not the other way around. Her hands settle on my tie, and once it's undone, slip down to the buttons of my shirt. She has me undressed in seconds. The blood-splattered white shirt hits the floor, and I cringe.

Dio, I almost killed Dante. I wanted to. For hurting her, for touching what was mine.

"I'm so sorry," I whisper. She shakes her head, new tears welling in her eyes. "This is all my fault." My gaze chases to the floor, to her bare feet. "I should've just told him about our business deal."

Her soft smile falters. "It's not your fault. You couldn't have known he would attack me. It's Dante's fault alone. He thought Bo had planted me here somehow, to spy on you, to screw with your business."

Fuck. This *was* my fault. After I'd beaten on Bo the other day, he must've fueled the rumor to get back at me.

Her gaze lingers on my chest, on the mess of scars, knife and bullet wounds and the tattoos inked across my torso to hide them. Now that the bandages across my shoulder are gone, a pinch of fear courses through my system as she nears the five numbers engraved across my heart. They're hidden well within the intricate patterns, but it's only a matter of time until she recognizes the date. A part of me wants her to find it already. Keeping this secret from her has weighed on my soul for years.

But I'm terrified she'll leave me when she discovers the truth.

So I cross my arms over my chest, shielding the date of Vinny's death. One day I'll tell her the truth, but not today. She's been through enough.

"Come on, let's get you in the shower," she whispers. "You've got blood on you."

I nod and slowly rise, then follow her into the bathroom. She flicks on the light, and my gaze lands on her nightie. "So do you."

She glances down at the crimson splotches, and her lips twist.

I step away from the shower and sit on the side of the tub instead. Turning the faucet, I watch the water fill the massive basin. I dump some bubble bath and fragrant oils into the churning water and draw in a deep breath of the calming scents. Then I turn to Stella and offer my hand. "Get in with me."

She shakes her head, dropping her gaze.

"It wasn't a question, princess." A hint of mischief laces my tone. I need this, and I know she does too, despite her reluctance.

Her eyes meet mine, and a flicker of light brightens those brilliant blue orbs. "And if I say no?"

"I'll punish you." I say it with a smirk, but perhaps it's too soon. Lowering my gaze, I stare at my split knuckles and wince. "Don't you think there's been enough punishment today?"

Her nostrils flare, and I regret my words. Dante deserved what he got. I'd cut him out of the business, out of my life for what he tried to do to her. Men that take advantage of women don't deserve to breathe. If I wasn't so scared of the backlash, I'd have him arrested. *No.* Tomorrow, I'd take care of this mess myself.

I stand slowly and creep closer. After what she's been through, I don't want to spook her. I offer her my hand again, and this time she takes it. With my thumb, I rub slow circles across her palm as I regard her. "What I did to Dante today was only the beginning. He's out. He'll no longer be involved in any aspects of the business or my life. What he did to you was unforgiveable. I want you to know that."

Her head dips as she sucks her lower lip between her teeth, gnawing on the soft flesh. *Dio,* I want to be those teeth.

"If there's anything you want to talk about …."

"No," she snaps. "I just want to forget about the whole thing."

That blinding rage rises again, and I grind my molars to keep it at bay. "Did he hurt you?"

She shakes her head. "He didn't get a chance. You came in right before—" Her words fall away, and I heave in another breath. "I don't want to talk about it anymore."

I nod and reach for the hem of her nightie before pausing. What if she doesn't want to be touched? When she doesn't withdraw, I drag it over her head. Slowly. I want to give her time to deny me.

But she doesn't, and it makes me happier than I have any right to be.

Until my gaze falls on those two hearts above her breast as she stands bare before me. They're a constant reminder of what Stella's lost, and one was my doing.

With a reluctant exhale, I drop to my knees and slide her

thong down her legs. She lets out a shudder when I glance up at her. I press my lips to her stomach and inhale a deep breath laced with her intoxicating scent. I haven't touched her in days, and it's been absolutely maddening.

I thought it would help to put some space between us, but I've been going crazy without her. Leaving the penthouse early to go to the gym, diving into work, spending late hours at the office, nothing helps. She's all I think about.

"*Cazzo*, I missed this," I whisper against her skin.

I can feel her heated gaze boring into me as my tongue slips between my lips and tastes her sweet flesh. I circle her navel, and a faint moan rumbles her chest. I'm hard as fuck just from that one little sound. Rising, I step out of my boxers and tug her toward the tub. Her eyes dip to my growing arousal, and heat flushes her cheeks.

Dio, I don't think I'll ever get tired of that look.

I help her into the tub, then get in behind her. The warmth blankets my body, releasing the remaining tension. Or maybe that's just Stella. She settles in between my legs, and I pull her closer, guiding her ass so that it's nestled against my cock. She leans back, her head against my heart, just over those five numbers that will forever torment me.

If she turned around and looked hard enough, she'd see them.

I snake my arms around her waist and pin her against me. She feels so good in my arms, too good.

"What are we doing, Luca?" she whispers on an exhale, her eyes fixed straight ahead.

"Fuck if I know, princess, but it feels too good to stop."

CHAPTER 32
ONLY ONCE

S tella

Luca wraps the plush towel around my shoulders, gently massaging my skin dry. A wicked grin curls the corner of his lip as he slips the soft fabric between my legs and pats my inner thighs. I'm so wet down there, he has no idea how futile his attempts are. After a thirty-minute soak in the tub with his cock pressed against my ass, muscled arms around me, I'm pulsing with need. After what Dante attempted, I didn't think it was possible. Less than half an hour in Luca's strong arms, and he's managed to erase all thoughts of the despicable act.

Straightening, Luca stands before me completely naked except for the towel draped around his neck, his impressive cock between us. My hand reaches for him, and I wrap my fingers around his silky hardness. He lets out a groan.

"Princess…," he growls. "What are you doing?"

"What I've wanted to do since the day you brought me to this damned penthouse." I take him in my palm and begin to stroke, up and down, up and down. He pumps against my palm and another moan parts his lips.

"After what you've been through today, I should be the one taking care of you," he rasps out.

The towel slips off my shoulders, and I'm bared before him. I fix my eyes to his as I continue to stroke, moisture dribbling from his tip making my hand smoothly glide over his hard length. "I want this," I whisper. "I want you to erase the feeling of Dante's hands on me. Please, Luca."

His mouth twists, and the anguish written across his face rips at my very soul. I don't want him to feel guilty for this. It wasn't his fault. "Are you sure?" he murmurs. A storm of emotions spirals through those midnight orbs.

I nod and tighten my fingers around his cock. With my other hand, I cup his balls, and he lets out a satisfying hiss. "*Dio*, Stella, I'm going to come in your hand in a second if you keep that up."

"Good." For some reason, seeing this powerful man crumble at my mercy sends a thrill up my spine. The ruthless king Luca Valentino reduced to a squirming mess at *my* hands. It's a high like no other. After feeling weak my entire life, this makes me feel strong, untouchable, invincible.

"Not yet, princess." He sweeps his arm beneath my legs and tugs me into his chest so I'm forced to release him. With a few long strides, he marches us into his bedroom. He drops me onto the mattress and his scent consumes me, the musky, spicy fragrance driving me wild. It's all over me, emanating from his silky sheets, from his skin as he hovers over me.

He crawls on top of me, and my gaze roams across that perfectly carved chest, those intricate swirling tattoos barely hidden by the towel still slung across his shoulders. My fingers roam beneath the soft terry cloth, and I pause at tiny digits buried within the black ink. Luca's hand claps over the spot, and his mouth captures mine. That wicked tongue tangles with my own, and all thoughts vanish as my lids drift closed.

"*Dio*, I missed those fucking lips," he murmurs before crushing his mouth to mine once more.

I moan against his lips as he deepens the kiss, his strong fingers fisting my hair while his free hand roams across my body. He finds my breast and palms the sensitive flesh until my nipple is so hard it could cut glass. His cock is heavy against my belly, and I sneak my hand between our bodies to touch him again. I can't get enough. "Luca," I groan. I want him inside me. But would this be it? If we have sex, will it be over?

A part of me knows that one time will never be enough. Already, I'm hopelessly addicted to Luca Valentino. And still, nearly two weeks of captivity remain. If I give into this, he'll ruin me for anyone else.

He crawls down my body, his tongue dragging down my torso so I'm forced to release him. Again. He's doing it on purpose. Teasing me.

"Mmm, princess, I've been dreaming about your sweetness. Just dying to worship at the altar between your thighs." He slides his nose through my dark curls and breathes me in. His eyes dart to mine, and a mischievous glint darkens his expression. "Just like I remembered it—"

"Sunshine and rainbows," we murmur together.

"Why do you always say that?" I rasp out.

"Because that's what you are to me, my brilliant light, the riot of colors that illuminates the endless night."

I'm so touched by his beautiful words I'm speechless. I open my mouth to say something, anything, but with his gaze still fixed to mine, his tongue slides between his lips and then disappears within my wet folds. I can't string together a single thought let alone a question. My back arches into him as fiery heat consumes me.

"I've never tasted anyone sweeter." The vibrations of his voice reverberate across my clit, and my blood thrums with need.

He sucks on the sensitive bud, and my hips buck against his mouth. Fuck me. *Dio*, I want him to fuck me so bad. I've never wanted, no, needed anyone like I need Luca. My fingers tangle in his thick hair; I'm so desperate to touch him.

He dips one long finger inside me, and the friction nearly sends me plummeting over the edge. In and out, in and out. He works me until I'm a writhing mess. Luca glances up at me from between my legs, his mouth covered in my arousal as his finger fucks me to oblivion. "I want to watch you come, princess."

I suck in a ragged breath. I'm so close.

He slides a second finger inside me, and I'm so soaked I can hear it with each thrust.

"Mmm, princess. Has anyone made you this wet before?"

"No," I pant.

"Good. Only for me, baby."

I rock against his palm, desperate for the delicious friction as his fingers curl inside me, finding *the* spot. Blazing heat scorches through every vein.

"Are you ready to come for me?"

I let out a whimper.

He dips his head between my legs once more, his eyes still locked on mine and with one perfect flick of his tongue, I fall.

"Oh, Luca," I shout as pleasure roars through me.

"That's right, princess." He pops up, his rough tone only intensifying the high. "You come only for me, got it?"

I nod as he crawls over me. His cock brushes the sensitive flesh at my entrance as he hovers over me, and another moan escapes. "I want to come again," I say on an exhale. "On your cock," I add before I lose my nerve.

He shakes his head. "Princess, you don't know what you're asking for."

"Yes, I do." *Dio*, was I going to do this? Was I going to beg this man to screw me knowing it'll only be once? Fully aware he'll leave me broken and ruined in the best and worst possible way?

Something unreadable flashes across his tense jaw. "You understand it will only be the one time?"

No. "Yes."

Again, that look. An internal battle is being fought beneath the dark surface. Luca's pupils are blown out and with that wild look in his eye, I'm not certain if he's going to fuck me or murder me, if he's happy that I'm giving into his rules or furious. A chill slides down my spine.

"Please," I mumble. My hands settle on his chest, and my finger runs along a dark spiral of ink.

"Turn around and get on the floor." The jagged edge has goose bumps cascading across my arms.

He leaps off the bed and digs through his bedside table. Finding a condom, he rips the silver pouch open and slides it down his hard length. *Dio*, he's huge. My lower half cramps in anticipation.

I slide onto the floor and flip onto my belly, and my heart hammers against my ribs. Luca's hands reach around my waist and tug my bottom half up until my ass is up in the air. His fingers dance along the seam of my thigh before finding my pussy again.

"Still drenched for me," he groans as he slides his fingers through my folds.

I focus on his touch, on the second wave of desire already pulsating across my center. But my mind whirls back in time to Caroline, to that day in the women's bathroom.

The rules.

Only once. Only from behind.

My ribs tighten across my lungs, and I drag in a ragged breath. *You can do this, Stella.* It's just sex. It'll be meaningless, mind-blowing fun. One day of pleasure you deserve after all the shit.

His cock presses against my ass as his thumb circles my

clit. His arms come around me, his entire body blanketing mine. Heat radiates from his powerful form as his head nudges at my entrance. He's so big and so hard a trickle of fear races up my spine. It's been a while since I've had sex, too long.

Dammit, if he doesn't do it now, I'm going to chicken out. I wiggle my hips and press my ass against him, urging him in.

His broad chest envelops my back and his warm breath skates over the shell of my ear as he leans closer. "Are you sure, Stellina?" For an instant, the hard mob boss, the ruthless C.E.O. is gone. The softness in his tone has tears pricking my eyes. I'm filled with the most overwhelming desire to turn around, to look at him. I need to decipher what's going on in that mind.

Cazzo, I'm terrified. I know the moment he thrusts into me we can never go back. But *Dio*, I've never wanted anything more.

"Yes."

CHAPTER 33
TELL ME YOU'RE MINE

L*uca*

"Yes," Stella breathes.

That one word unleashes a wave of emotions so powerful my entire body vibrates with need. *Cazzo*, what am I doing? Stella agreed to my rules. She's going to let me fuck her, agreed to just the one time. She's sprawled out in front of me, ass in the air, her perfect pussy just asking to be fucked.

And I'm paralyzed.

I'm so hard I'm certain I'll explode if I don't have her.

But just once?

I haven't even sunk my cock inside her, and already I know it'll never be enough.

Hell, I want her every possible way I can take her. I want to watch her as she rides my dick, gorgeous breasts bouncing, until her head falls back crying out my name. But I'm too damned terrified she'll see the date of Vinny's death stamped across my chest. Taking her from behind is the safest option, the only choice.

Fuck, I should've told her the truth.

She drives her ass back, and she's so drenched my dick nearly slips inside her dripping pussy. *Dio*, I want this. I've wanted her since the moment I saw those pouty lips scowling up at me in the back room of the pawn shop.

"Luca," she moans.

My thumb still circles her clit, and I can feel her tightening against me. She's going to come again, and I'll miss my chance. What if she changes her mind?

I've given her plenty of time to back out, to reconsider. She wants this as much as I do and I'm a fucking *bastardo* for taking it. My heart rams against my ribcage, the maddening tempo echoing the throbbing in my cock. My thighs tremble as I kneel behind her. *Just do it.* I palm her ass with my free hand and with a shaky breath, I thrust inside her.

She lets out a cry as I fill her. In and in and in.

"Oh princess, you are so tight," I growl. Even with the damned condom, her sweltering heat seeps into my skin. We fit so perfectly, her pussy wraps around my cock, drawing me in. Nothing has ever felt so right. I pull out slowly, then sink back in, giving her time to adjust. "Are you okay?" I rasp.

"Yesss. More …." She grinds her hips back, and I thrust again, deeper this time.

Her head falls back, and *Dio*, it's the sexiest thing I've ever seen. My finger works that pulsing nub as I pound into her. She's so wet, her pussy so hungry for me just the thought is enough to drive me over the edge. "Fuck, Stella," I groan as my hips ram into her perfect ass.

I'm home. She is it for me.

The errant thought squeezes the air from my lungs. I can't think about that, about her, about how perfect we are together. She'll destroy me, and I'll devastate her. She has no place in my world; she doesn't deserve the life I've chosen. I pick up the pace, plunging harder, deeper until she's a squirming puddle of desire beneath me.

I *must* stick to the rules. In my mind, I punctuate each word with another plunge. Fiery pleasure licks up my spine. I'm like a horny teenager with her. Biting my lower lip, I try to keep the orgasm at bay. *Calcio. My lawyer. The mountain of files I have to look over in my office.*

Nothing helps to distract me from the building orgasm.

I curl around Stella's back and drop kisses up her spine. I reach her shoulder and sink my teeth into soft flesh. Then I move to her neck and suck hard, claiming her. I want everyone to know she belongs to me and only me.

"You're mine," I growl as I plow into her.

She tips her head back, and I capture her lips. Our bodies are joined in countless places, and I can feel every single point of contact intensely. My mouth on hers, my hand cupping her breast, my fingers on her clit, my cock inside her pussy. I want to claim every inch of her.

"Say it, princess. Tell me you're mine."

"I'm yours," she moans against my lips. I swallow her cries, desperate for more. I want her screaming my name as she comes.

"I'm the only one that can fuck you, you understand?"

"Mmhmm," she murmurs. Her eyes snap open in the same instant I realize what I've said. I'd insinuated I would keep fucking her.

That this would be more than the one time I promised.

"Come for me now," I command, instead of meeting that hopeful gaze. I squeeze my eyes shut and drive into her as my fingers pinch her clit. She lets out a cry, and a tremor rips through her whole body.

"Oh, Luca," she wails as the second orgasm tears through and her pussy clenches around my cock.

It's all I can stand. The raging pleasure pummels me next and I jerk inside her, spilling my soul into the condom. Desire vibrates through every inch of me as the most powerful release I've ever had leaves me shaking.

Stella collapses beneath me onto the soft carpeting, flushed a gorgeous pink hue and still panting. After tearing off the condom, I fold my body around hers, snaking my arm around her waist and drawing her soft form against my chest.

"*Cazzo*," she mutters as her head sinks onto my arm.

"Yeah."

A warm laugh escapes her lips, and I nuzzle into the back of her neck. A deep purple mark darkens her skin at the crook of her shoulder, and a satisfied grin stretches across my face. I want everyone to know Stella is mine. A disturbing afterthought rises to the surface. I want her to be mine for good….

I stiffen, the terrifying idea icing my veins.

"What's wrong?" Stella cants her head back, eyes meeting mine.

"Everything." A rueful smile curls the corners of my lips.

"Then why are you smiling?"

"Because I've never been so happy to be wrecked."

She shakes her head, and her eyes slowly drift closed. "*Pazzo*."

Stella's right. I am crazy. I'm fucking out of my mind for her.

My hand splays across the flat planes of her stomach, and I imagine it round and full with my child. Squeezing my eyes shut, I force the image to the dark recesses of my mind. It can never happen. Bringing a child into this shitshow would be cruel and selfish. No, never, fatherhood is not in my future.

Focusing on her smooth, taut belly again, my fingers stretch until they reach the underside of her breasts. She lets out a soft hiss at the gentle touch. I palm her silky flesh, and my fingers close around her nipple.

She wiggles against me, and I'm hard again.

My hand moves down her body and settles on her hip. Fingers digging into perfect skin, I whirl her around to face me. Her hands move to my chest, and I panic. She's going to see that damned date. It's inevitable if we keep this up. But *Dio*, I want her again. And I don't want to take her from behind. I want to see her face as I wring out every ounce of pleasure.

I capture her lips as I work out the logistics in my mind. I could find a shirt and put it on, but that would seem strange.

Stella winds her leg around my hip and my cock blindly finds her pussy, nudging at the entrance. Mischievous eyes glance up at me, tempting, teasing as she rocks against me.

"If I fuck you again, it's not really breaking the rules," I whisper.

"Oh, no?"

I shake my head. "This is all part of the same time."

"Well, then I guess we better take full advantage." She smirks and crawls to the nightstand, baring her beautiful ass. She scours the drawer for another condom and turns to me with a heart stopping smile. "Ready?"

Stella

Wisps of light stream between my heavy lids as consciousness seeps in. Strong arms hold me imprisoned against a firm chest. That would explain the best night of sleep I've had in ages. Luca's scent consumes me, that manly musk mixed with a hint of the remainders of his expensive cologne. I release a sigh as my lids slowly open and take in the gorgeous naked male draped over me.

How had yesterday morphed from one of the worst days of my life to the best?

The ache between my thighs brings memories of the heated night rushing back. Luca hadn't just fucked me four times last night, he'd worshipped my body, made me feel cherished like no one else ever had.

And now it's over.

A rush of unexpected emotion tightens my throat. I inhale a deep breath forcing back the rising panic. It's over.... Tears burn the back of my eyes, and I'm not certain I can hold them in.

Luca shifts beside me, and his hard cock brushes my belly. His eyes snap open, and a wicked grin teases the corners of his lips. "Good morning, princess." The rough edge to his tone and the wild, sexy hair is just too much.

Oh, *Dio*, no.

I'd felt it coming for days. Had refused to admit the truth. But after last night and not just the sex, but everything before and after, I can't deny it any longer.

I am falling for him.

Desperately.

And now that he'd fucked me, we were done. Hell, I'd even agreed to it. *Stupid. Stupid.*

"Stella, what's wrong?"

I shove out of Luca's arms and search his bed for my clothes. *Cazzo*, I never had clothes here. I'd discarded my bloodied outfit in the bathroom.

"Where are you going?" he shouts as I scramble off the bed.

The heat intensifies behind my eyes, and my throat begins to close. *No.* I refuse to cry in front of him.

I race across his room naked, mumbling about a shower. I can hear him behind me, his footsteps echoing across the hallway as I sprint like a *pazza* to my room.

"Stella, wait!" he calls out after me.

I pump my arms faster, desperate to escape before the torrent of tears begins to fall. I whip my bedroom door open and slam it shut behind me. Once it's locked, I sink down to the floor and bury my face in my hands. The second I'm alone, the dam breaks free. Tears rush down my cheeks, and I release a gut-wrenching sob.

A soft knock on the door sends my heart leaping up my throat. "Stella, please …." Luca's pained whisper only intensifies the anguish. "Let me in."

"No," I murmur. "I just want to be alone."

"Please, Stella, don't shut me out. Let's talk about this." He wrenches the doorknob, and the hinges creak against the onslaught. "Tell me what's wrong, damn it."

"Leave me alone, Luca," I cry.

"Stella, *mannaggia alla miseria*, if you don't open the door, I'll break it down."

The door groans under his fist as he slams it against the thick timber.

No, I can't face him. I spin around and press my lips to the seam. Choking back a sob, I whisper, "Luca, if you care about me at all, please leave me alone."

He slams his fist against the door once more and exhales a frustrated breath. The slap of his angry footfalls echo across the hallway before the slam of his bedroom door sends a shudder through my heart. A crack races across my stupid, traitorous organ, and the tears begin to fall again until I drown in them.

CHAPTER 34
LOVE?

Luca

Miserable. I'm fucking miserable. I shove the files off my desk and let out a frustrated growl. It doesn't help. I reach for that stupid award for Businessman of the Year and throw it across the room. It shatters against the wall with a satisfying crash. Then I go for the stapler, my nameplate, everything smashes onto the floor, only exacerbating my rage. I reach for my laptop next as Clara races into my office.

"Luca!" she shouts as I hold the sleek device over my head. "*Che cazzo fai?*"

What am I doing? I'm fucking losing my mind that's what. One week after fucking Stella and I've lost every ounce of sense. She won't speak to me, she won't even look at me. She spends every moment I'm in the penthouse in her room. I watch her all night on the home security system like a *pazzo*. I haven't slept, I can't eat.

Her scent around my home drives me mad. Everything reminds me of her.

I've spent countless nights standing outside her room like a *coglione* trying to figure out what to say to fix this.

"Put your laptop down," says Clara.

I release a frustrated breath and set it down on my desk.

"You have to talk to that girl." She clucks her teeth at me like I'm some stupid lovesick teenager.

"I've tried," I snarl.

"Well, obviously not hard enough."

I skewer her with a glare. If Clara wasn't like a second mother to me, I would've thrown her out of my office by now. "You don't understand."

She saunters over in her hot pink Chanel skirt suit and waggles a perfectly manicured fingernail at me. "I don't understand that you're too blind to see what's right in front of you?"

"Watch it, Clara."

"I am, Luca. If I had it my way, I'd tell you what a *stronzo* you're being. That I've never seen you so happy as the moment Stella moved into your penthouse. That whatever you're too scared to admit is the only thing standing in your way of real happiness."

"It's not that simple," I hiss.

She corners me against my desk. "Nothing worth fighting for ever is, *figlio mio*."

"You know what my life is like. If I let her in, I'd only be hurting her in the long run. I told you what Dante did." Another wave of fury rushes over me. I still can't fathom my own brother attacking her.

"You're hurting her now and you're torturing yourself. Stop hiding out here and go home and tell her how you really feel. Apologize until she accepts it."

The idea is terrifying. My heart punches at my ribcage, desperate to escape this torture. I can't admit the truth, not to myself and especially not to her. I'd only be putting her in danger. I'd promised her *nonno* all those years ago I'd watch out for her and Vinny. I'd already failed her brother; I'd die before I let the same happen to her.

But I had to do something ….

I couldn't continue on like this.

"And by the way, in case you've forgotten, you have the Met Gala tonight."

"Tonight?" My voice rises a few octaves. *Cazzo*, how did I forget? This thing with Stella has my head on a tailspin. I could just not go ….

Clara shakes her head at me. "Don't even think about cancelling, Luca. You must attend the gala. You have a special table reserved with the mayor, remember?"

Shit.

Now I really have to find a way for Stella to forgive me. I need her at my side at the event tonight. As I stalk out of my office, I try to convince myself that's all I need her for.

Stella

I swallow down a bite of the meatball sub Magda made just for me and force a smile even though the hoagie melts to ash on my tongue. Just like everything else the sweet girl has made for me in the past week. She insists I've lost weight, and I have to eat to keep up my strength. For what though?

What do I need strength for? To wallow around the house in my pjs?

I am such a *stronza*. I knew having sex with Luca would ruin me. Why didn't I listen to my head instead of my lusty pussy?

At least before, my captivity had been going decent

enough. We'd fallen into an easy routine, and damn, I hated to admit it, but I was happy here. The playful banter, the wicked stares, the occasional flirtation, *Dio* I'd cherished those moments. Because obviously I've got a screw loose. Maybe it was one too many drunken slaps from my father. He'd broken something.

But it was nothing like the utter desolation I feel now. If my father had broken me, Luca had begun to mend the frayed edges only to rip apart my fragile insides once more.

I'd completely fallen for the ruthless mob boss, the cold C.E.O., and the fiery man beneath the icy surface.

Stronza.

I take another small bite as Magda's watchful gaze slants over me. Throughout my three weeks here, I've grown to like the girl, but I am also entirely aware she gives Luca a full report of my daily activities. I'd caught her spilling every single detail only two nights ago when I eavesdropped outside Luca's office door. I don't blame her obviously, but I also know I can't trust her. Not really.

The elevator dings, and the doors glide open across the great room. Luca's dark form fills the opening, deep lines carving into his jaw and somehow sharpening his beautiful features.

All the air vanishes from the room.

Shit. What is he doing home so early? He hasn't been back before dinner this entire week. I snatch my plate from the marble island and slide off the barstool. Keeping my eyes pinned to the remainders of my sub, I attempt to dart past him.

"Stop," he growls.

Ignoring him, I only quicken my stride.

"Stella!" He reaches for me, and if it weren't for that damned meatball sub, I would've been able to dodge his grasp. But Magda had slaved over the meatballs all morning, and the idea of them splattering across the floor has guilt spearing my chest. I'm such a sucker. His firm fingers close around my upper arm, and he spins me toward him.

"Let go of me," I hiss.

Dark eyes blazing, he glares down at me. "No." His fingers tighten, and I let out a squeal.

"You're hurting me, *bastardo*."

"Good." Rage flashes across those bottomless orbs. "I want you to know how I've felt for days."

I vaguely notice Magda scampering out of the kitchen as he uncurls my fingers from the plate with his free hand.

"What are you doing with my lunch?" I cry.

"You can't eat that in the bedroom. You'll drop it on the rug and that tomato sauce will never come out." He drags his hand through his hair, his expression so enraged it's almost comical. I've never seen anyone so angry about a non-existent, future stain.

"Fine, then I won't eat." I attempt to wriggle free of his hold, but his fingers only constrict another inch.

He drags me back to the kitchen and places the plate on the island once again, then clasps his hands around my hips and pops me back up onto the barstool. "Hey!" I squeal as his fingers dig into the bare skin peeking between my pajama top and bottom. They linger there for an endless moment, and the fire in his eyes morphs to something raw and much more deadly.

I don't dare breathe as he pins me with that menacing glare. His fingers sear into my flesh, branding me with each haggard breath.

Finally, he squeezes his eyes shut, and I'm released from those piercing midnight orbs. He draws in a breath and his hands fall away. "Eat," he mutters, taking a step back.

"I'm not hungry anymore."

"You're wasting away," he snarls. "All the dresses you bought won't fit anymore."

"What does it matter?" I cry. "We only have a week left

anyway." My throat tightens, and a strangled, choking sound erupts from my lips. I clamp my mouth shut and grind my teeth together at the embarrassing outburst.

His eyes grow wide, and the impenetrable darkness nearly eclipses the light. "You're upset about our time coming to an end?"

"*Vaffanculo*, Luca! I'm furious at you for many things, but trust me, that is not one of them."

The hint of a smile lifts the corners of his lips, revealing that elusive dimple. He steps closer, trapping me on the stool against the marble island. His hands clamp around my knees, and he forces my legs open. Heat races to my traitorous pussy as he squeezes his hips between my thighs.

"What are you doing?" I snarl.

"Something I should have done days ago." He threads his fingers through the tangle of hair at the back of my neck, fisting it so my chin pops up. His mouth captures mine, and I moan against his lips. My thoughts swirl, a tornado of emotions battling it out in my chest. *Dio*, I want this, dreamed about this since the last time he touched me.

But I can't ….

Summoning every last ounce of willpower, I slam my palms into Luca's chest and force him back. Our mouths come apart, and I'm already panting wildly. "No …." I shake my head, compelling the word out.

He cocks his head, an arrogant smile plastered across that unfairly handsome face. "Are you sure?" He inches closer again. "If I put my hand down your panties, I won't find you wet and ready for me?"

"Fuck you," I grit out. I squeeze my thighs together to squash the burning desire.

His hands frame my face, and I can't help but lean into his touch. Everything about him is so familiar, so much like home. I've never felt anything like it around any other man.

He leans closer, and his warm breath skates over the shell

of my ear, drawing goosebumps. "Princess, I love that you're always wet and ready for me."

Love? That word on his mouth short circuits something in my brain because instead of pushing him away, I lean into him as his lips move from my ear to my cheek, fluttering soft kisses along my jawline.

"Luca …," I plead. I'm not even sure what I'm asking for. To leave me alone or bend me over the couch and screw me senseless. The former would be the wiser option, but I can't deny how much I want the latter.

"I'm sorry," he whispers against my lips. "I'm sorry, Stella. I was stupid and wrong, *un vero coglione*."

My eyes snap open as I regard that hooded smile. "What?"

"Fuck my rules."

Again, I'm certain I'm hearing things. My mouth opens, but no sound comes out. I'm so shocked I can't string together an entire sentence.

"I want you so bad I'd break every goddamned rule on the planet. Please, forgive me for being so stubborn and arrogant. The other night, when I was buried deep inside you was the fucking best moment of my life. I was a complete *stronzo* to fool myself into believing once would ever be enough."

My heart freefalls. I draw in a shaky breath as his heated gaze locks on mine. I should say no, I should stick to my guns and protect my fragile heart, but when he's looking at me like I'm the only thing that matters in this entire world, I'm helpless.

Especially when there is nothing I want more than to be with him.

I should ask questions, I should clarify the details, but when I can't muster the words, his mouth descends on mine once again and I fall.

CHAPTER 35
COMING HOME

Stella

Luca's hands curl around my ass, and he lifts me up, wrapping my legs around his waist. I cling onto him like he's a lifeboat, my only chance at survival from the tempestuous sea of emotions threatening to drag me under. Are we really doing this? No rules?

He eats up the distance between the kitchen and the living room couch in a few long strides, his hot mouth never leaving mine. *Dio*, I could kiss him forever. He lowers me onto the supple leather sofa and gets to work on his slacks. I reach for his jacket and slide it off his broad shoulders. Once it's in a heap on the floor, my fingers undo the knot of his tie and trail down to his crisp button-down shirt. Before I get the third button undone, his hand clamps around my wrist.

"Uh-uh, princess, I want your hands here." He jerks my hand to his cock, and my fingers instinctively close around his hard length.

I suck in a sharp breath as I take him in. He's completely naked from the bottom down, that huge cock standing thick and erect, and with his perfectly starched shirt half unbuttoned, tie hanging undone from his collar, he's looking sexy as all hell.

He stands between my thighs, and I slide to the edge of the cushion and draw him closer. My eyes fix on that thick cock, and my tongue darts out. I've dreamt about tasting him, running my tongue over that silky smooth skin.

"I want to fuck you all over this penthouse, in every position I can come up with. But first, I want to claim that pretty little mouth, princess. Can you do that for me?"

I nod quickly. I flick the bead glistening on his tip and taste him for the first time. A groan slips free. It tastes like Luca: spicy, sweet and dangerously addictive. I glance up at him as I close my mouth around his erection, and his eyes roll back into his head until only the whites show. I inch down, farther and farther until I fit his entire length. *Cazzo*, he's huge. I'm impressed I can fit all of him in without choking.

He hisses out a string of Italian curses, only urging me on. "*Mannaggia alla miseria,* princess. I knew you'd be good, but fuck me, you are phenomenal." His hands dig into my hair, fisting the dark locks. "Do you have any idea how gorgeous you look with my cock in your mouth?"

I spin my tongue around his silky flesh and revel in his taste as he lets out another moan. *Dio*, there is something so satisfying about watching the powerful Luca Valentino fall to his knees for me. I bob up and down along his hard length, my eyes fixed to his. A raging storm of emotions flicker beneath the dark surface.

"You're going to have to slow down, princess, or I'm going to come in your mouth."

With my free hand, I close my fingers around his balls and give them a gentle squeeze. Then stare up at him with a wicked smile.

"Are you teasing me, princess?"

"Umhmm," I mumble around his dick.

"You want me to come in your mouth, don't you, you naughty little *puttana*?"

I move faster, his excitement intensifying my own.

He shudders, and his gaze turns feral. "Okay, you asked for it." He pumps his hips, forcing himself deeper into my mouth. I fist his cock and take him all in. I suck and swirl my tongue, licking him up. He guides my head up and down, up and down. He's so big his crown grazes the back of my throat with each thrust.

I cup his balls and squeeze again, and his cock jerks in my mouth. Sliding to the tip, I pause and shoot him a wicked grin. "Come for me," I mumble around his thick head.

His eyes widen and the hint of a smile curls the corners of his lips before his head falls back, and he moans my name. His warmth spills into my mouth, and I swallow every bit of it. I suck harder, needing to take all of him. *Dio*, I'm crazy about this man. No one has ever brought out this ravenous side of me before.

After I've taken every ounce of his pleasure, I slowly withdraw, licking up to his crown. He drops on his knees once I've released him, his chest rising and falling in a ragged tempo. His hands close around my knees, and he pushes them apart. His smirk turns savage as he drags my pajama bottoms down to my ankles.

"Now, it's my turn to feast." He's still panting and out of breath, and I'm wondering how the hell he's going to be able to—

He slides me to the edge of the cushion, and his tongue drags across my throbbing center. All my thoughts vanish. His mouth closes around my clit, and he sucks so hard my hips buck. "*Dio*, Luca…," I groan.

"That's right, princess. I am your god, and you are *mine*."

He slips a finger inside me as his tongue draws quickening

circles around my pulsing nub. In and out. In and out. He teases me, drawing out my orgasm. When he plunges a second finger inside, I wriggle harder, dying for the friction to find my release. I'm already so close.

Luca stares up at me over my dark curls, and those mesmerizing eyes capture me and hold me hostage. I dig my fingers into his wild locks, and he wraps his free hand around my bare ass, driving my hips into his face.

No one has ever drawn an orgasm out of me so quickly. "I'm going to come," I groan.

"Not yet, princess. You come when I tell you."

"I thought you said *fuck your rules*," I rasp out.

He grins mischievously. "I think you'll like this one." His tongue drives deeper inside me, sucking and licking, and I drag in a haggard breath. "The longer you hold out, the better it will be," he murmurs against my slick heat. The vibrations alone nearly throw me over the precipice.

His second finger glides further down my folds, dragging my wetness to the sensitive skin around the untouched flesh below. I stiffen for an instant, my ass virgin territory.

"Relax," he whispers, tongue still teasing as his finger explores further south.

Another wave of pleasure grips hold of me, the combination of his tongue and finger in my pussy and the other gliding across the space between too overwhelming.

"Luca, I can't hold on...," I pant.

"Just a few more seconds." He punctuates each word with another thrust of those dexterous fingers and spin of that tongue. I grind my hips against him, so desperate.

I'm whimpering, writhing with pleasure. "Please, Luca ...."

With a satisfied grin, he lifts his eyes to mine once more. "Okay, princess, now you can come for me. I want to watch you break apart with my tongue and my fingers inside your sweet pussy." He licks his lips and disappears between my legs.

I've never been with a man so hungry for me, and fuck, it's thrilling.

One flick of his deft tongue at my clit, a deep plunge of his finger and an increase of pressure along the ridge of puckered skin and I rocket over the edge. Heat surges through my veins like wildfire. I buck against his mouth as he continues to devour me through the raging pleasure.

I collapse against the couch and draw in a ragged breath, my heart racing so fast I'm certain it'll explode. Luca crawls over me straddling my legs with his powerful thighs. He draws my pajama top over my head, and my breasts tumble free.

"Mmm, I've been waiting for this part, princess." He licks his lips, my arousal shiny on his chin. "Have you ever tasted yourself?"

My head whips back forth.

"*Cazzo*, you don't know what you're missing." He drags his tongue over his lips then across mine. "Rainbows and sunshine," he whispers against my mouth.

I can't help but smile. The taste is sweet, musky and tangy, a perfect mix of us both. His tongue tangles with mine for a few seconds longer before his mouth descends on my nipple.

With the echoes of my orgasm still rippling through me, every lick is heightened, my senses on overdrive.

"I need you to come for me just one more time, princess. I want to watch you with my cock buried inside that hot pussy as you come apart for me. Only me."

"Right now?" I choke out. "Again?"

His gaze falls between us, and I follow his line of sight to his rock-hard cock. How is he ready to go again? I'm completely boneless, a shapeless sack of skin and raw pleasure.

"Unless you don't want to, of course?" He lifts a playful brow. "I thought you wanted me to break my rules for you? To fuck you face-to-face so I could kiss you while I nail you to the sofa?"

Dio, yes, I want that. Not even a month with this man, and I've become a total *puttana* for him. But dammit, I want him and his dirty mouth.

"Yes," I whisper.

His eyes light up, the flash of light through the endless darkness making my heart race. "Then spread your legs for me, princess. I'm coming home."

Luca

I sink into her, and I can't help the moan from tearing out as her pussy takes me in like we were made for each other. She's so hot and soaked. I want to feel her without this damned condom, and now that I've thrown all my other rules out the window, that'll be the next one to go. I'll get her on the pill, and I'll fuck her bare. I can't fucking wait to spill every bit of me inside her.

I thrust deeper and that sense of coming home fills my darkest depths. I'm selfish, I'm so damned selfish to drag Stella into this life after everything that happened with Vinny, but damn it, I cannot let her go now.

It was hard enough to walk away from her all those years ago.

My cock plunges again, and she lets out another whimper. Her hands clamp around my shirt, and I'm terrified she's going to rip the buttons off. She's completely naked, and I feel like a *cretino* with my shirt still on. How long can I put off the inevitable?

Her fingers close around the hem of my shirt, and she inches it up my torso. *Shit*. Grabbing her hands, I jerk them over her head and hold them with one hand as I plow into her.

I reach for the tie still hanging undone from my collar and wrap a quick knot around her wrists.

Stella's eyes widen as she regards me.

"Just say the word if you don't like it," I rasp out.

She snags her lower lip between her teeth and bucks against me. She *does* like it.

"That's my good girl." I slow my thrusts, going long and deep. Her breasts bounce with each plunge, just begging to be devoured. Even though I just came a few minutes ago, I'm ready to go again. Just the sight of her brings me back to my teenage years.

When my mouth closes around her pink nipple, her back arches. She squirms against my silk tie. "Keep your hands where they are," I warn.

With an irresistible pout, she wraps her legs around my hips and rocks up to meet me, plunging my cock deeper inside.

"You ready to come again?"

She nods quickly.

My mouth moves from her breast to her mouth, tongue entwining with her eager one. I could do this all day. I've never felt so at peace, so whole as when I'm inside her. The rest of the world could implode, and I wouldn't give a fuck. I'd give up everything for her.

The thought halts my frenzied heartbeats.

Too fast. Too soon.

But is it though? A part of me has loved Stella since we were kids.

Her legs tighten around me, urging me on. I must have stopped moving in my momentary panic. I glance down at her, and those brilliant blue eyes steal my breath. I kiss her again, hard.

"Come for me, princess," I whisper against her lips.

"Together," she pants.

My eyes slide closed, and I commit this moment to memory. The smile on her face, the utter fullness of my heart, the feel of our bodies intertwined.

With one final thrust, we plummet over the edge in perfect synchrony.

CHAPTER 36
OFFICIAL RELATIONSHIP STATUS

Luca

I haven't spoken to my brother in over a week. Not since he dared to touch what is mine. I've cut him out of my life in every way possible. Last I heard from Tony, the doc had patched him up, and he was alive. A deep, dark part of me wanted to kill him. I squeeze my eyes shut as images of his bloodied, battered face fill my mind. Now, I'm terrified he'll show up at the ball tonight. Stella and I are in such a good place right now, and I'm scared shitless to ruin it.

I broke all my rules for her. And as she snuggles up beside me in the limo, I want to break more. I want to give her my battered heart and black soul. But is there anything worthwhile to give?

"What's wrong? You're so quiet." Stella's hand grazes my inner thigh and even through my fine slacks, I'm instantly hard at her touch.

"I'm just thinking about all the ways I'm going to fuck you

tonight when we get home." A mischievous grin curves my lips.

A matching expression curls the corners of her perfect mouth. "You have quite a dirty mouth on you, *signore*."

"I do. And you love it, princess." I claim her lips, tangling my fingers through her long locks. She moans against me, and fuck, if we weren't already late, I'd have Mickey drive around for another half hour so I could drive my cock into her hot pussy right now. The way she's squirming as I kiss her, I already know she'll be drenched for me.

I force myself to release her, and she lets out a frustrated sigh. Her lips bow into an irresistible pout and damn, I just want to fuck that frown off her face.

"We'll make it quick tonight, princess. No dawdling like last time. We show up, take a few pictures to make the press happy, and I'm taking you straight to bed."

My hand lingers along her bare back, and a shudder races up her spine. "Your bed?" She raises a brow.

"Mmm, my bed." She'll be the first woman I've ever fucked there. Somehow, it's fitting. She was the first I'd let into my bedroom after all. And now she's sneaking her way into my icy heart….

"I'm looking forward to it." She smiles and *Dio*, my heart stops for an instant. I'm fairly certain I'm having a heart attack until it kicks up again.

This woman has ruined me.

And *cazzo*, I want her to keep doing it.

Stella

"Everyone's looking at us." I press my mouth to Luca's ear as we dance.

"So let them." He spins me in a tight circle, then dips me so low my hair trails the gleaming parquet. A high-pitched laugh bubbles out.

My cheeks heat as he pulls me back up and tugs me against his chest. Dozens of piercing gazes lance into the back of my head. "Why are they staring?"

"Probably because Manhattan's social elite has never seen me at one of these events with the same woman twice, let alone three times."

I can't help my mouth from puckering. His words are only a reminder that this thing between us has an expiration date. A quickly approaching one.

"What?" He draws me closer, leveling me with that dark gaze.

"Nothing."

"You should be incredibly satisfied that you're the first. I've broken nearly all my rules for you, princess."

I am pleased, but I'm also terrified. Every time we take a step forward it's quickly followed by a giant leap back. And it's that irrational fear that compels the words from my mouth. "What exactly are we doing, Luca?"

His eyes narrow, the heat from his gaze only intensifying. "I'm trying to give you what you want."

How could he know what that is when I can't even figure it out?

"Do you want an official relationship status? Should I confirm it on Facebook?"

I shrug, embarrassment flooding my cheeks. It sounds so silly out loud, but yes, I guess that is what I need.

He dances me back a few steps then twirls me around. A photographer stands before us, his camera inches from my face. Beside him stands a familiar reporter. The woman is all smiles as her eager gaze lands on Luca.

"Kerry, I need a good one, please, cover worthy, got it?"

Her eyes widen like she's just stumbled upon the Holy Grail of celebrity shots, and she nudges the cameraman. "You heard Mr. Valentino, Harry. The best you've got in you." She inches closer with a wry smile. "And remind me again, who is this beautiful woman at your side?"

Luca's eyes latch onto mine, and a mad flutter of butterfly wings assaults my insides. "This is my girlfriend, Stella Esposito."

"Girlfriend?" The reporter's smile only grows hungrier.

"That's what I said, didn't I?" He slides his hand down my lower back and entwines his fingers through mine.

"So does that mean you're no longer Manhattan's most eligible bachelor?"

"That's exactly what it means."

My breath hitches at his words. It's so stupid but they mean so much.

He gives her a panty-dropping smirk, and I clench my thighs together to stifle the rising heat.

Once we've posed for a dozen pictures, Luca thanks them and tugs me back on the dance floor, a shit-eating grin plastered on his unfairly handsome face. "Are you happy now?" he asks as he spins me into his arms.

"How do I know that was real? I was supposed to be your arm candy, wasn't that the deal?"

"It's never going to be easy with you, is it, princess?" He turns that blinding smile on me before he captures my lips.

A collective gasp resounds from every corner of the dancefloor. Or maybe it's just me. He kisses me so fully, my knees wobble. If it wasn't for his firm hold around my waist, I would've been reduced to a puddle on the parquet. He finally releases me, and I stagger back, or at least I try to, but his hold only tightens.

"Now are you convinced?" He nuzzles his nose against mine, and my breath hitches again. I'm so overwhelmed by him and that kiss, I'm considering reaching for my inhaler. "Anyone that knows me at all has never seen me kiss a woman. It's official, princess, you're mine."

"O.M.G., Stella!"

A familiar screech has my head spinning on a swivel. "Rose!" I wiggle out of Luca's embrace and race into my best friend's arms.

"What the hell are you doing here?" she squeals. "Your dad said you left for Florida. I've been trying to call you for the past month. What the hell, girl? I leave for a couple weeks to Long Island, and you vanish."

I can feel Luca's glare boring into the side of my face as I stare gaping at my best friend. "I, um, lost my phone and all my contacts." I chew on the inside of my cheek. "You saw my dad?" I'm such a sucker; I still worry about him sometimes. "How'd he look?"

She averts her gaze. "You know, okay."

Drunk, disheveled, looking like a homeless man most likely. How embarrassing.

Luca steps between us and offers a hand. "I'm sorry, I'm afraid this is all my fault. I've kidnapped your friend and kept her prisoner in my penthouse."

Rose giggles as his big hand envelops hers, and I let out an uneasy laugh. "You could kidnap me any day, stranger. Wait a second, you're—" She taps her temple. "Luca Valentino! You were on the cover of *The New Yorker* a few months ago."

"Guilty as charged."

"Ooh, that accent is so sexy." She leans close and whisper-hisses, "Holy shit. Are you guys together?"

"We are." Luca's arm settles across my shoulders, and he tucks me into his side.

Heat blossoms across my cheeks, and I'm sure I'm smiling like a *pazza*.

"Oh my God, Stells. How did this happen?"

"It's a long story," I mumble.

Rose rifles through her clutch and pulls out her cell. "Well, give me your new number! We have so much to catch up on."

I throw Luca a pointed glare over my shoulder. The

bastardo never did let me have my phone privileges back. He reaches for his phone in his jacket pocket. "Give me yours, and I'll send it to Stella when we get home."

I hold up my new sparkly Gucci clutch. "My new cell wouldn't fit in mine."

"Girl, that purse is gorgeous!" My friend's eyes nearly pop out of her head as they dart back and forth between us.

"Yup, I've been living the dream, Rose."

Luca rolls his eyes, but the corner of his lip twitches.

She squeezes my hands, bright green irises alive with excitement. "I cannot wait to catch up."

"Me too." I pause, my brain finally starting to function after this unexpected encounter. "Who are you here with?" I met my friend at community college two years ago, and she has no more business being here than I do.

She waves a nonchalant hand, motioning toward the bar. "Some guy who came into Dr. Winchester's office for therapy."

"Rose! Isn't that against work policy?" My friend is studying to be a psychologist, and I am fairly certain not dating patients is rule number one. Unlike my mob boss, my best friend is not a stickler for the rules.

Her dainty shoulders lift again. "He's not *my* patient. Not yet anyway."

I shake my head at my crazy friend. There's a reason she picked this field of study.

Behind me, Luca suddenly goes rigid. I feel every muscle in his body tense, and I follow his gaze.

Cazzo, Dante.

CHAPTER 37
MY COGLIONE BROTHER

Luca

"Fuck," I snarl as Dante approaches with Caroline wrapped around his arm. My *coglione* brother knows I won't make a scene in front of the woman. Her father is too important in the Manhattan business and social scene.

Stella's friend spins around as Dante nears. "Damn, he's hot." Her gaze flickers back and forth between us. "Is that your brother?"

"Mmm, it is," I mutter. I eye him as he makes his way toward us. The bruises have all but disappeared which leads me to believe my brother is wearing a shit-ton of makeup. Tony had said he looked like hell when he saw him the other day. I'm having my right-hand man keep an eye on the idiot.

Rose elbows Stella in the side and whispers a few decibels too loudly. "Hook me up, girl. He's almost as gorgeous as Luca."

She shakes her head, gritting her teeth. "Too bad he's a complete asshole. Stay away from him, Rose. Promise me."

"Okay, okay."

I tighten my hold on Stella as a shudder races up her spine.

"What do you want Dante?" I bark before he gets too close.

"I don't even get a hello?" Caroline purrs.

"Hello, Caroline. A pleasure to see you, as always." I reward her with a tight smile, but my insides are churning.

Her eyes narrow on Stella, then run down to my arm around her shoulders. "So it's true then? You two are really together?" Malice drips from her tone.

"Yes, Caroline. Stella is my girlfriend." Despite the thickness in the air, a hint of a smile curls my lips. I like the sound of it. "We're living together actually."

Stella gazes up at me, her eyes widening. *I'm all in, baby.*

"Living together?" Rose blurts.

"Apparently." She gives her friend a guarded smile.

Dante's jaw twitches, the tendon fluttering across his freshly shaven jawline. "Congratulations, that's quite a big step, *fratellino*."

"It is. We're very happy."

Rose stretches her arm out, jutting it between my brother and me. "I'm Rose, by the way, Stella's best friend."

Dante offers her a charming smile, the kind reserved for schmoozing. "A pleasure to meet you."

"O.M.G., you two have the sexiest accents!"

Caroline throws the girl a snarl, and another grin pulls at my lips. I can see how she and Stella could be friends. Rose is light-hearted, boisterous and sweet, everything my Stella needs.

Dante chuckles like he finds her absolutely enthralling. *Stronzo.* They chat for a few moments, the girl completely oblivious to the tension in the air. Finally, Dante turns to Stella, and his expression darkens. "I was hoping to speak—"

I jump in front of Stella, throwing my shoulders back to cut her off from his view. "No," I hiss.

"I only want to apologize—"

"I don't care. I said all I had to say on the matter last week at the penthouse."

"Please, Luca."

"No." I throw my hand up and plant it on my brother's chest. "*Vattene, se no ti ammazzo.*" I wasn't lying either. Fuck appearances, fuck the gala, I'd strangle him with my bare hands if he didn't get out of my face.

Tony appears at my side and places his hand on my shoulder. The man's like a wraith. With a gentle squeeze, he whispers, "Not here, not now, *capo*."

From the corner of my eye, I catch the circle of encroaching paparazzi. Clearing my throat, I drop my hand from Dante's chest. "We'll discuss this at another time."

"Fine," he grits out. "But I will have you hear me out. We're family, Luca, blood. This can't be it for us."

"We'll see." *Not in your fucking lifetime.*

With a polite smile at Rose, he places his hand on the small of Caroline's back and ushers her through the crowded dancefloor. The moment he's gone, Stella sags against me.

"*Mi dispiace*, princess," I whisper. I'm so sorry she has to deal with this bullshit.

"You okay, Stells?" Rose's wary gaze flickers between us.

"Yeah, just tired. Dante can be a little overbearing at times."

"With a face like that, I don't think I'd mind."

"Rose …," she warns.

"I know, I know. Hands off." She raises her palms in mock surrender. "I guess I should go find my date anyway."

"Yeah, probably."

Rose wraps her arms around Stella, forcing me to momentarily release her. I immediately feel the loss of her warmth. "Promise me you won't disappear again?"

"Of course not. I have a phone now and your number. Right, Luca?" Stella throws a pointed stare in my direction.

"Yes. I promise to give her your number as soon as we get home."

"Fantastic. Lunch date this week?"

I watch Stella's face for a reaction. Her smile is smooth, her demeanor calm. "I'd love that."

Her answer drives a pang of guilt into my chest. I've been a monster, keeping her captive in my penthouse. But the idea of losing her is enough to squeeze the remaining air from my lungs. We'd have to discuss the new rules, new boundaries of this relationship.

With another tight squeeze, Rose releases my girl and turns to me. "I'm sure you're a catch and all, but my friend is the best, so don't fuck with her, got it?"

An unexpected smile parts my lips. "Got it, Rose." Another wave of remorse crashes over me, but I maintain my cool grin. "I wouldn't dream of it."

"Good." She spins on her heel and disappears into the crowd.

Stella curls into my side, and I revel in the return of her warmth.

"She seems like fun."

"She's the best too. I hadn't even realized how much I missed her until right now." A look of longing furrows her brow.

"I'm sorry I've kept you so isolated. Things are going to change starting now."

She glances up at me, her brow curved. "Oh, are they? Now that I'm your girlfriend?"

"Mmm, princess, I like the sound of that a little too much." Truthfully, it didn't quite seem to encompass the magnitude of what I felt for her. Girlfriend felt trivial after all we'd been through.

She wraps her arms around my neck and presses her

breasts into my chest. Dipping my chin, I get an eyeful of cleavage. My cock twitches, and I'm instantly hard against her.

"You want to get out of here?" Even I can hear the rough edge to my tone.

"Yes, please." Her hand slides between us, and she throttles my cock. Even over my slacks, I groan at her touch.

"Careful, princess. Another few minutes of this, and I'll have to take you into the bathroom and fuck this naughty streak right out of you."

She releases my dick and takes a step back. "I'd like to see you try." She slants me a wicked grin that has all the blood racing to my cock. "Meet me in the ladies' room in five minutes, Signor Valentino."

Swinging by our table, I offer a quick goodbye to the mayor and his wife. With all the blood rushing from my head to the one below my belt, I'm surprised I remember at all. I give the couple a lame excuse of a headache when in reality my cock is just aching to be buried inside Stella's hungry pussy. I'd imagined claiming her in the limo, but the bathroom works just as well.

I'm practically sprinting by the time I clear the dancefloor. I turn the corner, rushing by the famous *Self Portrait With Straw Hat* by Vincent Van Gogh, to the hallway that leads to the restrooms when a dark form leaps in my path.

"*Cazzo*, Dante," I hiss.

"*Scusi*." He lifts his hands as he mutters the apology. "I *need* to speak to you."

"And I told you I have absolutely nothing to say." I shove past him, and at least he has the sense to get out of my way.

"It's about Stella's father." Dante's words send a prickle of unease down my spine.

I halt and spin around to face him. "What about him?" I growl.

"You know this thing with you and Stella has been driving me nuts…. And since you refuse to speak to me, you completely cut me out of the business and your life, well, I had some time on my hands."

"Get to the point, Dante."

"I did some digging, which was why I wanted to apologize to Stella. I was wrong about her being a spy."

"No shit," I snarl.

"Why didn't you just tell me, you *coglione*?"

It tore me up inside to admit, but I too shared the blame in what happened. This could have all been avoided if I'd only told him the truth about her. I press my lips together. I had no idea why I hadn't, other than wanting to keep Stella all to myself.

"I know about your little deal with Liam McKenzie," he continues when I don't answer. "And I've heard the lowlife doesn't have the money to pay up."

I could have guessed as much. I'd had Tony keeping an eye on him too and between all the drinking and wallowing in self-pity, I figured the *stronzo* hadn't rounded up the funds. It was just another thing I'd deal with when the time came.

"That name also rang a bell…." His eyes taper at the edges, and my heart kicks at my ribs. "This girl is Vinny's sister?"

A soundless scream tears from my lungs. I swallow down the pain and grit my teeth. I don't know why it matters, but I didn't want my brother to know. Even more so now after what he'd done.

"I get it now. Why this girl has gotten under your skin." He steps closer, and I take one back. I hate feeling cornered. The urge to run coils beneath my heated flesh. "She has no idea, does she?"

I shake my head, the faint movement barely perceptible.

"Fuck, Luca, I'm sorry."

I clench my lips into a thin line. "No," I grit out. "You don't get to do this. You tried to rape her!" My eyes widen as I realize how my outburst echoes through the museum's halls.

"I thought she was Bo's spy, *fratellino*. And I swear, I wasn't really going to sexually assault her. I was only trying to scare her." He drags his hands through his hair. "I fucked up, okay? I'll do anything to make it up to you."

"To me?" I shout.

"To her, whatever."

"Not whatever!" My fingers curl, nails cutting into my palms. I draw in a deep breath to keep the fury at bay. I'm about a second from losing my shit and attacking him again. "I can't do this right now," I hiss.

Dante backs off, holding his hands up again. "I'm sorry. I swear I'll find a way to make this right somehow, okay?"

Whipping my head back and forth, I barrel by him and storm down the quiet hallway.

CHAPTER 38
HOPE IS DANGEROUS

Stella

The slap of approaching footfalls sends my pulse skyrocketing. I lean against the vanity and draw in a breath. My pussy pulses with need, fiery excitement building in my core. She's such a little *puttana* for Luca. I've already discarded my lace thong, tucking it into my tiny clutch. It's a good thing it's a little scrap of indecent material or it never would have fit.

The door swings open, and Luca's imposing form fills the doorway. A faint groan parts my lips at the sight of him. *Dio*, he's gorgeous. And mine. At least until the week is up and my time in captivity ends.

"We're leaving."

Those two words douse the building flames racing up and down my center. "What?"

His hand wraps around my wrist, and he jerks me away from the vanity.

"Ow, Luca, you're hurting me."

He loosens his hold but continues to drag me out of the bathroom.

"What is the matter with you?" I screech as he nearly rips the door off its hinges.

"Dante ...," he hisses. I freeze and back into the upholstered wall. "He cornered me again. I just want to get you out of here, okay?"

My head dips slowly. Seeing him today was worse than a punch in the gut. One look at that *bastardo*, and I was back in the penthouse with my ass in the air and my face buried in the cushion. If Luca hadn't arrived when he did …. A chill skirts up my spine, and my shoulders tremble.

"He wanted to apologize to you. I guess he did his homework and found out the truth about your father and our situation."

Every muscle in my body goes rigid. *Apologize. My father. Our situation.* So many parts of that reply have my fancy dinner making its way back up my throat.

"He swears he never would have gone through with it." Luca shakes his head. "I'm sorry, I'm so sorry, Stellina." He pulls me into his arms, and his musky scent envelopes me. Just like that, the fear dissipates, and the dark memories recede to the murky corners where they belong.

"Let's get out of here," I whisper into his shirt.

☠

A warm breath tickles the shell of my ear, and my lids flutter open. Silky sheets cocoon me in luxury, but nothing makes me feel more treasured than the muscled, steel band across my waist or the thick thigh entangled between my legs. I inhale softly, afraid to breathe too hard and ruin this perfect moment.

It's only been a day since Luca's official declaration and already I could imagine a lifetime like this.

Which is stupid and so dangerous.

Nothing in my life that was ever worth it stuck around. Not my mom, not Vinny ... Luca would only be the last of a string of people who abandoned me. It's inevitable.

I stare out into the sprawling city below as the first rays of sunshine bathe Manhattan in all its glory. So many possibilities .... Here, sitting like kings atop this grand city, it's easy to imagine what life could be like. But hope is dangerous, and I must remember to guard my heart.

Too late, a dark voice invades my thoughts.

I run my fingers across Luca's forearm, drawing a trail through his dark hair. Tiny freckles speckle his skin and I trace patterns across the spots like a child's connect-the-dots. It's soothing and helps me force the growing anxiety down.

Cazzo, Stella, just enjoy the moment for once.

But the digital clock on Luca's nightstand catches my eye, and the flashing date only exacerbates the impending doom. Only three days left until the end of the month. What would happen then?

Luca stirs behind me and something hard and very familiar presses against my backside. "Mmm, good morning, princess." He nuzzles into my neck, and a wave of goosebumps ripples down my arm.

"It is a good morning." If I'm being honest with myself, I'd have to admit that the nights I've spent in bed with the mob boss have been the best sleep I've had in years.

"I can make it a better one." He slips under the covers and settles between my legs. I'm bare beneath his t-shirt as is he.

When he brought me home last night, we'd had sex for hours and he never took that damned shirt off. It was starting to bug me. He hovers over me, a wicked grin on those perfect lips. I wrap my hand around the back of his neck and jerk his mouth to mine.

I suck on his lower lip, so addicted to his sweet taste. As our tongues entangle in an already familiar dance, his hand skates beneath my—his shirt and finds my breast. Kneading it softly, my back arches at his touch.

Dio, just when I think this man cannot possibly coax another orgasm out of me, he has me soaked, ready and wriggling for his cock.

Luca lines himself up at my entrance and teases, running his head up and down my slick heat. "Mmm, princess… we need to get you on the pill. I want to feel your bare pussy taking all of me in."

A delicious shiver races up my spine. "I am actually on the pill."

His eyes widen, Adam's apple bobbing hard along the long column of his throat. "You are?"

"I have been for a while." A teasing grin parts my lips. "I just don't have sex with mob bosses that kidnap me without condoms."

"Oh really? Is that one of *your* rules?" He nudges into me, his tip pressing against my throbbing clit.

"It is. And a very important one," I rasp out. In a minute, I'll forsake every single rule myself just to have him inside me.

"Even for mob bosses who have religiously used condoms with every single sexual encounter and been meticulously tested for years?"

Figures the control freak C.E.O. would be all over that.

"I can show you my latest test if you want?" he continues.

Another smirk curls my lips. The fact that Luca wants me bad enough to break yet another rule brings me endless amounts of pleasure. I'm practically giddy.

He grips his cock and runs it up and down my entrance, asserting just the right amount of pressure. He glides between my folds, and my hips buck up to meet him. "Is that a yes, princess?" A glint of mischief sparks in those dark eyes.

I chew on my lower lip, pretending to consider.

"The answer better be a yes, or I'll have to punish you."

"You wouldn't dare."

"Oh, but I would. There's nothing I'd enjoy more than tossing you over my lap and smacking that perfect ass until it's a brighter red than your cheeks. Then I'd lick your sore skin, gliding my tongue over every inch of you."

Another shiver of excitement.

"I have a feeling you'd like it too."

I run my hands down his back and grab a handful of his muscled ass and drive him closer.

"Yes?" His lip twitches. "I need you to say it, princess."

"*Cazzo*, Luca," I groan. I'm going to come just from his tip teasing me.

He rocks his hips forward so that only his silky crown sinks in, and a moan escapes my clenched lips.

"More," I breathe, my fingers clenching around his ass and driving him deeper.

He fights me, his powerful thighs holding him steady.

"Pain in the *culo*," I grumble as I wriggle beneath him, desperate for more friction. "Yes, *cazzo*, Luca, I want you to fuck me without a condom. Happy?"

A shit-eating grin curls his kissable lips, and he plunges inside me so fast, my head falls back. I cry out his name. *Holy cannoli*, so much better without a condom. His hot skin sinks inside me, intensifying every thrust.

"That's a good girl," he whispers as he nails me to the bed. "I was right, this is so much better." His eyes roll back, lower lip caught between his perfect white teeth. "Your pussy is so hot and wet, just begging for my cock." He moans and *Dio*, I nearly come undone at the sound.

Instead, I try to focus on something else, anything else to extend the pleasure. He's still wearing his t-shirt, but I want to see all of him, his tattoos, even his scars. For some reason or another, I've never had a good look at his chest. Reaching for the hem of his black tee, I draw it up over his torso.

Luca freezes, balls deep inside me. "No," he grits out.

"No what?"

"Keep it on." A flicker of fear races across the murky depths of his irises.

"Why?"

"I—I'm all sweaty."

I arch a skeptical brow. "So what?"

His hand closes around my wrist, and dark eyes lock on mine. "Please, not yet," he whispers.

I'm so baffled by his request I can't summon a word out. Is he self-conscious about the scars? I couldn't imagine the cocky C.E.O. being insecure about anything. He starts to move against me, his cock hitting my clit at just the right angle and all other thoughts vanish.

I rock my hips up to meet his, harder, faster. I wrap my legs around his lower back, urging him on. He's so deep inside me I can't tell where he ends, and I begin. And it feels so damned right.

One more thrust and my pussy clenches around him, contracting as I ride out the best orgasm of my life. Just like the one before and the one before that. His cock pulses, and his warmth spills inside me. There's something so intimate about taking it all in. No awkward condom removal, just our haggard breaths as he collapses on top of me.

Luca presses his forehead to mine, noses touching. "You've ruined me, princess. And I want you to wreck me every damn day."

My throat tightens, and *Dio* I'm so happy I think I might cry. I quickly blink back the tears, so I don't look like a total *scema*. We only have three days left.

CHAPTER 39
A TICKING TIMEBOMB

Luca

Two days left.

The pit of unease grows in my gut with every passing moment. I haven't left Stella's side since the Met Gala. I spend half the day working and the other half fucking her across every surface of my penthouse. I was right all those weeks ago, she's instilled warmth in not only my home but every crevice of my dark heart and soul.

The idea of losing her is inconceivable.

Which is why I had Magda buy her this. I flip the white box around in my palm and stick the red bow my housekeeper bought on top of the gift. "Stella?" I call out. She should be dressed by now. After I fucked her in the shower, I left her to get ready while I went to grab the present from Magda. She's made herself scarce again like she has for the past few days since we've been screwing like rabbits. But I catch her knowing smiles. She's happy for us, and I don't know why it matters, but it does.

"Coming!"

I set the box on the marble island, the bright red bow standing out against all the white of the kitchen. Stella walks, in and her gaze darts to the gift. A heart-stopping smile parts her damned fuckable mouth, and her eyes lift to mine. "What's that?"

"A present. Long overdue."

Her brows furrow as she regards me. Inexplicable heat rises from my neck and spreads across my jaw. "Just open it."

So she does, like a good girl, for once.

When she pries the box open, her eyes light up. "A new phone!" She lunges at me and wraps her arms around my neck as she bounces up and down.

"It's got a new number too so none of your exes can harass you." *Namely, Bo.* She nods quickly and flips the power on so the sleek device flickers to life. "I already put Rose's number in there."

"Thank you!" She eyes the phone then me again. "So I can call her? Call whoever I want?"

"Yes."

She lets out a squeal, and my stupid heart staggers before firing back up. "I'm going to call Rose right now. We have a lot of catching up to do."

"Sure, go for it. I have to make a few business calls too."

She spins toward me and plants her lips against mine. Her entire body leans in, and my cock is instantly rock hard. She must feel it because she grins against my mouth. "Save it for later, Signor Valentino." With a wink, she saunters down the hallway, hips swaying to an invisible beat. It takes all my willpower not to run after her. I watch as she pauses at her bedroom in the hallway, then continues on to mine.

A storm of emotions batters my chest, a mix of ridiculous happiness and mind-numbing fear. I knew if I let Stella in, it would be over. One taste would never be enough. Now that she is in my life again, I couldn't let her go. But men like me don't get happy endings, we sure as fuck don't deserve them.

And if I hurt her somehow ... like Vinny ... I'd never forgive myself.

I release a howl of frustration and bury my face in my hands.

The ding of my cell phone distracts my dismal thoughts, and I eye the screen.

Tony: It's not looking good boss. The shithead is trying to take out another loan with the Red Dragons to cover what he owes you.

Merda. Of course, Liam McKenzie would try to find an easy way out. Owing the Red Dragons will only put Stella right back in the thick of it.

Me: Go to Jianjun and tell him to refuse. Under no circumstances is he to make a deal with him and spread the word around the city. No one is to give Liam McKenzie a loan, or they'll have to deal with me.

Tony: Got it, capo.

Fuck, why can't it just be easy for once? I stomp to the refrigerator and grab a beer. It's only noon, but I have a feeling I'll need it to get through today. Glancing at my phone again, I stare at the string of texts from Dante.

My *coglione* of a brother isn't taking no for an answer. He's insisting on apologizing to Stella, and I don't want him anywhere near her. Not now. Not when everything between us is so new and up in the air.

And perfect.

Not perfect, I remind myself as I press my palm to my heart. How many more times can I fuck her with my shirt on before she sees my tattoo? It's not just the sex, sleeping together complicates things further. I like to sleep naked, or with boxers at most. Falling asleep with a t-shirt every night feels suffocating.

Dark memories surface, the ones I've tried for years to forget. Pinned to the mattress. Shirt over my head. Trying to scream but my words are muffled by the fucking pillow.

I'd known getting initiated into the mob as a teen was going to be hell, but I'd never expected that. Or the rest of it. I squeeze my eyes shut, driving back the pain. After that day, I'd vowed never to be weak again.

And that's how I became the King.

I chug down a long gulp from the bottle, the bubbles going straight to my head and pushing away the grisly memories. I'd been tortured, beaten, and nearly raped. But somehow, I survived.

Now I'd focus all that anger, that rage, on protecting Stella. I'd never let anyone hurt her again. *Unless she gets hurt because of you.* That dark voice echoes through my mind, and fear's claws dig into my heart.

The sound of laughter drags me from the darkness and into the light of Stella's smile. She walks toward me, grinning so big my breath catches. She must still be talking to Rose. I lower the bottle of Peroni onto the countertop and wrap my arms around her middle. She giggles as I nuzzle her ear.

"Okay, Rose, I gotta go," she rasps out between fits of laughter as I dig my fingers into her sides.

"Remember, no hot Italian babies!" Her friend's warning reaches my ears before Stella ends the call.

Her cheeks flame as I regard her. "No babies, huh?"

"Not yet," she squeals. Then the enticing crimson hue only intensifies. "I mean, I wasn't saying we'd ever have babies … I just mean—"

I cut off her adorable ramblings with my mouth. The sick thing is nothing would make me happier than having a part of me growing inside her. To see her belly full with my child. The momentary joy is smothered by gut-wrenching fear. It's the number one reason for all my rules. It keeps everyone at a distance. If I don't care about anyone, I have nothing to lose.

And now with Stella, I have so fucking much to lose the terror is paralyzing.

She pulls back, eyes locked to mine. "Are you okay? You just went stiff on me." She reaches between us and cups my dick. "And I don't mean in the good way." A flirty smile flashes across that gorgeous mouth, and it settles the growing unease.

When I don't say anything for another long moment, Stella's hand envelops mine and she drags me to the couch. She pushes me down then crawls into my lap. The crushing pressure in my chest starts to relent.

"Tell me what's wrong." Her soft hand cups my cheek, and I'm filled with the most overwhelming desire to spill my darkest sins.

"You've often asked about my rules…," I begin.

Her lips purse, and something like fear flashes across the tranquil sea of blue.

"There are reasons for them."

She nods hesitantly.

"With the life I lead, love is weakness. Caring for anyone, sharing a life with someone, it only paints a target on their back." I pause and draw in a breath. "It's why I moved Ma outside the city, and I keep her far from the spotlight. And it's why I've always insisted on casual relationships. Ultimately, I inevitably hurt everyone around me, Stella. I closed off my heart so many years ago to keep the ones I love safe."

She shakes her head, tears welling in her eyes. Her hand slides off my cheek and rests over my heart. Directly over the date of Vinny's death. *Dio*, the guilt will drag me under if I don't admit the truth soon.

"You worry so much about others—who is there to take care of you?"

"No one, princess."

"Not anymore, *capo*." Stella brushes her lips against mine, and it's so achingly sweet and fiery, the layer of frost around my heart shatters.

I want nothing more than to give in to this woman, to make her mine forever. I know I don't fucking deserve her, but there is nothing I want more. Except her safety. For her to live a long, happy life. After all the shit she's been through, she deserves so much better.

As if she's read my thoughts, her mouth releases mine. A tear traces the perfect curve of her cheek, and I reach out to wipe it away. "Don't do this, Luca."

"Do what?" A jagged edge lingers in the air between us.

"Pull away from me in some misguided attempt to protect me."

The ghost of a smile tugs up the corners of my lips. She knows me too well. It's all at once disturbingly frightening and yet oddly satisfying.

"I've lost so much in my life," she whispers. "And at some point in the last four weeks, you became one of the few remaining things I can't bear the thought of losing. Please don't leave me. Especially not for my own good. There's nothing good left in my life without you."

Her words gut me. They carry the weight of all the pain she was forced to bear. Largely because of me. When Vinny died, not only had I robbed her of her brother, but also her substitute protector. I ran like a coward. Even after I'd heard her grandfather had died, leaving her truly unprotected, I never went back to check on her. I left her at the hands of fucking drunk Liam McKenzie. Somehow, I thought she'd be safer without me.

I was a complete *stronzo*. Seventeen and stupid.

No wonder she completely erased me from her memories.

"Promise me, Luca. Swear I won't lose you."

"I promise to always protect you, no matter what happens." It's the only vow I can make right now.

She eyes me for a long minute as if she's understood the difference in what she's asked and what I've promised. But she finally nods, somehow making peace with it. I press my lips to hers and show her how much I need her in the only way I know how.

CHAPTER 40
TIME'S UP

Stella

I stand in front of the mirror, gripping the marble vanity because it's the only thing keeping me upright. Time's up.

Today, my father is supposed to contact Tony to make his first monthly payment to repay the debt. Luca and I have expertly danced around the subject for the past two glorious days. We haven't emerged from the penthouse, have barely left his bedroom. It's like some unspoken pact we made to enjoy our final days together without any expectations.

But inside, inside I'm hollow.

Because *Dio*, I've gone and done the stupidest thing ever. I've fallen in love with Luca Valentino.

Every moment I spend with him I only fall deeper. He declared me his girlfriend at the gala, and I've stared at the shiny spread of the two of us in *The New Yorker* for hours. We appear to be the quintessential happy couple, but it's all based on a lie, on a debt owed.

A soft knock at the door shoots my heart up my throat. "Ready?" Luca's voice sounds garbled, but I'm fairly certain it's only a result of my thundering pulse across my eardrums.

Shit, Tony must have gotten the call. "Just a second," I squeeze out. A part of me aches to see my father, that's how stupid I am. I wonder if he's okay, if he's been drinking himself to death, if he held onto his last crappy job….

"Stella?" Even through the thick door, I can hear the concern in Luca's voice.

"Almost ready," I call out. Staring at my reflection, I take in my appearance. Despite the tears staining my cheeks, I look happier and healthier than I did a month ago. My dark hair is soft and sleek from the super-expensive hair products Luca spoils me with, my skin is practically glowing from the designer facial creams, and the dark hollows beneath my eyes have filled out from dreamless nights spent in the safety of Luca's arms.

The click of the doorknob twisting sends my heart aflutter. I hastily sweep away the remaining tears and splash some water on my face. Luca's arms weave around my waist, and he drops his chin on my shoulder. Through the mirror, his concerned gaze tightens my ribcage.

"You know I would never hurt you, right?" he murmurs against my bare shoulder. "That even if your father doesn't have the money, we'll come to some other agreement?"

"With him in a body bag?"

He shakes his head. "That *bastardo* doesn't deserve to live for what he's put you through, but I won't be the one to put him underground."

"What about Tony or Mickey?"

"It won't be under my order."

My throat thickens, raw emotion tearing up my airway.

"Everything is going to be okay, Stellina, I promise, just trust me." He twirls me around and folds me into his firm chest.

I want to believe him so badly. Breathing him in, I soak up that spicy scent that drives me wild and in the same instant, soothes my frayed nerves. He runs his hand down my arm, then entangles his fingers with my own.

"Come on, Mickey's waiting for us in the garage."

I must wince when the limo pulls up in front of the yellow awning of the familiar pawn shop because Luca's fingers tighten around my hand. I can't believe it was only a month ago I came here like a *scema* trying to save my dad. It seems like a lifetime ago.

Mickey opens the door to the backseat, and Tony's hulking shadow appears through the doorway. His thick, dark brows are gnarled. "He never showed, *capo*."

With those four words, my stomach plummets.

Luca lets loose a string of curses so vile even Tony's eyes look like they're going to pop out of his head. He motions to his right-hand man. "Get in, we're going to his house."

Tony folds his big form into a pretzel to enter the vehicle, then slides into the backseat beside Luca. They exchange a few words, but I can barely focus on their discussion over the maddening thunder of my heart.

He didn't even show up.

An entire month of no contact with his only daughter, and my dad didn't even have the decency to come in person and admit he didn't have the money. I'm not a complete *idiota*. I knew he had no way of scrounging up two thousand dollars. But to not come at all?

Luca doesn't even look at me as Mickey weaves the big ass limo through the crowded streets of China Town. His thigh pressed against mine vibrates with rage, his entire body stiff. An icy chill blankets my skin with each second he ignores me. I know he'd never hurt me, but what about my father?

The ruthless leader of the Kings couldn't let this sort of disrespect go unpunished.

That ten-minute ride is the longest of my life. When we pull up in front of *Nonna Maria's*, I dig through my purse until my fingers close around the small metal canister. Not pepper spray like last time. Only my inhaler. I turn away from Luca and take a quick puff, but there's no way he wouldn't hear the distinctive hiss.

Still, he doesn't offer a reassuring word.

Mickey opens the back door on Tony's side, and he and Luca slip out. I hurry after them, but our loyal driver is already closing it. "No!" I shout.

Luca's gaze remains trained straight ahead. "Don't let her out of the car," he mutters to Mickey.

"Luca!" I shout. "Don't do this!" I slam my fists into the door, screaming. "Please, Luca, no!"

Everything is going to be okay, Stellina, I promise, just trust me. His words from earlier echo in my mind with each punch to the unyielding glass. Knowing Luca, it's probably bullet-proofed. Not that he'd be stupid enough to leave me with a gun again.

I scramble across the backseat and search the secret compartment all the same. Empty.

Crawling back to the door where Mickey stands guard, I hiss out a volley of curses. "Mickey, please, let me out, please! I need to see my father."

The big goon ignores me, his broad shoulders blocking half the window. From the narrow rearview window, I can just make out Mrs. D. and her son, Giuseppe. Both are poking their heads out of the bakery take-out window.

Did they hear me?

I bang on the windows a few more times and wave frantically. Mrs. D. nods slowly and elbows her son. The pair disappears from the window and re-emerges a few desperately long minutes later at the front door of the bakery. Mrs. D. carries a plateful of cannoli, and Giuseppe follows a couple steps behind. If I wasn't so terrified, my mouth would've been watering at the sight of the fresh pastries.

"*Buongiorno*," says Mrs. D. and offers the plate to Mickey. "I make an extra batch. I know how Signor Valentino likes his cannoli."

Mickey reaches for one of the tasty treats, and Giuseppe nails him with a right hook. Damn. I had no idea Giuseppe had moves like that. Mickey's head bounces against the limo before his giant body collapses to the floor.

Mrs. D. wrenches the car door open, and I wrap my arms around her neck and press a kiss to each cheek. "Stella, *cosa è successo?*"

"Should we call the cops?" Giuseppe asks.

"No, please, you've done more than enough. I'll fill you in later, Mrs. D., I have to go." I release her and dart toward the entrance to my building. "Thank you both so much!" I call out over my shoulder before I race inside and slam the door behind me.

I've never taken the steps all the way up to the fourth floor so fast. My chest is heaving, but I don't stop for another puff of my inhaler. Fear blossoms in my heart, each step only intensifying the panic.

When I reach the fourth floor, I race across the squeaking wooden timber. Almost there. A shot rings out as my hand closes around the doorknob to my shitty apartment. Terror surges through my veins as I whip the door open.

Dad stands in the far corner with a gun in his hands and Tony trying to wrestle it away. My head swivels to the other side of the room, behind the open door, and I choke on a sob. Luca is on the floor. Deep crimson paints his crisp shirt and fine jacket.

God, no. I sprint for him and slide down to his side. His hands are clamped over the wound on his stomach. "Oh, *Dio*, what happened?"

"Well, your father, shot me, princess," he grits out.

I glance between the two mobsters and my father. No way drunk, pathetic Liam McKenzie got the slip on them. Luca must have warned Tony not to hurt him. Luca took a bullet for me instead.

"Luca …." My lip trembles. I place my hand over his to staunch the bleeding. The warm liquid pools between my fingers, and darkness consumes my vision. Vinny. Just like that, I'm twelve years old and back in that alleyway. My heart rebels against my ribcage, and my breaths come out in ragged spurts. I can't drag in a breath fast enough. My lungs refuse to pump.

I'm hyperventilating.

"Stella, breathe." Luca's soft voice cuts through the impending panic. "You're okay, and I'm going to be okay. It's just a flesh wound. I'll be fine."

A loud thud echoes behind me, and I spin around to find my dad on the floor.

Tony raises his hands innocently. "I just knocked the asshole out. He'll be fine, just a little knot on his head." He closes the distance between us and kneels down beside Luca. "How are you doing, *capo*?" Unbuttoning his shirt, he eyes the hole in his gut.

"I'll be fine as soon as the doc gets me stitched up."

Tony nods and pulls out his phone. He stands and moves to the bedroom to make the call. I can't take my eyes off Luca, the fear of losing him so acute I can barely sit up from the strangling emotions. Hot tears burn my eyes; a drop trickles over then another.

I draw in a breath. *Dio, please don't take him away from me. Not like Vinny. Not like Mom.*

"Just don't look at it," Luca hisses through clenched teeth. "Keep your eyes on me."

I should be the one trying to calm him, not the other way around. Tears stream down my cheeks, and I quickly swipe them away. "Never do that again," I cry. "You should've let me come with you. I could've handled it."

He shakes his head, anguish carved into the hard set of his jaw. "No, you don't need to see this *merda*. This dark side of my life." He reaches for my face, hand covered in his own blood, and still, I lean into his palm. "You are my light, Stella, you're everything good that is a part of me. I want to protect you from all of this shit. I hate that you have to see this, that you have to witness the reality of the monster that lies beneath the surface."

"You're not a monster, and I love you, Luca. And even if you were, I'd love you all the same." I slide my hand to his heart, and it beats wildly beneath my palm. Between my bloodied fingers, I can just make out black numbers hidden beneath the intricate tattooed pattern.

6.15.16

Ice water rushes my veins, and a whirlwind of flashing images race through my mind. Squeezing my eyes closed, I glance up. "Luca …?"

That piercing agony lines the corners of his eyes.

"Why do you have the date of my brother's death tattooed to your chest?" My voice is not my own, the eerie, icy calm belonging to a stranger. All this time with Luca and I'd never mentioned Vinny, not once. Why?

His lips press into a tight line, and he heaves out a breath. "I can't believe you don't remember me," he murmurs.

I blink quickly as a carousel of images spin through my mind. Vinny. Me. And Luca. My mom's funeral. The movie theater. Nights at the soccer field.

My stomach revolts, and I spin around just in time. I spew the contents of my empty gut all over the peeling linoleum. The warmth of Luca's hand spills across my back as he rubs slow circles. It's too much. Too much emotion, too much pain.

I whirl on him. "Why didn't you tell me who you were? Why did you disappear? Where were you all these years?"

His brows slam together, and darkness carves into his features. The tendon in his jaw twitches, his molars grinding so hard I can hear them.

"Tell me!" I cry.

"It was my fault Vinny died." Tears glisten through the bottomless midnight of his irises. "I was with him that night. I was supposed to protect him, and I failed."

I stare at him, my mind too numb to form words. Luca. My Luca? He'd been with Vinny when he died? There'd been no one there when I arrived. He was alone in a pool of his own blood.

"How could you?" I rasp out.

"I'm so sorry, Stellina."

"Don't call me that!"

Only Vinny called me his little star, and he was gone ….

I swallow hard, another wave of nausea threatening its way up my throat. "I—I can't …." I bury my head in my hands and force myself to stand. "I have to get out of here."

"Please, Stella, no. Let me explain." He tries to stand but his teeth clamp shut as the movement rips at the wound. "Please…," he murmurs. "Stella, I love you."

His words carve a hole in my vacant chest. He lied to me for an entire month. He deserted me when Vinny died. He'd left me alone with all that pain, all that guilt. "*Vaffanculo*, Luca Valentino. You abandoned me, you ran away like a fucking coward. You have no idea what love is, you *bastardo*."

In a blur of tears, I race across the tiny living room in a mad dash to the door. I vaguely hear Tony sprinting out of the bedroom. Then Luca's voice. "No, let her go."

CHAPTER 41
TORTURE

L*uca*

Dio, I feel like shit. If only the pain were skin deep. I glance down at the neatly wrapped bandages across my torso and wince. The bullet went clean through, avoiding all my vital organs according to the doc. Too bad it missed my heart. Damned thing hasn't been the same since Stella ran out on me a week ago.

"*Stella, I love you.*" The words I'd kept locked up for so long ring like mad across my mind.

"Vaffanculo, *Luca Valentino. You abandoned me, you ran away like a fucking coward. You have no idea what love is, you* bastardo." And her response. Also, not entirely wrong. Maybe Stella's right, and I really don't understand the meaning of the word. But *cazzo*, it sure as hell feels real.

The past week without her has been torture. I can't sleep, I can't eat, I can barely breathe. The penthouse is cold and empty without her, much like my heart. I'd been such a fucking idiot not to tell her the truth from the beginning.

A buzz draws my attention to my cell on the nightstand. With a grunt, I pick up my phone and scan the incoming message. Mickey. I've had him tailing Stella since the moment she ran out of her old apartment. I live for the occasional updates. For the past week, she's been holed up in her friend Rose's place. At least she's safe.

The girl lives in a studio in a decent part of mid-town. I had Tony run a full background check. No boyfriend, decent family from Long Island. She and Stella attend the same community college and like she'd mentioned, her friend is studying to be a psychologist. Maybe she'll talk some sense into Stella.

And she'll abandon me forever.

That would be the noble thing to do: let her go. For the record, noble hurts like hell.

A soft knock on the door pulls my lips into a frown. Magda has been doting on me, waiting on me hand and foot, and I just want to be left alone to my misery. "What?" I bark.

"Signor Valentino, Dr. Filippo is here."

Ugh. Another one who's giving me more attention than I deserve. I force myself to sit up, and this time the pain is minimal. Physically, anyway. "Fine, let her in," I finally grumble.

Magda opens the door, and the doc saunters in all ruby-lipped and high-heeled. I remember a time when the gorgeous doctor made my dick twitch. Now I feel nothing. Empty. Numb.

"Ciao, *bello*. You're looking better." She sets down her briefcase and pulls out the now familiar medical equipment. "How do you feel?"

"Like I was shot."

"Seems like your humor is progressing nicely."

"He won't get out of bed," Magda murmurs from the hallway.

I shoot her a traitorous glare. Maybe it's time to send her on that vacation she always refuses to take. A week or two alone could be just what I need. To wallow in self-pity.

"Luca, you know how this works." The doc looks up at me, stethoscope hanging around her neck. "The longer you remain immobile, the more difficult the recovery."

How do I tell her I don't give a shit? That without Stella I have no purpose, no reason to live. She's my shining light in the infinite darkness and damn it, without her the black is so thick I can't push past it.

She continues the checkup, gingerly removing the bandages to observe the wound. "It looks like you're healing nicely. I suppose that's the one plus to continuous bed rest."

I release a noncommittal grunt as she continues her quiet scrutiny.

How did I get here? Oh, right, I threw all my rules out the window and completely fucked up my world. That's why the rules were in place. That's why I'd gotten so far in life. One glorious month with Stella and everything had gone to shit.

The corners of my lips lift as images of her perfect pink lips, that fiery gaze, the feel of her against me fill my mind. *Dio*, I fucked everything up, but a tiny part of me would do it a hundred times over for that one month with her.

"Now that's what I want to see." Dr. Filippo grins as she gently replaces the bandages. "Whatever just made you smile, do more of that."

A rueful chuckle spills out. "I thought you said no sex until I'm fully healed."

She swats at me with her perfectly manicured fingernails. "I did. But that can't be the only thing that makes you smile."

No, it's not. Right now, just being next to Stella would be enough. Even if I could never touch her again, I'd survive if I just knew she was okay. A tornado of guilt lashes at my insides. She must hate me. And deservedly so.

I'd been such a coward abandoning her back then. Not only had I robbed her of her brother, I'd left her alone to fend against her asshole of a father. Sure, I was only seventeen back then, but I was a complete *stronzo*. I knew I was wrong. I'd promised Vinny I'd always protect Stella, and I abandoned her.

"Well, if you don't need anything else …." The doc stands, drawing me back to the present. "I'll be back next week to check on the stitches."

I slowly dip my head. "Thank you."

She squeezes my arm and offers a warm smile. "I've stitched you up more times than I can count, Luca, and I've never seen you like this. I don't like it."

"Just out of sorts," I manage.

"I hope you're back to your old self when I see you again."

I nod. I'm going to have to pull my head out of my ass before my empire crumbles. With Dante out, Clara has been manning the King Industries' ship, and the amount of stress I've laid on my executive assistant isn't fair. She's a tiger so I know she can handle it, but it's not right. I can't sit in bed forever.

I force myself to watch as Dr. Filippo sashays out, swinging her hips in that tight white medical coat, but I feel nothing. There's only one woman I want. And maybe I have been too much of a coward to admit it. I throw the covers back and slide to the edge of the mattress.

Magda lets out a squeal when I hiss from the pain, and I find her lingering in the doorway. "May I help you, signore?" she whispers and takes a step inside. Brave woman, considering the scowl I can feel twisting my lips.

"No," I snarl. "I have to do this myself." Slowly, I push myself off the bed. Another hiss escapes my clenched teeth as my torn skin stretches when I stand.

Muffled shouts coming down the hall put an end to my pity party. I stand up straighter and force my legs to the door. I recognize that voice. Pure, undiluted rage courses at the sound of it.

I march out into the hallway and find Albie and Dante in the foyer. My guard is trying to force my brother back, but he's being an asshole as always.

Albie catches my gaze over Dante's shoulder. "Sorry, *capo*. He wouldn't take no for an answer. He shoved right past me and got into the elevator before I could stop him. I didn't think you'd want me to shoot him."

A wry grin curls my lips. The first real emotion I've felt in days.

"*Cazzo*, come on, Luca." Dante spins on me. "I just wanted to check on you, *fratellino*. Tony tells me you were shot, and he won't say more. I've texted, called and you ignore me. Mamma's going crazy. You can't do this to her."

Another wave of guilt slaps me in the face. I never want to worry Ma, not her. She doesn't deserve it. "I'll call her as soon as you leave," I grumble.

"What the hell happened?"

"It's none of your business." I barrel past my brother, and my knees tremble from the effort. After a week of bedrest, all this commotion is too much. Weak bastard. Sinking onto the couch, my thoughts rush back to a week ago, to the first time I claimed Stella right here on this spot. I'd broken all my rules for her, and she'd broken me.

"This is about Stella, isn't it?" Dante glances around the penthouse as if he's finally noticed her absence. I feel it every fucking second. The emptiness, the chill. It's invaded my very bones. "What happened with Liam McKenzie?"

I snort on a laugh. The sound is high-pitched and slightly unhinged. "The fucker shot me."

"What?"

"I couldn't kill him. I wouldn't hurt Stella like that, so I took the bullet instead."

Dante slinks closer, like a hunter approaching a wounded animal. He folds down beside me when I don't bite his head off and releases a breath. Like he'd been holding it the whole time. "Where is he now?"

"Fuck if I know."

"And Stella?"

Her name on his lips is like a blade to my battered heart. "Don't fucking say her name," I rasp out.

"Luca, I don't know how many more times I can apologize. I was just protecting you. I thought the Red Dragons had sent her to fuck with you."

"You tried to rape her!" I shout.

"I was only trying to scare her, Luca, *lo giuro*. I thought if I roughed her up a little, she'd admit the truth. I swear I never would've actually assaulted her like that. What the fuck kind of monster do you think I am?"

I bury my face in my hands and huff out a frustrated breath. I can't go another round of this. Not right now. "I don't want to hear it, Dante. It's over."

"Where is she?"

It takes my final threads of restraint not to bash his teeth in. "She's safe for now. That's all you need to know. Anyway, it's probably better this way. The further Stella is from me, from us, the safer she'll be."

"*Dio*, Luca, you're in love with her."

His words slice me open, and I grit my teeth to keep the pain at bay. My molars are clenched so hard I'm certain I'll file them down to nubs.

He stands and paces a tight circle. "*Cazzo, fratellino*, I'm sorry. I thought she had you all twisted up because you hadn't screwed her. I had no idea you were in love with her."

"Stop saying that," I grit out. "It doesn't matter anymore. I fucked everything up. She knows about Vinny … she knows everything."

"*Merda*."

"Yeah." I drag my hands over my face, wishing I could

disappear. Admitting this shit to my asshole brother is the cruelest torture.

"Signore?" Magda peers up from across the kitchen island.

"Yes?"

"If I may speak honestly?" She wrings her hands before folding them on the counter.

Dante rolls his eyes, and if I wasn't so weak I'd slug him for his incessant disrespect of my staff.

"Go ahead, Magda," I say on an exhale.

"I've been working with you for almost five years now, and I've never seen you as happy as you were when Stella arrived." She pauses and fiddles with her apron, keeping her head down. "I don't know the details of what's happened between you, but it's clear to anyone with eyes that she loves you too. Fix whatever you've done and bring her back home."

My heart sinks. The penthouse never truly felt like home until Stella invaded it. She left her mark in every corner and now with her gone, it feels colder than ever before. "I don't know if I can fix this, Magda."

Dante shifts beside me, and I can practically feel his unspoken disapproval. My brother has a lot of shit to say about my love life, but his is no better.

"Of course, you can," Magda continues. "She loves you and love is the strongest thing in this world. Not money, not influence, not power. Love. You go find her, Signor Valentino, and you win her back."

I steal a glance at Dante from the corner of my eye. I wait for his rebuttal, but he remains silent for once.

I must be totally *pazzo* or maybe the doc slipped me something when she came because my chest is filled with hope. It's silly and ridiculous, but *Dio* I have to try, right?

CHAPTER 42
BECAUSE OF ME

S tella

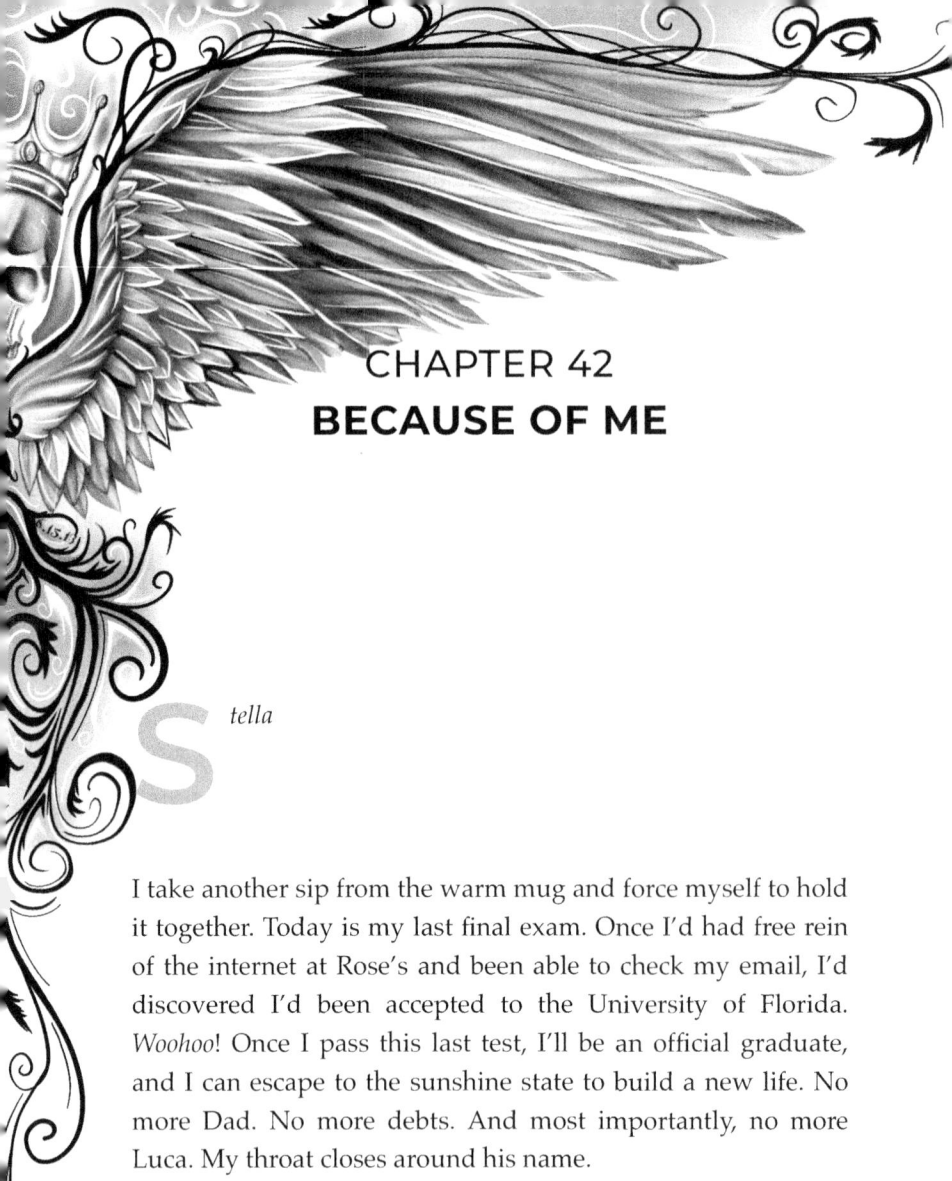

I take another sip from the warm mug and force myself to hold it together. Today is my last final exam. Once I'd had free rein of the internet at Rose's and been able to check my email, I'd discovered I'd been accepted to the University of Florida. *Woohoo*! Once I pass this last test, I'll be an official graduate, and I can escape to the sunshine state to build a new life. No more Dad. No more debts. And most importantly, no more Luca. My throat closes around his name.

How could I have been so stupid? Just call me fucking Lois Lane. I was so blind to what had been right in front of me the whole time. *Dio*, I'd adored Luca as a kid. He was my first crush. We'd spent practically every day together that summer before Vinny died. How could I have forgotten him?

According to Rose, psychologist extraordinaire, the memories were too painful, so I'd blocked them to protect myself. Sounded pretty insane to me, but it also explained so much. I'd felt an instant connection to that mobster *bastardo*. I'd blamed it on lust because the man was unfairly gorgeous, but at least now I understood it was more.

Only a complete *pazza* would fall in love with her captor.

And that's what I'd done. Tears fill my eyes, and I can barely keep them at bay.

I love you. Luca's words echo in my mind, the confession tearing at my fragile insides. I'd never wanted to hear those three words more than from his lips. But not then. Not when he'd just admitted to all the lies.

Dad had always blamed Nonno for Vinny's death. He'd thought his mafia dealings had led to the attack, and in a way he'd been right. Long buried memories flit to the surface. The dark alleyway, the pounding of my heart ….

"I want to work for Nonno too." Vinny.

My brows knit as I regard my brother. Our entire lives our mom had drilled into our heads that Nonno was dangerous. "You can't," I squeal.

Luca. A much younger version whips his head back and forth. "Absolutely not. That would be the opposite of keeping you out of trouble."

"But I want to be like you, Luca. I want to be strong and capable of protecting my little sister."

Vinny's words encircle my throat and tighten, strangling me. It wasn't Luca's fault Vinny died; it was mine. The only reason my brother started following Luca around was to protect me. He wanted to learn to fight, to be tough like him, so he could stand up to our abusive father.

Guilt crashes over me, threatening to pull me under. Vinny is dead because of me. That's why I'd blocked everything out. It's my fault. I choke on a sob as tears blur my vision.

The whine of squeaky hinges forces my gaze up. Rose saunters out of the bathroom in a plush pink robe. "You ready for your big test, girl?"

Blinking back the tears as she marches closer, I gulp down the rest of my coffee. "Yup."

She cocks her head, eyeing me. "Are you okay, Stells?"

Lower lip quivering, I clench my jaw to keep from bawling like a baby. Rose has been the most incredible friend. She took me in without question when I showed up at her door, teary-eyed and blood-stained. After hysterically crying for hours, I'd told her everything.

"It's my fault," I mumble.

"What is?" She sinks into the chair at the tiny table for two and scoots it beside me.

"That Vinny died." My throat closes around the last word, and my shoulders tremble.

Rose throws her arms around me and pulls me into a hug. "No way. It can't be your fault."

"He started hanging out with Luca to protect me. If it hadn't been for me, he never would've been in that alley that night. He never would've been shot."

"Stells, Vinny was your big brother. It's his literal job to protect you. It's not your fault. He loved you and that's what we do for those we love. It's like encoded in our genetic makeup. Trust me, I'm a future psychologist, remember?"

I appreciate her attempt to make me smile, but I can't summon the energy. Instead, I bury my face in her chest and sob some more. A part of me realizes the truth in her words, but if there's no one to blame then how does something like that happen? How could God take away my brother so soon after my mom? And on the same damned date! It just wasn't fair.

Rose frames my puffy cheeks with her slender hands. "You think you can hold it together for a few more hours so you can pass your final exam? Then we can have a girl's night and suck down bottles of wine and shovel heaping spoonsful of ice cream down our throats all night. What do you say?"

I force my head to nod. I've worked too hard to quit now. Just one little test and I'm free.

Rose helps me stand and with another tight squeeze, finally releases me. "Give me a second, and I'll walk you to class?"

"Nah, I'll be fine. You're not even dressed yet."

"You sure?" She squeezes my hands between hers.

"Yeah." I sniffle one last time and drag my finger under my eyes to wipe away the remaining traces of tears.

"Okay, but promise to come straight home so we can celebrate?"

"Deal," I mumble. Grabbing my backpack, I force my feet out the front door of the studio, my chest a tiny bit lighter than before.

Two hours later, and I'm almost happy. *I'm done*! I'd officially finished all my pre-requisites and assuming I hadn't failed any of my finals, I'd be the proud recipient of an associate degree from the Borough of Manhattan Community College. It sure as hell wasn't NYU, but I'd take it. It was my ticket out of here.

Pulling out my phone, I shoot a quick text message to Rose.

> Me: Finished! On my way home.
>
> Rose: Congrats! Wine is chilled, and ice cream is waiting.
>
> Me: You're the best.
>
> Rose: I know ;)

That dreaded weight on my shoulders doesn't feel quite so heavy as I weave through the streets of lower Manhattan. I try to picture a new life for myself in sunny Gainesville, Florida.

I've never been to the university, but the campus looks beautiful with ivy-covered red brick buildings nestled within the swamp. I'm not too sure how I feel about alligators, but they can't be any worse than the rats. Or the Red Dragons.

My thoughts instantly zip to Luca.

The idea of being so far away from him unearths a surge of panic. My chest tightens and I slow, reaching for my inhaler. For a few glorious days, I thought he was my future. That the mob boss and I could actually have our happily ever after. But he'd lied.

And I didn't have room for liars in my life. The men I'd grown up with had constantly hurt and disappointed me. Even Vinny, though of no fault of his own, had abandoned me. He'd been ripped away from me, but still. I didn't know how to trust a man.

How could I ever trust Luca after all the lies?

And still, as I envision my bright shiny future in Florida, a hole burrows deeper into my heart at that future without him.

The shuffle of approaching footsteps sends my head swiveling over my shoulder. Two guys in dark hoodies quicken their step when I spot them. I lengthen my stride, my eyes on the subway station at West 14th Street just ahead. The streets are quiet except for the slap of the males' footfalls on the concrete and the increasing tempo of my heartbeat.

Shit. What now?

I finger the small cannister tucked into my other pocket. Not my inhaler. Since I moved into Rose's place, I started carrying the pepper spray again. A girl can't be too safe, right?

The blue line comes to view, and I rush down the steps onto the subway platform. Three guys in red t-shirts stand by a graffitied bench. A familiar toothy smile sends chills down my spine. *Merda.* Bo's sneer only widens when he catches scent of my fear. I spin around to escape, but the two guys in hoodies block the exit. Feng, Bo's cousin, and another guy I vaguely recognize.

"Where you going, Stella?" Bo calls out. "I've been looking for you, ya know?"

I wrap my arms across my chest and glare down at him. From my spot a few steps up on the staircase, at least I can look down on the *bastardo*. "What do you want?" I hiss out.

"I heard you and your guido boyfriend broke up. Which I assume means you're fair game now?"

"I still wouldn't touch you with a ten-foot pole."

A couple of his buddies snicker, and his cocky sneer curls into a scowl. "From what I remember, you loved my cock."

"That was before I had a real one."

"Oooh." More laughter echoes across the silent platform.

"You'll pay for that, bitch." Bo lunges and catches me around the waist before I can reach for the pepper spray. His friends close in around me.

I scream and pummel his chest with my fists as he squeezes me hard against him. He grinds his hips against mine, and his tiny erection brushes my belly. Nausea sneaks up my throat, but I swallow it down and force out a sharp laugh instead. "Your cock's so small no wonder you never got me off. Not like Luca can."

A sharp sting bites into my cheek, and I let out a curse. That asshole slapped me. "Don't touch me!" I snarl.

"Oh, I'm going to do so much worse than just touch you, you little whore."

"Fuck you!" I howl then spit in his face.

Bo's eyes widen, the tiny slits rounding to full, white orbs.

The sound of a scuffle fills me with a swirl of hope. I spin around, and a familiar dark suit charges down the steps.

"Albie!" I cry.

Bo grips my face, jerking it toward him. He squeezes my cheeks, and I let out another squeal. He gets so close I'm terrified he's going to kiss me. Instead, his forehead rams mine and pain lances through my skull. I see lights for an instant, and then everything fades to black.

CHAPTER 43
PAIN IS BETTER THAN FEAR

L*uca*

"Just go, Dante." I stand at the elevator, leaning against the wall for support. I'd been a *coglione* hiding in bed for a week. Now, I could barely stand up straight.

My brother is parked in front of the elevator, his jaw set in a hard line. It reminds me of when we were kids. He was older and bigger, and he'd use it against me. Then I shot up past him, and the tables were turned. Now, we were back at square one.

"I'm not leaving until you tell me you'll at least try to forgive me."

"I can't!" I growl.

"We've been brothers for twenty-seven years, damn it, Luca." He drags his hand through his dark hair and when he looks up at me all I see is Papà. Whenever I run into Dad's old associates, they say I'm his spitting image, until Dante walks into the room. "I fucked up. I'll do anything to make it up to you. To Stella too. Please."

I'm about to shove him through the open elevator when my phone pings. I drag it out of my pocket and scan the message. Ice floods my veins.

> Albie: Bo and his guys took Stella. I tried to stop them, but there were too many of them. Sorry, capo.

My finger jabs at the call button on the screen as I curse the incompetent *cornuto* from here to kingdom come. He answers on the first ring, voice trembling.

"Where did they take her?" I bark.

"I don't know, *capo*. Bo and his crew knocked me out. They snatched her at the West 14th Street subway. I'm assuming they were taking the A line back to China Town, but I don't know. I'm so sorry, boss."

"Fuck," I growl.

"What's wrong?" Dante eyes me.

I consider my promise to Stella. I'd sworn to cut Dante out of my life, but right now I need him. He still had connections and maybe one of those could help me find her. She's all that matters. I'd rather have her alive and hating me than the alternative.

"Damned Bo and the Red Dragons snatched Stella." The moment the words are out suffocating fear blossoms in my chest. Oh *Dio*, if anything happens to her. I reach for the wall to steady myself. I take in a grounding breath, and I allow the icy calm to rush over me. Rage crowds out the panic, and I shove Dante out of the way. "If you're coming with me now's your chance. If you expect me to ever forgive you, this would be the moment to come through for me."

He nods quickly and reaches for his phone. He's shot out a

dozen messages before we reach the ground floor. I have no idea where they've taken Stella, but I'm starting with the Red Dragon; I'll shoot up the entire fucking place until Jianjun tells me where to find her. I send a frenzied message to Tony and the guys to scour China Town.

"Relax, Luca, we'll find her." My brother's hand lands on my shoulder, and it isn't until I see his hand vibrating that I realize my whole body is shaking with fury.

When the elevator doors open, I go straight for my motorcycle. No way faster through city traffic.

"You sure that's a good idea?" Dante eyes me and jerks his chin at my stomach. In the craze, I'd completely forgotten about my wound. The pain will only fire up the rage.

"I'll be fine," I grit out. "Meet me at the Red Dragon."

He nods and stalks toward his Beamer, and I round the Ducati. I swing my leg over the seat and biting pain races up my torso. *Merda*. Gritting my teeth, I slide my helmet over my head and fasten it. Pain is good. Pain is better than fear.

In seconds, I zip through city traffic, my head in a tailspin. If that asshole hurts a single hair on Stella's head, I'll gut him. I'll rip Bo Zhang apart and spread his entrails across China Town for all to see. Is he fucking *pazzo*, taking what's mine?

Oh *Dio*, Stella.

A spool of dread unwinds in my gut. *You let her go.* She's been unprotected for an entire week. *This is your fault.* That dark voice winds around my lungs, squeezing the air out. A horn blares, and I weave to the right, barely avoiding getting plowed into by a turning taxi cab. *Fuck.* I'm no good to her dead. Focusing on the road, I gun the engine and roar down the FDR.

When I reach the Red Dragon, I leap off the bike and hiss out a slew of curses as my stitches rip. I take a second to assess the damage, taking a peek beneath my shirt. Only a little blood dribbles from the wound. Minor setback. I race up the steps and find the same hostess from last week. At least it's before the lunch rush today, and the dining room is quiet. "Where's Bo?" I snarl.

"He's not here."

I reach into the waistband of my pants and pull out my handgun. "Where is he?" I hiss. "Think quickly. I don't want to hurt you, but I'm kind of desperate here."

Jianjun appears from the back, and I barrel past the hostess and train the gun on him instead. His eyes narrow as he regards me, but he holds his own.

"Where is your piece of shit son?" I bark.

His lips curve into a frown. "I do not know."

"Well, if you want him to survive the day, you better find him now." I barely register the jingle of the front door opening.

"Luca, *che cazzo fai?*" My brother howls.

I move closer to Jianjun and press the gun to his temple. "I warned you and your son if any harm came to Stella it would constitute an act of war. Is that what you want, old man?"

"No," he grits out.

"Then tell me where he is. I know where all your cocaine is stashed across Meatpacking. One word from me and it all goes up in smoke."

"I told you I have no idea where he is." He barks something to the girl at the front in Mandarin. "But I will be happy to help you find him."

"Would you really?" I press the barrel tighter to his skull. "Because I don't believe a fucking word out of your mouth."

More Red Dragons spill from the back of the restaurant.

"Luca, easy." Dante is behind me now, but I don't dare give Jianjun my back. He might be old, but he's as cunning as they come.

"I regret the poor decisions my son has made regarding your girlfriend, but I swear I had no idea of his intentions. You know I value our working relationship."

"Fuck our relationship. Fuck everything, Jianjun. I will raze the entire Meatpacking district if you do not return her to me unharmed."

"That will not be necessary." Tiny beads of perspiration line the old man's brow, barely perceptible. It only fuels my rage. I want this man on his knees pissing his pants from fear. "I will do everything I can to help find your girl," he adds.

"Yes, that's right, *my girl*. Mine." Crimson seeps into my vision, and I can feel my control slipping. "Fuck!" I roar. "Where is he?"

The hostess scrambles toward us, muttering in Mandarin.

"I'm sorry, but he is not with my men," says Jianjun, the picture of calm and collected. That used to be me. Now sweat drips off my brow, and my heart is like a sledgehammer against my ribcage.

I reach into my pocket with my free hand and slip my fingers through my custom brass knuckles. If Jianjun won't tell me the truth, I'll beat it out of him.

A few of Jianjun's men raise their weapons.

Dante's hand closes around my wrist. "No, Luca. Not like this."

"*Vaffanculo*," I rasp out. "You don't understand. I can't lose her." Nausea claws its way up my throat, and I barely keep the contents of my stomach down.

Black blankets my vision, and I'm back in that alleyway with Vinny in my arms.

The pungent, metallic scent of blood fills my nostrils. Hot tears spill down my cheeks, and my shoulders tremble with a sob. "Vinny, hold on. The ambulance is coming." I broke rule number one, never call the cops. But with one look at my best friend bleeding out, I knew I couldn't do it. Fuck the rules. "Hold on, amico, *please. Do it for Stella; she needs you."*

"Promise me," he whispers, nothing more than a gurgle of air. "You'll take care of her."

Another sob rips through my clenched teeth. "No, don't say that. You're going to be fine."

"*Promise me,*" he mouths.

I squeeze my friend's limp body to my chest, my insides caving in on me. "I swear it, Vinny. *Lo giuro.* I'll always protect her."

His head falls back, and his eyes glaze over as he stares into the night sky.

"No!" A shriek fills the silence, and I'm too fucking gone to realize it came from me. I hug my best friend tighter, his blood soaking into my shirt.

I'm trembling. A firm hand holds me steady. "Luca! Snap out of it." Dante gives me another shake. Jianjun coalesces before me, his wiry white brows tangled. My brother pries the gun from my hands and pockets it before he flashes his phone in my face. "One of my guys got a lead on Stella. Let's move." He shoves me toward the exit, my mind still swimming.

I don't even remember I've abandoned the Ducati at the Red Dragon until my hazy thoughts come to focus as we speed down the West Side Highway. Dante's driving, white-knuckling the steering wheel.

"We'll find her, I swear," he mutters.

Fuck. I'm having a mental breakdown, and now is not the time. Forcing my mind to sharpen, I focus on Stella. She trusts me. I promised Vinny to keep her safe. I failed him once; I won't do it again. "Give me my gun back."

Dante eyes me, a skeptical twist to his lips.

"I'm better now, *coglione*. Just do it."

He digs it out of his waistband and hands it over.

"Where are we going anyway?"

"Charlie said he saw Bo and some of his guys go into a warehouse in Meatpacking. He didn't see a girl, but maybe they had her hidden or something."

My gut twists. "Where's Tony and the rest of them?"

"Meeting us there."

"Good." I squeeze my fingers into fists to keep them from shaking. I bury the fear deep within the rage and allow it to flow freely. Then, I wait for the icy calm.

CHAPTER 44
PAYBACK

*S*tella

A pounding headache forces my heavy lids open. I blink quickly, shoving back the lingering haze as memories flit to the surface. The subway station. Bo. *Merda*. Metal bites against my wrists as I try to move. My shoulder blades burn from being forced behind my back. I sit in a hard metal chair, my legs and arms bound.

Fear lances through my chest as I take in the murky surroundings. Once my eyes adjust to the darkness, the sprawling warehouse takes shape. Soaring metal rafters overhead and massive rusted containers surround me.

We must be near the water. Right? They have to load these containers somewhere.

A strip of small windows lines the top of the vast space, but they're too small and too far to make out any details. I try to wriggle my hand through the metal cuff but it's too damned tight. My pepper spray sits in my pocket taunting me.

All that time wasted with Luca. I should've spent it learning how to fight like he did. Dark memories surge to the surface. Vinny, bullets in his torso, lying in a pool of his own blood. I squeeze my eyes shut to bury the images, but in the dark of this godforsaken warehouse, it's all I see.

Dad was wasted, too drunk to get out of bed when we'd gotten the call from the cops. So I'd gone by myself at twelve years old. More memories flood my mind. My small hands trembling. My heart racing so fast because I'd taken too many puffs from my inhaler. I'd called Luca on my way, and he'd never answered. Never returned my call.

He'd completely disappeared.

How had I not put it together back then?

Nonno died a few weeks after Vinny. A heart attack. Had it been guilt? Had he known all along that it was because of him my brother was dead? So many people to blame … and yet none of it mattered because nothing would bring him back.

A door whips open and light spills into the obscure space, tearing me from my twisted thoughts. I stiffen my lower lip and sit as straight as I can with the cuffs digging into my wrists.

"Ah, there she is, Luca's little whore." Bo's eyes gleam as they raze over me.

I must look like total shit. "He's going to gut you for this," I spit. "And then I'll dance over your entrails."

"Are you sure?" He stalks toward me and grips my chin, forcing my eyes to his. "I thought you guys broke up?"

"Fuck you."

"Soon." A twisted sneer curves the ends of his thin lips. "I've been waiting for weeks, Stella, waiting and waiting to catch you alone. Even when you moved out of his place, one of his guys was constantly on you."

My brows knit. He'd had me followed?

"For an entire week, I had your friend's apartment surveilled."

Of course, the one time I left Rose's studio was to take that damned test. I better have passed after all this. I glare up at him, steeling my nerves. "For just a whore, you sure seem pretty obsessed with me."

His fingers release my chin and tangle in my hair. He rips it back, but I bite my tongue to hold in the scream. I'll never give him the satisfaction.

"It's payback, babe. Luca Valentino is an arrogant guido, and it's time he's put in his place."

"It's your funeral," I scoff.

He steps closer still, that twisted grin growing wider. "Maybe, or maybe, he'll be so bent after I'm through with you he'll kill himself and do us all a favor."

Icy fear races down my spine. I'd been banged up quite a few times as a kid, hell even as an adult my dad had slapped me around more than I cared to admit. I'd put up with a lot, but there is no way I'm letting this motherfucker touch me.

He looms over me, and it takes everything I have to keep from shaking. Throwing my shoulders back, I glare up at him. "I'll never give you what you want."

"Oh yeah, and what do you think that is?"

"Me." I shoot him a saccharine smile. "After all this time, that's what you wanted, right? That's why you attacked me in the subway all those months ago. You wanted me back and I refused to return to your tiny, limp dick."

The slap ricochets across the thick silence. I bite back another scream, refusing to give him the pleasure of my pain.

"Shut your mouth, you little whore."

I force my lips to slide into a smile despite the sting. "What's wrong? You don't want your buddies to know what a terrible lay you are? That I faked it every time? Or maybe that Luca fucked me so good he erased every miserable time with you?"

A few of the guys chuckle, and rage flashes across Bo's

almond eyes until they grow to full furious circles. "I'm going to fuck that smile right off your face."

Bile oozes up, but I swallow it down forcing my expression to stay calm. I just need him to untie me, and I can reach my pepper spray. From there, I run. I'd rather be shot in the back than suffer his disgusting hands on me. "I'd like to see you try," I egg him on.

"Untie her," he barks at his cousin.

"Are you sure?" Feng's dark brows bunch together.

"I said fucking untie her."

Feng walks around behind me, and I drag in a steadying breath. I have to time it right, or I'll have five guys on me. He uncoils the rope around my waist but doesn't unclasp the cuffs. *Shit.*

Bo points at the chains around my legs. "Take those off too so I can spread her wide for me."

Oh, hell, I'm going to vomit.

Feng eyes his cousin before he moves in front of me and unlocks the manacles around my ankles.

At least I can run now.

"Get ready for the show, gentlemen." Bo jerks his chin at the table surrounded by chairs. The guys close in around it and fold into the seats. He turns to me and barks, "Stand up."

I do, throwing my shoulders back. I test out the range of my bound hands behind my back. I can just reach my side pocket now that I've been freed from the chair.

Bo drags the table into the center of the room, the sharp squeal of the legs against the cement floor grating on my frayed nerves. With a hateful grin, he moves toward me. Then he latches his finger in the first button of my shirt and yanks. It pops off and clinks to the ground. Then he grabs two fistfuls of my shirt and rips it open. All the remaining buttons clatter to the floor, leaving me exposed. I grit my teeth together to keep from gasping. At least I'm not wearing a cute lacey bra. The full coverage beige cups hide most of my breasts from the wandering pervy eyes.

I slip on that icy mask I've so often seen on Luca despite the riot of nerves in my gut. I won't break in front of these assholes.

Bo spins me around and wraps his hand around the back of my neck. He shoves me toward the table. With my back to the rest of the men, he hisses, "Take off your shorts."

"No." My pulse roars across my eardrums.

"Do it, or I'll do it for you."

Time's up. I have to act now, or my pepper spray will end up on the floor and out of reach. It's my only chance. Pretending to wiggle out of my shorts, I reach for the pepper spray and tuck it into my panties. My shorts drop to the floor, and raw adrenaline pumps through my veins.

I feel him behind me, inching closer. When his dick is up against my ass, I whirl around and spray. "Go fuck yourself!" I take off toward the door in nothing but my bra and underwear, arms pumping like mad.

Bo screeches behind me. "Stop her! I don't care if you fucking shoot her! Don't let her get away."

The warehouse door whips open, and a murky shadow fills the entryway. Every nerve-ending in my body stands at attention. Luca races toward me, fury carved into his beautiful face. Shots ring out, and I freeze.

A dark blur shoves me to the ground, and I hit the floor with a smack. All the air whooshes from my lungs against the concrete, and I struggle to slurp in a breath.

"Stella, Stellina, are you okay?" Luca's voice coaxes me from the darkness.

I force my lids open despite the crushing pain on my back. Warmth pools around me.

"I'm right here, baby." Luca's hand finds mine, fingers entwining like a perfect puzzle.

More shots ricochet across the warehouse. A cry, another

scream. A muffled curse. *Bang. Bang. Bang.* I cover my ear with my free hand.

"Save Bo for me!" Luca shouts through the chaos.

A faint groan alerts me of someone else's presence, and I glance up over my shoulder. There's someone still on top of me.

"*Cazzo*, Dante." Luca's panicked voice has my heart thundering back up again. He sits up and rolls his brother off me.

As soon as the massive weight is gone, I can breathe again. I search my body for wounds, but despite the puddle of blood, I'm whole. I hazard a glance at Dante, whose eyes have gone glossy. Three or four bullet wounds riddle his torso, and a lake of crimson pools around us.

"Tony!" Luca cries. He rips off his shirt and presses it to his brother's abdomen.

My eyes land on the blood seeping from Luca's stomach. "You're bleeding!"

He shakes his head. "It's the wound from the other day." He presses his lips into a hard line. "I'm fine."

It's only then I notice the shots have stopped. I glance around the warehouse and only Luca's men are left standing. From across the sprawling space, a familiar lanky form lays on the concrete, face first in a river of his own blood. I can just make out the glint of his tacky silver dragon ring on a bloodied finger. A part of me wants to see Bo up close, needs to see the remains of that asshole, but the fear on Luca's face as he watches his brother grounds me to the spot.

"Doc's on her way to your place." Tony slides to the floor beside Dante as Luca presses his bloodstained shirt to the wounds. "We have to get out of here. The cops will arrive any minute."

"He needs an ambulance." I fix my eyes to Luca's. I may not know much about bullet wounds, but there are a shit ton of them, and Dante's lost too much blood. Images of Vinny's body swim to the surface once again. I squeeze my eyes shut chasing them away before they pull me under.

"I—I can't. No cops."

"Go, then. I'll stay with Dante; he saved my life. I'll tell the police Bo kidnapped me. I'll tell them everything."

"My damned brother saved *both* our lives." Luca's head whips back and forth. "And no, I won't leave you. Never again."

"I'm not asking you." The wail of sirens breaks through the tense silence. "Go now, Luca. You can't be here."

"Come on, *capo*. We gotta go." Tony yanks on his boss's arm.

Luca's hand finds my cheek, his rough thumb drawing a slow circle. "Please, come back to me, *amore*."

Pressing my lips into a thin line, I dip my head. Everything is too raw, the wounds too fresh. I don't trust myself to speak.

Tony jerks Luca off the floor, and he drags him across the warehouse to the back door. The thick metal slams shut, and for an instant, there's only silence. I glance down at Dante's pale face and wait for the anger, the revulsion. But it never comes. Instead, I only see an older version of Luca. A dark and broken man.

A second later, the police arrive with guns drawn. "Hold on, Dante," I whisper as they surround us.

CHAPTER 45
LOVE KILLS

L*uca*

"I don't give a fuck about the optics, Jones. Dante's my brother. I'm going to the damned hospital to see him." I jab my finger at the red button and shove my phone back in my jacket pocket. The warehouse incident was a complete bumblefuck. If Tony hadn't called in a favor with the mayor last night, Dante's name and as a result, mine and King Industries would've been plastered across social media with mob implications.

Jones managed to play off the concerned bystander angle, but the rumors about my brother only echoed the truth. I'd managed to keep Stella's name completely out of the story. It had cost me a pretty penny, but it was worth it. I didn't need her reputation dragged through the mud along with the rest of us.

A seed of dread takes root in my gut. Bo, his cousin Feng, and three other Red Dragons are dead. It's only a matter of time before Jianjun retaliates. The kid might have been a *sfigato,* but he was the old man's only son.

I drag my fingers through my hair and heave out a weary breath.

Magda glances up at me from behind the marble island in the kitchen. The aroma of roasted coffee beans hangs in the air. She's perfecting my cappuccino, pouring the frothy milk over the double shot of espresso as I trudge toward her.

"How is Signor Dante?" she asks.

"Still in the Intensive Care Unit but stable."

She releases a soft sigh. "I'm happy to hear that."

A rueful smile lifts the corner of my lip. "You don't have to say that Magda. I know he's always been a *cap 'e cazzo* to you." A total shithead.

"Yes, but he's still your brother, and I was asking for you, not him." She hands me the warm cup and wipes her fingers on her apron. She watches me, wringing her hands as I take the first sip.

Magda has worked with me for long enough now that I know there's more on her mind. She's a delicate and respectful girl and knows when to hold her tongue. "Is there something else you'd like to say?"

A hint of crimson blossoms across her cheeks. "I was only wondering about Signorina Stella …. Will she be returning to the penthouse?"

Well, that is the fucking million-dollar question, isn't it? When Albie told me she'd been taken, it was like getting shot all over again. I'd never felt so powerless than in that instant. If anything had happened to her, I wouldn't have thought twice about ending it. I couldn't live without her.

As much of a *bastardo* as I am, I know she's a hundred times better off without me. What's that damned saying? If you love something set it free …. I've never loved anyone like I love Stella, but all I've brought her is misery and pain. Love is gentle, love is kind, but my love kills.

I swallow down a gulp of the cappuccino to buy myself more time to reply to a question that has no good answer. "I don't know," I finally murmur. Finishing it off with another gulp, I place the empty cup on the countertop. "I'm going to visit Dante then to the office. I won't be home until late so don't bother preparing dinner."

She nods. "Very well, signore."

The drive to the hospital passes in a blur, my maddening thoughts swirling. My heart and my head battle it out in an unending standoff. There's nothing I want more than to run to Stella and beg her to take me back, to forgive me for all the bullshit I put her through. But my mind, the rational, logical one knows that letting her go would be what's best for her.

But how could I lose the one good thing in my life? Stella is the other half of my heart and soul. Losing her would be like cutting off a piece of me. I'd done it before when I was young and stupid, and I'd regretted it every day since. How could I walk away from her again?

My thoughts race back to last night, to finding her beaten and half-naked in that warehouse. She'd almost been killed again because of me, and I'd been too weak to save her. If Dante hadn't rushed in, we'd both be dead. My *rompicoglioni* brother had saved us both.

Talk about a fucking twist. My brother the hero.

The car slows, and Albie's voice drifts to the backseat. "We're here, *capo.*"

I smooth down my tie and draw in a steadying breath. Two reporters are camped outside the doors of *NYU Langone*, only the best hospital for my *fratello*. Albie opens the back door, and I slide out. The reporters are on me before I make it halfway up the sidewalk.

"Mr. Valentino!"

"Mr. Valentino, a word?" The female is quicker and gets in my face with her mic and camera.

"I'm sorry, I'm in a hurry," I grit out.

"Just a few quick questions."

Albie moves between us, blocking her, and I zip past the second reporter and dart inside. Jones had been adamant about steering clear of the media, and for once, we're on the same page. A benefit of being one of the hospital's biggest benefactors is a speedy entrance. A nurse meets me at the front desk, and I'm whizzed past the line of visitors. Albie follows behind, his slow, steady pace particularly irritating at the moment.

We ride the elevator in silence, and for some inexplicable reason, my nerves are buzzing by the time we reach the ICU. The halogen lights flicker above, the scent of antiseptic thick in the air as we walk down the hall. When the nurse slows in front of a room, a new scent reaches my nostrils, a devastatingly familiar one, one that has a knot forming in my throat.

"Let us know if you need anything, Mr. Valentino." The nurse's words are muffled over the wild pounding of my heart. "Your brother is still unconscious, but it's what's best for him now. He needs as much rest as possible to recover."

I nod blankly and peer inside my brother's room.

Stella sits in a chair beside the bed, the chorus of mechanical beeps marring the strangely peaceful scene. I take a silent step inside, scared to ruin the oddly serene moment. The rhythmic whooshing of the ventilator steadies my manic heartbeats as I creep closer. Beside my brother's bed sits a bouquet of white calla lilies. I couldn't help myself; I had them sent over first thing this morning. Both of us could benefit from a little redemption, a rebirth.

Stella must be absorbed in her own dark thoughts because she doesn't seem to notice me at all. Or maybe she's ignoring me. The errant thought is piercing.

I round the chair and finally understand. Stella's eyes are closed, head lolling to the side. Did she spend the night here? I take in the hospital robe and her disheveled appearance and have my answer. Why would she stay with him after what he'd done to her?

Because Stella is good. *A kindhearted soul who is much too good for the likes of you.* That dark voice in my mind supplies the answer. The monster I try to keep buried knows me well.

She stirs as if she's felt me somehow, and my pulse skyrockets. Her lids flutter and she blinks up at me, the haze of sleep softening the typical fire in her eyes.

"Hi," I whisper, lamely.

She stretches her arms over her head and lets out a yawn. "Is it morning already?"

"Just past eight." My head dips. "You stayed all night?"

"Guess so." She wraps her arms across her middle, snuggling into the hospital gown.

I fold onto the edge of Dante's bed, careful not to disturb the complex tangle of tubes and wires. "Why?"

She shrugs. "I couldn't just leave him alone."

"*Dio*, Stella why do you have to be so damned good?"

Her lips pucker as she regards me with knitted brows. "Excuse me?"

"You make it so hard."

"Hard for what?"

"To be selfish with you. To take what I want. I've never wanted anything more than you." *Cazzo*, I'm rambling. No wonder she's looking at me like I'm a complete *pazzo*. I slide off the bed and sink to my knees. "Please forgive me for keeping the truth about Vinny from you. I'll do anything to have you in my life again. I know I have no right to ask, that I'm miles beyond deserving you, but *Dio* I love you, Stella. I always have. That day I met you in the cemetery when we were just kids, you changed me. You made me want to make something of myself. When Vinny died, I was a coward. I was so scared of disappointing you, I ran like a *minchione*. His dying wish was for me to take care of you, and I fucked that up so badly. But no more, whether you want me or not, I'm here for you. I'll protect you with my body and soul until *Dio* drags my weary bullet-riddled bones to *l'inferno. Capisci?*"

She nods slowly.

"*Ti amo, amore mio,*" I whisper.

I drop my forehead to her knees and wrap my hands around her legs. *Dio*, I love her so much it hurts. I don't dare move, don't dare breathe. Not until she says something.

The thick silence lingers between us, each passing second like another nail in my coffin. She's not going to forgive me. She won't take me back. How can I blame her after all the agony I've put her through?

A soft whimper breaks the silence, and I hazard a glance up. Those beautiful brilliant blue orbs are filled with tears. The breath catches in my throat as I take her in.

"Of course, I forgive you, you *stronzo*. I've been in love with you since I was ten years old."

Stella

Luca leaps up and jerks me into his arms. Tears run down my cheeks as he spins me in a circle, squeezing so tight I can scarcely breathe. But I don't want him to stop. I'm so stupidly head over heels in love with him; I'd rather die in his arms in this moment than have him release me.

I wasn't lying. I'd been in love with Luca Valentino from that terrible moment in the cemetery at my mom's funeral. He'd been my ray of hope on the worst day of my life.

What scared me the most about being with Luca wasn't all the terrible things he'd done, but that no matter how many times he did them, I'd still forgive him, I'd still love him.

He was beautiful and broken, scarred and savage, but he was mine.

CHAPTER 46
AMORE MIO

Stella

I tighten my hold around Luca's waist as he throttles the engine, and we zip around another corner on the sleek motorcycle. A wild laugh escapes from the adrenaline and the sheer happiness. It's been a week since I moved back into the penthouse, for real this time. Not that I had that many clothes to remove from my crappy old apartment but the few belongings that remained were important.

Dad was gone.

His side of the apartment had been emptied. He'd ran out on the last month's rent, his unpaid debt, and me. A few months ago, that would've broken me, but now with Luca at my side I could endure anything.

"Almost there, princess." Luca's shout distracts me from dark thoughts of the past.

"Where are we going?"

"If I told you, it wouldn't be a surprise, now would it?" I

catch a peek of his mischievous grin through the helmet's visor.

I focus on the surroundings, the lush green and quiet streets of the wealthy suburb of Eastchester. The neighborhood begins to look more familiar as he slows the Ducati and pulls up in front of a sprawling yard.

Luca cuts the engine and removes his helmet, then mine. He takes my hand and helps me off the bike then covers my eyes with his free hand.

"What are you doing?" I laugh.

He spins me around a few times until I'm dizzy and breathless from the nervous giggles.

"Luca!"

"Okay, okay." He presses his lips to mine, a slow, sexy kiss that has me panting for more. When he releases me too soon, I grumble a curse.

He lets out a husky laugh, hand still covering my eyes. "Are you ready?"

"Yes!" I hiss.

He turns me a quarter way then removes his hand. A huge lawn stretches out before us and a pad of concrete fills the central space. My brows knit as I regard the semi-familiar land. It isn't until my gaze settles on the pond with the small dock in the back and the thick trees that it all comes back to me.

"The picnic?"

A slow smile crawls across his face as he takes my hands. "I bought this land a while ago, but I was never quite sure what to do with it. I love my penthouse, and it's perfect for one of the city's most eligible bachelors but—"

My heart thumps out an erratic staccato as his eyes lance into mine.

"One day soon I'm going to ask you to be my wife, and this will be our home. I want to fill it with your warmth and laughter, and eventually, but not too soon, tons of our children."

Mischief sparkles in those dark eyes. "I hope your heart grows stronger with each day we spend together."

My jaw drops, and all the air evacuates my lungs. "Luca …" He'd said those exact words to me at the cemetery all those years ago, and it had gotten me through the first awful weeks without my mom. Heat burns my eyes, and my heart sprouts wings. It's the only explanation for the mad flutters.

"I love you more than there are stars in the sky, Stellina, *amore mio*. I can't wait to start this life with you. Do you like it?"

I wrap my arms around Luca's neck and smother his words with a kiss. "I love it."

"Good. Because Mamma is just dying to have us closer."

I smile against his mouth, the idea of a real family bringing more tears of joy to my eyes.

"It'll probably be another year or two before the house is complete, but I figured with you starting at NYU, it'll be easier to live in the city for now anyway."

My almost fiancé had of course insisted on paying for my next two years of university. A tiny part of me was sad to say goodbye to my dreams of sunny Florida, but I could never say goodbye to Luca. I didn't like the idea of him paying my way through college, so he agreed to a loan.

How I was to repay it was still unclear. He insisted on sexual favors, but somehow that just didn't seem fair since I'd be getting just as much out of it as he would.

He kisses me again, interrupting my musings, and I'm immediately swept away in the frenzy. His fingers dig into the hair at the back of my neck as he deepens the kiss. Fire builds in my core as he nibbles on my lower lip and moves lower, sucking on my neck. The man is like a teenager, constantly covering me with hickies. He insists it's so that anyone who sees me knows I belong to him, but the truth is I was his long before he marked me.

He pulls away to breathe against my lips, "Should we go for a swim?"

"Mmhmm," I murmur.

Luca sweeps me off the ground and swings me into his arms. I capture his lips again as he blindly stumbles toward the pond. I paw at the buttons of his shirt so that when we reach the crystal-clear lagoon, he's already half-naked. I pause as my fingers find the date tattooed on his chest. The one he tried so damned hard to keep hidden, but now means so much to me.

He stops when we reach the thick copse of trees, piercing gaze intent on mine as I run my finger over those five tiny numbers. "We'll always remember him. Together."

I nod and blink back the quickly forming tears. "*Per sempre.*" Forever.

His lips find mine, and he kisses me softly. Behind the cover of the thick trees, I undress him and he slowly strips me down until I'm bare.

Cradling me in his arms again, Luca runs across the dock and leaps in. I let out a squeal as the cool water envelops my heated flesh. His lips descend on mine before I can draw in a lungful of air. So I breathe him in, reveling in each nibble, every touch. He wades to the edge of the pond and wraps my legs around his waist. His hard cock nudges at my entrance as he glances at me beneath hooded lids. "I love you so much," he whispers, fingers digging into my hips. "*Ti amo, amore mio.*"

I sink onto him with a groan. His cock fills me so completely, my head falls back, and I moan his name. "Luca…."

"That's right, baby." Gripping my hips, he guides me up and down as we float at the edge of the peaceful pond. I press my body flush against his, but it's never close enough. I need to feel him inside me, next to me, everywhere. I clench around his cock, each thrust of his hips driving me closer to the edge.

"*Dio, sei bellissima, amore,*" he growls as he plunges deeper.

And I feel beautiful with him. I feel perfect through his eyes. No man has ever made me feel so cherished, so adored. I grind my hips against his, desperate for the friction, for the thrill of the approaching release. I'm hopelessly addicted; I need Luca Valentino like I need air in my lungs, my heart to beat and my soul to live.

Luca Valentino was my beginning, my middle, and is my perfect end.

EPILOGUE

Three Months Later
Dante

I never thought I'd see the day. My little brother with a woman on his arm, a woman he's so crazy about he's counting down the days to propose. A twinkle brightens his eyes as he watches Stella talk to her friend, Rose. Luca's hosting dinner parties now. Another thing I never thought I'd see. He's already bought a big fat diamond engagement ring too. It's been at my place for safe keeping. Stella insisted he couldn't propose until they'd officially dated for six months, and the month she spent as his 'captive' didn't count. And now they were halfway there. I'd even seen my brother's calendar with thick exes marking down the fateful day.

He's completely *impazzito*.

But damn, happiness looks good on him.

I watch Luca and Stella from across the room as they schmooze with the commissioner and his wife, then move on to the mayor and the missus. Luca was born for this shit. Stella, too, is perfect. Together, they'll go far.

Me, I'm just lucky they'd forgiven my inexcusable offenses.

It had only taken me four shots to the chest and countless weeks of rehab to prove myself. But I would do it ten times over to save my *fratellino* and his *amore*. I could be an asshole sometimes, but I still loved my brother and only wanted to protect him. It was one of the reasons I hadn't assumed my birthright, but that was another long story. I had no intentions of actually forcing myself on Stella that day. I just wanted to scare the shit out of her. Still, it was unforgiveable.

Truth was, I like Stella. I didn't want to, but I couldn't help myself. She's sweet and good and has been through so much shit, but somehow remains that way. Unlike my brother and me whose souls have long since withered away as a result of our dark pasts.

Stella is Luca's bright, shiny star. She illuminates all his murky shadows and finds the light. Every day he shines brighter.

And dammit, I am jealous as all hell.

Happy for him, but still envious that he's found something I'll never have.

I force a smile as the happy couple saunters toward me. "Please, don't let me tear you away from your fans, *fratellino*."

Luca smacks the back of my head. My little brother has made a terrible habit of hitting me constantly. I guess he has to release the rage somehow.

"Watch it," I growl. "You don't want the mayor thinking you're anything but his little golden boy, now do you?"

"Sorry." He throws me a sheepish smile. "Old habits die hard."

Stella snuggles into his side; the expression of utter adoration as she gazes up at my brother pinches at my cold heart. "Oh, everyone loves Luca, you know that, Dante. The commissioner is trying to get him to run for his office when he retires next year."

"Of course, he is." I fix my gaze to my brother's. "You gonna do it, little bro?"

"I don't know. I have enough going on with King Industries and our *other* activities." He whispers the last part.

After taking those gunshots meant for Luca and Stella, my brother welcomed me back into the fold. With Stella in his life, he's trying to take a step back from our less legitimate half of the business. He finally needs me.

Jianjun never did retaliate for his son's death, but it's like walking on eggshells around China Town. It's a powder keg ready to explode. Luca and Stella need to be far away from the shrapnel. Which leaves me mostly in charge.

It's my birthright after all. Now protecting them means going back on my word to our father.

"I could see it," says Stella, drawing me from my thoughts. "Commissioner Valentino." She smirks and presses a quick kiss to his cheek that has my brother preening like a damned peacock.

"That's King Commissioner Valentino." He chuckles and kisses her full on the lips.

If the penthouse wasn't full of guests, he'd devour her right in the middle of the living room. The happy couple fuck like rabbits. I'd experienced it firsthand on many an unfortunate visit. Now, I never stop by without warning.

"What's so funny?" Stella's friend Rose bounces between us, her perky breasts nearly tumbling out of her low-cut mini dress. Her long blonde hair cascades down her shoulders effortlessly. The girl looks like a damned Barbie doll.

"My brother likes to be referred to as the king," I offer.

Luca rolls his eyes. "That's not at all true."

"Only in bed," Stella counters with a wicked grin.

"I am the king in bed, am I not, princess?" He nuzzles her neck, and I quickly avert my gaze as she starts to giggle.

"Oh no, I have not had enough champagne for this." Rose tips back her flute and guzzles down the contents. "You two are nauseatingly cute, but I draw the line at sex talk."

A grin pulls at the corner of my lip. Rose is feisty and gorgeous, and the sight of her makes my cock stand at attention, but she's a fucking hot mess. She's nothing like the restrained, wealthy socialites I typically entertain.

"Why didn't you bring Caroline?" Luca asks as if he's read my goddammed mind.

Stella's mouth twists into a pout at the mention of Luca's one-time fling and my occasional hook up.

I jerk my thumb at his future wife. "That's why."

"What?" Stella's expression morphs into a look of exaggerated innocence.

"Please, we all know you hate the girl," says Rose. "She's a total snob and kind of a bitch." She swats at my arm playfully. "No offense, D. I'm sure she's a great lay."

Clenching my jaw, I suppress a smile. She's got Caroline pegged to a tee, but the only hopes I have of stepping out from behind my little brother's shadow is bagging an heiress. I can't live as Luca's second for the rest of my days.

It's enough that everyone believes Papà chose him over me.

A sharp squeal sends my heart catapulting against my ribs, and my hand darts to the gun stashed beneath my waistband. *Damned PTSD.*

"Oops, sorry." Rose rifles through her clutch and silences her phone, the ringtone the most irritating sound I've ever heard. It reminds me of a distress call from a ship. For a second, I was certain we were on the *Titanic,* and we were about to go down.

The second after she pockets the phone, it rings again.

"Shit," she mutters.

"Who is it?" Stella asks.

Rose shakes her head and adds in a dramatic eyeroll. "Remember that guy I was dating?"

"Please don't tell me it's another one of Dr. Winchester's patients."

Rose sucks in her lower lip and casts her eyes to the floor. "Yeah, um …."

"Rose! You're not supposed to be dating patients. That's so not the idea of real-life work experience. You could lose your internship."

She waves a nonchalant hand. "Dr. Winchester is super cool, and besides, I don't date the crazies."

"So why is this guy calling you nonstop?" I ask as the phone rings yet again.

She smirks up at me. "What can I say? Caroline's not the only one who's a great lay."

Stella groans and digs her elbow into her friend's side. "You have to be careful, Rose. You have no idea what these guys are seeing a psychiatrist for."

"I check their files before I agree to a date, duh."

"Oh, *cazzo*," Stella mutters. "You are so going to get fired for this."

The cell rings again, and I snatch it from Rose's hand, the ear-splitting noise making my temples throb. "Stop calling Rose," I growl over the phone. Both of the girls gasp.

"Who the fuck are you?" some douche asks.

"I'm her fucking boyfriend, you little shit. Unless you want me to rip your heart out with my bare hands, I suggest you delete her number and erase everything about her from your mind."

The line goes dead, and a satisfied grin curls my lips. Damn, that felt good. It's been months since I'd gotten into a good scuffle because of my injuries. Maybe it's time to get back to it.

I hand the phone back, and Rose tosses me a smile. "My hero."

I laugh, my entire chest vibrating. "I'm no one's hero, sweetheart."

And I had no intention of ever becoming one.

*** Keep reading for a sneak peek of Dante's story, *Savage King*, coming out later this year! Each novel in the Kings of Temptation series will feature a sinfully gorgeous King and the woman who makes him fall to his knees. For a chance to win an ARC and get exclusive sneak peeks of what's to come, join my FB group Sienna Cross's Heartbreakers or my VIP mailing list! You'll also get the *Ruthless King* prequel story for FREE!

CHAPTER 47
SNEAK PEEK OF SAVAGE KING

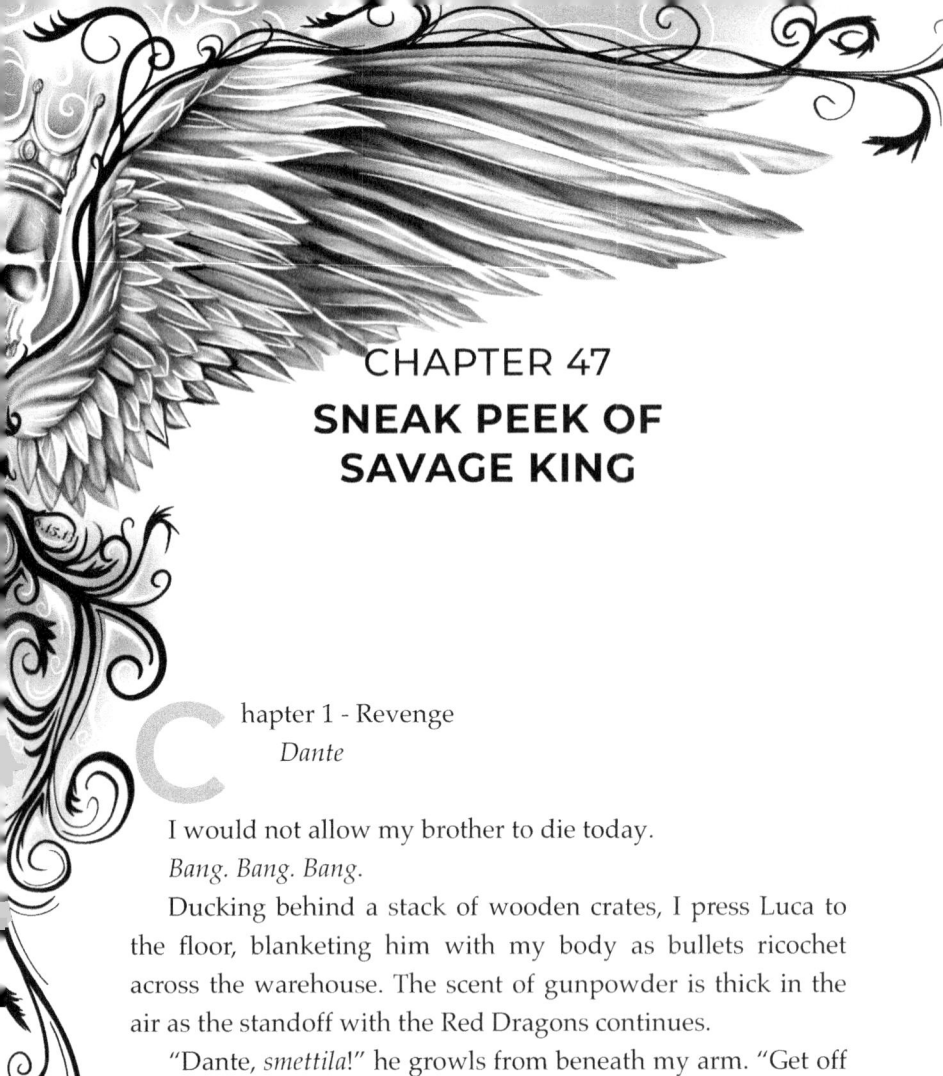

Chapter 1 - Revenge
Dante

I would not allow my brother to die today.

Bang. Bang. Bang.

Ducking behind a stack of wooden crates, I press Luca to the floor, blanketing him with my body as bullets ricochet across the warehouse. The scent of gunpowder is thick in the air as the standoff with the Red Dragons continues.

"Dante, *smettila*!" he growls from beneath my arm. "Get off me, I can fight for myself."

"No," I snarl, my finger closing around the trigger. I shoot off a hailstorm of bullets into the murky space. "Stella will kill me if anything happens to you. I already owe your fiancée enough. I don't need to add to the debt."

He remains silent for a blissful minute. My stubborn younger brother has always believed himself to be invincible. Until he met her. Now everything has changed. The idea of dying becomes much less acceptable when you're forced to leave behind someone you're fucking crazy about.

Lucky for me, I don't have that problem.

Luca shoves me off and crouches beside me, drawing out the handgun from his inside jacket pocket. As C.E.O. of King Industries, my *fratellino* doesn't have use for a weapon on most days. But today, those Chinese assholes got the drop on us.

"Where the hell are Tony and the other guys?" Luca hisses as another spray of bullets zings over our heads.

"On their way," I mutter through clenched teeth. I never should've let my brother come today. So much for a quick check on our supplies. How the fuck did Feng Zhang and his men know we'd be here? And unprotected?

"I still can't believe that *figlio di puttana* is still alive," Luca grits out.

I nod and squeeze out another round before reloading. Feng was supposed to be dead, along with his cousin Bo who'd nearly killed us three months ago. Bo's father Jianjun was the head of the Chinese Triad. His bastard son captured Luca's fiancée and my brother lost his shit. We thought they were all dead, then last week a fucking ghost appears.

Feng.

The thirst for revenge changes a man.

I know this well enough. After Papà died and Luca slid into the King's throne, vengeance was all I lived for.

The sudden silence jerks me from my musings, and I glance around the dark warehouse.

"Why'd they stop?" Luca whispers.

I inch up and peer over the edge of the bullet-riddled crates. Feng stands across the sprawling space with two men at each side. They're all in red from head-to-toe, the guys surrounding him wearing hoods.

"I've come to deliver a message." Feng's voice cuts through the unnatural silence.

Luca stands, but I wrap my fingers around his wrist and jerk him back down. "Stay down," I hiss. "You're too valuable."

"Oh, fuck off, Dante."

I throw a narrowed glare at my brother. "Stella," I mouth.

He huffs out a frustrated breath and shrinks down behind the splintering crate.

"We're listening," I shout back.

Feng clears his throat, then reaches into his pocket and something silver glints beneath the dim halogen lights.

"*Merda*," Luca mutters.

He creeps closer, hands extended palm up. His men trail him on either side, guns trained at us. As he nears, I finally focus on the silver circlet. A ring. Feng slides it onto his middle finger and squeezes his hand into a fist.

Then he glares at me from across the room, lips twisted into a snarl. "You slaughtered my cousin and his men, nearly killed me, and now you will pay. The Chinese Triad has declared war on the Kings."

"That's bullshit—" Luca leaps up and a bullet whizzes just past his head.

I shove him down to the floor again, muttering curses. "I told you to stay down, you *stronzo*."

A dark chuckle fills the tense air. "One more thing. The Triad has placed a price on Luca Valentino and Stella Esposito's heads. Dead or alive. One million dollars each."

"Fuck," Luca hisses.

Feng sneers, and I can feel the tension radiating off my brother in waves. "You'll have every low-life scum gunning for you and your precious fiancée."

Luca jolts up again, digging his elbow into my side when I try to stop him. "If you lay a hand on her, Feng, I'll tear you up from limb to limb, piss on your entrails and drag your remains across China Town."

"Big words from a mob boss gone soft, Luca."

"That's *Signor* Valentino," he snarls. "Or did you forget your place in the sewers, you little rat?"

"A lot has changed in the last three months, *capo*. The Kings don't rule the Lower East Side anymore. I do."

"Yeah, we'll fucking see about that," Luca spits.

"You've been warned." Feng dips his head, and his men move as one surrounding him in a red wave.

Heavy footfalls drag my attention to the opposite end of the warehouse. Tony, Mickey and half a dozen of our guys race in with guns drawn. Just as the Red Dragons slip out the back.

"That little shit, who the hell does he think he is?" Luca roars.

Tony moves in step beside my brother and gives him the once over before the tense set of his broad shoulders relax. "You okay, *capo*?"

"Yeah, I'm fine, Tony." My little bro gives his righthand man a tight smile. *Tony would be the most difficult to convince…*

I bite back the snarl on my lips. For years, Tony has coddled and fussed over Luca like he was his older brother. It pisses me off to no end.

I'm the older brother, that's my job. Sure, I might have fucked up a few things here and there along the way, but I'm on my game now. I can protect him. Which is why I know what I have to do next, no matter how much Luca will hate me for it.

***

The Frank Sinatra impersonator croons in the background as the guests filling my new penthouse ooh and ahh at his rendition of *My Way*. Ma's smile is so big I'm worried her lips will crack. Luca and Stella dance in the middle of the living room, the look in their eyes as they sway to the music nauseatingly sweet.

Everything is going according to plan. A dozen of my men are stationed in the penthouse and lobby, ready for my word. With so many dignitaries in attendance, their presence isn't questioned.

Besides, my brother is so obsessed with his beautiful fiancée, his head permanently buried between her thighs, he won't see it coming until it's too late.

Just like he didn't see the Chinese Triad slowly inching into our territory.

That's what love does to a man. The most ruthless man in New York City has gone soft, and now it's time for me to step in.

*** I hoped you liked that little sneak peek :) For more of Dante's story, *Savage King*, make sure you join my FB group Sienna Cross's Heartbreakers or my VIP mailing list! You'll get a FREE copy of the *Ruthless King* prequel story, *Ruthless Blood* and see how Stella and Luca first met!

ALSO BY SIENNA CROSS

Ruthless (Ongoing on Kindle Vella)

Kings of Temptation
Ruthless King
Savage King (Coming soon!)

ACKNOWLEDGMENTS

I'll let you in on my dirty little secret… Sienna Cross is my pen name, one I've been been dying to launch for a while now. I never would've even attempted it if it wasn't for the support of my husband. He's the only one in my family who knows about naughty Sienna. Thanks for pushing me to do all the things, honey!

A special thank you to my awesome V.A., Sarah, who has been such a huge help and also vault when it comes to keeping all of this a secret. And thank you to the incredibly talented Samaiya for the gorgeous art. You really make the story come to life! And of course my beta readers, Lydia, Sarah (again!), and Jena and my ARC team, you're all amazing! Some of you have been with me for years and I really appreciate all your feedback (thanks for keeping the secret too!).

And the biggest thank you to my readers! I could never do this without you :)
~ Sienna

ABOUT THE AUTHOR

Sienna Cross was kidnapped by mobsters, saved by her super-hot step-brother, then forced into an arranged marriage with a billionaire. From there, things got really interesting… She loves to write about dark, morally-gray alpha males and the captivating women that bring them to their knees. For all the inside info, join Sienna Cross's Heartbreakers on Facebook, like her page, and follow her on Instagram and Tiktok. She has a thing for stalkers ;)

www.siennacrossbooks.com

Printed in Great Britain
by Amazon